The Trackman By Karl Davis

This book is dedicated to my wonderful wife Stacey, and our
two captivating sons, Harry and Archie. Without their input
and influence, this book may well have been in print much
sooner, but my laughter lines would not have been quite so
pronounced, my hair quite as grey, nor my life so enriched.
They inspired within me the solicitude to continue writing
through my darkest times. I thank them eternally for their
support, giggles, cuddles, and their endlessly warming

presence in my life.

Thanks also to the very talented Lee Arnell for the cover design, and to my good friend, and fellow author/train driver Rob Reddan. His patience, generosity and good humour in terms of proof reading this book, as well as in terms of his unconditional friendship have been fantastic, and I am forever grateful.

I found the inspiration to write this book during a difficult period in my life whilst I underwent counselling. A middle aged lady, unbeknown to me, took the decision to end her life under the wheels of the train I was driving. In the pain, grief, chaos and helplessness that ensued, I drew strength from the support of my mother, Lynne, my brothers John and Terry, my best friend and fellow Train Driver Mike Keal, and my colleagues from around the globe, who spared the time, empathy and kindness to think of me, and to lend me their shoulders at a particularly arduous time.

If you are on the cusp of acting through desperation, or feeling hopeless and alone, please reach out. There is always somebody willing to listen. There is always an alternative for you, and for those who love you, and who would be left behind to mourn in your wake. You are not alone, and you are not beyond the help that you need.
Thank you.

The red flashing light emanating from the corner of the room made him paranoid. He felt vulnerable as he listened to slowed breathing, her hushed sighs filling the room. Like so many local street girls, she hadn't been willing at first to submit to his demands. He had managed to persuade her though, initially with more cash, and when she changed her mind, a swift injection of medazolene to her neck. On previous occasions, Steven had been forced to resort to violence to keep the girls he practised on perfectly still, and this had led to a shortage of willing subjects. This way though, was much better. She had obeyed him almost robotically during her ordeal, and he was feeling certain that he had found the way forward. She slept heavily, the soreness around her eyes gradually easing. As she shifted position, her bright pink lipstick smeared across the pillow. She mumbled quietly as she adjusted her aching form. He tore himself away from his thoughts to listen, as her breathy groans continued to puncture the silence.

"Mea Culpa" she whispered, her voice descending into soft cries. He smiled darkly, nodding in agreement and approval. Steven never usually allowed them to stay once he was spent, but such was his exhaustion, he couldn't help but roll over to face the wall and slowly drift into a troubled sleep, her pained sobs acting as a twisted lullaby. He continued to stare into the gloom, his eyes settling onto the sinister outline of the cupboard that occupied the far corner. It was almost as if the rhythmic pulse of the red light atop the camera was a warning. In the brief intervals of tainted light it looked like the cupboard was moving. He could not have anyone catching a glimpse of what was inside. He had a plan which was intended to deliver justice and redress the balance, and show the world how much he had been made to suffer! Turning back to the girl lying next to him, Steven watched her roll over with a whispered groan, the sheets riding up and exposing her thighs and buttocks. Worthless girls like her acted as the lid which kept this mental vortex hidden away. There were times when he wondered how he could have kept this constant anger buried inside him had he not been able to pay for the intimacy that kept him sane to the outside world. Rising from the bed and padding silently across to the bathroom, he turned on the light, and studied the gaunt face that looked back at him from the mirror. Twenty Nine years of vicious, hate filled dreams and harrowing flash backs were beginning to take their toll. Next to the sink were a handful of Polaroid pictures he had taken. Steven picked them up and flicked through them, reliving the evening. His heart rate quickened as he pored over the images of the girl who was now in his bed, her fear and suffering trapped in a freeze frame forever. Her eyes were taped open, and photographed at close range, the colour of her eyeballs transforming from white to red as each snap was taken. Glancing across towards the bedroom, the red flash from the camera caught his eye once more. His loins tingled as he thought of the footage he had shot. Usually, the act of photographing his prey was enough to peak his arousal. Being in a position of such complete authority, in a position whereby he and he alone could feel the thrill of restitution was more than sufficient to tip him over the edge of an almighty orgasm. But this time, mere photos were not enough. Yes, he had achieved release, but even after he came, noisy and wild, angry and ignorant of how he degraded her naked skin, he knew he needed more. It was in this moment that he had hurriedly grabbed his camera. Hastily erecting the tripod, he pointed the lens directly at her face and bare chest, and set about pleasuring himself over her immobilised form once more. Upon finishing for a second time, Steven had felt dirty. Such fetishes, mixed with a desire for justice had left a legacy of bizarre morality. The pictures seemed somehow safe, somehow acceptable. He knew though, that a line had been crossed from which he would not return. Steven licked his lips as he gazed at the picture of her dilated pupil, the terror she felt, masked by the drug he had forced inside of her. Turning his attention back to the mirror, his reddened eyes traced the stubble adorning his jaw line as his mind drifted back through the mists of the past.

He found himself amongst his friends and cousins once again, sitting cross legged on the floor of his grandmother's house, hurriedly passing a thickly wrapped parcel around the rough circle of excited children whilst nondescript music played in the background. He saw the blurred outline of the policemen as they knocked at the frosted glass of the front door. He saw his mum being immediately swallowed whole by trepidation as she answered, and the solemn face of the police officers as they followed her into the kitchen. He stared at the mirror that hung on the wall, watching reflections as his mother turn white, hearing her shrill cry as these grim faced officers informed her that his dad had been killed. He flinched, scrambling toward the sofa as a glass flew through the air, seeming to rotate in slow motion as it impacted with the mirror. The mirror shattered, shards and splinters projected randomly across the room as his grandmother shepherded the traumatised and confused children upstairs, grabbing him and holding him to her as they rushed out of the room. His eyes were fixed on the shards of mirrored glass that lay strewn across the carpet. The light seemed to dance on their edges, and Steven stared at the chaotic formations of the glass pieces as his mother let out another sickening cry. It was that horrible, empty scream, along with the sight of his mother collapsing into a sobbing heap that filled his mind with images that were the most vibrant, yet most numbing. These images resonated throughout his mind even now, 5:15 on a dark, Tuesday morning, 29 years later. That day, his seventh birthday, was the last day of his childhood.

-2-

Repeating the same ritual he practiced before commencing the last journey of each shift, Stuart Mallon reached inside his pocket and fished out a cigarette packet. Flipping open the lid, he smiled with relief as he counted the packet's contents. It was not that he was unable to complete a journey without a cigarette; he just liked to repeat the same sequence of events. Placing it back in his pocket, he groped for the light switch behind him, cursing under his breath as he scraped his knuckles on one of the many circuit breakers that lined the back wall of the cab. Stuart stifled a yawn before picking up the handset from the cradle in front of him and announcing the stations that the train would be calling at. He checked his watch, half squinting as he peered at the bright green luminescence of the clock. Peering out of the cab window of the train, Stuart watched as the platform staff completed their final tasks before the train departed. Having been given permission to leave the station, and having closed the doors, he pulled the brake lever back towards him, and opened the throttle. The electric motors responded, and the train began accelerating steadily away from the bright lights of the station, and into the pitched darkness of the night. As the train emerged from the protection of the station canopy, Stuart realised just how bad the weather was, as what little light there was began refracting through the rainfall that was hitting the windscreen with tremendous ferocity. With a shake of his head, he settled himself back into his seat, muttering under his breath as he always did just how bad these back rests were for his posture. Taking a sip from his drink, he stifled a burp, focussing himself on the route ahead as he peered into the wet, murky night that was being kept at bay by the rain soaked window.

-3-

It was only John's second day of training in a live signal box, and he was desperately trying to keep up with his new mentor.

"You see John" Jerry Pickford was saying as he stalked the

signalling panel almost effortlessly, "It's all about perspective" Jerry tapped his finger on his upper lip as he contemplated his next move, his other hand resting on his hip. "If you want to get good at this job, play chess" He walked over to the desk and shuffled some papers around, lifting the page he wanted from the desktop, and returning purposefully to the panel, picking up his coffee cup and using it as a makeshift paper weight for the evening rush hour schedule. A few years the wrong side of 50, Jerry was the type of guy who would still look scruffy when dressed in a £500 dinner suit. As John watched Jerry pacing the floor between the desk and the signalling panel he couldn't help thinking that Jerry looked almost as tired and outdated as the signal box they stood in. Although smoking had been banned from the signalling centre for a good few years, the jaded fascia and panelling were still dressed heavily in the nicotine stains of what seemed like centuries of pulmonary abuse. John had never been a smoker himself, and struggled to restrain an involuntary shudder as he imagined Jerry's lungs being in a similar state of disrepair. Jerry traced his finger down the left hand side of the page, tapping it on the text relating to the train fast approaching the nearby station. "The trick is to avoid treating them like trains" He said as he stood back from the panel, letting out a long, relaxed sigh as he mulled over the best route to send the train down.

John was standing near the desk, continuing to watch Jerry, still desperately trying to reconcile the lights and buttons adorning the signalling panel in front of him with the diagrams, videos, and training exercises he experienced at the training school. Things seemed to hurtle along at a hundred miles an hour here, even during the quiet times, and it felt as if he was travelling in Jerry's slipstream. At that point, Jerry stopped in mid action and pivoted on his heel to face John. He whipped a well chewed biro from behind his ear and pointed it in John's direction.

"What?" John nervously asked.

Jerry picked up a page from the evening schedule and handed it to John. He turned back to the desk and sifted through the pile of paperwork that was hiding the surface of the table.

"There's only one way for you to learn the job lad, and that's to do it" He paused as his left hand fished around in his overfilled trouser pocket for a packet of chewing gum

"Are you sure?" asked John, half hoping Jerry would say yes, whilst at the same time half hoping he'd say no. "Why not?" was the reply, accompanied by the customary shrug of the shoulders. John's throat had suddenly gone very dry, the sensation being interrupted by the shrill ringing of the phone. Pushing aside his feeling of trepidation, John strode purposefully over to the work station in front of the signalling panel and placed his hand on the receiver, pausing to look across at Jerry, who was now sat on the edge of the desk, rubbing the lenses of his glasses with one of his shirt tails, and pretending not to be taking notice. John took a deep breath and lifted the receiver from its cradle. "Mallington West" he said into the mouthpiece, grabbing a piece of scrap paper and a pen with his free hand.

"Come on then, what's Steven done now?" Graham asked, kicking his grubby canvas bag onto the floor, and putting his feet up on the table, his heavy plastic sandwich box clattering loudly in protest.

Raymond sat himself down on the edge of the table. Exasperated, he snatched his woolly hat from his closely shaven head.

"Oh, I only got up this afternoon to find that he'd gone and put a football through next doors kitchen window!" He stared at the ceiling, his eyes being drawn to the strip light, before following the cloud shaped nicotine stains that dulled its unnatural, blinking rays. Graham gave a wry smile and allowed his eyes to follow where his friends had just been.

"All part of his age though ain't it?" Graham mused.

"Try telling that to the wife!" snapped Raymond, his heavy, stomping footsteps echoing around the room as he marched over to the drinks machine, cursing loudly as he pushed the coffee button, only to be rewarded with a red 'out of order' light. "Fuck it!" he shouted, kicking the machine and putting a hefty dent in the front panel.

"I take it the little lady is a bit upset then!" Graham asked as he re-lit his cigarette, his face contorting as he drew back the sharp emissions from the tobacco.

"When isn't she upset?" retorted Raymond. He sat back down and pinched the bridge of his nose, closing his eyes. "Don't get me wrong" He said, his hand sliding down from the bridge of his nose and resting gently around his throat "I'm paying for the window, and it's not as if we can't afford it, what with the amount of overtime and rest days I've got in just lately" He leant forward, placing his elbows on the table and resting his chin on his hands. "I gave the lad a clip round the ear, grounded him for three weeks, and I even apologised to that smug bastard next door!" He allowed himself a brief grin. "Joyce thinks it's his fault for some reason".

"Not that I want to teach you how to suck eggs or anything, but you need to sit down and have a word with that missus of yours!" Raymond smiled thinly as Graham lent down and grabbed his bag from the floor beneath the table, keeping his overgrown fringe out of his eyes with his free hand. Raymond scratched an area of course stubble on his neck. The skin was reddening, and Raymond made a mental note that he must have a shave tomorrow.

"I don't know" Raymond sighed. "Anyone would think I kicked that ball myself" He put his hands behind his head and stared at the ceiling once again. "It's been like this since he was born. Everything he does wrong, it's my fault, I should've stopped him, and I should've taught him better or something. I know that she's protective, and I understand why!" Raymond gulped, forcing the last few words from his mouth, the pain of raw memories all too evident on his face as he picked up his hat from the table and examined the label inside, paying no particular attention to the writing on it.

"Evening ladies!" announced Ian Ellington. "We have ourselves a job" He grabbed his waterproof, and his sky blue and white metal armlet, denoting his position as being in charge of the men, a Controller Of Site Safety (COSS)

"What is it?" asked Raymond, following suit and grabbing his jacket.

"Does it matter what it is?" sighed Graham. "It's where it is you wanna be worrying about" Work had never been a close friend of Graham's, and he wasn't about to welcome it now, especially on a night with weather as bad as this. He fished in his pocket, his fingers finally coming to rest on his armlet. He wrapped it around his arm, making sure that the red metal plate was clearly visible with its white letters spelling 'LOOK OUT' He secured the straps in place, and then lit up another jailhouse style roll up.

"It's a broken rail" said Ian, nodding towards Raymond then pulling up his hood, and adjusting the woollen hat underneath it. "Hope you remembered your life jackets girls" said Ian. "We shortly set sail for Mallington"

"What?!" spluttered Graham "Mallington? That's at least 150 miles away!"

"You don't have to tell me that!" said Ian, his hands raised as if he were being held at gunpoint. "Think I like spending my working life on the motorway sharing a van with the likes of you? Fact is that we're sent wherever the work is!" Graham grunted in disgust. "If you put as much effort into your work, as you do into being a whining bitch, we'd probably be finished an hour or two early!" Ian turned away from the two men, and opened the door onto what seemed like a tempest growing more furious by the second. "Anyway ladies, the speedboat is waiting" He quipped over his shoulder as he disappeared into the incessant rain.

-5-

"You'd best have guts of steel tonight Jerry; we're down to our minimum staffing level!" Jerry ignored the comment as his temper finally got the better of him, the ragged and chewed end of his biro bouncing violently off the window pane. Gary Fenley, the terminally overworked shift supervisor looked up over the rim of his glasses, smoothing his tie as he tracked the flight of the pen, eyeing Jerry as he pored over a colleagues work station searching for another pen, gesturing to whomever was on the other end of the phone. If he were honest, Jerry wasn't a hundred percent sure who was on the other end of that phone line. In the preceding two hours, two of Jerry's fellow signallers had gone home ill with food poisoning, and he'd been called across from supervising John to cover for one of these colleagues who had gone home ill, and was having real trouble splitting his time between his eager, yet vulnerable charge, and the work of his colleague. As the person on the other end of the phone passed Jerry their information, he was eagerly scanning his own work station to see what John was doing. He was stood back from the signalling panel, scratching his head, engrossed in the running sheet as if it were a best-selling novel. John stepped forward, pressing buttons slowly and precisely that were setting a route for a coal train. The lights representing the route on the panel indicated that he had set the route correctly, and Jerry's shoulders lifted slightly as he returned his attention to the conversation he was meant to be having into the receiver.

"Sorry buddy, could you say again?" Managing to finally locate a pen, he grabbed a piece of scrap paper, and began hurriedly writing down the details that spilled from the receiver, ignoring Gary, who was shouting at him to answer yet another phone, on yet another work station, left unmanned by yet another casualty of the mystery illness. The only response

Jerry chose to muster was a shrug as he turned his back on Gary, once again keeping as constant a watch as he could on John who was busily scribbling on a piece of paper, repeating the information he was given back into the receiver in a text book fashion.

John seemed to be the calmest of the signallers on duty, despite his lack of experience. Gary, busily fielding calls from various people simultaneously, was waving urgently in Jerry's direction. A fault points failure had just occurred, and trains were already starting to back up. He mouthed a silent request asking how long until the repair crew were going to be on scene to fix the problem. Jerry grabbed yet another piece of scrap paper and scribbled in block capitals; 20 MINUTES?? Gary nodded, and turned back to his desk, cradling the receiver of the phone between his neck and shoulder as he searched frantically for another form that needed filling in. Jerry looked across at the ever more confident John.

"Take my advice boy" he said, nodding in Gary's direction. "Never take promotion"

"Come on you lazy bastard!" shouted Ian as he jumped from the minibus, yanking his hood back up over his hastily arranged woolly hat. As Graham blinked himself back to full awareness, he looked up in time to see the side door being slammed shut, as Raymond jumped out into the incessant rain. Grabbing his equipment, he swiftly followed suit. Bowing his head against the raindrops that were smashing into him at an almost horizontal angle, Graham walked as briskly as his idleness would allow him in an attempt to catch up with the other two. Ian was standing at the foot of a signal, talking to the signaller on the telephone, trying to pitch his ear to the receiver in a way that would block out the howling of the wind, and the constant sound of rain hitting his waterproof jacket, whilst Raymond was busying himself tightening the strings on the bottom of his waterproof trousers.

Ian returned the handset to the receiver, and closed the box that housed the phone.

"The line's been blocked lads" he bellowed, pushing his voice above the sound of the terrible weather. "What we've got to do is walk that way, the site is about five minutes away" he shouted, jerking his thumb over his shoulder.

"Points 243B" he recited, wiping away the rainwater that was collecting in his eyebrows. "Apparently the lateral bar has become loose, and the points haven't been setting properly" He looked across at Graham. "No need for the usual safeguards mate. As I said, the line is blocked; I've just spoken to the Signaller. He's confirmed all trains are diverted, so let's get it sorted, and get back into the warm eh?"

"You'll get no arguments from me there!" snorted Graham, fishing his torch out of his bag. "Get in, get it done, and get the fuck out!"

With that the three men set off down the track, their torches piercing the tempestuous mix of the sheer blackness, and the oncoming fury of the weather.

"What you doing at that panel boy?" asked Jerry as he returned to his work station.

"P-Way is on site" said John as he hurriedly returned to the panel he had been patrolling. "Just confirmed the block" Jerry snatched his mug from the overcrowded table, motioning to take a healthy mouthful of coffee, but briskly reconsidering at the last moment. He sniffed the contents of the mug, and after making a point of pursing his lips, returned it to the table, looking down at it forlornly and shaking his head.

"Did you do everything as it should've been done boy?" enquired Jerry.

"Yeah, it's all fine" said John, suddenly becoming irritated at Jerry's questioning. "I left the details on your desk, just near where you've put your..." His voice trailed off as Jerry turned to the desk, his left hand catching his mug and sending it toppling over, covering the seemingly infinite scraps of paper and forms in cold, dark coffee.

"Bastard!" shouted John as he leapt out of his seat and over to the window sill, grabbing the giant roll of paper towel, and covering the desk in it, heavily dabbing at the rapidly smudging reams of paperwork. The phone mounted on Jerry's panel started to ring. Jerry snatched the receiver from its cradle, barking the name of the signal box into the mouthpiece as he continued in his attempts to stem the flow of coffee that was invading all corners of the desk. As he pacified the first in a line of waiting and delayed drivers, Jerry sifted through the coffee soaked papers on his desk, and pulled from the brown flood the piece of paper that moments earlier, John had scribbled details of the conversation he had had with the P-Way crew. Unfortunately, largely due to the coffee incident, the writing John had left for Jerry was largely illegible. Jerry tried to decipher the details on the page, but after a few seconds of repeatedly rotating the paper through

360 degrees, he decided to give John the benefit of the doubt.

"Good work Johnny Boy!" said Jerry, finally picking out the words 'Up Relief' amongst the blurred inky lines, before screwing up the sodden paper, and throwing it at the bin, cursing under his breath as it hit the back wall and slid down to the threadbare carpet. "Just make sure that I'm there with you if anything like this happens again!"

John smiled thinly, half in relief at having managed the procedure correctly, and half in appreciation of the small praise that Jerry had served him. John loosened his tie as he returned to his panel, grabbing the receiver of the telephone as yet another shrill ring filled the air.

"Mallington West" he announced, glancing over at Jerry, who returned the smile along with an approving wink, and gave him a thumbs up gesture.

-8-

"Where the fuck, are these points then?" Graham shouted as he trailed a few steps behind Raymond and Ian.

"Shut up you bone idle bastard!" retorted Ian. "They'll be just along here!" Graham rolled his eyes, muttering under his breath as he held the front of his waterproof hood as far down over his face as he could in some vain attempt to stop himself from getting any wetter.

"Here we are you fucking moaning old woman!" snapped Ian, turning his torch beam full in Graham's face. Graham gave Ian a false smile, before setting off past the points in order to put in place the mandatory stop boards in the middle of the track. Ian opened up the bag of tools and accessories he had brought down from the minibus, pulling out two large lamps, and setting them up on either side of the points. Switching them on, he and Raymond began examining the points in earnest, both after a few minutes, exchanging confused looks as they surveyed the equipment before them.

"Dunno bout' you Ray" shouted Ian above the noise of the weather, sliding his hand under his hood to scratch his head

"But I can't see anything wrong with these!" Raymond replied by way of a shrug of the shoulders.

"I'll ring the signal box!" shouted Ian, standing himself up, and trudging across to the telephone a few yards away at the side of the track. Raymond continued to examine the workings of the points, oblivious to his surroundings, save for the blast of a horn coming from a passing freight train as it throbbed across the adjacent junction. Raymond raised his arm in acknowledgement, before returning his attentions to the mystery of the points.

-9-

Jerry's concentration was hijacked as the phone rang yet again. There was nothing unusual there, especially during this type of disruption. What was unusual, however, was the location that the call was coming from. Frowning, Jerry picked up the receiver.

"Hello Mallington!" boomed the voice at the other end of the line. "This is Ian Ellington, I'm down here at the location of the points failure you reported"

Jerry scratched his head, scrabbling through the myriad of papers strewn across the desk.

"Hang on a second mate" said Jerry as he finally laid his hand on the piece of paper he had faxed to the operations office earlier on concerning the fault on the points. "I've got the paperwork here. Why are you at the crossover on the southbound line mate? The fault is on the northbound line!"

"What?" exclaimed Ian, simultaneously rummaging through his pockets for the details of the job.

"We were sent to service the points at 243B"

"No mate!" insisted Jerry, "Its 243D" Jerry glanced across at the panel, and his stomach lurched sickeningly. "Shit!" he cursed as he lurched towards the panel, and threw the signal protecting the crossover where Ian was calling from back to red. It had been showing green. It was too late. Stuart Mallon's train had just passed the signal at around 65 MPH, and he was clueless as to the drama unfolding both in the signal box, and at the trackside just a few hundred yards ahead in the dark, wet, howling night.

"Get off the line now!" shouted Jerry down the phone. "The express from Victoria has just gone past the signal! I couldn't stop him!" Jerry slammed down the receiver, and set about making an emergency broadcast, his eyes glued to the panel as he prayed that the line would be clear by the time the train reached the points where the three men were.

Ian thrust the phone back into the box housing it, and took off back down the track, shouting a warning to Raymond that he had no hope of hearing

A hundred yards or so further along the track, Stuart Mallon's train hurtled past Graham before he could turn the lens on his lamp to red, in a vain attempt to warn the unsuspecting driver. For a brief second, Graham froze, the full horror of the potential scenario playing out before him. Returning sharply to his senses, Graham turned and made for the work site as quickly as he could, like Ian, screaming a warning to Raymond that was indistinguishable from the howl of the wind. Raymond was on his knees, minutely examining the mechanism of the points when he first felt the rumbling of the track beneath him. He barely had enough time to realise what was going on, the headlight of the train blinding him, and the deafening sound of the horn filling his ears, as the 160 tonne nemesis bore down on him. He scrambled to his feet, his last few seconds of life filled with the stomach churning squeal of metal on metal.

Stuart Mallon, having just heard Jerry's emergency message, threw the train's brake handle to emergency in a desperate and futile attempt to avoid disaster. Before Raymond could throw himself clear of the track, the train's coupler struck him squarely in the chest. Ian Ellington stood, frozen as Raymond's body separated into numerous pieces under the sheer force of the impact, being propelled through the air and down a steep embankment, his mutilated remains finally coming to a scattered and bloody rest in various areas of dense undergrowth. As Graham arrived back at the scene, the train was finally sliding to a violent halt in the distance. He sank to his knees as the reality of what had just happened dawned on him. Ian Ellington was still in shock, covering his ears as he stared at the red tail lights on the rear of the train in blank disbelief. Stuart Mallon was already on the radio, breathlessly relaying the horrific details of the incident by way of an emergency call to the signal box.

The signaller on the receiving end of that particular emergency call was Jerry Pickford. As he ended his conversation with the distraught Stuart Mallon, he looked up at Gary Fenley, who was already on the telephone to the Regional Operations Manager.

"Best get a Rail Incident Officer dispatched Gary" said Jerry, just managing to stifle his obvious distress. John Tierney, realising that he too had played a part in this most horrifying of events, ran for the exit, pressing his hand across his mouth as he tried to make it to the toilets, before he vomited the contents of his stomach onto the floor.

-10-

Steven drummed his fingers on the top of the steering wheel as his mind hurtled along at breakneck speed. The world seemed to dance carelessly past the window, as oblivious to him as he was anonymous to it, and all those disrespectful bastards that filled it. Peering across the road, his eyes remained fixed to their target, devouring every piece of information they could receive. Girls in skimpy dresses flirted and shrieked as they tottered along the uneven pavement, glitter and fake diamonds twinkling in the light cast outward from pub after pub. He sat slouched in the tired seat of his nondescript car, a vehicle that shared his anonymity, as well as his untidy appearance. Running his hand nervously through his hair, he checked his watch.

"Not long now" he muttered. Closing time loomed in the building opposite, the building which housed his prize, and a feeling of anticipation was brewing in the pit of his ulcerated stomach. Steven smiled as he rehearsed mentally what he was about to do, almost salivating at the thought of the release that for him was so near. Reaching over to the dashboard, he took a neatly folded piece of paper in his hand and smoothed it tenderly, studying the names that were arranged methodically across it. His mind was briefly elsewhere as his fingers traced the letters of his orderly, but intense writing, before he folded the paper and placed it back on the dashboard, his trembling fingers resuming their metronomic beat on the worn steering wheel.

Across the emptying street, the building which had been the subject of his gaze was slowly winding downward into darkness. His heart began to beat a little faster as, by now, only one room remained lit. Knowing what his target was, and where it was located, he steeled himself in preparation for the task that now loomed imminent. Scooping up the camera from inside the canvas bag sitting on the passenger seat next to him, he checked it to make sure it was ready to capture the evidence then returned it to the bag. He nervously slipped his hand down into the rear foot well, groping around in the darkness, grabbing a large Perspex box. Taking a furtive look in the car's rear view mirrors, he gently opened it, staring almost lovingly at the contents. Reaching in, he ran the tip of his finger along the ridge of a jagged piece of glass. The moon and the streetlights conspired to make the glass glint and sparkle as he studied it. There were 7 pieces in the box, all working in partnership to throw gentle light displays of blue, green and red against the stained upholstery of the car. He studied the glass pieces for a moment before choosing one, and placing it on the passenger seat next to the canvass bag. Absently, he stroked the reflective surface of the glass as he watched the final few stragglers exit the building, pausing a second to chat on the steps before dispersing in differing directions. His gaze not leaving the building's exit, he fished from the canvass bag an ageing plastic tube. Slowly, he unscrewed the lid, his eyes scanning the thinning lines of revellers as they made their way towards the kebab shops and taxi ranks. Dropping the shard into the tube, he screwed the lid back on and pushed it into the corner of the bag and closed the flap, carefully securing one of the buckles. Slowly opening his car door, he threw the strap of the canvass bag over his shoulder and checked the street in each direction. Crossing silently, he ducked for a second into the alleyway that ran between the two buildings that were now casting ominous shadows onto the street. Taking in a deep breath, he exhaled as opened the bag, reaching inside and producing a small black case. Flipping the lid of the case open, he tenderly picked up a large syringe, sliding off the protective sheath and examining the slender needle as it glinted in the moonlight. His heart pounded as he carefully replaced the sheath and placed the needle back into the case. Returning the case to the bag, he began to move away from the cover of the alleyway. A shrill sound threw him back against the wall. "Shit!" He hissed as the darkness that now dressed the empty street was sliced open by the piercing blue of the flashing lights of a police car. He watched from around the corner as the car pulled up across the road. Two officers got out, grabbing their caps and rushing down the street to an open gate which lead to playing fields. As he observed, he knew only that he wanted this so badly. He yearned for release, for satisfaction, for justice. After a few seconds his head won the argument with his heart, and with his fingers trembling, he slinked out of the alleyway and back to his car, opening the door and placing his bag carefully on the passenger seat. He got in without a backward glance, carefully and quietly closing the car door and starting the engine. Checking his mirrors, he nosed the car into the road, and disappeared easily into the night

-11-

Detective Sergeant Joe Tenby looked around the CID office as he settled himself into his chair. The office was deserted. His appointment to CID had only been confirmed the previous day, and he wasn't officially due to start work there until the following Monday, but a hunger to impress his new Chief Inspector combined with a lack of anything else to do had led Joe to come in and familiarise himself with his new work environment. He hadn't anticipated there being nobody in the office when he arrived, and as such, he wasn't really sure what he should do. Having acquainted himself with the layout of the office, and made sure that his log in details for the police intranet worked from his new computer, he was just standing to leave when a constable bustled through the double doors at the opposite end of the room, spying Joe, and stopping in his tracks.

"Constable" Joe nodded as he put on his coat.

"It's unusual to see any of you lot in here on a Friday afternoon!" The constable said.

"Detective Sergeant Joe Tenby" Joe said with a smile. "I've just moved across from Traffic"

"PC Andy Mills" said the constable as he adjusted the bundle of envelopes tucked under his arm. "I've just brought up the mail. It's a little bit late getting here I'm afraid." Placing the envelopes on the table, he quickly sorted through them before picking one up and handing it to Joe. "There you go Sarge!" he said. "You're getting fan mail already!" Joe frowned as he looked at the small brown envelope. His name was clearly written across the front, but it didn't look the right size to be anything internal or official.

"Cheers Andy!" Joe said with a forced smile.

"No problem!" Andy said over his shoulder, already on his way back through the double doors. Joe sat down, continuing to study the envelope. The address was neatly handwritten, and the envelope had been delivered by hand. Joe carefully ripped it open and tipped the contents onto the desk, a recordable DVD with the same handwriting on it as the envelope. Joe moved to pick the disk up, stopping before he touched it and reaching into his pocket, taking out a paper napkin and gingerly lifting the disk up. He frowned as he read the words out loud, looking nervously around the empty office as he struggled to pronounce the words properly.

"Acceptet est eius culpa"

Joe gulped as his mouth instantly began to dry out. "Is that Latin?" he asked himself. Whatever language it was, Joe knew that the content of the disk would not be nice. Hesitantly, he opened the disk drive of the computer and placed the disk inside. Closing the drawer, he clicked play and waited.

"What the hell?" he whispered to himself, unable to tear his eyes from the screen. The footage was of a naked female. Kneeling, she was staring at the lens; her eyes taped open, her eyeballs red and pained. The film seemed to be savagely edited, the shot lurching from extreme close up of her eyes, to views of her bare skin. Liquid glistened under the artificial light as gravity pulled it slowly earthward, it's journey marked by sticky trails across her forehead, cheeks, neck and breasts. A shadow cast across her shoulder was silhouetting a man masturbating, and as more liquid ran down her face and body, the shot closed in on her lips. She appeared to be saying something. Every part of the short film seemed to be cut so as to be too close to the woman's face for her, or her surroundings to be identified. Joe briefly considered the possibility that this was a porn clip downloaded by his mates in traffic and sent as a prank, but quickly discounted that theory, electing instead to replay the footage with sound. In the background, a man could clearly be heard grunting and moaning. As his groans became more intense, he was muttering something. Joe tilted his ear towards the speaker but couldn't make it out. He replayed the clip again on full volume. The grunting male voice had been slowed down, the tone deep and subhuman. Listening hard, Joe averted his gaze to the ceiling in a bid to clear his mind of everything but that voice. Suddenly, the words became clear.

"Say it, bitch!" came the growling command from out of shot. All this time, the woman's facial expression had not changed at all. She had not flinched, nor had she even tried to blink. Even as he had orgasmed all over her face, neck and chest she had not reacted. "Either she is a great actress, or this is some form of torture!" he said to himself as he began sweating slightly. Looking at the double doors, Joe locked the computer, scooped up the envelope and ran, bursting into the corridor and frantically looking left and right. Sprinting down the corridor, he hurried to the stairs, bounding to the front desk.

"Andy!" he spluttered breathlessly. PC Mills spun round.

"Hello Sarge!" he said. "Can I help you with anything?" Joe put the envelope on the counter.

"Did you see who delivered this?" Andy glanced down at the envelope, shaking his head and shrugging.

"Sorry Sarge" he said. "It was in the letterbox with the rest of the mail." Joe sighed.

"Please tell me there is a camera on the front of the building!"

"I'm afraid not!" Andy replied with a slight shrug."

Ok, thanks anyway" Joe said, turning away from the desk and making his way back towards the stairs. As he walked, he opened his phone, scrolling through his contacts list. Realising he didn't have his new Chief Inspector's phone number; he shoved the phone back in his pocket, swearing under his breath. Rushing back upstairs, he snatched up the receiver to the phone on his desk and stabbed the number for the operator into the keypad. "This is Detective Sergeant Tenby, Amelia Park CID" he said briskly. "I need you to get me a contact number for Detective Chief Inspector Evan Whindle!"

-12-

The urge to make good this burning injustice was growing inside him. Lately it had been more of a struggle to contain these urges, but now it was all too obvious that he was swimming against the tide.

"Things have to be made right!" he hissed as he continued to study Tina. Missing out on his first full taste of justice had made him angry. His hand shook with desperation as he consciously tried to calm his erratic thoughts. Dipping his hand into the canvass bag, he felt his away along the lining until his hand came to rest upon the lid of a box. Lifting the box, Steven removed the lid and felt the ridges of each shard of glass. He had to keep reminding himself that the sharpness of these pieces was being dulled by the gloves that clung to the flesh of his fingers as he settled on a long and thin piece, removing it from the box and studying it intently. The glass felt cold through the material of his trousers as he laid it gently on his knee. Reaching inside the bag, he produced the plastic tube, unscrewing the lid and slipping the shard inside. Looking down at the station, he screwed the lid of the tube back on and returned it to its concealed home inside the bag. Next to the tube lay his syringe box. Opening it carefully he checked the syringe, and the small vial stored carefully within. The seal was intact. Securing the box, Steven focussed on the scene below, satisfied that all was well. The station was almost empty. Reaching inside another pocket, he produced a piece of paper, grubby, yet meticulously folded. Opening the folds out, he studied the contents, running his latex covered finger along a line and tapping it gently.

From his carefully chosen vantage point he could see the hypnotic glare of the CCTV monitor as it illuminated the far corner of Tina's ticket office. Having traced the route of the cable that powered the cameras, Steven watched keenly as he awaited an opportunity to cut that wire and avoid any recording of him on the scene. His right hand gripped a pair of wire clippers as he waited for the right time. He couldn't afford for her to become suspicious that anything was amiss or worse still, report a fault that would prompt a visit from some engineer! Tina continued to sort paperwork and close down machines one by one. When it came to the CCTV monitor, she didn't even look at the screen. She just reached behind her and flicked off the power switch. High up in the undergrowth, Steven gratefully accepted this as a signal to act, cutting the power cable for the cameras and maintaining his covert surveillance. The last train of the evening had just come to a gentle stand at the platform, and its passengers were still busily filing out from its doors and milling around the station exit, waiting for their turn to filter through. It was obvious that Tina was by no means ready to leave. Suddenly, she stood up from her desk and disappeared from view. He made to follow suit, but hesitated, deciding instead to see what she did next. The darkness of the platform was interrupted by light coming from inside the ticket office, as Tina emerged from the fire exit. He looked on as she walked to the front of the ticket window and pulled down the shutter, obscuring the inside of the office from view. She duly returned to the fire exit, pulling the door after her. Concentrating hard, he peered at the door, his ears being pricked by the sound that the door made as it swung closed. "That door didn't shut" he whispered to himself. The decision was made. He would make his way down to the station sooner rather than later to get a better look. Slowly and deliberately, he fed the strap of the bag through the buckle and pulled it tight, securing the flap in place and starting his delicate descent down towards the station.

"I never did like wearing black" muttered Joyce under her breath as she fixed her late husband's favourite brooch into position over her left breast. Eyeing herself in the mirror, she scanned along the lines furrowing her temple and forehead, down to the jowls of her neck that seemed to grow a little larger every time she dared herself to look. Joyce diverted her attention momentarily from her ageing form and inspected the imitation mahogany trim that completed the oval shaped looking glass.

"Even after all these years, this mirror is immaculate" she thought to herself as she absent-mindedly smoothed a trembling hand over her greying hair. Briefly, she allowed herself a smile at the longevity of her husband's last gift to her before his untimely passing, before that distant, gnawing pain that existed in the pit of her stomach forced that briefest of smiles from her lips, returning her delicate features to their usual expression of serenity, tinged with an inner sadness. Joyce had long since learned to cope with life as a widow. One thing she had not been able to do was to get used to it. With her steadily advancing years however, it was as if she had built a crutch from the wisdom and experience one gets from raising two children almost singlehandedly. No matter how relentless the sands of time seemed to drift past however, Joyce never did reconcile the fact that her husband was really gone for good, even after 29 years. Fighting back the urge to give way to her building emotions, Joyce reached for her black tailored jacket, suspending it from her index finger as she gave it a final brush with her other hand. With a well-practiced movement, she slipped the jacket on, and observed her reflection once more as she fastened the two gold buttons on the front. Trying to practice an expression that indicated she was at least comfortable wearing these clothes, she once again wished she could feel at ease wearing anything other than black for her visit to her late husband's graveside on this, the anniversary of his death. Her train of thought was interrupted by the sounding of a car horn. Pushing the net curtain to one side, she looked out of the window, waving her acknowledgement to the taxi driver.

"I really do not like wearing black" she muttered to herself once more, before striding purposely across the living room towards the door, picking up her bag from the highly polished table as she went.

-14-

Steven had taken full advantage of Tina's preoccupation, sneaking up to the fire exit that she had failed to close properly, and managing to slip a small piece of wood into the door to make sure it didn't cheat him of justice by locking him out. Guaranteeing entry into the ticket office was only going to make tonight's job all the easier. Steven looked on from the shadows, pulling a pair of overalls from his bag, and slipping them on as Tina continued, blissfully unaware that she had sealed her fate by failing to ensure that it locked behind her. He felt the adrenaline rise within him as he pulled out his piece of paper from his jacket pocket. His fingers trembled slightly as he unfolded it, taking a pen and striking a careful line through a line of text. He returned the paper to his pocket, and opened his bag, taking the syringe from from its case in readiness as he silently approached the door. The time for justice was near.

The station platforms were now in darkness, the lights having been turned off twenty minutes after the last train had departed. So as far as anyone was concerned, there was nobody here. Tina was preoccupied with the paperwork that covered her desk. Maybe it was because she had been at work for 14 hours straight. Whatever the reason was, it resulted in what could only be described as the direst of consequences for a tiny mistake. Tina stopped in mid scrawl, listening, but remaining completely motionless, her emerald green eyes darting back and forth, scanning the desk as she listened to the room behind her. Slowly, she looked up at the security glass, reacting at first with confusion, and then terror as her eyes met the reflection of a man stood over her, clad in a fluorescent orange boiler suit, wearing what looked like a white hood and paper mask across his face. Her eyes were drawn to his right hand. Without saying a word, he sank a syringe into her neck, depressing the plunger and emptying the contents into her bloodstream. Instantaneously, the tension that had caused her to freeze simply melted away, her body going limp and her head lolling forwards onto the desk. Opening his bag and putting the syringe back into the case, he stood over Tina, studying her intently, his penis straining in unexpected arousal against the material of his clothes, and his breath making the skin on his face moist as it rebounded off the inside of the mask. Lowering his bag carefully to the floor, he unbuckled it and produced a roll of surgical tape. Yanking her head back, he forced her eyes open, one after the other, securing the tape to the upper and lower eyelids. After savouring the sight of her naked eyeballs, he knelt next to her, stroking her cheek gently.

"Come on Tina" he soothed. "Time to wake up darling!" Her cheek muscle twitched slightly, her mouth giving a quiet groan. "Come on babe!" Gradually, her eyes flickered, struggling to find focus as her hands automatically went to her eyelids. "Sit up Tina! Hands by your side! Face straight ahead!"

"What? Who are you?" Tina asked, frantically trying to blink.

"I'm a friend!" Steven said warmly. "I've come to help you with your eyes"

"Why?" Tina said. Steven didn't reply.

Tina frowned. "Why can't I blink?" She asked. "My eyes hurt!"

"That is why I'm here to help you!" Steven said, patting her arm. "You just face straight ahead" Kneeling down for a second he scooped up his bag and set it down on a nearby chair. Producing his camera, two cotton pads, and a roll of bandage which he set down on the desk, he turned the camera on, and opened the viewfinder, taking care to make sure that Tina's face was central to the shot. Returning his attention to the contents of the bag, Steven took out the syringe case and opened it. Beneath the syringe and its foam padding sat a small glass vial filled with small dark coloured flecks. He picked up the vial and placed it in front of Tina, motioning to open it but pausing to make sure his gloves were properly covering his hands. Checking again that the camera was recording, he looked into the lens as he opened the vial and emptied the contents equally between the two cotton pads, gently pressing the small pile of grain like flecks into the wool. Deftly securing the cotton pads to a length of bandage using the surgical tape, he positioned himself behind Tina who continued to look blankly ahead as he leant over her, his forearms resting on her shoulders, the cotton pads only inches from Tina's eyes which were now weeping.

"Tina babe" he whispered softly, his throbbing groin pressing into her back.

"Yes?" Tina replied, oblivious both to his arousal which was rapidly increasing, and the mortal danger she was in.

"I'm going to put something on your eyes that will help" he said.

"Will it stop the pain?" she asked. Licking his lips, Steven leant into Tina's ear.

"It'll help you see things as they really are, I promise you that!" Before she could reply, he pressed the cotton pads against Tina's eyes, bringing each end of the bandage together at the back of her head and tying them neatly in a tight knot. She sighed, the cotton pads giving the briefest of respite from her inability to blink in reaction to the harsh office light. Within microseconds however, the abrasive flecks on the cotton pads began burning into Tina's eyes, her body shaking as she emptied her lungs of air with a shrill, blood curdling scream "Please!" she screamed, her voice descending into unintelligible sobs. "Make it stop! Make it stop!" Seizing the moment, Steven grabbed the knot of the bandage and yanked her head back sharply. His heart was pounding, and he was so exhilarated by the proximity of justice that he could feel his pulse beating a rhythm within his erect penis.

"I'll make it stop when you take responsibility!" he snarled, lifting her from the chair as he pulled the bandage ever tighter. "Say it!"

"Please! I'll say anything!" she wailed. "Just stop it! My eyes!"

"Say it!" he screamed, yanking again on the bandage. His fury was spiralling and giving way to a primal urge to take what he wanted, what he needed. "Take the blame!"

"I'm to blame! I'm to blame!" she shrieked, her body shaking with increasing violence, her voice now a heaving soup of grunts and sobs. "I'll say anything! I'll do anything!"

Repositioning himself squarely behind Tina, he looped his free arm around her stomach, pulling her violently against his crotch and punching her hard in the ribs. As she gasped for breath through her sobs his lips were touching her neck as he spoke.

"You'll do what I tell you!" he hissed, checking the viewfinder on the camera. Her agonised face dominated the screen. Tina tried to cry out but his vicious punch to her lungs had drained her of air. So pained was her body and so heightened were her senses that his breath almost burned her neck. "I own you Tina! I take whatever I fucking want so you pay the debt you owe!" Before she could react, Steven slid his hand from her stomach down to the belt on her trousers, ripping at it furiously. As Tina shrieked in protest, her body still virtually paralysed thanks to the injection Steven had given her, he tore at her buttons, easily conquering them and her zipper, before wrenching her trousers earthward and kicking her legs apart. "No! Please! I'm begging you!" The medazolene had rendered Tina helpless, and they both knew it. Steven pulled a condom from his pocket, tugging at his overalls and trousers. He opened the condom wrapper and expertly rolled it down his shaft before slamming her head down against the table. Before she could react, Steven was inside her, deep, uninvited and thrusting viciously. Tina's body instinctively spasmed as she clenched her muscles hard. Steven responded with another punch to her ribs, knocking the breath viciously from her body, along with her will to fight.

"Please! Why are doing this?" she asked in agonised whispers, the pain of Steven's thrusts taking her breath away.

"Louder!" Steven barked, without warning he hacked at her blouse with the glass shard, slashing the material and yanking it apart, exposing the flesh of her back. Tina screamed as he ripped through her bra strap. She was begging for her life.

"Please! Please don't kill me! It's my fault! It's my fault!"

"Mea Culpa! Mea Culpa! Mea fucking Culpa!" he screamed as his arousal suddenly began racing away with him. He began slamming his hips against Tina as hard as he could. She cried out as the force of his exertions smashed her stomach and pelvis against the desk, and as he stared down at her naked back, his lust for vengeance took over, sending him barrelling towards a growling orgasm as he dug the glass into her back and pulled hard, cutting savagely into her flesh.

"Here! Let me spell it out for you so there's no mistake!" The air filled with a cacophony of high pitched screams and orgasmic grunts, Tina's back teeming with blood, her body twitching and bucking, Steven crashing over the brink and climaxing inside her, his overalls turning a dark red from the warm torrents that poured from her jagged wounds. As Tina lost consciousness he continued to thrust mercilessly.

Noticing the limpness of her body, he grabbed a handful of her hair, the glass shard protruding menacingly from just below her right shoulder. With his free hand he ripped the cotton pads away from her eyes, checking the viewfinder to make sure that Tina remained central to the shot. She mumbled incoherently, her voice reduced to a lethargic roll of shallow gasps as the agony of the air touching her eyes roused her. Still wedged deep within her, his body trembled as he breathed deeply.

"What do you say Tina?" he whispered, yanking sharply on her hair. Trying desperately to talk in a vain attempt to escape with her life, she murmured. "Mea Culpa"

"Good girl!" Steven whispered. Without warning, he pulled the glass shard from beneath her shoulder. She cried out as the wound spilled yet more blood across her desecrated skin.

"Say goodnight Tina" he said, lining the tip of the glass shard with the space between her bottom two ribs. Before she could respond, he drove the shard into her, ramming it as far inside her as he could, and twisting it with such force that it broke. Tina let out a grunt as her body fell forward onto the desk. Steven pulled himself from within her, letting out a satisfied gasp as he paused for a second to appreciate his work. He observed dispassionately as her dying body twitched and jerked. The last embers of Tina's life faded before him as he watched the camera's viewfinder, licking his lips as blood oozed from Tina's mouth, her blistered eyes glaring grotesquely. Adjusting his clothing and fastening his trousers, the full condom was clinging to his wilting shaft. As much as it felt awful against his skin, he couldn't risk removing it and leaving biological traces. Steven stood back from Tina's prone corpse as a lethargic torrent of blood pooled on the desk and then fell toward the threadbare carpet. He surveyed the scene, breathing heavily. The exhilaration of what he had done was causing him to perspire. He examined her lifeless face and once green eyes, now blistered, reddened and clouded, her bloodied mouth shaped as if to ask why it was her life had been so cruelly snatched away. Revelling in the scene for one final time, Steven heaved her expired form over his shoulder, and staggered out of the door and into the cold, dark, night air, heading towards the shadows that shrouded the ramp at the far end of the now long deserted platform.

-15-

As soon as the gates swung open, Joe sped into the yard, just managing to slow down enough to drive over a speed bump without smashing his head against the roof of the car. Regaining his composure, he swung the car into the first available space, coming to an unceremonious halt between two immaculate patrol cars. Grabbing his briefcase, Joe jumped out of the car and started force marching across the yard, pausing only to punch the access code into the keypad on the door and straighten his tie.

"You must be the new boy!" boomed the voice from inside the Duty Inspector's office. Joe paused, summoning up his best business like stride as he approached the office door.

Inspector Goodman was crammed into a ragged brown swivel chair that was fraying on the arms, and squeaked at a ridiculously high pitch every time he moved. Joe stood almost at attention, struggling to avoid being distracted by the burgeoning collection of football trophies, and a photograph of the inspector stood next to Alan Shearer that filled a shelf behind his head. Staring at Joe, Inspector Goodman preened his moustache as he reached across the desk and took a folded piece of paper from one of the neatly arranged trays, and placed it carefully on the table top. Joe cleared his throat.

"I'm actually running a little.."

"Late, Detective Sergeant Tenby?" asked the Inspector, his thick eyebrows raised high as he returned to his slow and steady typing. He picked up the piece of paper, pressing the crease between his thumb and forefinger before handing it across the desk. "From the DCI" he said, once again returning to his typing. Joe scrutinized the page.

"A body on a railway line sir?" he asked, confused as to why this was not being pursued by the British Transport Police.

"That's right Detective Sergeant, a body on a railway line" replied the Inspector, sounding a little bit frustrated as his eyes scanned the computer screen in front of him.

"Am I right in guessing that the deceased wasn't killed by a train then?" asked Joe. The inspector stopped typing again, looking up from behind the desk with a tolerant smile that would usually be spared for dealing with people of much lower intelligence.

"Like it says on the paper, the deceased has injuries consistent with being impacted by a train. However, there are signs of head trauma that are inconsistent with the same cause. Do me a favour DS Tenby, hit the ground running, and get to the scene!"

"Don't suppose you know where this scene is, do you sir?" asked Joe.

"No" came the flat reply. "No I do not"

Coming to terms with the fact that he had definitely not made a friend, Joe turned away and made once again for the corridor.

"DS Tenby" shouted the inspector.

"Yes sir" replied Joe, electing this time not to go back into the office.

"Three things" he continued. The gentle and constant tapping of computer keys could be heard in the background as he spoke. "Firstly, the traffic garage is at the end of the yard. They'll sort you out with directions"

"Cheers Sir" replied Joe.

"Second thing" he continued, cutting Joe off. He pointed a meaty finger at Joe's chest. "What tie is that?"

Joe looked down at the bright red tie. "It's Hull Kingston Rovers sir, Rugby League"

"I know who they are Sergeant!" retorted Inspector Goodman. He studied the three crowns of the club's emblem for a second. He shrugged. "At least it's not Man United" Joe forced an awkward smile.

"One last thing Mr Tenby" Joe's smile faded.

"The speed limit in the yard is 10mph for a reason. If I catch you driving like a lout in my yard again, the results will not be pretty. Are we clear Detective Sergeant?"

"Yes Sir" replied Joe, swiftly turning on his heels and walking back down the corridor in search of the traffic garage, the echo of his steps on polished floor filling his ears as he went.

-16-

Anna Brown's delicate hand gently cradled her jaw as her slender face illuminated with a dazzling smile that was mirrored in the face of the athletic young man whose hand was tracing the soft skin of her forearm. Her other hand played absently with a spoon which nestled in an oversized coffee cup. A barista fussed over an overheated jug of milk as he poured lattes. In the corner, a group of teenage girls shrieked and covered their faces as they feigned embarrassment at the pictures they showed each other from their mobile phones. She could never have known, but right across the busy street was a man who wanted her. He wanted her for his own peculiar, dark reasons. Steven hunched down into his seat, observing Anna Brown as she shared a flirtatious joke with her boyfriend. Subconsciously he licked his lips as he studied her petite and feminine form. Anna's boyfriend called the barista over and handed over money, smiling as he took his change. Leaning into her he kissed her lips, a kiss that she returned passionately, her fingers tracing at his pronounced jaw line. Grabbing his coat, he headed for the door, pausing and turning to her and waving, before hurrying away and disappearing into the steady stream of shoppers.

Across the street the surveillance continued. Anna gazed out of the window, looking past the throngs of shoppers, deep in contemplation as she sipped at the remainder of her coffee. Steven continued to analyse her every expression, studiously ignoring the people passing his car, yet remaining acutely aware of the fact that he was staking out his next victim in an exceptionally public place. He readied himself to move as he watched her slip her coat on and pick up her bag, handing over her now empty cup to the barista and walking out into the busy street, making a call on her mobile as she went. Across the street, her stalker switched on his engine, and drifted into the afternoon traffic.

Driving up and down the narrow lane was getting repetitive. Joe was looking for a tiny access path, but couldn't see anything lining the roadside, with the exception of a constant green army of angry looking plants and bushes. Squinting in the glare of the late morning sun, Joe was getting increasingly frustrated at his inability to locate the scene, and the fact that he was still running late.

Muttering under his breath, Joe pulled the car sharply into a lay by at the far end of the lane, deciding to trace the hedgerow. Stepping as far into the roadside as possible to escape the path of an approaching bus, Joe fished his mobile phone out of his pocket. No reception. Looking up to the opposite side of the road, he noticed a slight parting in the vegetation with a natural path that had been worn into the ground by the passing of feet over many years. Looking left and right, he darted across the road, gingerly stepping into the void between two bushes. The sun was casting strange and wonderful shadows on the narrow path as he made his way down the bank that fell sharply away from the road. He could see that the pathway widened a little further down, and could just make out the fluorescent yellow of a constable's jacket. He was half an hour late, his shoes and trousers were caked in mud, and he was sweating to the point that his shirt was clinging to his back. Today was not going to go down as a great first day.

Joe flashed his warrant card at the constable whose jacket

had guided him down to the gate, and stepped under the police tape. The bank's steep drop evened out below and merged with the grey ballast of the railway line. The track was a hive of activity. A mix of florescent yellow jackets and white forensic suits busily tracked back and forth between Upper Charleston station, about 100 metres away, and the white tent that indicated the location of the deceased. On the far side of the track, the usual bland grey concrete of the retaining wall was serving as a backdrop to the macabre work of the forensic specialists and police who were diligently combing the area, inch by inch. Joe carefully walked the last few steps to the crime scene, and it dawned on him just how eerily quiet it was here, especially considering that normally, trains would be speeding through here every few minutes. Collecting his thoughts, he walked up to the side of the tent, coughing nervously as his hand hovered over the zip that was keeping the inner crime scene free from prying eyes. Here at the bottom of the bank there was a slight breeze, and it was making his sweaty shirt feel as though it had been doused in iced water as he shivered, realizing just in time that he wasn't wearing a forensic suit.

"DCI Whindle" Called out Joe, feeling somewhat awkward.

"Go and see Jessica Hopewell DS Tenby" replied a disembodied voice. "She's up at the station. She will issue you with a forensic suit."

"Yes sir" replied Joe, looking at his mud covered shoes in the absence of an actual person to direct his speech at. Trying to separate his shirt from the skin on his back, he shivered again as he turned away from the tent and looked towards the station, its modular 1960s style buildings rising awkwardly from the ballast.

Standing over his father's weather worn gravestone, Steven stared down blankly at the mud and grass that housed Raymond Kilkis' final resting place, his mind a heavy dust cloud of naked rawness that still ate at him. He glanced at his mother, who was standing between her two sons, her eyes gently closed, her hands crossed at her front as if deep in contemplation. He always wished he could conduct himself with the same kind of dignity and calm that she managed. She looked at him, smiling reassuringly, in the same way she did when he was 9 years old, looking on forlornly as his father's coffin was lowered into the ground. Joyce studied Steven closely as his eyes returned to the gravestone. Always such a troubled and insecure child, he had been a twin, although his brother had died aged only a few days, and despite the best efforts of both his parents, he never seemed to feel quite complete. In many ways, her guilt over the effect it had on Steven had prevented her from accepting it fully herself. Steven looked across to Robert, his younger brother who was born after Raymond was killed. Despite his never having been held by their father, or played in the garden with him, his sense of loss seemed razor sharp, and Steven couldn't help but admire his younger brother for that. Just then, his thoughts of admiration for his younger brother were disturbed as his peripheral vision picked up the figure of an old man. Clad in sombre black, Graham's hair was grey and untamed, wildly and disproportionately flying in all directions under the attentions of the gentle afternoon breeze. The bulky overcoat he wore failed miserably to disguise the frailty of body that belied his advancing years. As Steven watched Graham approach, he felt his fists start to curl up and clench as a wave of anger washed over him. Joyce looked up at the reddening face at her son, and stepped forward, intercepting the approach of the unwanted, yet familiar visitor. Steven's rage was only heightened as he watched his mother's gloved hand lay gently on Graham's shoulder. The anger pulsed through his veins like white hot lava as he saw Graham's hand come to rest on the small of Joyce's back.

"Did you know about this?" barked Steven at his brother.

"About what?" spluttered Robert, shaken from his thoughts, and scrambling to get a hold on what was going on. "What are you talking about?"

Steven lurched at his brother, grabbing violently at the lapels of his grey overcoat, yanking and shoving him back and forth as the material clamped between his gloved fingers strained.

"You've fucking lost it Steve!" shouted Robert as he shoved his brother back in attempt to break free.

Seeing the struggle that was erupting beside her husband's grave, Joyce Kilkis rushed from Graham, slapping her hand onto the top of her head in an attempt to stop her hat from tumbling from her head as she went.

"Stop it!" she bellowed, her voice cracking as the tears welled up in her eyes, and cascaded down her cheeks. Graham followed as quickly as his frailty allowed, trailing only a yard or two behind Joyce as she gripped her son's shoulder with all her might.

"Steven, please!" she shouted. At that moment, Robert shoved his brother in the chest, causing him to lose his grip on the lapels of Robert's jacket, and fall backwards, crashing down onto the grassy surface of their father's grave, taking his mother, and the Graham, who had just managed to drag himself to the aid of Joyce, with him. The three of them landed in a heap on the grave, the air filled with Joyce's tears, and Steven's almost incomprehensible screams of rage. Robert stood there, looking at them, his hands over his mouth as he searched for some kind of appropriate words, but none came.

"Come on Steven!" pleaded Graham, gingerly bringing himself to his feet, and doing his best to help the sobbing Joyce up from the ground.

"Shut it!" spat Steven. "You don't have the right to speak to me!" He jabbed a finger accusingly in Graham's direction.

"Steve!" exclaimed Robert. "Don't speak to him like that!"

Steven span on his heels, glaring at his brother.

"Have you gone out of your mind?" said Robert, staring at Steven, half in disgust, and half in disbelief that he could lack such respect on such a day. "What could Graham have done that's made you so angry?"

"Good old Uncle Graham killed Dad!"

Robert looked across at his mother and Graham, who were still standing on Raymond's grave, looking at the floor.

A silence stonier than the headstones that surrounded them permeated the brisk air.

Robert looked at his mother.

"Is this.." his voice trailed off.

"No it certainly is not" replied Joyce sternly. "Graham was.."
she paused momentarily as she searched for the right way to explain.

"I was working with your father" offered Graham, his eyes still not meeting Robert's as he spoke.

"Right?" demanded Robert as he tried to look the old man right in the eye.

"On the night he died" Graham rubbed his eyes with an ageing hand.

"On the night you killed him!" shouted Steven. By this point he was pacing up and down as his mind desperately tried to unscramble itself.

"What are you talking about Steve?" said Robert, half turning so he could see his brother.

Graham cut in once more. "I was the look out on the section of track where the train hit your dad." He looked briefly at Joyce. Her eyes were fixed on the engraved letters of Raymond's headstone. "I could've done something" he whispered, his voice cracking with emotion.

"You couldn't" hissed Joyce as she patted his arm. "The inquiry cleared you! They blamed the railway! Nobody blamed you! We still don't blame you!" Her hand lingered on Graham's for a second, a gesture that was observed by both brothers.

"I blame you" muttered Steven, fixing Graham with a cold stare. "I always will!"

Robert was reeling. Graham had always been around, for as long as he could remember. He never knew. His mother always told him about his dad, and all the good times they had, but neither she nor indeed Graham had ever spoken about the accident. It had always been too painful for Steven for Robert to ask. He felt betrayed, and as if he had been kept on the outside of some grandiose conspiracy, but he didn't feel blame for Graham. He needed time to think.

As Robert brought his mind back to his father's graveside,

Steven was making a move towards Graham.

"That's enough!" shouted Robert as he stepped into his brother's path. "How dare you be so disrespectful?"

"Disrespectful? Me?" spluttered Steven. "She is stood there with the bloke who killed our dad as if they're high school sweethearts and you can't see what's wrong? She was shagging him before dad was even dead! It wouldn't surprise me if that's where you came from!"

"Bastard!" he screamed. "Don't you ever!" He swung his fist at his older brother, catching him squarely under the chin, sending him barrelling over a neighbouring gravestone and spinning a small plastic bottle filled with brightly coloured flowers across the grass, scattering its contents. Joyce let out a cry, burying her face in Graham's chest, sobbing relentlessly as Robert walked over to wear his brother was lying. He crouched near his brother's reddened and grazed face, glaring down.

"I don't care what deluded fantasies you've got in your twisted little brain Steven, but I can tell you that whatever happened that night, Graham Crosbie is more of a man than you could ever hope to be, so I think it's best you go!"

Steven stared back at his younger brother, his eyes intense and unblinking. He dragged himself to his feet and ran a hand through his hair, straightening his suit.

"Look at you!" he snarled. Graham and Joyce stared back at him, still numb with shock at his actions. He looked down at their feet which were still on the grass covering Raymond's grave.

"At least you're not dancing on it, that's something I suppose!" he stared at his mother for a moment, holding eye contact until she broke the gaze, shuffling uncomfortably.

Turning back to his brother, Steven fixed him once again with the same intense gaze.

"Ask them!" Spat Steven, his hand outstretched as if he were trying to pull Robert into some kind of conspiracy. "Ask them why she asked me not to tell dad, ask them Robert!"

"Just go!" ordered Robert, still slightly breathless with anger.

"But you don't understand" replied Steven. He turned and began trudging away, his fists clenched tightly at his side as he marched through the graveyard.

"Steve!" shouted Robert after him. He stopped and turned.

"You ever talk to our mother like that again, and I'll kill you"

His eyes locked with Steven's as his older brother took on board what he had said. Deciding not to reply, Steven turned away and stomped towards the gothic stone gate at the eastern end of the cemetery.

-19-

Upper Charleston station, usually a place of steady and uninteresting activity, was now a crime scene. The station car park, usually crammed with the cars of London bound commuters, was cordoned off by police tape. A small crowd of curious onlookers had gathered at the tape, eager for a ghoulish glimpse of what was taking place inside the building. Inside the ticket office, Jessica Hopewell, scenes of crime officer, or SOCO as the Police called them, was on her hands and knees under the desk examining the threadbare carpet for blood spatter.

"Miss Hopewell!" said DC Glen Violet, allowing his eyes to travel along the outline of her bottom as the material of her forensic suit stretched across it. Beneath the desk Jessica rolled her eyes.

"What do you want?" she sighed as she continued examining the carpet.

"Just had the railway children on the phone" he replied as he continued staring at her backside. "Apparently they're not too pleased about the fact that their forensic people have been frozen out. What's the official story?" He went quiet as he imagined the type of underwear Jessica was wearing.

"If the case is investigated by the Metropolitan Police, it's best that all the forensic work is done by the associated forensics officers as well. It makes it harder for a clever defence brief to question the evidence continuity when the case goes to court" she replied in a matter of fact tone. "If the British Transport Police have a problem, tell them to speak to Dr Rothesay!"

"Oh, right" Glen stumbled for a reply as his fantasies about Jessica's underwear were interrupted by a vision of the rotund, bearded Dr Rothesay.

Glen turned towards the door, his gloved hand resting on the door handle.

"Oh, and Glen" called Jessica from beneath the desk.

"Yes" he said, pausing for a second.

"Last night some poor woman was brutally attacked in here and murdered. I don't think it's the time or place to be checking out my arse, do you?"

She could almost hear his face redden as the door closed clumsily behind him, Glen making coughed excuses as he went. Giggling to herself, she continued with her minute examination of the carpet.

As Joe trudged along the track, he managed to pick out the unmistakably feminine figure of Jessica Hopewell. He paused for a second, watching her as she turned and closed the door she had walked through only seconds before. She was now bent over a red plastic box at the back of a white van emblazoned with the words 'FORENSIC SUPPORT' As he started to climb the ramp at the end of the platform, Joe tried not to stare at the taught white fabric that was stretched across her buttocks, instead focusing on the splashes of mud that were covering his shoes and trouser bottoms.

Straightening himself up, he stood directly behind Jessica as she continued to rummage in the box. Without looking up, she snapped the latex gloves that she was wearing from her delicate hands and threw them into a yellow sack that was hanging from a frame on the inside of the van door, before reaching back into the box and throwing a plastic package at him.

"DC Tenby I presume. I reckon that should be about your size." The package impacted with Joe's chest, and he trapped it, grabbing the wrapping and clenching his fist as he lowered it, looking at the pristine forensic suit that was inside. For a second, Joe was genuinely confused.

"How did you..?" he stammered, still looking at her buttocks, this time, his mouth slightly open.

"Forensic scientists know everything Joe!" she giggled. "I can call you Joe, can't I?" she said, turning to face him with a wide smile.

"Joe's fine." he said, his weight shifting from foot to foot for a few seconds as he stifled a blush. "That was quite impressive

Miss Hopewell"

"If you think that was impressive, all I can say is that you are way too easily pleased" she retorted, their gazes meeting for a second as Joe set about ripping open the packaging from the forensic suit. Infuriatingly, the size of the suit was correct.

"My standards are much higher than that Jessica" responded Joe, gathering his game, and returning the visual compliment by slowly and deliberately looking her petite, almost feline frame up and down, in much greater detail than she had examined him. Jessica's eyes flicked downward and she examined her white training shoes for a second. "I can call you Jessica, can't I?" Joe said, with a touch of irony. Jessica blushed.

"Anyway" she retorted, pulling a hair grip from the back of her head and re-inserting it into her immaculate black locks "How do you know I'm a Miss?"

"Sorry?" Joe replied, momentarily jolted from his revelling.

"When you called me Miss Hopewell" she said. "How did you know I'm a Miss? I could be married." She said, a sly grin slowly spreading across her face again.

"That was really quite simple" he said. "Your ring finger on your left hand is empty."

"I could've just taken it off, or be allergic to gold or silver!" she said, crossing her arms.

"Not really" he replied, warming to the task of impressing her. "If you really were allergic to metal, you'd probably wear your wedding ring around your neck. Given that you don't have an allergy, the skin tone on your ring finger is the same as the rest of your hand. If you wore a ring but took it off for work, the skin under the ring would be lighter than on the rest of

your hand, and the texture of the skin would be different too!"
Her arms dropped to her side in defeat.

"That was quite impressive Mr Tenby" said Jessica.

"If you think that was impressive, all I can say is that you are way too easily pleased" he replied with a wink. Laughing, she stepped back toward the van and picked up a clipboard.

"Okay, okay. I think you'd best get back to the DCI before he comes hunting you down!"

"You're probably right" he said, turning to walk away.

"Oh, and by the way" Joe was speaking over his shoulder.

"Yes" she said, looking up from her clipboard, her composure regained.

"It's DS" he said casually.

"Come again?" she mused, looking up quizzically

"When I walked up, you called me DC Tenby. It's DS Tenby" he said, stopping and turning to her with a smug smile.

"In that case I am so very sorry Detective Sergeant!" she said with mock remorse.

That said, he strode back toward the crime scene, unfolding the forensic suit as he walked.

"Well don't just stand there DS Tenby" boomed the voice of the DCI, "Get in here!"

Joe grabbed at the zip of the forensic tent, yanking it up hard and folding himself inside. As he fully immersed himself in the parallel world within the grisly confines of the tent, he turned to face the person from which the hitherto disembodied voice of the DCI came.

"I do hope you're not squeamish DS Tenby" he said. Joe took a deep breath as he cast an eager eye over the crime scene, processing all of the information that was laid out before him within what was now the final inner sanctum of the deceased. An older detective once told Joe that, if you can think of any way in which one human can hurt or kill another, no matter how horrible, or how deranged, it's probably already been done. He also said that, given the wrong circumstances, and the wrong pressures, anyone is literally capable of anything if they're in the wrong place at the wrong time. The DCI was standing in the corner of the tent, dispassionately observing whilst another man bent over the body of the deceased, a clipboard lying on the floor just near the left foot of the bloodied corpse. A third man was hurriedly packing a camera into a metal carry case, folding the straps and leads into the box and clicking it shut, leaning over to the man bending near the body and passing him a piece of paper which he signed before handing it back. The photographer slid the paper into a compartment at the back of his carry case, stood up and turned to the DCI, nodding and making for the exit, gesturing to Joe as he passed. Joe waited for him to leave before carefully zipping the entrance to the tent firmly closed. Turning his full attention to the ghastly scene, Joe tried to take in as much detail as he could whilst fighting the urge to be sick. The body was that of a middle aged woman. She was approximately 5ft 2 to 5ft 3 in height. She had peroxide blonde hair, and was lying face down. Her trousers were unfastened. The body of the deceased was straddling the left hand rail of the Coastal bound track, the torso separated from the lower body at the small of the back. The rail was covered in tissue, blood and body matter where it intersected with the corpse, and beneath the body, the ballast was stained a deep red, as was the back of her white blouse. "Jesus. I hope she wasn't alive when the train hit!" he motioned unnecessarily as he crouched next to her. Her head was lying to one side, and as Joe glanced at her face, his breath was taken from his chest.

"I can tell you indeed that Mrs McBride was not alive, Detective Sergeant!" said pathologist Dr Tom Rothesay as he handed Joe a paper towel. "Just in case" he said with a tired smile. Joe looked blankly down at the paper towel in his hand, and then back at the horrifically disfigured eyes of the victim, electing to hold it to his mouth, more as a precaution than anything else.

"Mrs McBride?" asked Joe.

"Tina McBride Detective Sergeant" Joe turned to face DCI Whindle. "According to her ID she worked in the ticket office up on the platform" Before Joe could reply, DCI Whindle's phone vibrated. Snatching it from his pocket he turned away as he answered the call. The brief conversation was over. Turning back to the body, he shuddered. As a seasoned traffic officer Joe had acquainted himself with the grisly adornments of brutal death. This however, was altogether different. These injuries were not the consequence of misfortune, they were overtly sadistic, and it had caught Joe off guard.

"Look here" said Dr Rothesay, pointing at the pooling of congealed blood beneath the body with his biro. "Had she been alive when this happened, the blood would have pooled in a much different way. The manner in which the blood has left the body is indicative of gravity, and not of the major arteries being severed whilst the heart was pumping blood" Joe stared up at the pathologist as he slipped the biro back into his top pocket. Dr Rothesay continued. "Further to this, the fact that there is not a huge spray of blood across a wider area confirms our thoughts that the deceased was assaulted in the ticket office, and then dragged or carried here" As the pathologist spoke, Joe tried to focus on the bloodstains that Dr Rothesay was referring to, but he couldn't divert his gaze away from those eyes.

"Corneal Leukoma" said Dr Rothesay. Joe managed to tear his gaze from the eyes of the deceased long enough to look across at the pathologist, who was busily scribbling on a form attached to his clipboard.

"I'm sorry?" Joe replied from behind the paper towel. Dr Rothesay finished the sentence he was writing with a full stop, which he announced with an emphatic stab of the form with his pen.

"The damage to the eyes" Dr Rothesay replied as he placed the clipboard on top of his bag and slipped the pen into his top pocket. "Those injuries were caused by chemical burns." He knelt beside the body, as Joe looked on. "This whitening of the eye in the area of the iris and pupil is known as porcelainisation DS Tenby"

"What type of chemicals?" asked Joe. Stuffing the paper towel into his trouser pocket, he reached inside his jacket and produced his notebook and a pen. This type of injury is caused by a high concentration of an oxidising agent being applied directly to the eyes, either in liquid or powder form"

"Would it be possible for the deceased to have perhaps been exposed to a chemical and then in a panic, blindly stumbled down the platform and in front of a train?" Dr Rothesay shrugged.

"Possible, but highly unlikely. I say that for three reasons. Firstly, the severity of the damage to the eyes, secondly, the unlikeliness of a platform office having the required chemical type" Dr Rothesay paused.

"Thirdly?" Joe enquired as he looked up from the notes he was taking. The doctor knelt beside the body and slowly pulled Tina McBride's blouse up, revealing the savagely carved wounds to her back.

"Wow!" Joe said, sighing loudly as he exhaled, leaning his head to one side as he studied the bloodstained and torn skin. As Dr Rothesay moved to pull the blouse back down, Joe stepped forward.

"Hang on" he said, continuing to stare. "Are those wounds arranged in a pattern?" "I'm not sure Joe" replied Dr Rothesay. To be fair, there is too much blood on the skin. We'll get her cleaned up when we get back and have a proper look then." Joe nodded as he continued taking notes.

"Regarding the chemical used in the attack on the eyes. Any hunches?"

"Well, I have tentative good news on that front!" said Dr Rothesay. I discovered a small quantity of coarse powder from around the eyes. I took samples and will send them to Miss Hopewell for analysis. From a cursory glance, I'd hazard a guess at Potassium Permanganate" Joe shrugged as he looked at the doctor blankly. It's an oxidising agent Joe, used for all sorts of things, from waste water cleaning, to treatment of fungal infections. It's even used to prematurely age TV & theatre props"

"It sounds like a widely available product Doc" sighed Joe, his shoulders sagging. "I don't suppose there's much chance of forensics?" Joe asked, as he turned and looked at the DCI. DCI Whindle was still standing in the corner of the tent, phone call now finished and looking on moodily as Joe quizzed the pathologist.

"Not good I'm afraid" replied Dr Rothesay "I would say that the killer had a good idea that leaving a body in a situation like this would maximise the chances of contaminants interfering with the body, as well as perhaps being a clumsy attempt at hiding the cause of death? I have to say that it is an unusual location to leave a body. The attacker could be someone who knows about trains if the trackside is his home turf. At least we'll know more about the victim after the Post Mortem"

Joe frowned. Something didn't seem to add up here. The body was laid horizontally across the rails. The injuries caused by the train were at the opposite end of the body to the horrific attack on the eyes, as well as the stab wounds, and this bothered him.

"I don't get it" muttered Joe, his eyes repeatedly scanning from the blood soaked ballast that lay beside Tina McBride, and the contaminated white of her blistered eyeballs..

"Don't get what?" asked the DCI. Joe turned and faced him. The mixture of curiosity and impatience in his voice made Joe a little worried, though the fact that he had been acknowledged was at least progress.

"The only reason the killer would dump the body on an open railway line would be to disguise the fact that it was a murder. Why would they position the body so that the only mutilation that took place was above the waist? It is still abundantly clear that this lady was murdered, so to place the body here would seem pointless"

The DCI and Dr Rothesay looked thoughtful as they mulled over what Joe had just said, the only things filling the air inside the tent being a tangible silence, along the smell of stale blood.

"Maybe it was personal" DCI Whindle mused.

"Or maybe he was disturbed" Joe offered.

"How do you mean?" he asked.

"Dr Rothesay said that this was probably a man who knows about the railways" The DCI nodded thoughtfully. "What if he wasn't expecting a train to pass through here at the time of the body dump?" Joe reached for his notebook. "According to the incident log, the alarm was raised at 05:13 this morning by the Driver of an empty train. The thought is that it was his train that inflicted the second injury to the deceased. But what if it wasn't?"

The DCI stroked his chin.

"Okay DS Tenby, get onto the rail authorities and see if this theory of yours holds up. If forensics are looking patchy, we'd best explore other possibilities. Take DC Violet with you"

"Yes sir" said Joe, reaching for the zip, and starting to undo it slowly. "Where will I find DC Violet?"

"If he's doing his bloody job he should be still around the station buildings DS Tenby, though no doubt he's sniffing around Jessica!" said the DCI, looking across at the pathologist. Dr Rothesay nodded sagely.

"Not a problem sir, I'll track him down" said Joe, grateful for the chance to leave. He paused for a second. "What about CCTV footage from the station?"

"The power cable to the security system was cut" DCI Whindle replied curtly, once again fiddling with his phone. "We have the system up and running on a generator, and we're downloading the camera footage now. Will there be anything else, DS Tenby?" Before Joe could reply, DCI Whindle stabbed at a button on his phone and crammed it to his ear. Joe looked across at Dr Rothesay who smiled, reinforcing Joe's assumption that his cue to exit the tent had arrived. As he walked away, inhaling the fresh air of the trackside, the DCI's voice boomed through the side of the tent, disembodied once more.

"DS Tenby!"

"Yes sir"

"Have you made any progress on this CD movie thing you received?"

"Forensics came back negative Sir! The CCTV cameras at the police station failed to catch anything, there were no fingerprints on the disc, and there was no DNA on the envelope!" Joe replied.

"You'll probably find it was a practical joke by one of those speed camera monkeys you used to work with!" shouted the DCI.

"Perhaps it was sir" Joe said, unconvinced.

"Either way, get yourself to the station car park and rescue Jessica Hopewell from DC Violet!" Joe started to walk away.

"That wasn't a bad call for your first day! Keep it up and we will get along just fine!"

"Thanks Sir! Joe said, fishing his radio from his pocket as he started the walk back toward the station.

"Why didn't I know that you were the look out on the night

Dad was killed Graham?"

Graham shook his head gently, his eyes still fixed downward as his mind raced, searching for the right words.

"We felt it was best at the time dear" Interjected Joyce. It was now her turn to feel the intenseness of Robert's searching gaze. "Poor Steven reacted so badly. He's blamed Graham since day one. We just thought it best to, well, leave things as they were"

Robert's gaze returned to Graham.

"What happened?" Spat Robert.

"Come on!" said Joyce "You know what happened. What is the point in going over it again?"

"I want to hear it from him" said Robert, his voice a mix of malevolence, and sheer coldness.

Graham took a deep breath, finally lifting his gaze to meet the eyes of the angry young man who sat before him.

"That night was like nothing I'd ever known in 25 years on the tracks before that night, or in the 21 years after it. The weather, the wind..." His voice trailed off as Robert rolled his eyes.

"We were sent out on a long distance job to a place called Tangston North, up on the West Coast Main Line" Graham looked up at Joyce, who was now perched on the arm of his chair, looking almost right through the far corner of the room, her eyes distant as she relived the memories of the worst time of her life. "Only, on the way to the job, the office told us to turn around and head to Mallington, a points failure. Problem was, we were sent to the wrong set of points because of a mix up in the messages being passed on, and your dad was crouching in the middle of an open stretch of track."

"But you were the look out!" Robert interrupted. "You should've seen the train and warned him! That was your job!" Graham's gaze returned once again to his shoes.

"I was on his way to the look-out point when the train went past me. I didn't have time even to put a red lamp to the Driver. We thought the line was blocked. We were told the fault was at Points 243B. Really it was at 243D, and that was the stretch of line the signal box had blocked. They didn't know we had the wrong location, and neither did we. The train was doing 60 and the driver didn't have a hope of stopping...your dad, well he..." Graham's voice faltered as the emotion welled up inside of him

."He didn't stand a chance son" said Joyce slowly. Robert's tear filled eyes moved away from the old man, and onto his mother, who met his gaze with a forlorn and wretched expression of her own.

"I couldn't even see your father before his burial because he wasn't in one piece" She winced as she spoke the words as if they tore at the back of her throat. "But his faith in the higher powers, and his memories of the good times me and your dad shared together kept me going, and the lord gave me back some of what he had taken away when I discovered I was expecting you" She smiled a half smile that her son returned. The tears began streaming down Robert's cheeks.

"So what was all this about you two seeing each other behind Dad's back?" Robert whispered as he battled hard against a wave of tears.

"It was a one off, drunken mistake" said Graham, finally breaking his silence. Joyce was once again staring into some distant place, trying desperately to remove herself from reality in the hope that somehow it may all go away. But she knew deep down that her son needed answers. He deserved them.

"Your dad and I were having problems" Joyce said softly. "When your brother Gavin, Steven's twin died, I shut down. Your dad tried and tried to reach out to me, but the more he tried, the higher I built the walls." A solitary stream of tears rolled gracefully down her cheek. "You have to understand that the pain I was feeling, that we were both feeling was so sharp, so intense. I just wanted to curl up in a ball and die. I didn't want to even look at Steven because he reminded me of Gavin. I blamed myself for not keeping one of his babies safe, and I blamed your dad at first too. I just felt so guilty, and so inadequate that I pushed your dad, Steven and the rest of the world away! Your dad never gave up on me or our marriage. He never stopped trying to heal the wound, but despite everything, the pain was causing us to slowly drift apart. Your dad took refuge in work, and I just caved in on myself and shut out everyone and everything"

Robert struggled to take in what he was being told.

"I get the grief mum, really I do, but I cannot see how you go from being grief stricken at the loss of a baby to cheating on dad!" His words carried a sharpness that shocked Joyce.

Graham, sensing her unease, stepped in.

"It was a Friday night, myself and your dad were meant to be going out for a couple of drinks, but he got a phone call from work, asking him to go in. Being a bit strapped for cash, in he went" Robert prompted Graham to continue. "When I turned up, your mum invited me in. She offered me a drink."

Robert motioned as if to leap from his chair.

"Are you trying to tell me that my mother seduced you?"

Graham recoiled in his seat. "No, not at all!" he stammered. "We were both feeling vulnerable at the time, for different reasons. I'd just been served divorce proceedings by my wife, and your mum and dad were under pressure in their relationship because of everything she just told you"

"I desperately needed someone to talk to son" Interrupted Joyce, absently fiddling with her necklace as she spoke. "Graham was there at the wrong time"

Robert glared at his mother, tears welling up in his eyes. "I really don't know what made me do it, but I ended up spilling everything out to Graham about how I was feeling, and what with your dad working all hours, I just felt so alone"

Once again, Graham interceded as Joyce started to cry.

"After I'd listen to your mother get everything off her chest, I made her sit through the sorry tail of my failed marriage. As we both got drunk and more depressed, I think we just ended up falling into each other's arms for comfort"

Wiping the tears from his eyes with the back of his hand, Robert lunged at Graham from his chair, grabbing the old man by his shirt and propelling him across the room.

"Comfort?" He shouted, his face, now contorted with rage was millimetres from Graham's.

Joyce leapt to her feet, pulling at Robert's arm in an effort to prize him away from Graham, who was gasping for breath.

"Robert, please!" She pleaded, still trying in vain to pull him away.

Robert sneered. "I reckon Steven was right yesterday!"

He released his grip on Graham, letting him slide down the wall, nearly causing the picture that was hung above him to come crashing down. Robert stormed out of the room, wrenching the back door open, and disappearing into the garden, where he paced round and round in a circle, his fists clenched by his side as his chest heaved with anger.

Joyce rushed into the garden after him, leaving Graham alone in the front room, still crumpled in a heap on the floor.

"How dare you?" she said as she burst into the garden. Robert stopped pacing.

"More to the point" he replied "How dare *you*!" He ran his hand through his hair as his mind raced.

"What's done is done son" she said, her eyes fixing him in place as she stepped closer to him. "Do you really think that I wake up every morning and feel anything other than shame at what Graham and I did?"

"But what if Steve is right? What if I'm not dad's son?" muttered Robert, his gaze now on the damp grass. Joyce placed her hand on her son's shoulder.

"Believe me son, there is not a chance that he is not your father" She smiled at him, but he did not reciprocate.

"But you're his mother" he said, almost to himself. "And I've had to listen to you telling me about when you cheated on his Dad with him in there" He jabbed a disdainful finger in the direction of the open door.

"Yes, I am your mother" she replied, once again holding his gaze as she spoke. "But I'm also human. Humans make mistakes Robert. This is nobody's fault. I'm not perfect son, and not a day goes by when I don't torture myself over what we did. I am truly sorry, but I can't go back and undo it, otherwise I would do in a heartbeat." Robert stared at one of the fence posts as he pondered his mother's words.

"This is just immense" he whispered, his voice cracking with emotion as he turned away from Joyce "I need a minute"

Deciding not to say anymore, Joyce quietly went back inside, switching the kettle on as she passed through the kitchen, returning to the living room to check that Graham was okay. After a few moments of awkward silence, Robert appeared at the kitchen door, busily trying to compose himself. Joyce looked anxiously across at Graham, and then at her son. He stepped forward.

"Sorry Mother" He sighed through his tears. "Sorry to you too Graham, truly I am"

Joyce got up and crossed the room to her son, allowing her arms to fall around his heaving shoulders.

"I'm glad you've been able to let it go son" She said as he sobbed against her.

"I only wish your brother could do the same. It worries me that he won't allow himself to let his father go. He's been bottling up this hatred for all this time!" She tightened her arms around her son as he looked over at the old man, managing the briefest of smiles. Graham returned the smile, basking in the forgiveness that he had craved for so long.

Having managed to access the station car park, Joe stared out of the windscreen. He had reverse parked the car into a bay that faced the exit, partly so as to be ready for a swift getaway, but also as an opportunity to study the throng of curious locals and mischievous reporters trying to sneak inside the police cordon. A smartly dressed blonde woman was waving in Joe's direction, smiling. He recognised her instantly, making a conscious display of ignoring her gestures. His eyes were drawn to a man filming the police operation on a small handheld camera. He was smiling, as if revelling in the hustle and bustle of the crime scene, and that just didn't seem right. After a few seconds of Joe's intense stare, the man with the camera became aware that he was being watched. Scowling in Joe's direction, he switched off the camera and scuttled away from the cordon. Joe continued watching as the man got into a tatty blue Volvo and drove swiftly away. Reaching into his pocket, Joe took out his notebook and scribbled the car's registration number on a fresh page. Making a mental note to check the vehicle details once back at the office, Joe glanced down at his watch. More than ten minutes had passed, and he was considering whether or not he should go into the ticket office and remind DC Violet exactly who was in charge. Thinking better of it, he moved his hand from the door handle to the volume dial on the stereo and turned it up. *Crawling Up A Hill* by Katie Melua was flowing melodically through the speakers like a soothing summer breeze. Joe was always transported to another place by this song, a much worse place professionally and personally. A place when he was in a job that he hated, a job that had no prospects. He had no drive, no direction. A very wise old man who used to drink in the same pub as Joe once told him

"When you feel that you've hit rock bottom, you really haven't. You have to make a choice. You can keep sinking until you really do bottom out, or you can kick yourself up the arse, and make yourself into the person that you want to be." With hindsight, Joe thought that he was politely telling him to get a grip, and either change what he didn't like, or stop moaning about it. Either way, Joe had taken his advice, enrolled in the open university, studied for a Psychology degree, applied successfully to join the police force, and been accepted onto the force's High Potential Development scheme. Because of this Joe had gone from PC to Detective Sergeant in four years, something that many resented, but gave him an immense feeling of personal pride and achievement. He smiled as he compared his experiences with the lyrics of the song, before shaking these analogies from his mind and putting in order all of the information regarding the case. Despite DCI Whindle dismissing the film he had been sent as a prank, Joe couldn't rest with such an easy explanation. There was no doubt in Joe's mind that the film clip was something altogether more sinister. He could not see the police officers he used to work with risking their careers to send a pornographic film as a joke. He could see that, and he was angry that DCI Whindle seemed blind to it. Now, Joe's mind was also questioning whether the killer of Tina McBride was disturbed in the sense that he had been interrupted during the act of disposing with her body, or whether he was disturbed in terms of being mentally unbalanced to the extent that he would dump her body on the line in order for her remains to be mutilated still further, just for the sake of it. He had learned quickly never to assume anything during investigations. The level of physical strength required would all but rule out a female, and this was a crime that had shown intense, almost unimaginable rage. The fact that Tina McBride was face down where she was dumped may have indicated a sense of guilt on the part of her attacker, placing her in that position so that he could not see her face as he surveyed the crime scene. Nothing was obviously symbolic regarding the positioning of the body, or its location, and the Police could not interpret anything really until they had accurately determined whether or not dumping Tina McBride on the railway line was a deliberate act of further mutilation, or a reaction to an unexpected event. The sheer volume of unanswered questions was head spinning, especially given the creeping suspicion he was feeling that the murder he was now investigating, and the CD he had received were somehow linked. Joe's thoughts were interrupted by a tapping on the window.

"DS Tenby?" Joe looked up at the man looking at me from the other side of the glass. Joe motioned toward the passenger door. He briskly walked around the car to the passenger side and got in, adjusting his suit jacket as he settled into the seat.

"Glen Violet" he said, offering his hand in greeting.

"Joe Tenby" reciprocated Joe. Swinging the car around, he pulled away from the station forecourt and headed down the road, both men sitting silently as the stereo played the jazzy rhythm of *Mocking Bird*, albeit at a much lower volume. Joe decided to concentrate on driving as he remembered that he was still annoyed with DC Violet for his lateness. Glancing across at him, Joe could see that he was feeling somewhat awkward.

"You'll have to excuse me if I'm a little slow on the conversation DC Violet" said Joe, checking his wing mirror. "It's just that I'm probably a good ten minutes ahead of you, what with my waiting around for you for ages back there." Joe looked across at him briefly. Glen's face reddened slightly.

"Look Glen" said Joe, deciding to lift the tension. "Not many things wind me up. But I do get annoyed when people are late. That's just me I'm afraid." Glen nodded.

"Fair enough" he said. "I apologise" The car fell into an awkward silence. "Got anything a little more lively?" He asked, examining the controls on the stereo closely as he tried to build bridges with Joe.

"How about this?" Joe replied with a smile, and flicked the control on the steering column, changing the CD and filling the car with the opening bars of *Fake Tales Of San Francisco* by The Arctic Monkeys.

"Much more like it" beamed Glen, relaxing into his chair. Joe felt able to relax as well, satisfied that the pecking order had been clearly established. Satisfied that he had made good start, Joe turned his mind back to the task in hand of checking train movements from the previous evening. He had identified that the portion of line concerned was controlled by the signalling centre at Posternby Central, some 20 miles or so from the crime scene. That was where the two men were going. "There's a possibility that the mutilation to the victim wasn't caused by the train whose driver reported the body this morning. If another train came through last night that was unexpected, it could've disturbed the killer" Joe said, his eyes fixed firmly on the road. Glen's face was a mixture of confusion and intrigue.

"So what's that going to prove?" he asked, his left foot idly tapping in time with the music.

"If the killer wasn't expecting a train to pass through there, rather than proving the theory that our killer has no railway knowledge, it means that he has knowledge of the railway system doesn't it? That narrows down the pool of suspects by a fair way" Glen sat for a moment, digesting what had just been said.

"I suppose there could be something in it" he said, clearly annoyed at being shown up by the new sergeant. Joe smiled to himself, indicating left and leaving the motorway as they headed for the small town of Posternby. As they approached a large roundabout, the music changed and Joe turned up the volume, both men smiling at the irony as *Drops Of Jupiter* by Train pumped from the speakers.

Finally managing to locate the signalling centre at the back of a small industrial estate, Joe found that the small car park was full, and there were no spaces anyway immediately nearby. Electing to set a good example, Joe decided against disregarding the double yellow lines, scanning the immediate vicinity for any available space. Turning the car around in the cramped car park, Joe drove back up to the other end of the road, parking outside of a graphic design company. Both men got out of the car and walked the 400 metres or so back to the signalling centre. Neither spoke for the duration of their walk from the car. Joe's mind was racing as he busily thought through the possibilities of gaining some useful information that could really get the investigation going. He'd certainly get off to a flying start in the eyes of his new boss, which was exactly what he had set out to do. Glancing across at Glen, Joe thought that he was still trying to convince himself that this expedition wasn't a complete wasting of time. Approaching the security gate, they both gave the building a quick once over. It was all metal panelling and steel girders, with the upper floor clad in glass. A white metal fence standing at least 8ft in height surrounded the structure, with electronic gates controlling entry into the inner yard. The two men found themselves standing at a steel turnstile, complete with a card swipe reader, the whole complex being surveyed constantly by a phalanx of CCTV cameras watching from all manner of angles.

"Blimey" remarked Glen. "I thought signal boxes were wood panelling and flowerpots"

"Maybe they were fifty years ago!" replied Joe sarcastically, pressing the 'call' button on the panel next to the turnstile. The intercom crackled into life, and a tired sounding middle aged voice simply said "Yes?"

"Detective Sergeant Tenby and Detective Constable Violet, Metropolitan Police. We're here to speak to the DSM regarding an ongoing investigation" said Joe, adopting an official tone. The man at the other end of the intercom paused for a few seconds. The intercom crackled again.

"Ok gents, show your identification to the camera please" They both took out their warrant cards, holding them up for the scrutiny of the faceless man inside the building. A buzzer sounded.

"Push the turnstile gents" said the voice, the intercom clicking then going dead. They filed through the turnstile, walking up to a dark blue door made of thick wood with a metal handle, a small double glazed window three quarters of the way up being the only route in for the light of the outside world. Another buzzer sounded, and Joe pulled the handle, the heavy door swinging open, allowing access to a grey air conditioned corridor with a staircase at the far end. They walked in, the door swinging slowly shut behind them. For a second the two men stood exchanging looks of uncertainty, not being entirely sure where they should go next. Just then a middle aged man in a beige suit came walking towards them, his hand outstretched.

"Gentlemen" he said. Joe responded by taking his hand and shaking it.

"DS Tenby" he said, introducing himself. "This is DC Violet"

Glen nodded at the man, and he returned the gesture.

"Come this way" he said, turning on his heels and heading back down the corridor towards the staircase. As they started following him Glen leant in towards Joe.

"What's a DSM?"

"Duty Signalling Manager" Joe replied as the man stopped at the foot of the stairs to wait for them.

Joe smiled amenably as the two men quickened their pace and caught up. Joe and Glen followed him across another corridor and into an office, decorated unremarkably, the room filled with generic office furniture, and covered with notice boards bearing all kinds of papers, notices and charts. There was a large window behind his desk, the top of the huge security fence being just visible. He motioned for them to sit, which they did. The building overlooked the main line to London. Joe was sure that usually there would be trains speeding past the window every few minutes, but what with the crime scene being right in the middle of the railway, all services were cancelled owing to the line being closed for the Police to complete their investigation. The three men sat looking at each other for a few seconds, none of them really sure who should break the ice.

"Simon Roberts. Duty Signalling Manager" the man said, lurching from his chair and offering both men his hand in turn. Joe smiled, shaking his hand a second time, making a mental effort to avoid introducing himself again.

"We're here in connection with the body at Upper Charleston" Joe said in an attempt to move things along. Mr Roberts' expression switched from joviality to a mix of seriousness and confusion.

"Forgive me, but why are the met involved in a fatality?" he asked, sinking back into his chair.

"Well it wasn't a straight forward fatality as it turns out" said Glen, sitting forward. Mr Roberts' gaze switched from Joe to Glen.

"We're taking the lead on this one" Joe said.

"Okay" said Mr Roberts, "What can I do to help. Every hour we've got that line closed, it's costing a fortune, so whatever I can do" He jerked his thumb over his shoulder towards the window, and the silent, static railway line beyond.

"We were wondering if there were any unusual or unscheduled train movements in the Upper Charleston area last night" Joe said. Mr Roberts thought for a second.

"As a matter of fact there were" he said, rising from his seat. "Come with me!" Heading out of the door and turning left, his footsteps echoed as the two men scrambled to their feet and followed.

They caught up with Simon Roberts at a set of doors halfway along the corridor. He produced a swipe card and ran it through a reader. The doors opened and they hurried through. "The security here is impressive Mr Roberts" Joe remarked, watching as the doors closed behind them as they made their way to another security door where the whole ritual was repeated.

"Can't be too careful Detective Sergeant" said Mr Roberts, ushering them through the second set of doors. The three men emerged onto a balcony overlooking a large open plan space inhabited with work stations positioned in 6 circles, each one being attended to by a man sitting at a control desk wearing a headset, each station being covered with screens, keyboards, and a large tracking ball. In the centre of the room was an elevated booth, in the middle was sat a man who was watching a number of computer screens that were positioned all around him, along with a bank of telephones. It was obvious that he was in charge. Mr Roberts saw Joe and Glen looking around the room, observing the guy in the central booth as he typed furiously on a keyboard.

"Posternby Central controls all lines between London and the Sussex coast, including Brighton, Gatwick Airport, and parts of Surrey too. It's ideal in terms of a target for terrorists." Both men nodded, agreeing with the logic, and being surprised at the sheer scale of the area covered by the people working on the floor below. Mr Roberts went to a phone mounted on the wall and picked up the receiver, pressing three buttons and waiting. "Janet, could you bring a copy of the train register for the up slow lines please for yesterday evening. Everything from 2045 until 0530" He looked at Joe, asking silently if that was acceptable. Joe nodded his approval and Mr Roberts thanked the woman on the end of the phone and replaced the handset. They stood in silence for a few moments, watching the whole seamless process of moving trains from one place to another being acted out before them.

Drifting in and out of consciousness, Steven shifted awkwardly as he moved his hips in time with the attentions of the girl knelt between his thighs. He glanced down at the top of her head as it bobbed slowly up and down, his eyes flicking back and forth beneath the thin cover of his clamped eyelids. No matter how he tried, he couldn't seem to relax into the attention he was receiving as the ravages of endless night terrors coursed through his body in a heady cocktail of pleasure and mortifying pain. Grainy images flashed through his mind, glimpses of wispy black hair along with the sensation of unwelcome breath against skin, the reflection of his own body, a time long ago when he was much younger, looking back at him from a grubby mirror as he repulsed at what was happening, the calloused surface of a hand on his thigh, his waist, his neck. His stomach lurched and churned as he felt the limpness of surrender to the dark desires of someone stronger, larger, somebody impervious to the effect of what they were doing.

"No. Please." He whispered, his head thrashing left and right, his throat opening and closing as he gulped air.

On the carpet in front of him, the girl looked up as his head turned from side to side, his eyes shut tight and his mouth opening and closing. Like so many prostitutes plying their trade in the back streets, she knew very little English, and simply assumed she was doing what he liked. Tightening her grip around his swollen hilt, she doubled her efforts, sliding her mouth further down him, hollowing her cheeks as she glanced down at her watch, being mindful of the time as she worked him hard in an effort to hurry events along so she could move on to her next 'customer'

"This is special pleasure for special boys" said a gravelly, male voice in his head as that rough, calloused hand moved further up his thigh, dislodging the lower edge of his underwear. Steven's body stiffened as his mind replayed the feeling of intense pain and traumatic intrusion that followed as the hand continued on its unspeakable journey. The girl between his legs was now working feverishly, her fingers and mouth exploring every inch of his manhood as she dragged him towards his orgasm.

"Please baby" she whispered in a Russian accent. "I want you cum now" Suddenly, the heavily accented words penetrated his daydream, his eyes snapping open and his gaze fixing on the blonde haired, blue eyes that looked up at him intensely, her hands and lips bullying him towards a guilt-ridden, twisted bliss, her words mixing in her mind with the masculine tones of that gravelly voice.

"You know you like it!" the voice hissed sleazily. With a jolt he exploded, her voice muffled as she completed her work, his primal grunts filling the room as she closed her eyes tightly, her free hand sliding into her pocket and squeezing the bank notes that she had counted, and then folded neatly before she rang the doorbell and ushered inside. Slowly, his body calmed, the first sight to fill his vision being the exhausted weave of the sofa's backrest. Cleaning herself up, she looked up at him smiling.

"You like?" she asked. Almost by reflex, he lurched forward, punching her in the face. She squealed as her body recoiled, her mouth filling with blood as she lay on her back staring at him, the language barrier, the shock and the pain making her speechless.

"Do I fucking like it?" he snarled, grabbing her ponytail and pulling her to her feet.

"Please! Please! I sorry!" she cried in broken English, her head bowed in an attempt to minimise the pain of her hair being viciously yanked.

"I'm not like that! I'm the fucking opposite of that! You understand?" she stared into his eyes. His expression was so intense, his pupils wide and his lips curled. She had no idea what he was saying, but her instinct was telling her to agree with him. The rage within him bubbled as it rose from the pit of his stomach; his face became more snarled with abject fury as the adrenaline reached the farthest extremities of his body.

"Don't even look at me you filthy fucking whore!" He screamed. She let out a yelp as he clasped a hand around her throat, reddening the skin of her neck around his hand as he squeezed her windpipe. Staggering backwards, she grabbed at his hand desperately, her eyes wide and pleading. Steven breathed hard, forcing air out of his lungs through his nose, then sucking in mouthfuls with enthusiasm as he studied her face, noting how the pallor of her skin subtly began to change as her brain became starved of oxygen. Looking away from him, she stared into the dirty mirror that stood above the fireplace. She could see the fury in his eyes, a burning intensity that transcended the borders of language. The expression on his face was one of hatred. She could see her own strength fading from her body. She was transfixed to the reflection in the mirror, as if she were watching her own death on a cinema screen. Her eyeballs were flickering in all directions, her throat producing a soft gurgling sound as the strength began to seep from her. Watching her life begin to dissolve, he hesitated, realising that the need for her services had to overcome his increasing desire to kill. Swearing under his breath he clamped his eyes shut and forced his hand to release the grip on her neck. Falling onto the floor, the girl managed to get herself onto her hands and knees, drinking in air and sobbing as she cradled her stinging neck.

"I not understand! You pay me! I please you!" Steven looked down at her, continuing to study her before looking away.

"You have a pocket full of cash from the other cocks you've sucked tonight! I pay you when you get me what I need!" Steven snarled. The girl looked up, her fright replaced by anger as she rubbed her swollen throat.

"Fuck you!" she screamed. "You try kill me!" Steven aimed a hard kick at her stomach. Crying out, she rolled onto her back as she curled into a ball.

"Don't forget Olga!" Steven spat as he leant over her. "I know where you live! I know where you work! You carry on helping me, or I find you!" She looked up at him, her eyes still watering. He disappeared momentarily into the kitchen, reappearing with a grubby scrap of paper. Throwing it at her, he pointed. "Get me as much of that as you can!" She read the paper and looked back at him questioningly. "Get out" Steven said quietly. He did not repeat himself, and it was clear that he did not care about what he had just done. Deciding not to speak again, she grabbed her handbag and her coat. Backing towards the door, she edged out of the room before rushing down the hallway. Thrusting one hand into her pocket, she held her evening's earnings tightly, as her free hand grasped the door handle. Throwing the door open, Olga rushed into the cold air, thankful for her freedom. Steven looked towards the empty doorway, before studying his reflection in the mirror. Sighing loudly, he grasped the vodka bottle from the fireplace as he walked back to the sofa, unscrewing the lid as he fell backwards onto the ragged cushions. Thankfully, sleep began to envelop him, his heart rate slowing in pace and intensity. The relative silence of the room was rudely disturbed by the shrill ringing of the telephone. "Fuck it!" he murmured to himself, forcing his aching body to move. Scrambling about the dirty floor for the phone, he finally found it, and with hands still trembling from the horrors of the night's sleep, pressed the call accept button as yet more debris from several nights of drink were sent spinning across the room. Slowly he raised the phone to his ear. "Yeah" he murmured.

"It's Robert. Are you ready to apologise to Mum for the other day yet Steve?" he asked accusingly.

"What?!" spluttered Steven, his feelings of pain and sadness suddenly being replaced by a growing sense of fury. He stared at the receiver of the phone, his hands beginning to tremble.

"You heard me!" replied Robert. "You were out of line! Deep down, I think that you know that."

"The only person who is out of line here is you!!" shouted Steven, his words shooting down the receiver like bullets from a machine gun.

"Come off it!" countered Robert, caught off guard by the viciousness in Steven's voice.

"All three of you are out of line!" Steven screamed, his chest heaving in anger. "Mum, for fucking Dad's best mate, him for killing Dad, and you for swallowing their bullshit!"

"Mum told me everything!" snapped Robert.

"She told you what she wants to believe! You might be happy enough to forgive what she did to us and go and play happy families with the bastard that took my Dad away from me, but I'm not!" Steven paused. "If you can't see what is going on here, then I don't want anything to do with any of you!"

Before Robert could reply, the line went dead as Steven launched his phone at the wall, an incoherent stream of noise bursting from his mouth. The phone smashed into the wall, its components showering the cluttered floor in every direction, as he sank back onto the sofa. He closed his eyes tight, trying to shut out the world. Instead, all he got was the echoes of his brother's voice, and then the sound of his Dad, shouting. Steven tried to escape the sound that rattled around his aching brain. The voice of his father was getting louder, clearer, his anger and disappointment more pronounced. All of a sudden, Steven was 7 years old. He was looking regretfully up at his Dad who was shouting at him, pointing his enormous finger at him as he told him how stupid he was, how much the next door neighbour's window was going to cost, how we couldn't afford to go to the seaside now, and how it was all Steven's fault. Steven could see the football resting against the other side of the garden fence, nestling amongst the long grass of their neighbour's garden, shards of broken glass, in various sizes strewn across the concrete.

"I'm sorry dad" said Steven, as his Dad glared at him. "I'm sorry, I'll be good from now on, I promise!"

Slowly, the image of his father slipped away and was replaced by a kaleidoscopic light show of as Steven's eyes remained tightly closed, his body once again cramming itself as far as possible into the corner of the sofa. Slowly, he opened his eyes, his vacant stare falling upon the corner of the room, passing the fallen vodka bottle, and the forgotten beer cans. "I'm sorry" he whispered, as tears rolled mournfully down his now expressionless face. 'I'm so sorry"

-24-

The remains of Tina McBride were resting on a stainless steel trolley, positioned in the middle of the long rectangular room like some kind of strange centrepiece for this, one of the most macabre of gatherings. The room was an almost blinding mixture of brilliant white, and stainless steel. The smell of industrial sanitiser hung in the air. Deliberately ignoring the remains, Joe looked around the room, its tiled walls adorned with row upon row of stainless steel racks and cupboards, their contents assembled symmetrically in identical rows. Glancing briefly at Dr Rothesay, Joe wondered whether this would explain the absence of spirit in the pathologist's eyes. Joe had seen it in many people who worked in Dr Rothesay's profession, the kind of emptiness that makes every smile somehow hollow.

"Nice, is it?" DCI Whindle said, shaking Joe from his thoughts.

"Sorry guv?" replied Joe, somewhat confused.

"Whichever planet it is that you are currently inhabiting, Detective Sergeant Tenby!" snapped DCI Whindle "Because whichever bloody planet you're on, it certainly isn't Earth now, is it?"

"My apologies!" Joe replied. His eyes were drawn to the circular window which was usually concealed by a white blind. Jessica was passing the window, looking in as she cradled an over filled red binder in her folded arms as she went. Catching Joe's eye, she smiled. Joe's cheeks reddened slightly. The DCI sighed loudly, fixing Joe with an icy glare, before turning his attention to Dr Rothesay.

"Well, following the post mortem on your victim, my preliminary findings seem to be correct Chief Inspector" He moved toward the trolley in the centre of the room, where an oversized halogen light hovered over Tina's body. He bent over her head, grabbing his glasses from the chain around his neck and slipping them onto the bridge of his reddened nose, swearing under his breath as he stretched across the trolley, and flicked on the switch to the imposing lamp overhead.

"To be fair we were pretty much on the money at the crime scene gentlemen, but I have found a few surprises", he said as beckoned the two men over to the corpse. Unwillingly, Joe followed the lead of the DCI and moved closer, still consciously ignoring the ghoulishness of the situation as he blinked in reaction to the harsh beams of light that bounced randomly between stainless steel and glass. Tina McBride lay face down on the trolley; the uniform pageant blue of the sheet that concealed her seemed comforting and unsettling in equal measure. Dr Rothesay grabbed the nearest corner of the sheet, pausing for a few seconds whilst Joe and DCI Whindle shuffled grudgingly to a suitable vantage point. Joe carefully reached into his inside pocket and fished out his notebook without breaking the stare that was fixed on the pathologist chubby fingers.

"First thing to note is that the chemical used on the eyes was Potassium Permanganate as I suspected" stated Dr Rothesay as he slipped the sheet down to the nape of Tina's neck, his voice remarkable by way of its lack of any discernible emotion.

"I also found traces of adhesive on the skin in a line between the temples and the bridge of the nose, and small amounts of cotton wool". By this point, Joe was busily filling a page in his notebook with scrawling notes. He suddenly became aware of the DCI's glare. He had been watching Joe as he scribbled, his eyes switching between the notebook and Joe's face.

"I take it that would not have been the injury that killed her doctor?" Joe asked. Dr Rothesay shook his head.

"Cause of death was blood loss caused by multiple stab wounds." Joe immediately recorded the details in his notebook. "However, it is at this point that things really get interesting." Dr Rothesay gently drew back the blue sheet until Tina's back was fully exposed. Joe's mouth fell open as his eyes traced the jagged path of the wounds covering Tina's back.

"Jesus" he whispered.

"Certainly makes things interesting, eh?" said Dr Rothesay. Joe nodded blankly, transfixed. He knew then and there that the killer had chosen him.

"Sir!" Joe said quietly, his mouth running dry. DCI Whindle looked up. "The CD I received had a message in Latin!"

"So?" DCI Whindle replied with a shrug. "Mea Culpa." Joe said, motioning towards the trolley. Dr Rothesay looked down at the wounds and then back at Joe.

"Evan, its Latin. It means 'my fault'" he said quietly. Before DCI Whindle could reply, Joe stepped forward. He wasn't sure entirely why, but it was becoming increasingly clear that the DCI was not taking to him. Joe paused, choosing his words carefully before speaking. "Sir, I know that this is going to sound crazy, but I think that the CD I received may have been sent by Tina McBride's killer" DCI Whindle fixed Joe with a quizzical, almost mocking expression.

"You're right Sergeant Tenby!" he said. "It does sound crazy! You think that someone would do this just to get your attention? You've been reading too many fucking Ian Rankin novels!" Joe managed to stifle a sigh. "

"Without a doubt Sergeant Tenby" replied Dr Rothesay, "I would go so far as to say that death would've been pretty much instantaneous. A mercy, given the events subsequent to the attack, I'm sure you'll agree"

Joe smiled in agreement. The silence was interrupted by the door opening. All three men looked at Jessica and she paused for a second. The harsh, artificial lighting made her appear even paler of skin, and this only served to make her look even more delicate than before. Her slim arms were folded across a yellow clipboard. Joe caught himself staring at her as he realised that he could well end up falling for a perfect stranger. Jessica looked back at them, unfolding her arms and removing the paper from the clipboard. Deciding to break the uneasy silence that hung in the air, she stepped forward to the foot of the autopsy table and cleared her throat.

"I have the results of the forensic analysis I carried out on the items and samples taken from the scene Dr Rothesay" she said.

"Anything usable Jessica?" Joe asked, stepping forward. The DCI glared at him.

"Nothing much I'm afraid" she replied as she turned to the flipped the top page of the papers on her clipboard over. "The only clearly identifiable sample in terms of what could be a foreign material that we recovered, other than the usual office based wastage and litter, was this"

She held up a small evidence bag that contained a thin orange thread. "It's a polyester based material. Judging by the colour, I'd say it is most likely that it came from.."

"A safety vest!" Joe exclaimed.

"You seem very knowledgeable on this Mr Tenby!" said DCI Whindle, flatly.

"My Dad was a railwayman" said Joe. The DCI huffed, but said nothing more.

Joe couldn't help but be intrigued by this find. He couldn't help but think that they were looking for somebody who was employed within the industry. He did consider whether the attacker knew the victim, given the fact that the body was face down, and the severity of force used in the attack, if of course, the body was deliberately placed face down.

"HVV" Joe murmured to himself.

"H V what?" asked the DCI.

"HVV guv." he replied. "High Visibility Vest. It's what safety vests are called on the railway" Clearly irritated, DCI Whindle ran his hands through his hair, exhaling loudly.

"So what we're saying, is that the only piece of forensic evidence we have so far is a thread from a railway vest that just about any one of thousands of people carry with them very day, including the victim?" Joe couldn't understand why the DCI was reacting like this, especially considering that there was precious little else to go on. In Joe's mind, the pool of suspects was, although still very large, being reduced gradually as the investigation uncovered more information. He was growing increasingly concerned that they were a good way into the critical first 48 hours of the investigation, and was getting anxious at the thought of what could be a deranged serial killer out there.

"There is one more thing" Dr Rothesay said. He reached down and moved Tina McBride's head to one side, her eyes now closed, but her eyelids visible to everyone.

"During the post mortem we found that the deceased's eyes and the skin around them were very reddened and irritated."

"That's interesting!" Joe said as he jotted down the details in his notebook.

"So she had dust in her eye before she was carved up!" DCI Whindle huffed. "Big deal! When you get anything remotely usable and relevant, call me!"

"DCI Whindle made for the door, shoving it open with the flat of his hand, causing it to slam against the wall with a bang that echoed down the seemingly never ending corridors beyond. Joe got the sinking feeling that he had given the wrong answer.

"With me please, Mr Tenby" he commanded over his shoulder.

Joe's eyes fell to the floor as he rubbed at the slight stubble on his chin, shrugging at nobody in particular.

"Nice knowing you Joe!" whispered Jessica playfully, a mischievous smile spreading slowly across her delicate features.

Sighing, Joe trudged out of the room and into the highly polished and lifeless corridor, pausing to making sure that the door to the autopsy suite was closed firmly behind him.

Anna Brown stood facing her father across the kitchen table, her hands on her hips, and her stance defiant. She stared at him in disbelief.

"I don't care how old you are Anna, this is not a knocking shop, and he is not staying over! End of discussion!" Ken Brown looked at his daughter over the top of his coffee cup, his eyes holding her gaze.

"Dad, I am 22 years of age! I have a career, my own car. It's not as if I'm 16. I'm a grown woman for god's sake!"

Ken shrugged.

"Like I said, the answer is no." He looked tired. He always looked tired. The hair on the top of his head had long since departed him, leaving only a band of greying hair around the back and sides. Crow's feet emanated from his eyes, his thin, angular face ageing him beyond his 53 years. Anna on the other hand was youthful and vibrant. Her long wavy hair flowed from her head in vibrant red locks, her green eyes shining like beacons. She was slight in build, standing no more than 5ft 2, with gentle curves that were almost perfectly in proportion for her diminutive figure. Her china like fingers were playing with the tassels on the end of a plum coloured glittery scarf that was wrapped repeatedly around her neck.

"This is ridiculous!" she shouted, turning away from her father and stooping to grab her shoes which were next to the kitchen door.

"That's another thing" said Ken, over his shoulder as he turned the page of his newspaper "Put those bloody things under the stairs will you? I nearly went head first over them earlier!"

Anna scowled at the back of her father's head as she crammed her tiny feet into her best, attention grabbing high heels. Grabbing her coat and her car keys, she snatched open the door to the hallway.

"Where are you going?" said Ken, still half engrossed in the newspaper.

"Out!" she shouted as she opened the front door. "And no, I won't be telling you where I'm going, because it's none of your damn business!"

As the house returned to silence, Ken let out a heavy sigh, and opened the sports section of the paper.

-26-

DCI Whindle was facing the wall, pinching the bridge of his nose as Joe walked up to him, wondering what would be his best strategy in tackling the situation. The DCI turned and looked at Joe, stepping forward.

"DS Tenby, what the fuck was that?" he spluttered, his voice matching the anger in his face, his voice bouncing of the smooth walls and glass of the corridor.

"Guv?" said Joe, looking blankly back at him.

"Latin?" spluttered DCI Whindle. "I don't follow" replied Joe. "It's really very simple DS Tenby! Point number 1! I am aware that Mea Culpa is Latin! Point number 2! This is not some dating agency! Point number 3! When we are investigating a murder, we are bloody well focused on that, and that alone, not trying to figure out what the girl from forensics would look like in her bra and knickers!" Joe felt a mixture of embarrassment and indignation well up inside him. Whilst Jessica Hopewell was a very good looking woman, Joe couldn't help but felt insulted to be accused of allowing any feelings of attraction to get in the way of his professional duties. Joe had come up with the only lead that the team had to work with so far, and was busily trying to construct some sort of idea that could provide a head start in tracking down the man who did this.

"If there's nothing else sir, I'll carry on working on my theory regarding the lead we got from the signalling centre" Joe said, trying to subtly highlight the fact that, so far at least, he was making the running on this investigation. Ignoring Joe's attempts at subtle self-promotion, the DCI leaned forward, gently pressing his finger into Joe's lapel.

"Stop flirting with Miss Hopewell, stop undermining me in front of Dr Rothesay, and earn your salary! Are we clear?" he spat. Joe looked down at his finger, looked him in the eye, and nodded. That said, DCI Whindle turned on his heels and marched down the corridor, slamming open the exit, and disappearing into the outside world. Slumping back against the wall Joe stared into space, his mouth slightly open.

-27-

So engrossed was Anna Brown in both, the hunt for the keys, and her rage at her father, she did not see the shadowy figure watching her from a short distance further down the street. He smoked slowly and deliberately as he watched her, just as he'd watched her for the last three days. She hadn't noticed him, why should she? He drove a dark blue Toyota Carina, an unremarkable car, and instantly forgettable. Having finally located her keys, Anna unlocked her car, the lights flashing as the alarm deactivated. He continued to watch her, feeling invincible as he leant back, dissecting her every move and studying it intently. He was ready. She had to make amends, and he was ready to help her. He had already chosen which piece he wanted from his box of glass. The piece was securely stowed in the plastic tube in his pocket, and the box was safely stowed back behind his seat. Pulling the folded piece of paper from his pocket, he opened it and stared momentarily at the names, caressing the thick black line that ran through the middle of a piece of text. He had positioned himself so that he would be facing the rear of her car as she drove away from the house and toward the city centre, so he didn't have to worry about being seen in the glare of her headlights. Slowly and carefully she drew forward from the driveway and into the road, turning her little red car left, and gently accelerating to the end of the road, the small stuffed rabbit attached to the rear window by suction cups gently swaying as the car sped up. Waiting for her to turn right at the end of the street, he started his engine, and pulled away, switching on his headlights only when he was sure he was not within the reflection of her mirror.

Checking her watch, Anna looked around the bar, as she waited for her boyfriend. Dressed in a black tailored blazer, a pair of tight blue jeans and burgundy high heels, Anna was relieved that she wasn't over or under dressed for the venue. Traffic had been fairly light, and the journey had only taken her twenty minutes. She smiled as she watched a couple sitting at a table as they kissed tenderly, before focussing her attention on the bar's decor. The walls were the palest cream, the neutrality of the colours offset by a series of coloured lights embedded in the walls that subtly changed colour, along with lights hung from the ceiling of differing shades that all colluded in giving an ambience usually found in back street jazz clubs. The bar had a black shiny bar top, with silver panelled frontage, and pale blue down lighting. A large painting hung in the middle of the wall, illuminated by its own spotlight, portraying a naked woman posing sexily, cupping her breasts, almost offering them to the viewer in the way that a glamour model would in a top shelf magazine. For a moment, Anna debated the picture in her head, reasoning her distain for the use of a woman in such a sexual way against the very real quality of the painting. As the barman poured her drink, she took a tube of lip balm from her pocket, and unscrewed the cap. Delicately, she pressed some of the contents onto her forefinger and carefully spread the balm across her bottom lip. She smiled in thanks to the barman, and paid him. Taking a sip from her drink as she put her change back into her purse, her face creased up in reaction to the sour sensations that were passing through her. Glaring at the glass of orange juice, she was just about to complain to the barman when she stopped, and plunged her hand back into her pocket, pulling out the tube of balm, she glared at the label.

"Silly cow!" she said, shaking her head as she realised it was apple flavour. "Apple and orange do not mix"

"That is the first sign of going mad you know!" Anna turned to face the man who was setting himself down on the stool next to her and making himself comfortable. She was just about to give him one of her pre-prepared brush off lines when she noticed what a charming smile he had. His face was kindly, and his eyes warm. Dark hair framed his face that, although wasn't classically handsome, was appealing in a strange sort of way. He was dressed in a black shirt with a pair of designer jeans and a brown leather jacket. Realising that she must have been caught obviously checking him out, she shot him her most dazzling smile, hoping it would hide her embarrassment.

"What is the first sign of going mad?" she asked, offering her hand in greeting.

"Talking to yourself!" he replied with an equally dazzling smile. He oozed self-confidence as he accepted her hand, shaking it cordially as he made deliberate eye contact with her.

"Anna" she said, gesturing to herself and continuing to hold eye contact with the man. Her initial reaction was to back away from Steven's advance. After all, she did have a boyfriend, a boyfriend whom she was in fact waiting for. Still, she had no intention of letting anything happen, and if she was honest, she always enjoyed a bit of harmless flirting.

"What harm can it do?" she thought to herself as she gave him her best wide-eyed expression. He smiled, and ordered a double vodka and blackcurrant from the barman, taking a measured sip almost as soon as the barman had finished pouring. He nodded, and then turned and faced the bar, smiling to himself as he made a deliberate and physical ploy to ignore her unspoken attempt to learn his name.

"Teetotal then?" he asked casually as he eyed her drink.

"Oh god no!" she said, softly pushing her hair back behind her ear. "I'm driving tonight!"

"I admire that" he said, examining his glass. "I'm the same. Never drink if I've got the car. It's a taxi for me tonight" he swallowed the remaining contents of his glass, and put it back on the bar, catching the barman's attention and calling him over.

He turned to her. "Can I get you another drink Anna?"

"Thank you, but I'm waiting for someone" she said.

"By the looks of things, he's running late" Steven said.

Glancing down at her watch, she couldn't help but agree.

"Being a true gentleman, I could not leave a beautiful girl to wait alone now, could I?" he said, his hand resting gently on her knee. She looked down and smiled.

"Okay, thanks." She said. Rising from her stool, she picked up her handbag.

"Same again?" he asked.

"Yes please, she replied. "Just nipping to freshen up" she said, and turned, walking away, her hips swinging as she felt his eyes tracking her from across the bar.

As soon as he was sure she was out of sight, he paid for the drinks, and whilst the barman was getting his change, he took a quick look around. Once satisfied that nobody was watching, he dropped a tablet into the orange juice, examining it closely as the tablet dissolved in the liquid. Knowing that the vast majority of clubs and bars concentrated their security efforts on the till, and areas where staff would otherwise have an opportunity to steal money, drinks, or both, Steven allowed himself a brief smile of satisfaction at the fact that his plan had so far gone without a hitch. As Anna returned to the bar, he raised his glass, and she reciprocated, both of them holding mutual eye contact as they sipped their drinks, him paying particular attention to her swallowing the now tainted orange juice. Putting the glass on the bar, she scrambled for her phone as it rang.

"Sorry" she mouthed, answering her phone and turning away

from him as she spoke into the mouthpiece. A conversation in hushed but harsh sounding voices followed. From the tone of the conversation she was having, he was guessing that she had in fact been stood up.

"Well, thanks very much! Idiot!" she hissed as she snapped the phone shut.

"Problems?" he asked.

"My so-called boyfriend!" she answered. "Apparently he's been drinking all afternoon with his work mates and doesn't fancy coming out now" she rolled her eyes, and took another sip from her drink. He couldn't resist watching her soft lips taking in the cold juice, complete with his own special ingredient, nor could he tear his eyes from her smooth neck as he imagined the liquid making its way through her body. His anticipation at what was to come next was building.

"I'm Steven" he offered, smiling as he held out his hand.

She laughed. "Better late than never I suppose" She downed the remaining contents of the glass, and placed it back on the bar.

Looking down at his rugged, hairy hand, she reciprocated, offering hers, both of them laughing as they realised that they had already gone through the hand shake a few minutes earlier. Steven's eyes swept down to her fingers as they intertwined with his. Finishing his drink, he decided to make his move. Leaning over to her, he whispered softly in her ear.

"Shall we have another drink here, or do you fancy moving on somewhere else?" Instantly she recoiled from their intimate pose, her mind racing for a second as she considered going off with this man who was, after all a stranger. She didn't make a habit of going off with random men,

"But he is really nice" she said to herself. She thought about her boyfriend. "It's not like we're serious or anything" she reasoned. "If he wanted me that much, he'd have made the effort to be here!" Her stomach lurched slightly as she made her decision. Mustering up all of her confidence, she lifted herself from the seat, picked up her handbag, and began to stride toward the door, her hips once again swinging in feminine confidence. Steven was caught slightly unawares, for a split second thinking that she may have seen through him. Before he could say anything to her she stopped and half turned, fixing him with her best wide eyed look as she said "Come on then, what are we waiting for?"

-28-

Jessica giggled to herself as she looked at Glen. He was stood in front of the desk with one hand on his hip as he looked at a manifest of all material collected from the crime scene. His shirt sleeves were rolled up to his elbows, and his top two shirt buttons open, revealing just a hint of chest hair. Up until this point, Glen had been engrossed in the contents of the list he was holding.

"What's so funny?" he asked her, his eyes leaving the page for the first time in about twenty minutes.

"You!" she replied. "You're just so macho!" she said in a mock girlie voice, tensing her arms like a bodybuilder for effect.

"That's real funny Hopewell!" countered Glen. He tossed the list he had been reading onto the table in front of Jessica.

"Don't you think you went a little overboard with the crime scene?' he asked, almost accusingly.

"How so?" she asked, idly looking at the contents of the page

Glen had just tossed on the desk.

"Look at what they collected!" he exclaimed. "We have assorted Bracken, numerous articles of ballast like rock material, a rusted speed sign, and even a broken shard of mirrored glass!" Jessica's eyes moved from the page, and met Glen's stare. She knew that he did not like her holding eye contact with him, and this time was no exception. Almost instantaneously he diverted his eyes, and examined the carpet as Jessica spoke in a calm, steady tone.

"This is precisely the reason why Police Officers do not undertake forensic and scientific work!" She swivelled the list around so that it was facing the right way for Glen to read it. "One of the fundamental rules of Crime Scene Operations is that evidence without context is not evidence at all. As we do not yet have any context within which to place the Crime Scene debris, we cannot exclude any of these items as irrelevant." Glen ran a hand through his hair as he mentally processed Jessica's last statement.

"But come on!" he protested "A fucking piece of broken mirror?"

"Here endeth the first lesson Glen!" she said slyly, ignoring him entirely as she stood up, her face illuminated with a smile that aroused a mixture of fury and sexual attraction within Glen. With her victory hanging in the air, Jessica pivoted on her left foot and marched triumphantly out of the room as Glen went back to studying the list, trying to glean from it something significant that the killer may have left behind.

Finally they reached their destination. Steven carefully parked the car, ensuring that it wasn't easily visible from the main road that passed to the right. Slowly, he reached behind his seat, producing the plastic box and opening it. He gazed lovingly at the glass shards that lined the box, briefly forgetting about his passenger. Selecting a piece of glass, he paused as his own reflection stared partially back at him from the smooth, mirrored surface. From the passenger seat he grabbed his plastic tube, unscrewing the lid and slowly dropping the glass into place. Securing the lid, Steven opened the car door, remaining vigilant for any sign of life on this usually deserted lane as he slid the tube into his pocket. Walking around the car, he opened the boot and leant inside, opening his green holdall and producing his orange overalls. Efficiently, he unfolded them and slid them on over his trousers, forcing his arms into the sleeves and then fastening the buttons that ran down the overalls from his collar to his crotch, then taking from the bag a miniature video camera, a small microphone which he clipped to the front of his overalls, and a laptop computer. His eyes flicked from the computer screen to Anna as he turned on the three devices and linked them via Bluetooth. He scooped up the camera and aimed it, opening the rear door of the car and tilting it until he could see Anna's face on the laptop screen. Allowing himself a few seconds to enjoy the picture, he suddenly slammed the laptop closed, and stuffed the camera into his pocket as he clambered into the backseat of the car. Staring longingly into Anna's eyes, he stroked her face gently, smoothing the tape down that was clamping her eyelids apart. Her cheeks were moist with enforced tears. Without saying a word, he gripped Anna's upper arm and motioned her to get out of the car. He gently smelled her neck as she stood there, her chemically created daze suspending her like a marionette. Revelling in her scent for a moment he closed his eyes, breathing deeply as the first flushes of adrenaline began to pump about his body. He knew that the time for his plan to be put into action was very near.

Steven leant into Anna and whispered. "As you've been a good girl Anna, I'll take you to see your daddy!"

"D-dad" she murmured, her body numbed and disabled by the drugs that were coursing through her bloodstream.

"Come on, this way" he said gently as he stepped toward a gap in the trees. Anna responded, taking his lead and walking as if her body were stuck in neutral, navigating around the kissing gate that Steven had just passed through.

"Your dad is this way, you'll want to see him after your argument won't you babe?" Steven whispered.

"Yes" she replied, her words slurring "Need to say I'm sorry"

"He's sorry too" said Steven soothingly, dropping back a step to walk beside her. The hand that was holding her arm now rubbed it reassuringly before dropping momentarily to her waist, gently guiding her onward.

"Why won't my eyes close?" Anna mumbled. Steven ignored her. As they walked, her bare feet struggled to grip onto the muddy and uneven country lane, Steven grabbing her hips as she started to fall. They continued their walk in a silence that was fuelled by a mixture of drug induced hypnosis, and the focus of a man who was contemplating and relishing what he was about to do.

"Where's my dad?" asked Anna as they emerged from the trees at a small foot crossing at the side of a railway track, the diffuse light afforded by a solitary lamp forming a blurred sphere on the ballast and footboards of the muddy crossing.

"It's okay" Steven soothed. "Your Dad went for a walk to clear his head. He said he wanted to meet you here to talk"

Anna looked at him, her eyes, now streaming with moisture were blank, yet somehow questioning. "He's just over there babe" whispered Steven. "But you need to do something for me before you go and make everything better" He reached inside his pocket and produced the miniature camera and the earpiece. Switching both on, he pointed the camera at the floor, adjusting the focus until he could clearly see the mud-soaked hems of Anna's jeans, and her feet. The nail polish was still resolutely intact, despite her barefoot walk through the forest. In the distance he heard the warning horn of a train sounding, and he knew it would be rounding the bend in no more than 3 minutes. Handing her the camera, he leant into her body, taking one last chance to fill his lungs with her sweet aroma. He could feel the need to take her building deep within him, the material around his crotch tightening as he imagined how it would feel to be inside her. He knew though that he didn't have the time. Anna's beauty made her the perfect vehicle for communicating his message. Forcing sexual desire from his mind, he attached the earpiece to her ear, carefully smoothing her hair out of the way. The tracks were slowly beginning to hum with energy as the train got closer with every passing second. Pointing to the deserted clearing at the other side of the crossing, Steven leaned into Anna. "If you want to tell your dad how sorry you are, how really sorry, you'll have to listen to me and do as I say! He's waiting for you Anna! He wants to tell you its okay!"

"How do you know where he is?" she asked, her eyes once again meeting his in a mix of neutrality and question.

"Easy" he answered, his face beaming that confident smile that gained her trust a few hours earlier. "I know everything babe!" Steven winked as he pushed her gently out onto the crossing, as if freeing a small boat from its mooring. Anna turned away from Steven as he retreated behind the barrier, smiling darkly, unable to free himself from an overriding feeling of arousal. She slowly started walking toward the middle of the track.

"Can you hear me Anna?" he said softly, directing his mouth downward toward the microphone.

"Yes" she replied.

"Stand there" he commanded. She stopped, peering into the vacant clearing for a split second.

"Dad!" she called out in a hollow voice, "I'm here! I'm sorry!"

"Anna! Concentrate!" he snapped. "If you want to see your dad, you need to do as I say!" Her silence signified that she had yielded to his will. He breathed deeply, calming himself before continuing. "Anna, lift up the camera and look into the lens" She raised the camera until her face filled the viewfinder.

"Okay. Now what?" she said. The darkness of the woods began to lighten, the brilliant beam of light from the train's headlight appeared, and began growing rapidly. Steven licked his lips as he slipped his phone from his pocket and opened it, punching a few keys and grinning as Anna's face stared back at him from the screen. He was receiving a live feed from the camera to his phone, and he couldn't wait to replay the recording from the safety of his own bedroom.

"Now, you look right into that camera and you say everything I tell you to!" Steven said, ensuring that he was out of sight. "Turn to your left Anna" he instructed. Silently she did so. Once he was satisfied that she was staring into the lens, he let out a small groan as he gazed at his phone. "Repeat after me" he said. As Anna Brown spoke into the camera, the dark tranquillity around her erupted, its emptiness suddenly filled with the roar of oncoming metal, the crossing beneath her feet rumbling as the oncoming train rounded the corner. Anna continued to speak into the camera, even as the front of the train appeared over her right shoulder on the viewfinder. Steven smiled darkly as he watched the screen on his phone fill with light, and a beautiful young woman was transformed into nothing more than an intriguing silhouette. His arousal almost peaked as the driver sounded the horn of the locomotive, its bellowing cry failing to drown out the sound of the train impacting with Anna, her slender body exploding under the sheer force of the impact. Steven observed the scene via the phone, his hands trembling, and his arousal beyond the point of return. His hands, his face, his orange overalls, and his phone were covered in a fine spray of blood and body matter. Managing to temporarily stifle his exhilaration, he stepped onto the crossing, staring intently into the distance as he heard the distant squeal of brakes, the cumbersome freight train finally managing to stop more than a mile along the track. Steven's heart was beating a solid rhythm as more feelings of arousal flooded his body. As he savoured his work, enveloping himself in every detail of the scene, his heart skipped, his attention drawn to the unmistakable shape of a disembodied female hand, laying a few feet from the crossing at the side of the track. Listening keenly for the sound of the inevitable response, he walked briskly over to it. Absently, he touched his crotch as he studied the pale skin and dark finger nails. Sliding his hand into his pocket, Steven pulled out the plastic tube, opening it and taking careful hold of the glass shard. Studying it in the moonlight, he saw his own face, the tone of his thoughts obvious from his expression. The glass was fairly thin, with chaotic angles at the bottom, and a broader part at the top, almost like the outline of the Italian mainland. Steven smiled, returning the container to its hiding place as an idea overtook his mind. Stooping, he picked up the hand, marvelling at the softness of the palm, and the neatness with which the brute force of the freight locomotive had managed to amputate it from Anna's arm. Carefully, he pressed the glass into the hand and wrapped the fingers around it, satisfying himself that the hand was holding the glass in place. Walking back to the crossing, he set the hand down on the floor, angling the glass until its reflective surface made the moon visible. He took out his phone again and activated the video camera, filming the hand as it lay in the very centre of this muddied and blood soaked crossing. Once more, the material of his overalls was stretched around his groin as he continued to film. He could no longer avoid the urge. With a free hand, he tore at the buttons of his clothing, ransacking his overalls and trousers until he could free his erection, gasping as the cold air caressed his hot, swollen skin. He began to pleasure himself prim ally, grunting and whispering obscenities as he stared down at Anna's lifeless, severed hand, his arm quickly adopting a breakneck rhythm as he reached a messy climax in minutes. Looking down at the warm stains on his left leg and shoe, he laughed to himself as he stopped filming, shoving the phone back into his pocket, and carefully pulling out the piece of paper that was at the epicentre of his mission. Steven produced a pen, methodically crossing out a line of script before refolding the page and sliding it back into his pocket. Calmly and slowly, he walked back to the barrier, looking and listening for any signs that someone was nearby. Down the line, he saw the wavering beam of light that was coming from a hand held torch, probably belonging to the driver of the freight train. Steven knew he had to leave. He pulled out a cloth and wiped the barrier clean of any fingerprints he may have left behind. Turning and walking away from the crossing, towards the safety of the secluded lane and his car beyond, Steven took a final deep breath as he left the scene, relishing the smell of death that permeated the evening air.

-30-

"I'll bet this is Violet" whispered Joe to himself, irritated as he bounded the stairs. "What's he doing, ringing me at this time?"

"Tenby" he said into the mouthpiece breathlessly.

"Hi Joe, Its Jessica" she said, sliding herself gracefully onto one of the stools in her pristine kitchen. Joe smiled to himself as he listened with pleasure at the conspicuous girlie quality in her voice.

"Hi Jessica" Joe said, his face transforming from an expression of alcohol fuelled fatigue to a wide grin in an instant.

"Joe" she said, catching his full attention with her dramatic pause. "I probably shouldn't be ringing you before I've spoken to DCI Whindle, but I got a call from a guy who I know who works with the transport police, and apparently they just cleared a scene over in Bansholt. Young woman hit by a late express last night."

"Okay" said Joe, his mind still trying to fight its way through the fog. "So?"

"So" she said condescendingly, "He thought he'd give me the heads up about it" Joe could almost see her eyebrows rising as she spoke.

Realizing that he was standing in the middle of the landing, Joe walked slowly back into his bedroom, closing the door quietly behind him. "Don't you people have enough work to be getting on with?"

"Trust me Joe, we have plenty of work to be getting on with!" she replied. "I think you'll agree that this one is of particular interest"

"Right" Joe snorted, realizing that he was cold, sitting there in just his boxer shorts and a t-shirt. "What could be particularly interesting about some girl walking out in front of a train? She probably had too much to drink, split up with her boyfriend and went off at the deep end!"

"How about if I told you that she was a railway employee?" asked Jessica, smiling slightly as she checked her hair in the glass door of the oven.

"Okay, I'm listening!" Joe said. "Fancy a pre-work excursion? See if the local plod on the cordon will give us any info?"

"We should really inform DCI Whindle" Jessica replied hesitantly. Joe remained silent as she mulled the proposal over. "On second thoughts, let's go! Perhaps it'll put a smile on his face if we can drop a fresh lead on his desk!"

"Great!" Joe said with a grin. "I'll pick you up!"

"I'll text you my address" Jessica said, feeling slightly naughty.

"So how come you've got the railway children running around giving you tip offs all of a sudden?" Joe asked her, walking over to his wardrobe and opening the door.

"He was one of the transport police officers who turned up at the station murder" she replied. "I think he thought it might have got him a date, bless him"

"Now that is interesting" Joe said, smiling to himself as he grabbed his trousers from a hangar, cradling the phone between his ear and shoulder as he put them on.

"What is?" asked Jessica, almost laughing. "The information, or the guy chasing me?"

"Both!" Joe replied with a smile, snapping his phone closed and grabbing a clean shirt from the open wardrobe.

An hour later, Joe and Jessica were sitting in Joe's car, parked half way down a country lane that meandered along a steep hill overlooking a busy road. A constable from the transport police manned the cordon opposite and glared defensively at them as they sipped lukewarm coffee. Beyond the tape lay a narrow pathway that lead down to the railway line. It was a predictable scene of organised chaos, with police officers, forensic technicians and detectives busying themselves diligently. They sat in awkward silence as they waited for someone from the transport police to grant them permission to pass the outer cordon. Joe distracted himself from the subtle fragrance of Jessica's body spray by scouring the lane and the vegetation immediately bordering it. The road followed an uphill gradient past where the constable grimly stood guard, and as Joe gazed beyond the fluorescent yellow of the constable's jacket, he thought he could see a headlight sticking out slightly beyond an untamed hedge.

"What's that?" he said, unclipping his seatbelt and reaching for the door.

"What?" asked Jessica.

"Wait here" he said as he got out of the car and walked slowly towards the hedgerow. As he got near, he could see that the driver's side door of the car was open. Peering over the top of the hedge and through the passenger side window, he could see that the keys were in the ignition, though the engine was not running. A man was leant on the top of the car. He had positioned a digital camera on the roof and was smiling excitedly as he studied the viewfinder. Realising that the car was a Volvo, Joe instantly recognised the man from the station car park at Upper Charleston. Looking in the direction that the camera was aimed in, Joe could see clearly the crime scene on the railway line as the narrow lane charted a course downward, affording a perfect vantage point from the lane.

"What are you doing?" asked Joe as he stepped from the cover of the hedgerow. The man looked up startled, and without replying he jumped into the car, started the engine and drove away. Running out into the lane behind him, Joe squinted at the licence plate, cursing himself as he realised that he had taken note of the number at the previous crime scene and not asked for a check to be made. Snatching his phone from his pocket, he made a call to the control centre as Jessica got out of the car. She looked down the lane as the suspect vehicle disappeared from view before looking back at Joe.

"Get in the car!" he said. "We have to go!"

"What about looking at the crime scene?" Jessica asked as she got back into the car and fastened her seatbelt.

"We may not need to have a look!" Joe replied as he followed suit, slamming the driver's door and starting the engine. "The car that has just sped off was at Upper Charleston. I took a note of the number because the driver was filming the crime scene! I can't believe I didn't run a check on it!" Spinning the car around, Joe gunned the accelerator, banging the top of the steering wheel with his fist. "I knew he didn't look right! He was filming the crime scene up here as well!"

"Calm down Joe!" soothed Jessica. "He could have been a journalist!"

Joe shook his head dismissively as he worked the car through the gears.

"No way" he said. "I can tell a journalist from miles away! He was just odd!"

"Well, let's hope that the vehicle checks come up with something!" Jessica sighed. "By the looks of it, it isn't just DCI Whindle who could do with a cookie and a nap!" Joe glared at her, his dark expression melting quickly into a stifled laugh as she smiled slyly at him.

31

"I was wondering, Detective Sergeant Tenby!" snapped DCI Whindle. He was facing the huge whiteboard on the far end wall of the CID office. "I don't suppose you would know what the Latin translation would be for the phrase 'poor timekeeping'?" It appeared that Joe was the last member of the team to arrive, and the DCI was already a good way through the morning briefing. Joe had remained in the car for a few minutes so that Jessica could discreetly take her position in the main office, so as not to make it obvious that they had travelled in together following their 'of the cuff' excursion. He stood by the door for a few seconds, observing as DC Violet stood by the whiteboard under the watchful eye of DCI Whindle, his silver tie already loosened from the collar of his dark purple shirt. He scribbled details of the girl who had been hit by a train the previous night on the whiteboard, occasionally referring to a pile of A4 papers cradled in his left forearm. Slowly Joe made his way to his desk, throwing his suit jacket over the back of his chair, and failing to see the small brown envelope that sat on the desk as he debated what to do regarding the fact that Jessica had tipped him off before speaking to the DCI about the potential new lead. Should he come clean and tell him the details that Jessica passed on? Would that mean trouble for her? It was obvious that the team were all aware of the fact that the murder had taken place, so what harm would it do to just keep his mouth shut? What about the check he had requested on the suspect blue vehicle? After a brief moment of indecision, Joe elected to be upfront.

"Come on then Tenby!" hissed the DCI, pre-empting Joe's decision. "Care to share? Or do you and Miss Hopewell intend to claim spousal privilege?" Joe straightened his posture, looking the DCI in the eye. Mustering his strongest sense of indignation, Joe faced DCI Whindle square on.

"I beg your pardon sir?" he said, as slowly and deliberately as possible without sounding monotone. DC Violet had stopped writing and was now facing the pair of them, the marker in his hand now idly at his side as he watched the stand-off. Joe shifted his stare to him. Glen rapidly got the message, being conspicuous in returning to the task of transferring the data on Anna Brown from the file to the whiteboard, and ignoring the conflict that was unfolding next to him. DCI Whindle took a step forward, his forehead shimmering slightly with perspiration.

"DS Tenby, I do not want you to beg your pardon! What I also do not want you to do is go behind his back and strike out like some renegade on this case!" DCI Whindle's face was rapidly colouring under temper, and he wiped angrily at his forehead with the sleeve of his suit jacket, never once breaking the gaze that he had fixed on Joe.

"Renegade, sir?" Joe asked.

"I want to know why Jessica Hopewell is contacting you instead of me! Have you been promoted at my expense since close of play yesterday?" DCI Whindle hissed. Joe countered his rising anger at DCI Whindle blatantly ignoring his reply, instead watching his boss position himself on the edge of DC Violet's desk and fold his arms.

"Not to my knowledge sir" Joe replied softly. He was trying to placate his anger by not giving DCI Whindle a reason to wind himself up still further.

"Come on then Tenby!" demanded DCI Whindle, his confidence growing at the same rate as his anger. "Tell me why you and Miss Hopewell saw fit to saunter down to a crime scene being investigated by another force, without my authorisation! What is the lightning bolt of inspiration that prompted such a waste of police time?"

"Our latest victim is also a railway employee, there could be a connection between the two victims!"

DCI Whindle scoffed, shaking his head as he laughed to himself.

"You forget one key thing Tenby" Joe didn't speak, instead choosing to maintain eye contact with the DCI. "You have no proof! Unless of course, the killer has been sending you secret messages again!" Looking around the room to ensure that he still had a captive audience, DCI Whindle continued. "One of the most basic tenets of good police work is substantiating a theory. You come in here, spouting your theories, driving a bus straight through the chain of command and you expect to get carte blanche in return? This isn't a parking offence Detective Sergeant! Things you encounter in murder inquiries are not black or white. That is why this is no place for some careerist chancer better suited to chasing tax disc thieves and speeding teenagers!" Joe wanted to extricate himself from this confrontation so that the rest of the team, who were watching every move, and drinking down every word, would give a positive account of his handling of it when the particulars were recycled in the canteen later.

"I can assure you, Detective Chief Inspector, my abilities compare with any person in this room, including you! As for Miss Hopewell, I don't know why she contacted me!" Joe said, pausing for a second. "Maybe she tried to contact you beforehand"

"DS Tenby, please do not insult my intelligence!" DCI Whindle said, as he got up from the edge of DC Violet's desk and walked briskly toward his office door, which was creaking steadily as it blew in the breeze from the open window.

"Look, DCI Whindle! I have a potential lead on a suspect vehicle! I saw the driver and the car at Upper Charleston, filming the scene! He was there again this morning! I've asked for background checks!" Joe snatched his notebook from his pocket and tore the page out, throwing it down onto the desk. DCI Whindle walked back to Joe's desk and scooped up the paper. Glancing at it, he screwed it up and thrust it into his pocket, waving his hand dismissively.

"I know all about your little checks Tenby! You forget that I have eyes everywhere! I will be talking to Miss Hopewell regarding protocol! In the meantime, get yourself over to the labs, and get me the full story on this girl! If there's a crackpot on the loose, we need to make the connection before the press do!" As he reached his office door, DCI Whindle stopped and turned. "And Mr Tenby, try and concentrate on the bloody case, and not on phantom cars and Miss Hopewell's backside!" Flushing with anger, Joe remained static for a second, his fists clenched tightly. DC Violet turned away from Joe, grinning to himself in the mistaken belief that he couldn't be seen. "Oh and DC Violet! Get me some bloody lubricant for this door! It's doing my head right in!"

"Sir!" they both said, exchanging quizzical glances as the DCI slammed his door shut. Joe grabbed his jacket from the back of his chair, heading for the corridor.

"Where you going Sarge?" called DC Violet as Joe walked away.

"Forensics Glen" he said "Toxicology results on our second victim will be due anytime.

"What should I tell the guv if he asks where you are?" he asked. Joe stopped at the door and turned around, thinking about the most appropriate response to give.

"Tell him that I'm doing as I'm told!" Joe said with a smile, turning on his heels.

32

Joe's phone had vibrated a couple of times, but he had decided to ignore it. He was not in the mood to talk to anyone. The caller was Amber Rawson, a journalist who was clearly desperate to get any information regarding the case that she could. Like the unknown man with the Volvo, Joe had seen her hanging around at Upper Charleston. He decided quickly that he had enough trouble to deal with without risking further problems by dabbling with the press. Joe was always paranoid about the noise of his footsteps when walking down these types of corridors. He always walked with a lighter step than usual, trying unsuccessfully to walk silently. Reaching the open door of Jessica's office, he knocked lightly and entered. Jessica was sitting at her desk typing. As usual, the office shone with cleanliness and lack of personality. Joe always found himself getting depressed if he stayed in these kinds of places too long, but he was struggling to concentrate as his eyes kept returning to the meticulously maintained dark hair that framed Jessica's features as she looked up from her computer screen. Unconsciously his hands fidgeted as his eyes darted about the room. Jessica slid her chair away from the desk and rose to her feet.

"Detective Sergeant Tenby" she said with a smile, breaking the awkward silence as she turned to the filing cabinet behind her, selecting a bright red box file from the shelf and opening it. "I take it that DCI Whindle has sent you for the toxicology results?" Joe nodded. "Well" Jessica said through a grin, it seems that you have a few more questions to answer!"

"How do you mean?" Joe asked. Jessica handed Joe the papers.

"The toxicology screen found vastly elevated levels of Medazolene" she said, walking around the desk and standing behind him, reading the papers over his shoulder.

"Didn't your mother ever tell you that reading over somebody's shoulder is rude?" Joe said. Her scent was filling his nostrils, and he was becoming seriously distracted. Forcing himself to concentrate on the file, Joe focused on the bold text at the bottom of the first page.

"Medazolene" he read aloud, deep in thought.

"It's a drug used in certain branches of mental health practice, similar to benzodiazepine" Jessica replied. Joe watched her as she gracefully returned to her chair. She tapped expertly on the keyboard for a brief second, and swivelled the computer screen around so that Joe could see. He tried to digest the paragraphs of information on the drug.

"You'll have to forgive my ignorance Jessica" he said apologetically "Is this drug recreational?"

"Not really" replied Jessica, her attention drawn momentarily from Joe as she sifted through another pile of papers.

"It's a tightly controlled drug Joe! This isn't the kind of teen drug we normally see in overdoses!" The statement pricked his interest, and his attention was wrenched from the screen "Besides" said Jessica, her brow furrowed slightly. "I thought you had a degree in Psychology. Surely you know your mental health drugs!" Joe smiled, making a note of the fact that she had obviously been researching him.

"Psychology studies tend to focus on the physical and emotional causes of illness and sickness. They don't tend to study in any great depth the pharmacological remedies available. That is what psychiatry students study"

"Fair enough" she said, a sweet smile escaping her lips.

"So was Miss Brown being treated for any kind of medical condition?" he asked.

"No. The only medication she was taking was the contraceptive pill" Jessica handed Joe the papers and he gave them a cursory glance, placing them on the desk for now as he tried to make sense of the data being displayed before him.

"So, how would somebody get hold of this kind of medication?" he mused. They stared thoughtfully at the screen for a few seconds. "This is getting weirder and more complex!" she said, almost under her breath. "How does an ordinary middle class girl turn up with such a rare and tightly regulated drug in her system?" Closing down the browser on the computer, Jessica re-opened the document that she had been working on when Joe came in.

"It's like I said Joe, this kind of drug is tightly controlled. It's hard to get hold of" Joe continued his mental search for an answer as his eyes lost themselves in the documents she had given him.

"Something else though" she said. "One of the effects of this drug is that can induce a state of chemical hypnosis"

His eyes snapped up from the papers she had given him. Joe looked her directly in the eye as an alarm bell started to ring in his mind.

"Chemical Hypnosis?"

"The drug affects the brain and induces a state similar to hypnosis whereby the subject is highly susceptible to suggestion and direction" Joe moved his gaze to the ceiling, exhaling loudly.

"So we're saying that she was given this drug so that someone could make her do what they wanted?"

Jessica met the question with a neutral stare. "But surely the obvious motive for that would be sexual?" Joe asked. "Why else would someone want to incapacitate, a young girl like this?" Jessica's expression remained unaltered as Joe spoke. "I'm assuming the rape kit came back negative?" Jessica nodded grimly.

"That is one area where we were lucky Joe" she said. "The pelvic area and abdomen were just about the only parts of the body that were intact upon recovery." Joe shuddered.

"So if she didn't take the drug herself, and she wasn't sexually assaulted, why was it in her blood stream?"

Jessica shrugged. "Maybe sex was the motive" she mused.

"Maybe he was interrupted before he got the prize"

"Either way, I think we can safely rule out accidental death or suicide" Joe said, pulling out his mobile phone and dialling a number. "By the way" he said, pausing before making his phone call. Jessica looked up at him.

"Was Tina McBride tested for Medazolene?" Jessica paused for a second, pursing her lips as she thought.

"No she wasn't" Jessica replied.

"Why not?" Joe asked, frowning.

"Dr Rothesay saw no need. It was only after the Anna Brown murder that the drug became an issue, and we can't conduct the test without.."

"DCI Whindle!" Joe sighed.

"I'm afraid so!" Jessica said, returning her attention to the computer screen. "On the subject of your mysterious Volvo!"

she said. "What did the checks come up with?"

"Your uncle has blocked them!" Joe said, his voice sharpening in frustration.

"Nobody said he was user friendly!" said Jessica as her fingers effortlessly worked the keyboard.

"Thanks Jessica" he said in a muted whisper, electing not to comment further on DCI Whindle. He turned and strode out of the room. Once outside, he took a deep breath and calmly informed DCI Whindle of the news as he headed back to his car.

-33-

"But I don't want to go!" pleaded a young Steven, his hands pawing at the black tie that he felt was strangling him. He was looking up at his mum, flawless in her black tailored overcoat and court shoes.

"Remember what your dad told you about doing your duty" replied his mother, straightening his tie for the fifth time in as many minutes as they stood in the hall. His throat narrowed and his eyes filled with tears. He missed his dad so much. Every day seemed to make his memories a little thinner, a little further away and it hurt. Puffing out his chest and trying his hardest not to cry, he nodded.

Sitting in the courtroom, Steven was in awe. The sheer number of people was staggering to such a young child. An official from his father's trade union was saying something to his mum, and occasionally looking down and smiling warmly at Steven. He replied by grabbing his mum's dress and hugging her leg. The whole place smelled funny, and everybody seemed very old and serious. Looking around the room, Steven saw Graham, his dad's boss, and another man with a beard who bit furiously at his nails. They all looked ashen, and never once so much as glanced at each other. The man biting his nails looked scruffy, and half of his shirt wasn't tucked in. He had a bushy beard and kept running his fingers through it. Steven's eyes locked onto Graham. Sensing that he was being watched, Graham glanced across at Steven, managing a smile before looking away.

When the judge walked in, everybody stood. Steven couldn't understand what was going on. The air seemed to be filled with long words that he had never heard before. The room smelled of cold, and Steven shivered. Noises bounced around the room, filling his young head, along with the posh voices of the barristers, and the constant sobbing of his mum. Steven did manage to understand that the judge was telling Uncle Graham and his dad's workmates that they weren't to blame. Sitting wide eyed, he was numb. That numbness began to give way to anger and fury as the sound of his mother's sobs became all-consuming in his mind. Recoiling from the waves of despair that spilled from his mother, he gripped on to her hand as tightly as he could.

As this dreamscape gave way to the grey light of his living room, Steven realised that he wasn't gripping onto his mother's hand at all. It was the ragged arm of the sofa that he held onto so tightly. Making a half-hearted attempt to raise his body up, he submitted to the pain that was coursing through his head, staring at the dusty sheen of the mirror as it threw refractions of light across the room. Grunting, he relaxed his body as sleep once more overtook him. He punched the cushion he was hugging with what little energy he had left as his eyes slowly closed, the grey light of the TV casting shadows that acted as his toneless lullaby.

-34-

Questions surrounding the death of Anna Brown were swarming around Joe's head like angry bees. Could someone really administer such a rare drug and cause a chemically induced trance? Were the deaths even connected? Was it merely a coincidence that Anna Brown and Tina McBride were both railway employees? What about the video of Tina that Joe been sent? He had a strange hunch that these were not separate incidents, and with each passing minute, he grew more certain that the video was the work of Tina McBride's killer. Add to that the mysterious man in the blue Volvo, and Joe was struggling to contain himself. The street outside was unusually quiet, and usually where Joe would be grateful for the peace and quiet, the silence that was filling the room in place of the usual sounds of passing traffic was making a louder noise than any logical answer his mind could construct. A loud 'BEEP' shook him from his thoughts. Turning over, he saw that Jessica had sent him a text message.

"Get in!" said Joe as he read Jessica's invitation to meet up for breakfast. Hurriedly he typed out a reply, and within one minute a meeting was arranged for the police canteen. Hardly a glamorous location, but it as the best he could do before the start of the working day. Snapping the phone shut, Joe leapt to his feet, grinning to himself as he grabbed a towel, casually walking out of the bedroom, relishing the thought of a hot shower to set him up for what was hopefully going to be a great day.

The canteen was bustling as always. Groups of officers sat at tables, exchanging jokes, station gossip, and markedly similar complaints and stories about the people who had crossed their paths during their shift. Joe selected a table nestling in the back corner of the canteen, choosing this spot in the interests of privacy. From here, Joe had the advantage of being able to see what was going on around the room, as well as being in direct line of sight of the door. After half a dozen anxious glances at the increasingly busy entrance, he started to become annoyed with himself as he looked up, only to see the back of a shaven head instead of Jessica. He was still mentally rehearsing how he was going to ask Jessica out. This definitely was not the ideal location, but Joe had decided to seize the opportunity, and he was allowing himself to be quietly confident about his chances. Suddenly, his mobile phone rang. Looking at the screen, he rejected the call and swore under his breath. Seconds later, a message appeared on the phone screen. It was Amber Rawson.

"DS TENBY. I ONLY WANT TO CHAT WITH YOU OFF THE RECORD. NO TRICKS. JUST WANT TO REPORT FACT. CALL ME. AMBER"

Joe fiddled with the phone as he read the message. He knew that speaking to any journalist off the record was a bad idea, even worse considering that he didn't know how she had managed to get hold of his mobile number. Nevertheless, he still had to deal with the issue of the video clip he had received and the mysterious cameraman in the Volvo, and was already growing frustrated with the pace and direction of the investigation. Despite his only being a member of the team for a matter of days, he knew that the case was heading for stagnation, unless something could be done to rip open the straightjacket that DCI Whindle seemed to have wrapped around everything. As he talked himself out of replying to the message, his fingers tapped a rhythm out on the table, his mind unaware of Jessica's silent arrival.

"Love the tie!" said Jessica, throwing Joe off guard. She stood at the other side of the table, a short black jacket folded over her crossed arms. Standing up, Joe attempted to be chivalrous by motioning for Jessica to sit down, managing to knock his phone off the table in the process, his head dropping as it came to a rest next to the foot of a startled WPC, who handed it back to Joe with an awkward grin. Dumping himself back into the ageing plastic chair, Joe offered up a pensive smile, clearing his throat as he prepared to take the plunge and ask Jessica out to dinner.

"Joe" she said, setting her coat down in one of the seats on the opposite side of the table, and slowly sitting down in the seat next to it. Swivelling the chair slightly, she eased her legs from under the table, and crossed them. "The DCI called me in yesterday afternoon and he wasn't best pleased over me tipping you off! Even less so about us going down to the crime scene!" Joe intensely examined the back of his phone. He was pretty sure that he knew what was coming next.

"I really like you, but I'm up for promotion next year, and I really need to keep people like DCI Whindle on side. I think it's best if we maybe step back a little here" Attempting to recover the situation, Joe leant forward, motioning to touch her hand, but thinking better of it as he remembered where he was.

"Come on!" pleaded Joe. Changing tactics, he embarked on one last effort to turn things around. "A few drinks, maybe dinner? Does it matter whether the DCI thinks that we're well suited or not?" Joe mustered his most convincing smile. Their eyes met for a second, but Joe knew that he was beaten.

"It's not as simple as that Joe!" she said, her hand resting briefly on Joe's. Her skin felt so soft, her touch so delicate. "DCI Whindle is my uncle. I think that is why he's being so rough on you. You do know that he has put a stop on any background checks you request from now on?"

"What?" spluttered Joe. "He'll be confiscating my access card for the car park next!"

"He's always been protective" Jessica sighed. Joe smiled in defeat.

"Glen Violet is all over you!" he retorted. "How come Whindle isn't hanging him out to dry?" Jessica smiled, squeezing his hand.

"Maybe because he knows that Glen wouldn't have a chance with me" she spoke softly.

"I like you. But crossing DCI Whindle could affect my family and my career. Both are important to me Joe!" Gathering up her coat she stood up and turned to leave. Joe looked at his hand, where just a second ago hers had rested. He dropped it lamely into his lap and fixed her with a deflated look.

"I'm sorry Joe" she said, smiling sympathetically. Joe forced his facial muscles into a half smile as she adjusted the shoulder strap on her bag. Having straightened it out, she turned to walk towards the door, pausing for a second. "Meet me tomorrow night." She said soothingly. "We can talk more freely away from work." Joe nodded. "Anywhere you'd prefer?" she asked.

"The Milward Club" said Joe.

"I think I know it. I'll be there at 7:30" Jessica said, placing her hand gently on his arm. He looked down at it briefly, before looking away as she walked towards the door, leaving him staring at the bright 'Wet Floor' warning sign that was standing against the wall in the far corner of the room.

35

"Detective Sergeant Tenby!" Instantly Joe straightened up, standing with square shoulders and offering a professional smile. Commander Hayley Carlton returned the smile in the same professional way. Standing 5ft 4 inches in height, she was an attractive woman, with a steely glint in her eye. Known for not suffering fools gladly, she was another product of the High Development Programme. Aged only 37, she already had responsibility for the whole of south eastern division. Meticulous about everything, she was complimented by the tailored tunic of her uniform. Commander Carlton stood with her hands clasped in front of her, her hat tucked neatly under her arm along with a folded newspaper. Joe's eyes flicked down to her highly polished shoes that announced her arrival so loudly. He could see the outline of one of the ceiling lights in them.

"Morning Ma'am!" said Joe.

"Shall we walk Mr Tenby?" she said sternly. Joe followed as she turned. Silently she strode ahead, leading Joe down the corridor and through a set of double doors, pausing only to swipe her access card through the reader. Within a few steps they were in Commander Carlton's office. She sat down in a large leather chair, her desk orderly yet busy, the four document trays healthily loaded with case files. The room was airy, with two sofas positioned near a coffee table. Through a side door, the Commander's secretary busied herself at her desk, typing diligently as she spoke into a telephone receiver. Commander Carlton motioned for Joe to sit down. He complied, silently questioning where this meeting was going to lead.

The Commander leaned back into her opulent chair, examining Joe with a steely stare. After a few seconds the stare faded to a smile.

"Joe. I wanted to have a talk with you." She began, editing her words before announcing them. Joe listened, dreading whatever was coming next.

"How are you finding life in the middle of a major case?" she asked, leaning forward.

"It's a challenge ma'am!" He replied, managing a tense grin.

"Joe, I haven't called you in here to carpet you!" said Commander Carlton. She paused for a moment before passing Joe the newspaper she had been carrying under her arm. "The press are already crawling all over this one! I've managed to deflect most of the more mischievous questions, but there's one hack who won't take no for an answer! Amber Rawson! She's behind this piece of journalistic shrieking!" Joe unfolded

the paper and read the front page, his lips pursing as he took
in the headline;

THE TRACKMAN CLAIMS 2ND VICTIM!

Joe scanned the accompanying article for a second before
refolding the paper and sliding it calmly back across the desk.
"Your thoughts Detective Sergeant?" she asked.
Joe exhaled, electing for brutal honesty.
"Well, it could be said that Amber Rawson is a lot closer to
solving this case than we are ma'am, if what she claims to
know is true!"
"Are you telling me there is an issue with the Senior
Investigation Officer Joe?"
"I'm not making any such claims at this early point in the
investigation ma'am." Joe countered as diplomatically as he
could. "I have to confess Commander, that Amber Rawson has
been leaving me messages recently. I haven't replied to her,
but I can't be the only member of the team she has managed
to reach. These newspaper claims must either be as a result of
inside information, or just complete fabrication." Commander
Carlton nodded as she pondered Joe's words.
"Not to mention a great deal of poetic licence!" added Joe,
motioning to the headline with his hand, allowing himself a
smile. The smile was not returned.
"Detective Sergeant Tenby, your decision to avoid press
comment shows a sound judgement, and your ability to play
politics is promising for your career, but please do not be
misled into thinking that this is in any way a joking matter!"
Joe recoiled at the sharpness of Commander Carlton's words.

"I need you to be honest with me Joe! I have certain, issues, with DCI Whindle. He may well have the support of certain senior officers, but he lacks perspective at times! This is an investigation that cannot be allowed to run off course! I will be watching everybody very closely and monitoring the press for any sign of information being handed over. What I want from you is for you to keep quiet about it! You've shown independence, judgement and diplomacy Detective Sergeant. Now show some discretion please." The Commander continued to fix Joe with her stare, her lips pressed firmly together in a grim expression.

"Yes Ma'am" Joe compiled.

"Joe, your CV at first glance doesn't shout from the rooftops! I gave you this chance because your mentor from the High Potential Development programme was impressed by you, your performance and assessment reports are outstanding"

Joe nodded in gratitude.

"The fact that Whindle doesn't like you puzzles me, because he told me that you were the best candidate for him! His main problem though, is that he's a dinosaur who thinks he's Gene Hunt!" At that point the Commander's phone rang. Not breaking eye contact with Joe, she slipped her hand into her bag and pulled out the phone, sliding it open and speaking curtly into it "Carlton."

Sensing that the conversation was at an end, Joe quietly lifted himself from the chair and made his way to the door, carefully opening it as he replayed the Commander's words in his head.

"The DCI wanted me?" Joe exclaimed inwardly. Commander Carlton had finished the call and was returning the phone to her bag.

"Joe." She said. He paused and turned.

"Ma'am?"

"I need results, and I took a big risk on giving you this post. There is more than your career path riding on the outcome of this case. This is your opportunity. Don't waste it!"

"Yes ma'am" said Joe as dutifully as he could.

36

Steven sat in the driver's seat of his dark blue saloon, smoking as he surveyed the neglected buildings and depot car park from across the street. The roof of a slow moving train was just visible from his vantage point, and Steven found this to be briefly distracting. The driver gave a mournful greeting to the workers inside the shed with a blast of the train's warning horn. Reaching behind him and picking up his plastic tube, Steven picked out a broad, chunky segment of glass, its edges jagged and seemingly random in the directions they pointed to. Re-sealing the box, he placed it back behind his seat, realising that he had very nearly missed his victim emerging from one of these fire exits. A skinny man, with an unruly head of jet black hair and a jaw covered in stubble, Sean Grant stood in the open doorway, looking back into the shed as he pushed earphones into his ears and switched on his iPod. Sean had left at almost exactly the same time every day this week, and he had stopped and done the exact same thing before getting into his car every time too. Predictable behaviour makes it easier for a predator to accomplish his aims. The familiar rush of adrenaline and butterflies swept through Steven's body as Sean made his way over to the far corner of the car park and slid his key into the driver's door lock of his white BMW. It was fair to say that the car had seen better days. The interior of the car was strewn with fast food packaging and old papers and the back seat was home to an array of grimy tools and dirty orange overalls. Steven had carefully stalked his young victim over the preceding few days, and had become quite familiar with the habits of Sean Grant. He had at first been confused as to why it was that Sean always elected to park his car in the far corner of the car park. Managing to establish that there were no working cameras covering the area, Steven sneaked into the yard and made his way to Sean's car in an attempt to understand something of the young life he was about to snuff out. It was now that Steven learned of his prey's slovenly ways. He also noted that the tax disc in the window was valid at first glance, but when Steven scrutinised it, he discovered that it was actually for a motorcycle! He had also since learned that the car park was overlooked by the Traffic Warden's offices for the area. Steven reasoned that the car was probably uninsured too, and the tax disc was, in all probability the reason why Sean parked all the way over in the shadows. Well, at least Steven hoped there would be shadows when he finally took his chance.

As he watched Sean open the car door, Steven remained calm. Dusk was in full flow as the moon seemed to suck the daylight from the air. Sean switched on his headlights, and then turned the key in the ignition. The engine spluttered and struggled before falling into silence. Sean tried again, turning the key and pumping the accelerator in vain. Three more times Sean attempted to start the car before he got out and opened the bonnet. Steven opened his car door and crossed the street, subtly turning himself away from the glare of headlights as a bus grumbled past him, its engine seemingly as miserable as the commuters packed on board. Glancing up at the Traffic Warden's offices he noted that all lights were off and all the traffic wardens were safely at home and off duty. Silently he walked over to the white BMW where Sean was still puzzling over why his car wouldn't start, too distracted to notice him as he made his way around the back of the car and positioned himself to approach from behind. Taking one final glance around, and satisfying himself that he and his victim really were alone, Steven stepped forward, coolly and calmly reaching around Sean's neck with his right arm, shoving a cloth into his mouth with his left hand. Sean struggled against Steven's forearm for a few tense seconds, before finally giving way to the chloroform that Steven had bathed the rag in beforehand. Sean's body slid ungraciously down the front of the car, and Steven lowered him gently onto the gravel. Steven slipped his right hand into his coat pocket, pulling out two spark plugs. Examining them for a moment, Steven smiled to himself, basking in self-satisfaction as he looked down at the seemingly lifeless body of Sean Grant.

"One of the golden rules of motoring Sean" he whispered at his unhearing victim. "Always check your spark plugs!"

Joe studied the grainy pictures that lined the walls of the Milward Club as he drained the frothy remnants of his glass. The brickwork had been exposed, but was covered subsequently with white masonry paint, probably in an attempt to give the illusion of greater space. Deciding that he preferred the snug and cosy look to the more spacious aspirations of Phil, the owner, Joe returned his attentions to the case files he was scouring whilst he waited for Jessica. As the emptiness of his findings grew louder, so his frustration rose. The same could be said for his personal life. Jessica had made it clear that she wasn't going to let things advance any further between them, but Joe couldn't help but be hopeful that she was somehow giving him the chance to persuade her in a more private setting.

"Murderers I understand. Women I will never fathom!" Phil sighed as he scooped up Joe's glass from the table. Allowing himself to become distracted from the files, Joe found himself drawn to a giant reproduction of a picture of a whaling ship as he became aware that Phil was hovering. Its crew were standing on the deck, clothed head to foot in the clumsy waterproof suits of the day, their faces almost indistinguishable through their thick black stubble and long moustaches. They all looked happy. "Simple pleasures?" muttered Joe to himself.

"No matter what anyone says Joe, life for them lot was simpler than we have it!" said Phil as he wiped a neighbouring table. Phil was a shabby looking man, no taller than 5ft 6 in height, with chaotic black hair and a scraggly beard protruding in random directions from his gaunt face. A veteran of the 60's rock music scene, Phil had played guitar in a long defunct band who toured briefly with David Bowie and Mick Ronson. Being a northern lad in London, Joe was drawn to Phil after coming into the club for a cheap drink shortly after moving south from Hull. The two men shared a common love of all things to do with their home city. They argued furiously over rugby league, with Joe supporting Hull Kingston Rovers, and Phil following Hull FC. Joe would often come into the club dressed head to foot in the red and white of his beloved team, with Phil covering much of the wall space with historic photographs of old Hull FC players, and pictures of Hull's infamous Hessle Road in its heyday. Looking beneath the table, Joe smiled warmly as a furry head nestled itself on his thigh. Reaching down he stroked the dog's head as his swishing tail beating out a busy drum beat on the table leg. "Hello boy!" Joe whispered. The drum beat quickened. Gently ruffling the dog's ears, Joe looked up as Jessica walked gracefully across the bar, two drinks in her hands. Her hair was scraped back meticulously, as normal, but was arranged in a clip at the back which fanned out just above the nape of her neck, the gentle sculpted curve accentuated by the contrast of dark hair on pale, flawless skin. Jessica lowered the drinks onto the table and sat down opposite him, crossing her legs with a poise and precision that seemed to draw him in just as much as the scent she was wearing. The dog immediately left Joe and went to her side, looking up at her adoringly as his tail hammered out chaotic rhythms on the wooden floor.

"He's yours?" asked Jessica unnecessarily as Joe smiled at her, trying to aim his grin at the dog as he continued to run his eyes up and down her body as discreetly as his desires would allow.

"Meet Sully!" Jessica gazed down at the dog as his eyes darted from her to Joe and back again, his tail now swishing across the floor, sweeping the dark stained floorboards clean as it went.

"As in Toy Story?" asked Jessica, laughing.

"As in Sullivan! Clive Sullivan" Joe and Jessica both looked up at Phil in surprise.

"Clive Sullivan?" asked Jessica.

"I forgot that I have to deal with philistines down here!" continued Phil with an exaggerated roll of the eyes. Joe gave him a look aimed at indicating that he was not welcome in the conversation. Phil answered with a mischievous smile. "Sir Clive Sullivan is the finest sportsman to have played for Hull FC!"

"I didn't know any footballers had been knighted!" Jessica said, suddenly fascinated.

"He was a rugby player, and for the record, he played his best rugby for Hull KR! You know it Phil, I know it! Let it go man!" Phil ignored Joe's retort.

"You'll have to get this fine young man to, err, take you up there and teach you all about it sometime! For the record, the dog is mine!" he said, revelling in Joe's unease.

"Yes thank you Phil!" interjected Joe, shooing him away. Jessica smiled as she watched Joe flush with embarrassment. Sully walked over and dumped his head in Joe's lap, exhaling loudly. Looking at the papers on the table, Jessica paused for a second.

"Homework Joe?" she enquired. Joe smiled uneasily, his frustration at his lack of progress on the case returning.

"I'm just coming up against a brick wall here!" He said as he absentmindedly stroked Sully's nose. The dog narrowed his eyes and nestled his head into Joe's thigh. "These cases are linked! I know it!" his tone was sharper, the conviction of his belief punching through as he spoke. Jessica's eyes fixed on the papers that were spread across the table.

"Have you found fresh evidence?" Joe lounged back in his chair. The dog flinched ever so slightly, but didn't move.

"Not yet! But there is a link between the victims that is right under our noses! Call it a gut instinct!" he said flatly. She locked gazes with him as he spoke but remained silent. "The railway is a very small place Jessica, trust me! Two incidents of such violent nature within that bubble can't be isolated, unless we're talking about the mother of all coincidences!" Jessica smiled. "Then factor in the video clip I was sent, and that weirdo in the blue Volvo! For some reason the DCI just won't accept that it could be connected to the murders! If only I could get him to pull his head out of his arse!" His voice trailed off as he remembered he was talking to Whindle's niece. "Sorry" he said with a tense grin, his hands held up in a gesture of contrition. Jessica accepted the apology with a warm smile that melted the awkwardness of the moment. Forcing the case to one side for a moment and deciding to seize the initiative, Joe recovered himself.

"Look, about what we talked about before" he said, starting purposefully before trailing off before he could finish the sentence.

"Joe, it's okay, you really don't have to say anything." She said, smiling warmly.

"But I do!" Exclaimed Joe, desperate to make her see how deeply he was drawn to her.

"Look. There's no need to feel awkward" she said, continuing despite his best efforts. "We can still be friends. We have a real connection, and I don't want to lose that, but I can't risk my career or my family life, I just can't." Joe nodded. "It's just all too awkward Joe. You've arrived at a pretty bad time!" Jessica laughed gently. Joe sat motionless, a hostage to Jessica's fears about her family and of workplace politics. "If we weren't on the same case, and if my uncle wasn't the Senior Investigating Officer, maybe things would be different, but instead we're going to have to settle for being friends." She leaned across and kissed Joe's cheek, his entire body warming as a pulse of electricity coursed through it.

"How can you be so sure we can be friends?" he asked, "You hardly know me!" Anna gazed into his eyes, disarming his sense of injustice. "I know you're a good copper, and a decent man." She soothed. "I also know that Sully likes you, and trust me when I say that dogs are very good judges of character!" Joe looked down at the dog, whose head was still nestled into Joe's thigh. Joe's forefinger was still tracing the line from Sully's nose to the top of his head. His eyes were shut tight and he was seemingly oblivious to what was going on between Jessica and Joe.

"Friends?" she asked, offering Joe her hand. Joe examined its delicate dimensions. Sighing gently, Joe took it, gently cradling it within his own grip.

"Friends" he replied, mustering a half smile. Sinking back into the chair, Joe brought the drink Jessica had bought him to his lips. The cold liquid was just nestling against his lips as he took a mouthful, when his attention was drawn to the unmistakable sound of high heeled shoes beating a staccato rhythm on the wooden floor. Joe and Jessica looked up from their shared gaze, Jessica's was one of conciliation, almost pity, Joe had thought. Joe's was one of resignation, bordering on defeat. Jessica frowned slightly as she looked over Joe's shoulder. Joe reacted by swivelling in his chair to face the source of the sound.

"Joe Tenby?" asked the woman standing before them. Joe looked back at Jessica. She shrugged.

"I am" Joe replied flatly as he faced her, taking in the features of her face, the wide, blue eyes, the golden blonde hair, the engaging smile and the dazzling white teeth, and consciously ignoring the generous amount of bronzed, bare leg her skirt was showing.

"Amber Dawson" the woman said as she offered Joe her manicured hand.

"What can I do for you Ms Dawson?" Joe enquired as his hand encased her slender fingers, the dark red nails accentuating the paleness of Joe's skin.

"I've been leaving you messages Detective Sergeant. I need to talk to you about The Trackman inquiry" Joe felt his blood pressure raise slightly as he became annoyed.

"How did you know I was here?" Joe said coldly.

"That's not important" countered Amber as she stepped towards a vacant chair. "I'm here now and I need to speak with you. Do you mind if I join you?" As she spoke, she motioned to pull the chair away from the table so she could sit. Joe put his hand on the back of the chair, holding it in place and fixing Amber with an angry look.

"As it happens I do mind!" he hissed. Amber stepped back in surprise. "I only speak with four categories of people Ms Rawson; People I need to talk to in order to catch killers, my colleagues, my family and my friends. You're not in any of those categories, and following me during my personal time will only decrease the chances of you making it into one of them!"

"Joe!" she said, placing her hand on his shoulder. He looked down at her hand before staring at her in a way that made it clear, that removing it was advisable.

"Listen, Ms Rawson! I don't know where you're getting your information, but you won't be getting any comment or insight from me! You may find it easy to sweet talk coppers into letting information slip out, but it will take a lot more than tanned legs, a manicure and a doe-eyed smile to get round me!" Jessica stifled a laugh as she watched Amber grope for a persuasive comeback.

"I need you to realise that I am not the enemy here Joe!" Amber said.

"Ms Rawson, I am having a private conversation, with a friend, and I have no desire for your company, now or in the near future!" Joe turned back to face Jessica.

"I think it best you leave now" Jessica said to her. Without a further word, she turned and walked as sassily as her bruised ego would allow out of the bar.

"You certainly told her!" Jessica said with a laugh. "Her and her tanned legs!"

"Did she have tanned legs?" Joe spluttered, not wanting her to think he found Amber attractive. "I have to say I really didn't notice!" Jessica giggled and rolled her eyes.

"Oh Joe!" she sighed, shaking her head. "Finish your drink!"

Having arrived at his chosen parking place, he had quickly donned his overalls before unloading his haul from the boot of the car. The extra layer of fabric was causing him to sweat furiously, and his clothes were hugging his soaked skin. The hitherto lifeless bundle that lay prone across his broad shoulders had given out a twitch or two, signalling to him the need to act quickly. His path was strewn with randomly sited rocks and stones, and now and then his foot caught one of them, forcing him to desperately shift balance. From beneath the heavy canvass wrapping emanated a muffled and disorientated moan.

"Fuck!" He hissed, forcing himself into a brisk march, angling his body against the incline as he pushed on.

At the top of the hill, the path widened a little. He paused for a brief moment, fishing a water bottle from his pocket and drinking thirstily from it. He froze as he heard rustling in the undergrowth. "Shit!" he said to himself as he steeled his body. A fox scampered across the path, pausing for a second to inspect him before disappearing into a hole beside a large oak tree. Up ahead, the path turned into a thin trail that disappeared into a copse of trees via a left hand bend. The sound of leaves and branches scraping and rubbing against the load he was carrying filled his ears, along with the sound of his own breathing and heartbeat. Negotiating the bend, he let out a large sigh of relief as he emerged from the copse to the sight of an old railway bridge, its orangey brick work flaking against the ravages of time. "Thank fuck for that!" he whispered. Resting his package momentarily against the side of the bridge, he dumped down his holdall that had been carried across his chest, and roughly yanked at the sleeve of his jacket, stabbing his finger at a small red button on the side of his watch, his eyes fixing on it as the face illuminated sharply against the pitch darkness. He knew that nobody would be around. "23:07" he whispered. Kneeling next to the holdall, his ears listened keenly for any sound that could give notice of unwelcome eyes. He unzipped the bag, pulling out his small black syringe case, his own camera, a metal towing cable with a medium sized weight attached to it, and a headset with an adjustable camera mounted on it. Having placed everything on the floor in a neat line, Steven stepped toward the bundle that he had rested against the bridge wall, and aimed a swift kick at the middle of it. The package fell heavily onto the floor of the bridge, sending a small plume of dust into the night air. Pulling the plastic tube from the inside of his overalls, he opened the lid and pulled out a shard of glass. Steven placed his knee onto his now prone cargo, muffling the pleading voice within for a second. Slowly and methodically, he sank the jagged edge of the glass into the canvass, its fibres protesting loudly as the blade snapped them, thread by thread. Hysterical howls poured from inside the material, their volume increasing with every inch of the glass' journey. Twisting the shard, he pulled it violently toward his kneecap, stopping just a few inches from the material of his own trousers. Pulling back the ripped material, he moved his knee and looked down, smiling. Sean Grant's eyes focussed on the brickwork next to his head, and then on Steven, his chest heaving as tidal waves of adrenaline flooded his body. Sean tried to move but his arms were tightly strapped behind his back. He was naked.

"What is this?" pleaded Sean, his throat sore from the presence of Steven's knee. "Who are you?" Steven stared at him, his body motionless. Sean began to struggle.

"Don't fight it Sean!" Steven soothed, setting down the glass and reaching for his surgical tape. "It's not worth it!" Sean's eyes bulged, as Steven carefully placed the tape across his victim's open eyelids, his lungs expelling as much air as they could as he bellowed a cry of hopelessness.

"Please!" he whispered, his breathing now short and shallow. Steven lowered his finger to Sean's lips as he became suddenly aware of a familiar feeling in his groin.

"Shhh" he whispered. "You have to accept what's coming Sean! You have to pay!" Steven swivelled Sean onto his side, dragging his body from the canvass. Sean furiously tried to blink as he shivered against the evening breeze. The dust that was still swirling in the air was hanging thickly, and it irritated Sean's eyes. Brandishing the shard of glass, Steven hovered above Sean's prone and bound form, a menacing expression on his face. Steven calmly reached for his black syringe case. Opening the lid, he withdrew the syringe he had methodically filled earlier. Holding it up to the sky, he squinted, checking the contents as best he could. Aiming the needle towards Sean's neck, Steven pressed it slowly against Sean's skin with an increasing the pressure until the needle had punctured the surface. Sean let out a moan of protest as his body absorbed the drug that diluted his bloodstream and dulled his panic. After a few seconds, he became still, his eyes staring into a dark emptiness. Placing the syringe back into the case, Steven secured the lid and returned the case to his bag. Hauling Sean onto his back, Steven took a second to appreciate Sean's passive and compliant eyes as they stared eerily into the night sky. Coldly, he ignored Sean's laboured breathing as he picked up his camera and turned it on, zooming in on Sean's motionless eyes. Strangely, the administering of the drug had managed to pacify Sean's body without removing the pain and horror from his gaze. Steven smiled widely, seemingly revelling in the experience of extolling such extreme terror on somebody he considered to be so deserving. Kneeling beside Sean, Steven positioned his mouth close to Sean's ear.

"Do you want to live Sean?" Steven asked, aiming the camera at the face of his victim. Sean didn't reply. "Answer me Sean! Do you want to live?"

"Yes" Sean said robotically.

"If you don't want to die Sean, beg me to let you live!"

"Please" he whispered. "Just tell me what you want!"

"You're boring me Sean!" Steven hissed wickedly. "Make me believe it!"

"Please! Please! I want to.." Sean drifted into unconsciousness, but Steven wasn't listening anymore. He placed the camera on the ground, and scooped up the headset, putting it on Sean and adjusting the camera so that it was aimed squarely the unconscious man's face. Turning it on, he reached into his trousers for his mobile phone, opening it, and typing as quickly as his thumb would allow. The phone switched from text to video, Sean's slumbering face filling the small screen. Having satisfied himself that the camera was linked to his phone so he could once more record every second of his crime, Steven put his phone away and heaved Sean upright, bending him over the bridge wall.

"Wake up!" Steven snarled as he punched Sean hard in the

kidneys. Sean let out a howl, his body lifting under the force.

"What do you want?" Sean hissed.

"I want you to tell me the truth! I want you to put right what has been wrong for too many years!" Sean let out a groan as his stomach and thighs grazed against the rough bricks of the structure.

"You're a fucking maniac!" Sean gasped.

"Tell me the fucking truth!" Steven barked as he leant over Sean, grabbing his hair and pulling his head back as he tried to ignore and suppress the sexual ache from deep within. "Tell me it's your fucking fault!" As much as he wanted to, the drugs in Sean's bloodstream were stopping him from putting up any form of resistance, and despite his near paralysis and naked vulnerability, he was angry.

"Fuck you!" Sean grunted. Steven stepped back and punched him again, this time in the small of the back. Sean's body tensed for a few seconds, before flopping onto the brickwork.

"This is your fault!" Steven screamed, "It's all your filthy fucking fault! Say it!"

Spit dangled from Sean's chin as he gasped for air.

"I'm not saying anything, you fucking pervert!" Steven's eyes bulged with rage. He snatched at Sean's restrained hands, pulling his body away from the wall and standing him as upright as his injuries and fatigue would allow. Sean grunted as Steven hissed in his ear.

"Don't think for a second that I don't control you boy!" Sean managed a defiant, sarcastic laugh, the effect of the drugs maintaining his deadpan expression, despite his agony. "You don't believe me Sean? Maybe it's about time I showed you who is in command!" Steven pushed Sean as hard as he could against the bridge wall, knocking the wind out of him again as his body impacted with the brick. Steven felt a sexual energy running through him that transcended normal borders. He had been challenged. His veins coursed with the need to dominate, to emphasise his superiority in a way that could not be questioned, and that need had made him more aroused than he had felt in a very long time. Simplistic urges took over, and he hurriedly undid his overalls and trousers, throwing them to his ankles. Stooping, he reached inside his pocket and produced a condom, opening the packet and rolling it briskly down onto himself. Reminding himself of the presence of the towing cable, Steen grabbed it and looped it around Sean's neck, his erection pressing onto the small of his naked back.

"What the fuck is this?" Sean screamed.

"Call it a lesson!" Steven snapped as he pulled the cable tighter around Sean's neck, forcing his body away from the bridge. Pushing him down so his chest was on the top of the wall, Steven lined himself up with Sean's naked buttocks, and slowly pressed himself between them, taking care to find his target before viciously thrusting until Sean's anus surrendered and allowed entry.

"No! Please no!" Sean squealed, his face defying his every effort to contort in agony. His eyes grew wider with every thrust, his brain unable to comprehend the level of intrusion and pain he was suffering. Steven thrust into him mercilessly, forcing his battered and naked body against the cold bricks of the bridge again and again, pulling the cable around Sean's neck tighter as his orgasm approached. Loosening the cable for a few seconds, Steven punched Sean in the ribs.

"Tell me! Tell me now!" he growled, not breaking the rhythm of his thrusts even for a second.

"I don't know what you want from me!" Sean sobbed, his body beginning to go limp again through a mixture of exhaustion and trauma.

"Say it's your fault!" Steven replied breathlessly.

"It's my fault! It's my fault!" Sean screamed. Steven didn't reply. Instead he quickened his pace as his climax began to sweep through his body in a slow, undulating wave. His voice lowered into an almost unintelligible growl.

"Mea Culpa!" he grunted in between long, dramatic breaths. "Say it!"

"Mea Culpa! Mea Culpa!" Sean shouted, silently pleading for the ordeal to come to an end. Steven continued his onslaught of thrusts, saying the words in time with Sean, his voice heightening in pitch as he came to a deep and violent finish. Stepping away from Sean, Steven stood over him, fastening his trousers. His expression was one of disgust at what his quest for justice had forced him to do. Gathering himself together, he snatched at the towing cable, yanking it hard and forcing Sean to his feet. Pulling the cable along the floor, he snatched up the weight that was attached to the end.

"Please! No more!" Sean whispered, his face stained with tears. As he turned to face Steven, droplets of blood fell from between his thighs, and this seemed only to spike Steven's rage as he watched them mix with the dust.

Look what you made me do!" Steven growled. "Why couldn't you just admit it? Why did you make me do that?" Sean swayed as he looked down at his feet, moisture from his eyes running down his cheeks and along his jaw line. A trickle of blood had oozed half way down his leg before falling onto his ankle. His reddened eyes traced the blood's journey backwards and forwards as he shivered, partly through his naked body being exposed to the wind, and partly due to shock.

"Mea Culpa" he whispered repeatedly. His teeth chattered each time he took a breath, and the wind stung his eyes as they filled with tears.

"Answer me!" Steven raged. "Look at me and fucking answer me!" Sean continued to stare at his blood stained ankle.

"Why?" Steven screamed as his emotions boiled over. Stooping, Steven grasped at the glass shard he had left on the ground a few minutes earlier. "You made me do it!" he snarled as he plunged the glass into Sean's chest, dragging it diagonally down across his chest from just below the left shoulder, almost to the opposite kidney. "You made me do it!" he spat again, brandishing the glass shard once more and plunging it into Sean. Sean's mouth fell open as he screamed, his legs wobbling as Sean attacked for a third time before throwing it at the floor and smashing it into pieces.

"Please!" Sean sobbed. "I'm begging you! Just stop!"

"Quiet!" Steven hissed, leaning into Sean so their mouths and noses were only an inch apart. Steven seared with anger at the fact that Sean seemed to be so lucid, despite the healthy dose of medazolene he had received. Sean looked aimlessly at the floor, his eyelids flickering, desperate to close. "This is just another thing to blame you for!" Steven shouted. Clutching the weight he had been holding, he swung his arm, connecting with the side of Sean's head and sending a thick spray of blood into the air and all over himself. Still Sean didn't move.

He swayed viciously under the force of the impact, Steven's tight grip on the towing cable around his neck preventing him from falling. Suddenly the power lines spanning the railway below started to hum and vibrate, wrenching Steven's gaze from his immobilised and wounded victim. Knowing that the vibrations signalled the imminent approach of a train, Steven knew that the time had come. Blood was running down Sean's chest, coating his stomach, genitals and legs. It was obvious that he was on the verge of unconsciousness. Steven lurched forward, grabbing him by the neck, pulling the cable that hung around his neck as tight as he could and turning him to face the bridge, pushing Sean forward until only his grip on the cable was preventing him from plunging headlong onto the track below. Sean peered hazily into the night. He was distracted momentarily from the agony in his chest, neck and anus by a low, constant hum that filled his ears. His eyes were drawn to a dim light.

"Train!" Sean whispered, as he gasped for air. "Oh fuck!" As the light became larger and brighter, Sean's senses heightened. He couldn't tear his eyes from the oscillating wires as his mouth went dry. "No!" he screamed, jerking and thrashing as best he could, causing his body to sway violently. Managing to steady the swaying, Steven took a step back, dragging Sean towards him slightly. The swaying eased as Sean succumbed to exhaustion, his body still weak from the Medazolene. He started to hyperventilate, his panic heightening as the darkness was cut away by a harsh light, and the deafening scream of electrical motors.

"Yes! Come on!" shouted Steven, his grip on the cable tightening still further as he braced himself. He stared unblinkingly into the glare as the headlight of the onrushing train filled the desolate cutting with harsh light. At the top end of the headlight's reach, Steven could just make out the train's pantograph, bouncing against the underside of the wires below. The train was travelling at 125 mph, its Driver oblivious as to what was about to occur just feet above the roof of his locomotive. Sean too, stared into the light, his eyes as wide as they had ever been in his brief life. If anyone were able to look at his face they would have seen the traces of tears, glistening across his cheeks and nose. They would have seen his silent plea for help. They would have seen his mouth, slowly and noiselessly begging for his mother.

Judging the distance and speed of the train, Steven, exhaled fully before stepping into Sean's bloodied body, shoving him violently at the bridge wall and throwing the weight as far as he could into the path of the train. As the weight fell, and then gained velocity, the cable tightened and Sean was slammed against the brickwork, crying and screaming as he impacted with the parapet and plunged over the side. It seemed for a second that nothing happened. Then Sean's body impacted with the wires and the pantograph of the train simultaneously, showering the entire area with sparks, squeals, and flashes of blue light. Slamming on the train's brakes, the Driver threw himself instinctively onto the floor of his cab, covering his head as the night sky sprang to life in a terrifying display of chaos and unleashed power. The head of the pantograph cut savagely into Sean's back, severing his vertebrae and spinal cord, killing him instantly. The wires wrapped around his mutilated torso, cooking his wounded flesh, slicing his legs from his body and sending them careering down onto the track, coming to rest at the foot of the steep embankment. As the wires fell from their mountings, they took Sean's remnants down with them, spreading him over several hundred yards, the smell of cooked flesh and violent death filling the air, along with the shrill sound of squealing metal.

In the midst of all the sparks and noise, Steven had turned and watched the train disappear under the bridge. He had seen Sean's body being ripped apart by the wires as they tore at him like starving dogs. Whilst all of this had happened he had not blinked. He slowly reached inside his pocket and took out a folded piece of paper. From his other pocket he took out a miniature torch, and twisted its neck, the lamp blinking into life. Unfolding the paper, he aimed the torch at the page and smiled calmly, fishing out a black marker from his coat and aiming the light at the centre of the page. Striking a thick black line from one side of the page to the other, Steven refolded the paper and placed it back in his pocket. He switched off the torch and silently walked back down the trail, merging effortlessly into the darkness as the undergrowth and woodland assumed ownership of the night once more.

39

Reaching into his inside pocket, Joe took out his phone, unlocking and scrolling through the menu. Selecting his email inbox, he opened the new message that had announced itself loudly to the inhabitants of the bar. It was Commander Carlton.

"DS Tenby. I would like you to pay particular heed to my specific concerns centring on the direct operational issues which we discussed, and their potential ramifications. There is an awful lot at stake, and I would loathe to for you to forget that. I trust you require no further clarification"

Joe exhaled loudly as he read the message again. Closing the phone, he took a healthy swig of his beer, and stared blindly at the television that was suspended above the bar.

The self-important chimes of the introduction jingle for the news shook him from his thoughts. The screen lingered for a second on a panoramic view of the London skyline taken from the top of the Shard building at London Bridge, before the screen switched to an immaculately dressed brunette sitting on the edge of a desk, her face sober yet inviting.

"Good Evening, and Welcome to the news at 7." She said, a gentle smile puncturing her sober expression.

"Good evening to you my darling!" said the barman, looking up from his stock list, a sleazy smile occupying his face. He looked over in Joe's direction, offering the smile to him as an opportunity to agree. The scowl on Joe's face as he strained to hear told him that no agreement was forthcoming.

"Breaking news tonight!" announced the newsreader as the camera slowly closed in on her in a smooth motion. "Rail services in the north east are being heavily disrupted still following a suspected murder on the main railway line between York and Newcastle. British Transport Police are making no specific comment regarding the details of the incident, said to have taken place late last night. Although details are still unclear, a source has suggested that the alleged victim was hit by a train. We'll bring you more on this story as we get it."

"This has got to be linked!" Joe said to himself, thrusting his hand inside his jacket and fumbling for his phone. Summoning the DCI's number from the phonebook, he hurriedly pressed 'Call', tapping his foot as he waited to be connected. After a brief pause, the DCI's phone started to ring, before being switched to voicemail. Joe swore under his breath before leaving a hurried message. Ending the call, Joe swallowed the remaining liquid in his glass and made for the exit, acknowledging the barman's expression of gratitude with a wave of the hand as he disappeared through the door and into the street.

40

Joe knew that the DCI had deliberately snubbed him in ignoring his message. He was probably waiting for Joe to go in all guns blazing, giving him an excuse to side-line him further, or worse, get rid of him altogether. Collecting his thoughts, he remembered the E-Mail from Commander Carlton. Not for the first time following their recent conversation, he had paused to consider the strangeness of DCI Whindle choosing him as the best candidate for the job, and then being seemingly determined to make his life hell from the minute he had arrived. Focussing on the issue at hand, he considered going directly to the Commander with his hunch, but dismissed the idea just as quickly. She needed to know that he was trustworthy, that he had the strength to solve problems without running to her every five minutes.

"Just remember Detective Sergeant, there is an awful lot at stake, and I would loathe for you to forget that" she had written. It was an observation not lost on Joe.

"This is your big chance Joe" he whispered to himself, straightening his tie as he checked his appearance in the rear view mirror. "Don't let him ruin it for you!" Filling his lungs with air, Joe sprang from the car, grabbing his jacket and briefcase from the back seat and striding toward the building, ordering himself not to rise to the inevitable bait as he went.

Joe calmly pushed open the double door to the CID Office, and walked purposefully toward his desk. Jessica was just walking across the room towards one of the side offices where had based herself for the day. Awkwardly, they hesitated as they passed each other, both of them feeling the mutual effect, like orbiting moons repelling and attracting each other as they circled a strange planet. DCI Whindle was stood in front of the desks in the general office area, smiling mockingly as Joe made his way to his desk.

"Parting is such sweet sorrow" he said, imitating a stage actor, making an oversized gesture with his hands.

"It'll be nice for you to get to work at some point Detective Sergeant!" Motioning to speak, Joe stopped himself, resisting the urge to be pulled into this game as he spied the envelope that was sitting on his desk, his stomach lurching. Somehow, he knew that the envelope was a follow up to the video clip he received previously. He smiled tensely, making a show of placing his briefcase on the desk and opening it. He reached inside the case and pulled out some paperwork, placing it slowly and deliberately on the desk as he casually picked up the envelope, steeling himself for the inevitable. "Did you get my message guv?" he asked as he unbuttoned his shirt cuffs and rolled them up.

"I get lots of messages DS Tenby!" said DCI Whindle over his shoulder as he walked nonchalantly into his office and swung the door closed behind him. Joe breathed deeply, before tearing slowly at the envelope, peering inside.

"Oh shit!" Joe whispered as tipped the contents onto the desk. It was identical to the first that had been sent to Joe days earlier. As with the first picture, there was a small note which read simply

"Lustitia Colitur"

Looking across the main office, Joe saw Jessica sat at her desk. He grabbed a latex glove from his jacket and slipped it on. Scooping up the disc, note and the envelope they came in, Joe hurried across to the side office she was in, knocking on the door and slipping inside.

"Joe, what's the matter?" Jessica asked, looking over his shoulder for any signs of her increasingly erratic uncle.

"You're white as a sheet!"

"I think I've received another disc!" Joe said.

"From the killer?" Jessica asked. Joe nodded, showing her the evidence he held in his gloved hand. Setting the envelope and the note down on a sheet of paper, he stooped to the computer and opened the disc drive, gently placing the disc in the tray and sliding it closed. Shutting the blinds, Joe felt sick as he waited for the disc to load. Suddenly the screen burst into life, the clip edited in the same savage style as the last one. Tina

McBride sat at her desk, eyes taped open, her facial expression blank. Without warning, the picture lurched, the clip overlaid with Tina's pleading for her life.

"No! Please! Stop!" bellowed the computer's speakers as Joe watched the screen with his mouth hung open. The video jumped to Tina leaning over the desk, her eyes covered with pads. Her attacker was behind her, his trousers down and midriff bare. Tina was being slammed forward repeatedly. Joe covered his mouth with his hands as he realised he was watching a rape. Jessica stared at the screen, her head shaking slowly in disbelief as she watched. On the screen the attack continued, as did the haphazard manner of the footage, the scene jumping and lurching chaotically, with Tina's increasingly desperate voice pleading for her life, and for her ordeal to stop almost simultaneously, the grunts and words of her attacker distorted beyond recognition. The speed of the footage seemed to increase suddenly, the screen jumping and changing at an ever increasing pace, Tina's attacker hacking at her body with a large piece of broken glass, until he brandished it menacingly, plunging it into her. The footage switched to slow motion as blood oozed from her mouth, coating her chin and neck. Over the footage, a deeply distorted voice rumbled.

"Say goodnight Tina"

"Goodnight" came the desolate reply. The screen then filled with a haunting picture of Tina, the cotton pads now removed, her eyes naked and tortured. Her expression, and the damage to her eyes had conspired to make her look almost like a gargoyle. The camera zoomed in on those eyes as a caption scrolled across the screen that made Joe shiver.

Joe and Jessica exchanged stunned glances. Without saying a word, Joe grabbed the envelope, snatching at the door handle. He strode into the centre of the room. Turning around to face everybody, Joe held the envelope up. "Did anybody see who delivered this envelope? It came by hand!" he asked. Sighing in reaction to the blank looks and shakes of the head, he knew that DCI Whindle had to accept now that the disc sent to Joe previously was no prank. Catching DC Violet's questioning look. Joe's unspoken answer was clear; "Keep your head down". Steeling himself, Joe walked across to DCI Whindle's office door, raising his knuckle to the glass to knock, but thinking better of it. Taking another deep breath, he grasped the door knob and opened the door, marching into the office.

"What do you think you're doing Sergeant?" demanded Whindle, rising from his desk in protest. Joe's eyes drifted from DCI Whindle, taking in the office. This was the first time he had been inside. It was bland. The usual dark coloured office furniture occupied most of the space. Two filing cabinets a cupboard and a bookcase were positioned around the perimeter of the office, its windows dressed in metal blinds that seemed to remain permanently closed. Joe scanned the walls, bare except for a decorative mirror that looked as if it had been neglected by the station cleaners for quite some time. Centrally positioned towards the rear of the office was the desk. On one side sat DCI Whindle in his high backed swivel chair, on the other were two standard plastic seats, no doubt used to intimidate whoever was foolish enough to visit. Returning his gaze to DCI Whindle, Joe could see that he was far from happy.

"This needs to be sorted!" replied Joe, his voice flat and calm. "I left you a message last night, an important message with direct relevance to this inquiry"

"I got your message Sergeant!" retorted Whindle as he slowly sat back down again.

"It's Detective Sergeant!" said Joe, his gaze hardening. DCI Whindle sniggered as he busied himself with the papers that littered his desk. "Sir, I've received another one!" Joe said, gently placing the envelope in front of DCI Whindle. Whindle looked at it for the briefest of seconds before turning his attention back to his papers.

"Your little friends in traffic are as persistent as you are annoying!" he said.

"What is your problem?" said Joe, his voice rising as he struggled to maintain his calmness.

"I beg your pardon DS Tenby?" The DCI's tone was now more of a warning than a jibe.

"How can you still think this is a prank? Inside this envelope were a disc and a note! The note looks like it's in Latin! The disc shows the rape and murder of Tina McBride, in brutal detail! There is a caption on the end of the clip that mentions me by name! You'd see as much for yourself if you could be bothered to look!" Whindle sighed. "Wake up!" Joe said. "These clips are a kind of trophy for this guy, as well as serving as a message! They were delivered by hand and addressed specifically to me!"

"If you say so" Whindle said, still not looking up.

"How did whoever sent them know I was in this department? It was sent before I officially started work here!" Joe leant forward, placing his hands on the desk. "For some reason, the killer is trying to communicate with me" DCI Whindle rolled his eyes.

"Look at the note!" hissed Joe. "We have video evidence of a rape and murder! What kind of copper are you to sit there and ignore it?" DCI Whindle looked up in fury. He sprang from his seat, navigating the desk and grabbing Joe's tie, thrusting him hard against the office wall, sending papers and various binders flying across the room as he went.

"Listen to me you annoying little prick!" whispered Whindle as he clutched Joe's tie tightly, his other arm across Joe's shoulders and neck.

"I cannot stand overgrown traffic wardens! I especially cannot stand you! You are not a Detective! You will never be a Detective! You haven't earned the right!" Joe forced himself not to cough or splutter. Instead, he stared straight into Whindle's eyes.

"You listen to me!" countered Joe, mustering all of his strength and shoving Whindle as hard as he could. The DCI fell backwards, stumbling to avoid the corner of his desk, and crashing heavily into the bookcase that stood against the back wall. DC Violet shot up from his seat, throwing the door open. "Everything alright?" he asked nervously. DCI Whindle picked himself up gingerly, brushing down his suit jacket and straightening his tie.

"Everything's fine DC Violet" said Whindle. "Go back to whatever it was you were doing" Glen looked at Joe. "Are you deaf?" shouted Whindle. "Get the fuck out!" Not needing a second warning, Glen briskly shut the door. Joe seized the initiative.

"I make no apologies for being promoted quicker than you were! Yes I'm on the High Potential Development scheme, but I had to prove my worth to get on it, so I will take no lectures from the likes of you on my merit, DCI or not!" The DCI sat expressionless as he listened, the veins in his neck still standing out, the skin a deep red. "I notified you of a potential investigatory development relating to this case. You failed to act! You failed to even order a test on Tina McBride's blood to see if she had been drugged as well as Anna Brown! That isn't just poor police work, its professional misconduct!"

"Are you threatening me?" The DCI rose from his chair again. Joe put up his hand.

"All I am saying is that I have brought to your attention a number of matters that require your attention. The blue Volvo you blocked the background checks on, these videos, and the notes! They need investigating, as does the potential lead in Newcastle! The DCI sat back down again. Joe felt as though he had the upper hand.

"Convince me!" DCI Whindle said.

"I just think that the railway industry is a very small world, so to speak. I have a contact at Newcastle Central within the BTP, a DC, and I'm sure he'll be.." DCI Whindle held up his hand.

"On second thoughts, I don't care for your reasons Tenby! Go to Newcastle! Find out what you need to find out. That way at least, I get you out of my hair for a couple of days. These clips are pranks sent by bored traffic wardens who should know better, or some sort of crank who's as desperate for recognition as you are! HR will sort your train travel. Now get out, leave me alone, and leave the real detectives alone to do some serious police work!"

Joe chose not to reply, instead turning away and opening the door slowly, offering a fake smile to the DCI before emerging into the general office, still frustrated at the attitude of the DCI with regard to the video clips, but triumphant at his small victory.

"What's occurring?" whispered DC Violet.

"I'm going to Newcastle" announced Joe, picking up his briefcase and flicking open the catches.

"Newcastle?" repeated DC Violet.

"Possible lead Glen" said Joe, smiling as he slipped some papers into the briefcase. "Someone needs to move this investigation forward." That said, Joe turned on his heels, picking up his jacket and briefcase, and strode across the floor to Jessica's side office. Having breathlessly relayed details of what was happening, he gave her the envelope and hurriedly signed evidence bags as she placed it, alongside the disc and the note into them, carefully sealing them and placing them into her bag for processing. With a tense smile, he left Jessica, closing her door behind him, bustling across the main office towards the exit, and heading down the stairs.

-41-

Luckily the train carriage wasn't that busy. The lack of passengers had left plenty of room for Joe to occupy, spreading papers across the table to study them, but being careful not to display sensitive information or photographs. Swearing often under his breath, he shifted the papers about, trying to find some kind of pattern, some kind of link between the victims, the locations, anything. No matter how many times he rearranged them, or how intensely he studied them, he just could not seem to come up with any kind of common factor that could bring these seemingly random people together, other than the envelopes and discs he had been sent that were so quickly dismissed by DCI Whindle. Was it really possible that two violent murders could take place separately in such quick succession? Was there just the one killer? Were there 2 killers working in partnership? Why had the videos and notes been sent to him? Who was the man with the Volvo? As he considered the questions, he became certain that the killings were connected. He was also angry at himself for letting DCI Whindle take the paper he had written the registration number of the Volvo on. It didn't matter that much, as he was able to remember it and write it down again, but nevertheless, he was angry at this crucial piece of evidence being left to rot in the pocket of an arrogant and incompetent policeman. Taking a quick break, Joe settled his gaze on the passing scenery as the train passed over a viaduct. He watched impassively as the undulating green of the fields fell away to form the belly of a spectacular vista. A lazy river meandered, bending and twisting its way into the distance where it sliced through the middle of a small market town. Joe was oblivious to its name, or where he was relative to his destination. It was just good to focus his mind on matters other than the case, or Jessica. Sitting back into his seat, he picked up his phone, studied the screen, and then threw it back onto the table. Trying to convince himself that he wasn't desperate for Jessica to call or text him, he turned his attentions back to the case. Commander Carlton's words still weighed heavily in his mind too. The clock was ticking. Results were needed, and fast. Just then, his phone vibrated into life. It was a text from Jessica. Opening it, he allowed himself a little smile.

"R U TRYING TO TURN ME GREY LOL?"

Hurriedly, he tapped out a reply.

"DON'T KNOW WHAT U MEAN! ;-)"

Her reply came through before he even had chance to place the phone back onto the table.

"U AND MY UNCLE! SURE IT'S NEWCASTLE HE'S SENDING YOU TO? MORE LIKELY SIBERIA! TALK TO YOU LATER x"

He let out a stifled laugh as he looked longingly at the kiss. Forcing himself to close the message and concentrate, he once more scanned the profiles of the victims. Reaching for his phone, he opened the phone book and selected DC Violet's number. He answered on the third ring.

"What's up Sarge?" asked DC Violet.

"Glen, I need you to do something for me." Joe said, getting straight to the point. "I need you to run background checks on the victims"

"We already did" said Glen as he took a mouthful of coffee.

"We need more detail though" countered Joe. "I want to know about their families too. I want to know about colleges, clubs, jobs, and hobbies, anything you can get your hands on! There is a link between them Glen, we just need to look in the right place to find it!"

"Sure thing Sarge" said Glen.

"One more thing Glen" said Joe. "Can you run a background check on this blue Volvo? We need to find that driver!"

"I can't!" replied Glen. Sorry Sarge, but that vehicle has been flagged so that DCI Whindle is notified if anyone tries checking on it!" Joe sighed.

"Okay Glen. Well, if you can get on with the other checks, I'd appreciate it. Keep this one under your hat though. I'm not on the guv's Christmas card list right now. I don't want you sucked into the shitstorm."

"No problem Sarge" said Glen.

"Let me know what you find" said Joe, ending the call briskly and throwing the phone back onto the table. Exhaling loudly, he stared out of the window once more, watching a seemingly endless line of empty trailers attached to a freight train as it throbbed along the adjacent line. Closing his eyes, he took a deep breath, before picking up the papers that were in front of him and carefully reading through the text once again.

Bringing his car to a smooth halt, Steven applied the handbrake. Leaving the engine running, he sat staring at the living room window of his mother's house. The constant hum of the car's heater, coupled with the rhythmic tapping of raindrops on the windscreen was providing background music for his increasingly erratic thoughts. His gaze switched back and forth almost constantly from the window to the letter he held in his hand. It was from his mum, pleading with him to 'open his heart' He sneered as he read the contents of the letter over and over again, the edges of the page becoming dog eared from the constant massage from his dirty fingers. Yet, despite his disdain, he couldn't draw his eyes away from the writing. No matter how hard he tried to hate her, he couldn't. That was just another failure, and that failure made him angry. Chewing on his lip he saw Robert's car pull up a few yards down the road. Watching his brother get out of the car and walk casually down the driveway, Steven furrowed his brow as he watched.

"What's he doing here?" he said to himself. His hands were shaking gently as he studied the letter one more time. He hesitated, unsure as to whether he should drive away, or make the walk along the driveway, and go inside. "Maybe she had realised how wrong she had been all these years" he thought to himself. "Maybe she was finally ready to admit to what she had done, and to say sorry!" Grabbing at the door handle, he opened the door and lifted himself from his seat, exiting the car. Locking it, he pulled the lapels of his jacket up as far as he could, leaning into the falling rain, and walking briskly across the road and down the gravel driveway, pausing at the door to collect his composure once more, before ringing the bell.

-43-

"Ladies and Gentlemen, this train is now approaching Newcastle Central. Change here for Alnmouth, Berwick upon Tweed and stations to Edinburgh" The shrill tone of the conductor's voice wrenched Joe from the shallow sleep he had drifted into. Case notes were spread across the table, although thankfully they were still in discreet piles, and weren't able to divulge any information sensitive to the inquiry. Chiding himself for being so foolish, he started gathering up the papers and loaded them into his briefcase, mindful of the fact that the train was now slowing to a smooth halt next to the platform. Managing to successfully stow all of his papers, he scooped up his jacket and overnight bag, making for the exit before the Conductor closed the doors again for the train's onward departure.

The impressive Victorian architecture of Newcastle Central station imposed itself on the eye, dominating the platforms and roof with high arches and thick iron pillars, dressed heavily in a combination of opulent decoration and functional paint. Its grace and splendour seemed to lose itself in the clamour and bustle that filled its confines. Streams of light poured in through the glass roof, the curve of the station playing tricks, spreading those light beams into elliptical patterns on the walls and on the sides of standing train carriages. They gave some passengers an almost angelic aura as they stood obliviously within them. Staff busied themselves answering queries and questions, hurrying from one end of the platform to the other, slamming train doors as they went. A cleaner swirled a tired looking mop lethargically in circles against the glossy floor, one eye on the task in hand, and the other on one of the many digital clocks announcing the countdown to home time.

"DS Tenby?" Joe spun around, seeking the source of the voice through the commotion of the station.

"DC Kevin McDonnell" said the tall suited man as he offered a confident hand of greeting. Kevin had been a contact Joe had made through the High Potential Development scheme, although the two men had not previously met. They had both been paired together as 'distance partners' on a project, and had spent many hours talking by phone, largely about criminological strategies, sociological contributory factors in crime and crime reporting, and public order management methods. They had also spoken at length about rugby. Kevin was an avid follower of the Newcastle Falcons, and was a font of knowledge regarding all things Rugby Union. Joe, on the other hand was fanatical about Rugby League, and all things Hull Kingston Rovers. They shared a mutual admiration of each other's knowledge and passion for their respective codes, and had debated the merits and drawbacks of the differing versions of the game on many occasions. Despite never having seen each other, Joe felt as if Kevin were a friend. "Glad you could make it" he said, his voice mixing a deep Geordie tone with a touch of gravel.

"No problem. Nice to put a face to the name!" replied Joe with a smile as he straightened his tie.

"How was the journey?" enquired Kevin as he grabbed Joe's bag, starting for the car park.

"Fine" Joe replied noncommittally as he followed, checking his phone for messages as they walked. Both men maintained a professional silence as they crossed the station, exiting the main doors, and turning left, where they walked down the street for a while, stopping next to a green VW Passat parked in a hatched area marked 'POLICE VEHICLES ONLY' DC Kevin fished the keys from his pocket, motioning Joe to get in.

Kevin opened the boot and dumped Joe's bag inside as Joe clambered in and fastened his seatbelt, taking a second to watch the bustling throngs of foot traffic as people went about their business. Kevin opened the driver's door and dumped himself in the seat, turning on the ignition, and indicating before merging carefully into the traffic, his eyes flicking from mirror to mirror as he accelerated.

"So you're checking out this Overhead murder?" enquired Kevin, his eyes busying themselves with monitoring the mirrors still.

"Murder! You're calling it then?" asked Joe quizzically. Kevin shrugged his shoulders as he changed gear. "Suppose I am!" Joe replied thoughtfully with a sigh as he became suddenly weary of the burgeoning complications that were presenting themselves. "We've got a case down our way that we're investigating on behalf of BTP involving a member of station staff being murdered. She was placed on the track and hit by a train after being raped and stabbed" Kevin's face screwed up in an expression of distaste. Joe remained deliberately impassive as he watched him drive. "I know it's a bit of a cheek, me just dumping myself on you like this, but I had to give you a ring when I saw the news report" added Joe.

"Sounds like a rage killing" mused Kevin, indicating right as he pulled to a halt at some traffic lights, his eyebrows rising as he mulled it over.

"Exactly what I thought!" agreed Joe, allowing himself a smile as he watched a group of five young boys in Newcastle United shirts heading a football to each other down a side street. The weather was starting to change. The morning had brought a piercing sun, combined with a pronounced chill, but now the clouds were gathering. Somehow the weather seemed appropriate.

"We released the news of the body being found to the press by saying that it was an unexplained death" said Kevin, his gaze reaching past the white Renault in front. "We didn't want the crackpots or the press sniffing around more than necessary" Joe looked at him, nodding in agreement. "Trouble is, one of the TV stations got wind of the unusual circumstances and managed to tap up somebody connected to either the investigation itself, or the incident response" Kevin paused for a second, shaking his head in disapproval as a taxi lurched rightward, turning viciously across oncoming traffic without indicating. "So you obviously think that our case and yours have a connection?"

"I do" replied Joe, staring at the reflection of the rear passenger door in the wing mirror. "On the one hand we have the rape and murder at the station. On the other hand though, we also have a young girl who was killed by a train at a crossing" Kevin flicked Joe a quick look as the traffic lights changed. He didn't catch onto the connection.

"Hardly seems the same" he said, accelerating onto a dual carriageway.

"Yeah, but it turns out that she was drugged" said Joe, delivering the latest nugget deadpan. Once again Kevin raised his eyebrows "She was also a railway employee. She was a management trainee" Kevin nodded slowly, appreciating the reason for the two crimes being combined in terms of the investigation. Suddenly a grave expression spread across Kevin's face. Checking his rear view mirror he spoke quietly. "The victim of the overhead murder was a fitter at a railway maintenance depot." Joe gulped as discreetly as his blood ran cold. His feeling of foreboding was, as it turned out, justified. Slumping back into his seat, he covered his face with his hands for a second, puffing out his cheeks. He had suspected from the time of the second victim that these cases were linked, a suspicion only underlined by the second video! He should have been feeling vindicated, that his instincts as a Police Officer and as a Detective were being proven to be sound and robust. But vindication was not the emotion that dominated his mind. He felt somehow as if the validation of his theory had made the mountain he stood at the foot of even bigger than it was before, as if the peak had reached another thousand feet through thick cloud and howling winds. He also felt anger. DCI Whindle had scoffed at him, and had done his best to scupper his work. The thought flashed through his mind that, if this third killing was linked to the previous two, DCI Whindle would have blood on his hands.

"I take it this is a bad one?" asked Kevin. Joe was gazing out of the passenger side window, completely ignoring the passing scenery as his mind raced. He didn't bother to turn his head as he nodded in reply.

"I've also received two video clips!" Joe said, his eyes fixed on the window. "Each had a note. The footage was edited in the same way, really chaotic. They were on CDs addressed directly to me, delivered by hand to the police station!"

"What did your DCI say?" asked Kevin.

"He's wrote the first one off as some kind of prank from my old traffic unit! Joe shrugged. "He's still sceptical about the second. The arrogant bastard hasn't even watched it yet!"

"What?" Kevin spluttered in disbelief. Joe was starting to feel slightly out of his depth. Fighting the notion that he was hopelessly beyond the limit of his capabilities, he forced himself to think about the sequence of killings in an orderly, fashion, applying the handbrake of logic as firmly as he could. "At least we have a firm connection." He said to himself. All of these seemingly unconnected victims were railway employees. What possible motive or motives could a person hold that would drive them to kill, even execute railway employees in such gruesome ways? Were the suspects connected at all? Joe reached down into the foot well and grabbed his briefcase, snapping open the locks and sifting through the profiles of the victims, searching desperately for any commonality that corroborated this new connection. None of them even did the same job. One was aged in her forties; one was nineteen, and the latest twenty four. There simply had to be a reason for these people being selected. The manner in which they were murdered could not be classified as an opportunist killing in the way that people have been stabbed by sociopaths on buses and the like. These killings showed premeditation, cunning, and a relish for the act of killing that was beyond anything Joe had seen professionally, or during his studies. He had felt since early on that these acts even beyond the escapades of the criminally insane featuring frequently in the case studies of criminological study. Couple that with the fact that the suspect quite obviously possessed some level of railway knowledge, and there were the foundations of an as yet unidentified motive. But what was that motive? And why was the killer choosing to send these videos to Joe? He had been silently considering all of these things for the last ten minutes, silently and unsociably staring out of the window as Kevin navigated effortlessly through the streets.

"I know you're not into proper rugby like, but Newcastle Falcons are playing Bath tonight if you fancy it?" Kevin said, breaking the silence. Joe shook his head, smiling at the good natured insult Kevin had just thrown his way.

"I don't know," Joe said "I'm on thin ice with my DCI as it is. I don't want to give him an excuse to accuse me of slacking off. I'm meant to be here on a murder investigation after all!"

"Come on man!" said Kevin as he laughed, his smile almost conspiratorial. "All work and no play! Besides, I'm under orders to take you to the infirmary tomorrow morning! I'm not doing that if either of us have hangovers!" Joe hadn't arranged any visit to the infirmary, which is where the mortuary is located, and he raised his eyebrows in silent question. Laughing again, Kevin explained.

"DCI Whindle requested we make the pathologist available to you who conducted the post mortem on the overhead guy" Joe nodded his agreement, wondering why it was that, even in death, some people struggle to have others remember their name. 'Overhead guy' as Kevin had referred to him was actually called Sean Grant. "Besides" continued Joe. "If you're going to embarrass yourself by showing me girl's rugby, we'd best get ourselves sorted and ready. I don't want to miss any of the on field cuddles you lot call tackling!" Kevin glanced at Joe and swore under his breath, smiling as he overtook a lorry.

The two men made the rest of the journey to Kevin's house almost in silence. He lived in a quiet side street in the Jesmond area of Newcastle, just round the corner from the trades club. As Kevin's car rolled slowly past the entrance, Joe gave the building a quick inspection, its porch occupied by two old men wearing flat caps, pointing and gesticulating about something as their beer sloshed violently around in their glasses. Joe chuckled to himself as he thought of Phil, and the run down state of the trades club back in London. Kevin glanced questioningly at Joe.

"Reminds me of my local" said Joe, jerking his thumb towards the building.

"Not really my scene I'm afraid" said Kevin as he indicated left, swinging the car into a narrow cul-de-sac and stopping smoothly outside of a semi-detached house with a small garden covered in pale blue stone and gravel. The house stood out from the majority of the neighbouring properties in that the double glazing was obviously brand new and the brickwork was brilliant white. Overall the house looked tidy, its recent renovation giving indication that its owner enjoyed a larger disposable income than most of the residents in the street. Without saying a word, Kevin got out the car and walked up the path, leaving Joe to get his case from the boot. Having retrieved his case and closed the boot, Joe turned and walked toward the path as Kevin aimed his car fob at the vehicle and locked it from inside the hallway.

"Come in man!" he called as he walked towards the kitchen.

Joe stepped inside the door, closing it quietly behind him. From deeper within the house he could hear the sound of a kettle being filled and cups being rescued from a dishwasher. Kevin emerged from the kitchen.

"I'll show you the spare room mate" he said. "You can get sorted out whilst I make a brew"

"Nice one Kev, cheers!" said Joe, finally beginning to relax. Bustling past Joe, Kevin walked up the stairs, motioning for Joe to follow him. He opened the door to the room at the back of the house that overlooked the bare, concrete yard. The walls were magnolia, and the bed was dressed in plain white linen. The carpet was beige, with the only furniture a combined wardrobe and dressing table and a plain black plastic chair, very similar to the type found in canteens and offices. Joe pondered the likelihood that the chair began its life in the canteen of the police station, or perhaps the CID office. It was plain to see that this room was not often used, but was nevertheless well maintained. Joe made a point of looking admiringly at both the room, and the view from the window.

"Nice" he said. "It's in much better shape than my spare room!"

"Ah, well!" said Kevin with a smile, "I always like to be prepared!"

"Prepared for what?" asked Joe.

"Anything" said Kevin flatly. Before Joe could think of a reply, Kevin had turned and was descending the staircase, calling over his shoulder. "Get yourself changed and relaxed man! We can't have any distractions from the rugby! I'll make the brew!" Joe obeyed Kevin's direction, throwing his black casual coat over the hook on the back of the bedroom door, and undoing his tie and removing his shirt and trousers. Opening his case, he pulled out his favourite rugby shirt, slipping it over his head. Then he grabbed the jeans he had packed, quickly assessing whether they were too creased to wear. Deciding that they weren't, he pulled them on, adjusting his shirt so it hung in the most flattering way over his seemingly ever expanding stomach. Feeling much more relaxed, he sat down on the double bed that occupied one corner of the room. Taking a few deep breaths, he tried to purge his mind of everything, of the case, of Jessica. But the harder he tried, the more prominent those thoughts became, his mind once again plunging itself into the conundrum that was the motive for these brutal killings, and how on earth he was going to set about catching the monster who was responsible. Joe was hesitant at the thought of saying the words out loud to other people, even fellow detectives, but inwardly there was no doubt in his mind that they were now hunting a serial killer. Clicking open his briefcase, he thumbed through the assorted papers, picking out a black plastic document wallet. He slid out a picture of the first crime scene. Tina McBride's body had been removed when the photo was taken, but the deep red stain of blood on ballast, and tell-tale remnants of tissue and body matter on the rail head told the main gruesome narrative. Joe tried to imagine the assailant, to mould him into a physical form, as if that would make it somehow easier to catch him. "You're not going to neatly tick the boxes on a profiling form for me are you mate?" Joe asked. Exhaling loudly, He placed the photo back inside its wallet and placed the wallet in turn back inside his briefcase, and lay back onto the cold duvet. After a few minutes of peaceful contemplation, Kevin shouted up the stairs that a cup of tea was waiting. He stood up, grabbing his coat from the hook on the back of the door. Putting it on, he was just making to open the door when his phone rang. He took the phone out of his pocket, looking at the screen. It was Jessica.

"Hey" he said casually.

"Hey" she answered. There was a brief, not to mention awkward pause.

"I was just calling to talk to you about a couple of things, mainly the DCI" Joe rolled his eyes, but appreciated the gesture all the same.

"I know what you're going to say" he said, trying to cut the expected lecture short as politely as I could.

"I'm not joking!" she scolded. "He's a serious player, and you don't want to be getting on the wrong side of him, especially so soon after you've arrived. It's not just me who should be thinking about career implications Joe." Joe sat silently as he listened, Jessica's reference to their conversation in the police canteen causing him to wince in embarrassment. Sensing this, Jessica continued, her voice warmer.

"Look. You're on the fast track. I'm up for promotion. The one thing we've both got in common is that DCI Whindle could make problems for both of us". Joe knew she was right, and it hurt.

"Come on!" said Joe "We've got more than that in common surely?" His jovial tone was lost on her as she sat in silence.

"In all seriousness Jessica, I know what you mean, and you're right" Joe sighed. Feeling the need to discipline himself for letting his mind be blown off course, Joe hauled himself back onto the subject at hand, namely that there was, somewhere, a mad man, who was going around killing people, seemingly on account of the fact that they earn their living on the railway. Joe couldn't help thinking that in that respect, DCI Whindle was right. He did have to start earning his salary. That hurt too. Jessica realised this and changed the subject.

"How's Newcastle?" she asked.

"Cloudy" he replied. "A DC from the CID here has put me up in his spare room. Apparently he's going to show me what proper rugby is like" she laughed that girlie, carefree laugh that he found so intoxicating, and it was with real effort that he again dragged his mind clear of that delightful sound, moulding his face into seriousness.

"You boys and sport!" she said. Joe could almost see her shaking her head as she giggled.

"Seriously though, it seems we've got a serial killer" Jessica took a deep breath as Joe spoke, breaking through her gentle laughter.

"I can't say I'm surprised Joe, now I've seen the second video" she was whispering now, the edge of her words harsh.

"This murder, the guy on the overhead power lines?" Joe prompted, phrasing it as a question.

"Uh-huh. Sean Grant." she replied. Joe could hear tapping in the background, realising that she must be typing as they spoke.

"He's railway staff" Joe looked forlornly at the neatly framed window as Jessica digested the news. "I can't see another link like that being coincidental" she said thoughtfully. "It seems like this is just confirming the serial killer possibility to me. What are you going to do?"

"I'm not ringing the DCI just yet" he said. "All I have is the occupation of this third victim. You know what he's like, that will not be anywhere near enough to satisfy him" Jessica nodded. "I'm due to speak to the pathologist who carried out the post mortem tomorrow, then look at the crime scene. I'll see what he has to say. Hopefully I'll have some ammunition when I check in"

"Be careful!" Jessica said.

"What else did you want to talk to me about? Joe asked.

"I think it sort of underlines what we've just been talking about Joe!" she said. "Glen asked me to tell you that you've got a letter"

"Shit!" Joe hissed.

"Shall I open it for you?" Jessica asked. Joe considered his options, quickly realising that he couldn't afford for the envelope to sit on his desk until his return.

"Yes please!" he said. "Can you run the usual tests on it and let me know ASAP?"

"Sure thing!" she said. "Fingers crossed!" Leaning back against the door, Joe folded the phone shut and dropped it into his jacket. Checking to make sure he had remembered to pick up his wallet, Joe headed downstairs in search of that promised cup of tea.

44

Raising his cup to his lips, Steven took a mouthful of hot, sweet tea. As it ran down his throat it warmed him. The sensation took him back to happier times. His mum always made her tea exactly the same way. He didn't usually take sugar, but his mum always used to put one spoonful in everyone's tea, and an extra half spoon for 'her sweet boy' Whenever he was ill, or if he hurt himself or felt sad, a cup of sweet tea always seemed to do the trick. He smiled a smile which matched the tea in its warmth as he stared into the bottom of the cup, consciously trying to take his mind to another place.

"You look like you've been in the wars son" said Graham from across the room. Being wrenched back into reality by Graham's words, Steven shot him a look.

"What's it got to do with you? I'll shave when I want to and not before!" Graham looked down into his tea awkwardly, then across at Joyce. She smiled gently, her eyes telling him that patience was the key. All of a sudden, the familiar rage began to brew in the pit of Steven's stomach. He looked at his mother, sitting demurely as she nursed her teacup. She was looking back at him with an expression that only a mother could give. Her face told a story of pain and worry, of regret and sadness. His anger calmed momentarily before the words whipped up a dust storm in his mind. "How could she? Fucking bitch!" His thoughts bounced around in his head as his hands trembled with temper. "If it wasn't for her being such a whore, Dad would still be here!" Looking up, he realised that his mum, Graham and Robert were all staring at his hands as they trembled, making the cup vibrate at a high pitch against the surface of the saucer. Angrily he dumped it down on the coffee table, making a fist with his right hand and resting it against his lips, closing his eyes as he calmed himself once more.

"I told you this was a bad idea Joyce" said Graham as he sat uneasily in his chair, his eyes flicking back and forth between Steven and Joyce.

Steven looked up, his fist still positioned against his mouth. "What was a bad idea?" he asked, the fires within him beginning to grow.

Robert placed his cup gently on the table. "Come on bruv" he cautioned, standing slowly.

"Stay out of this!" snapped Steven, his eyes fixed on Graham. "I know you're in on whatever little scheme these two have cooked up, but stay the fuck out of it!"

"Steven Kilkis! Have some respect!" snapped Joyce.

"Don't you dare lecture me about respect!" he shouted, his voice become hoarse as fury spilled out of his mouth. "You wouldn't know what respect was if it came up and kicked you in the face! You and that scheming old arsehole!" Joyce's hand shot to her mouth. She inhaled sharply, her son's words cutting her deeply. A tear ran down her cheek as she crumpled into her chair. Robert was incensed, grabbing at Steven's shoulders, he gripped the material of his grubby overcoat and pulled him harshly, swinging viciously with his fist, connecting with Steven's jaw and sending him stumbling across the room. The force of the blow sent Steven crashing into the coffee table, upending him, causing him to fall face down onto the rug. Instinctively he picked himself up, rounding on Robert and punching him with every ounce of venom he could muster. The force of the punch broke Robert's nose and split his top lip, sending small droplets of blood into the air, as Robert fell backwards, slamming against the nearby cabinet and knocking it over with an angry thud, the ornaments and photo frames which had been sat proudly atop, now spinning across the carpet. A river of warm, claret liquid oozed from his nose, flooding his mouth and making him suppress the urge to vomit as he picked himself up.

"Why do you have to do these things Steven?" shrieked Joyce. "Why do you hate us all so much? Graham and I are together! We're a couple! We love each other and have done for years. It's about time that you accepted that it isn't going to change!"

She rushed to Robert's side, inspecting his injuries then rushing to the kitchen, returning seconds later with a cold wet tea towel which she gently placed on his nose.

"I don't hate you!" he replied, his voice now cracked with emotion. "I just can't believe you would poison Dad's memory by shacking up with that! I just want you to see him for what he is!" As he spoke with rising sharpness, he pivoted on his heel and pointed angrily at Graham. He sat motionless in his chair, save for a slow shaking of his head, his gaze set firmly to his lap. "You need to face up to what you've done you twisted old Bastard!" spat Steven. Robert was sitting against the wall next to the overturned cabinet. He dabbed his bleeding lip with the back of his hand, his eyes trained firmly on Steven.

"I think you'd better leave" he whispered. His ability to pronounce words was severely impacted by the blood in his mouth and the swelling to his nose that seemed to be quickly taking hold.

"Don't worry!" snarled Steven "I'm going!" He looked down at the debris littering the carpet. A treasured photograph of his dad looked up at him. Stooping, he picked it up from the floor. Inspecting it, he saw that it was undamaged, despite the fracas. "I'll take this with me. You don't need it anymore!" Thrusting it into his jacket, he stepped over Robert's legs, crushing a teacup under his heavy boot as he stomped from the room, shoving Graham's chair from his path, causing the old man to cry out. His mother sobbed quietly, her shoulders rhythmically heaving as she tended to Robert's bleeding wounds.

45

Joe's bed for the evening was comfortable and firm and he had enjoyed every minute of slumber. Despite sleeping well, he had not satisfied his craving for rest. He hadn't managed to fall asleep until the small hours, having spent a good hour or two laid staring at the flawlessly white ceiling, his brain refusing to surrender as the particulars of each grisly crime flashed before him like a slideshow at a university lecture. Breakfast had been much better, Joe spending the best part of half an hour stretching and yawning as he listened to Kevin's tuneless singing bouncing off the kitchen walls and into the dining room, the wonderful aroma of sausages and bacon slowly filling the house. Joe had thoroughly enjoyed the match, even though he battled almost constantly to push the case into the back of his mind. Kevin had made it clear that he didn't expect any 'shop talk' whilst the game was being played, and out of courtesy, Joe had complied. After a little while, his natural love of rugby had overtaken and he had to admit that his first rugby union match had been entertaining, even if Bath had come away as clear winners. Some of the fans sitting near Joe and Kevin had spied Joe's Hull Kingston Rovers shirt. The red and white of the fabric had stood out starkly against the sea of black, white and silver. Some of them had even thought that he was wearing a Sunderland shirt! Once he had reassured them however, their attitude toward him had warmed and he had found himself enjoying copious amounts of banter, both about the friendly rivalries between rugby league and rugby union, and about the fishing histories of the respective regions. He was in a massively positive mood, even though the case loomed over him constantly. Sitting at the dining room table, he was forcing himself to concentrate on the smells of breakfast. As he stared at the morning news, he found himself salivating. Joe was hungrier than he had first realised. Both men had taken the decision to stick to coffee during the game, but Joe felt ravenous as if he had been drinking all night. Kevin breezed in from the kitchen with the welcome hot food. Bacon, eggs, sausages, hash browns, beans and toast covered both plates. "Dig in!" said Kevin, placing the meal in front of Joe. Nodding his thanks, Joe immediately began attacking the food, pausing only to add ketchup.

"Woken up hungry then!" said Kevin through a mouthful of food.

"This is good!" said Joe, stabbing half a rasher of bacon and swirling it in the pool of beans. "So what got a Geordie boy interested in Rugby?" he asked, his mouth crammed with food.

"I started playing at school!" Kevin said. "I had the chance to have trials with Northampton, but injured my shoulder! Mind you though, if I'm being honest, I've still got it!"

"Whatever!" Joe snorted with a laugh, pointing at the gentle outward curve of Kevin's stomach. Kevin shook his head as both men shared the joke, their laughter fading as they ate in silence, the only noise being the scraping of cutlery on plates, and the swill of tea. For the first time since the investigation had begun, Joe was feeling a little contented. He had watched a great game of rugby, experienced a modicum of solid sleep, and was now filling his stomach with an excellent breakfast. Despite this, the faces of the mysterious killer's victims, and the videos he had been sent were standing large and illuminated in his thoughts as he absently nursed a strong coffee.

Throughout the journey to the hospital, Joe had been silent, and DC McDonnell had not seen fit to challenge that silence. "Dunno bout you Kevin" said Joe, breaking the quietness as he got out of the car, "But I don't think I'll ever get used to being around autopsies." People tended to assume that, being in such a job, Police Officers would have gotten used to being around the dead. Whilst many take solace from the fact that they play a pivotal role in bringing justice to the victims, the thought of standing in a room with a dead body lying on a steel trolley is enough to bring a dark tone to the day of even the most experienced and hardened detective. Joe and Kevin made their way into the hospital, approaching the main reception desk and hanging a left. As they walked, Joe continued to mull over the case. Wrenching himself back to reality, he turned his attention to Kevin, who had snatched his phone from his suit jacket as it had begun to ring, and was now babbling on about last night's game. He had originally bought the two tickets for himself and a friend, Joe having stepped in after the friend had cancelled at short notice. Kevin was discussing the game with his absent friend at length, and was obviously more than a touch preoccupied with the eighty minutes of rugby as he walked past a large sign on the wall advising that mobile phones were to be switched off. Despite his reticence, Joe was eager to talk to the pathologist that had conducted the post mortem on the latest victim. The much vaunted saying that the most important part of any investigation is the first 48 hours is, to an extent true.

As the trail of evidence cools, and then eventually turns cold, the chances of finding solid, tangible evidence linking crime to criminal diminishes. This was bothering Joe. Whilst not usually a slave to the tired hook lines that are born from the scripts of trashy American crime dramas, Joe couldn't help but become increasingly worried, at how quickly the hours were passing since the first murder had taken place. Despite the videos, the inexplicable attitude of DCI Whindle towards them, and Joe gave the case a feel of there not being much in the way of evidence, or even solid leads. Kevin continued to ramble into his phone as they walked into the elevator, and Joe continued to zone him out as he brooded over the lack of progress.

The smell of disinfectants seemed to grow stronger as they ventured further, and the lights seemed to become even more artificial, each corridor smelling more pungent, the light harsher on the eye than the last. Eventually they arrived at a set of double doors, the paint on them chipped and scraped from a lifetime of being smashed aside by the hospital's army of trolleys, a scratched and worn Perspex window casting filtered light onto the grey security doors beyond that stood guard over the autopsy suite. Joe stopped for a second, pausing before plunging himself into the world of steel trolleys and death. Pushing the door open, he walked with Kevin to the security door and pressed the button on the intercom mounted on the wall. Loosening his tie, Joe was feeling increasingly claustrophobic. He spoke into the front of the intercom, and with a buzzing sound the door released.

"You must be DS Tenby" said the man at the far end of the room, his broad Scottish accent bouncing off the tiled surfaces and sterile brickwork of the autopsy suite. Dressed in blue scrubs, he was wearing a white lab coat, and was hunched over a desk against the back wall, scribbling furiously on a notepad. The room was long and thin, the walls clinical, with adornments of silver equipment and tubing that disappeared into voids behind the brilliant white brickwork. The place stank of disinfectant, and seemed to be filled with an almost subterranean feel, as if they were somehow in a different world, even though life rattled busily on in blissful ignorance just the other side of the wall.

"I am!" said Joe with a half-smile. He looked across at Kevin who was busily checking his reflection in the glass door of a cupboard, oblivious to his surroundings. Shrugging off the muggy sensation of claustrophobia that clung to him, Joe stepped forward, fixing the trolley that took centre stage with distaste as he stepped around it. The cadaver that lay on the trolley was covered with a large white sheet, and Joe was hopeful that he had arrived just in time to miss the main event. Throwing his pen dramatically onto the desk, the pathologist spun round, walking forward toward Joe with a broad smile, his large hand outstretched.

"Dr Ross Marvell" he said, grasping Joe's hand and shaking it energetically. Joe forced a smile as he imagined the depths to which those hands had explored the poor soul covered by the sheet lying on the trolley. Forcing the thought from his mind, Joe pressed on with the reason for his visit.

"I'm here about Sean Grant" Joe said, again allowing his eyes to roam across to the trolley.

"Aye, I know that son" replied Dr Marvell, his face still in smiling mode. "The police told me you'd be calling. I've got him ready.'"

"Pardon?" Joe said, the comment catching him somewhat off guard.

Dr Marvell motioned with his hand.

"Mr Grant" he said. "He's ready." Grasping the corner of the sheet, he looked up at Joe and smiled wickedly. "I do hope you've skipped breakfast DS Tenby" Before Joe could answer, he whipped the sheet back, exposing the gnarled and mutilated remains.

-46-

Joe reluctantly pulled the handkerchief from his mouth as the door to the mortuary swung shut behind them, the grey polished corridor reverberating with the sound of door on frame. Kevin was already a good half dozen paces in front, his free hand in his trouser pocket as he spoke quietly into the mouthpiece of his mobile, no doubt completing his interrupted match report from earlier. The vivid images of mangled, smashed and gruesomely disfigured human remains were busily engraining themselves into Joe's mind. Kevin was still concentrating on his phone conversation, and Joe was concentrating on ignoring him. The pathologist had taken the best part of an hour to fully explain the extent to which Sean Grant's body had been decimated by both pantograph and power cable. He had mentioned that portions of the body had shown signs of laceration, a fact that had instantly rang alarm bells. Joe had spent the entire time trying as hard as he could not to throw up his breakfast, and was grateful as he stood in the coolness of the corridor that Dr Marvell had supplied him with a paper copy of his initial findings. Sliding the pathologist's report under his arm, Joe fished his notebook from his inside pocket and flicked it open, rustling through the pages until he found the scrawled notes he had managed to make whilst recoiling at the gnarled remains of Sean Grant. Dr Marvell had conducted a toxicology screen using tissue samples. Initial findings had suggested that Medazolene was present in Sean Grant's blood. This pointed to a further connection in Joe's mind, but he knew that the DCI would not be impressed, and would no doubt judge the trip a waste of time, despite the fact that two of the three victims had been exposed to the same drug, had shown evidence of suffering lacerations, and that all 3 victims were railway employees! Joe took the pathologist's report in his hand, resolving to push for a toxicology screen on the body of Tina McBride as he plunged his notebook back into his pocket. Flipping open the report, Joe studied the seemingly endless details of injuries to the deceased with a cool academic detachment. Despite the utter annihilation Sean Grant had suffered at the hands of the wires and train equipment, there was nothing surprising about the injuries mentioned in the report. He stared thoughtfully at the writing on the page, the almost mechanised whirring of his brain disturbed by a pronounced cough. Looking up, he realised that he had completely forgotten that Kevin was waiting.

"You can read that in the car Joe" he said, jerking his thumb over his shoulder in the direction of the lifts.

"Sure" Joe replied, furrowing his brow as he walked. Kevin turned away and walked a few steps ahead, stopping at the lift doors and pressing the button. Scratching his chin, he looked at Joe, chuckled, and shook his head.

"What's so funny?" Joe asked defensively.

"You really don't like death and mortuaries do you Joe?" he asked, the smile still spread across his face.

"Does anyone?" he replied. Kevin stabbed the 'call' button with his finger another four times for good measure.

"True enough" he replied, once again straightening his tie. Cutting him off before he could speak, Joe stifled a rising cough as the lift doors slid open. Stepping in, he studied the artificial lights in the ceiling, trying to gain some sort of foothold in terms of achieving progress in the hunt for someone who, at least in his own opinion, was a twisted, psychopathic and highly dangerous serial killer.

" I need a breakthrough on this Kevin" Joe said softly, the various details of the killings swimming around in his brain as he closed his eyes and rested his head against the wall.

"It'll come" he said reassuringly. Whilst grateful for the sentiment, Joe remained unconvinced.

"I'm heading back south today" Joe said, checking his watch. "I need to be able to tell the DCI that I have something, *anything*"

"You've seen the reports yourself" said Kevin. "You can only report back on what you've got. You have the drug link! You have the railway link! You have the videos! There has to be some mileage in that lot! I know that you're the new boy at your nick Joe, but you can't let your 'guvnor' get away with ignoring such a big chain of evidence!" Kevin was right, and Joe knew it. He couldn't help but feel a rising sense of desperation, both in wanting to get the DCI off his back, and to take him on and force him to view the increasingly obvious links seriously. He knew though, that he needed to remain calm and disciplined if he were to have any chance at stopping this killer before someone else dies horribly. "Look, we've got to go down to the crime scene now Joe. Trust me when I say that we have been over that stretch of track with a fine tooth comb and a magnifying glass, but you never know, you may think of something, find something. Don't go getting all negative so early on mate. That's how the Falcons have gone so long without silverware!" The two men shared a smile as the lift doors slid slowly closed.

-47-

It struck Joe how peaceful everything seemed as they stepped down toward the main railway line that links London and Scotland. There were high banks on either side of the tracks, and the top of each bank was covered in lush greenery and densely vegetated trees. The sun was only just managing to break through the natural roof of green that hung above their heads, and the whole area seemed to have an almost magical feel to it, as if it were taken straight from a story book. The two men were being guided down to the trackside by a rather portly middle aged man called Doug Porter.

"Have your guys noticed anybody hanging around here of late Doug?" Joe asked. "Anyone repeatedly driving down access roads? Any new spotters about? Doug looked thoughtful for a second.

"Not that they've mentioned to me" he replied.

"Anything on the track bed that wouldn't normally be there? That could have been associated with the fatality?" Joe persisted hopefully.

"This line was looked at pretty closely Mr Tenby" said Doug with a shake of his head.

"Would you mind if we were to walk down to where the fatality actually took place?" Joe asked, more out of a creeping desperation. Doug looked at Kevin in search of guidance. None was forthcoming.

"What?" he spluttered, his face reddening. "You're asking me to cause an awful lot of disruption Mr Tenby!" he said as he rubbed the back of his neck. Joe held up his hand.

"I appreciate what you're saying Doug, but this is a murder investigation. If it were a relative of yours, I'm sure you'd think the delay well worth it!" Doug looked away, shifting softly from foot to foot.

"We'll have to arrange for a block on both lines. I'll phone the signaller." He sighed, relenting to Joe's request as he made his way back up the staircase, his phone stuck to his ear. Joe turned his attention back to the immediate area. Out of nowhere, an express train thundered past them, its horn blaring. Kevin raised his arm in acknowledgement as the cutting in which they stood seemed to literally fill with deafening noise. Joe watched, transfixed on the train's tail lights as it disappeared around the gentle right hand bend, seemingly dragging that intolerable sound along into the distance with it. Joe just about managed to stifle a scream, and nearly had a heart attack as he felt a hand on his shoulder.

"We've got the block Sgt Tenby. This way, though we need to be as quick as we can. Stopping trains isn't a cheap exercise!" Doug led Joe and Kevin down onto the trackside. This seemed to amplify tenfold, the eeriness of where they were. They walked for a while, their feet yielding unwillingly to the sharp edged ballast until they were standing underneath an imposing brick bridge. All trace of the horrific events had been quickly and expertly removed, the power lines that stretched overhead and their associated equipment glistening in their newness. Joe couldn't help but shiver.

"This is where the incident took place" said Kevin as he scanned the horizon in both directions. Joe concentrated on the ballast immediately in the vicinity of the bridge. It was stark in its contrast to the tired and weather worn stones that neighboured it. Joe's heart sank slightly. Kevin was right. The area had been gone over closely. Staring up at the bridge, Joe had an idea.

"Can we have a look up there?" he asked Doug.

"Sure thing" he said with a relieved smile. "It'll be much cheaper than keeping the lines blocked!" The three men turned and made their way up the line to the access stairs, and away from the trackside as Doug stabbed at the number pad of his mobile phone, desperate to open the railway lines to traffic as quickly as he could.

Arriving at the bridge, the sheer loneliness of the place seemed to jump out immediately. It felt so remote, so disconnected from the world beyond the railway below, and the trees towering above, that it would be easy to feel able to commit an unspeakable act, and then slip away into the night. Remembering what he had said to Kevin after their visit to the pathologist, Joe diverted his attention to looking for any and all signs of useable evidence that he could present to the DCI with the hope of strengthening his case. The equipment involved in the murder had been replaced within hours of the line being returned to the railway authorities, and the scenes of crime officers had gone over the line, and all surrounding areas in minute detail. Accepting the inevitable truth, Joe began to concede that he was trying too hard to swim against the tide. He turned to Kevin.

"I think we'd best make a move back to the station. I can't magic the evidence out of thin air. I'm only delaying things"

Without a word, Kevin turned on his heels and started down the bridge and onto the access path, walking over to Doug and thanking him for his time. Doug nodded, looking across to Joe and smiling pleasantly. Joe donned a false smile and waved, before forlornly making his way toward Kevin, his eyes fixed on the floor. The sides of the pathway were littered with used condoms, crushed beer cans, and even the odd needle and syringe paying testimony to its usual patrons. Joe scanned every inch of the path, more out of a mixture of habit, and creeping desperation, than any expectation that any kind of result would be yielded. It was as he scanned across another bend in the path that he saw a glimmer of light reflecting off something that was wedged at the very foot of the retaining wall. Crouching down, Joe frowned as he realised that it was a small piece of glass. Deciding to play safe, he pulled out his phone, selecting the video option, and filming the immediate area, and the glass itself, stating his name, rank and location, as well as the date and time for the benefit of the phone's microphone, so as to verify the particulars when the clip was played back. Licking his lips subconsciously, Joe pulled an evidence bag and a pair of tweezers from his coat pocket, and carefully picked up the glass, examining it for a brief second, before dropping it into the bag, and sealing it. Something was not right about it. The glass seemed completely out of place. Looking up from his crouched position, Joe saw that Kevin was turned away, once again engrossed in whatever conversation about rugby he was having. Straightening up, Joe made to walk across to Kevin, but paused, checking himself. Protocol required that he declare the find to him, but with the exception of the video clips that were being so stubbornly dismissed by DCI Whindle, Joe had the only physical forensic evidence the investigation had produced to date, disappearing into some storage locker in Newcastle. Walking across to him Joe raised his hand as Kevin looked up. Finishing his conversation, he closed his phone as he looked down at the evidence bag that Joe was holding.

"What's in there?" he asked, trying to examine the contents through the coloured plastic.

"It's a piece of glass" Joe said, trying to keep his voice sounding casual. "Found it over there, just by the bend in the pathway" Joe motioned with his head. Kevin's eyes followed Joe's gesture and he looked over his shoulder at the dirty and dingy pathway that snaked into the trees behind them.

"I don't think it's much" Joe said, lying as he held up the small bag for them both to scrutinise. Kevin grinned.

"Don't take this the wrong way Joe" he said. "If you didn't think that was much in the way of evidence you wouldn't have taken the trouble of filming it. " Joe flushed slightly, embarrassed at making such a poor attempt at deceiving a fellow detective. "Tell you what" he said "How's about I allow you to take that piece of evidence back south with you, file chain of evidence paperwork, and give you a head start with that demon DCI of yours, and you keep me in the loop with how the investigation goes, maybe make sure that some credit finds its way to me "

"Sounds like a hell of a deal to me!" Joe said. "Why are you doing this though Kevin?"

"Well" he replied, throwing his hands up in the air in a Gallic display of indifference "I think we both know that the investigations that are currently underway are going to be merged, and you lot are going to be given the lead on it, I'm only cutting out the middle man, and if it catches the sick bastard, so much the better!"

"Thank you Kevin" Joe said, shaking his hand. "I appreciate it"

"No problem" he said. "Besides, I'm overdue my stripes, and any brownie points I can get will be most welcome, thank you very much!" They stood there for a few seconds, awkward silence hanging in the air. "Hadn't you best let somebody know?" Kevin asked. Automatically Joe's hand fished out his mobile, and he opened it, selecting DCI Whindle's mobile number from the phonebook. Just as he was about to press the call button he paused. The initial desperation to find some kind of news that would assuage the DCI was being replaced by a desire to find something altogether more concrete before Joe put anything on his desk. Joe looked down at the phone for a few seconds, and as he continued to stare at the phone's screen, he had made his decision. Selecting Jessica's number from the phone, Joe dialled, speaking quickly into the mouthpiece, relaying to her the details of the find and telling her to keep it quiet for the time being. Before Joe could end the call, Jessica gave him the news he was dreading.

"I opened your letter" she said quietly. "It was another one Joe. Just like the first two!"

"Was it Anna Brown?" Joe asked.

"I can't make a positive identification because of the lighting conditions, but the woman in the footage has the same hair colour and build as Anna Brown, and the clip was filmed on a railway crossing, so on the balance of probabilities, I would say so." Pausing briefly, she spoke softly. "Joe, it's really messed up!"

"I'm heading for the train now so I'll be back in a few hours! You can bring me fully up to speed then!"

"It's not pleasant viewing!" Jessica said. The distress in her voice was audible. "Joe, there's something else. She spoke on the clip. She was speaking to you"

Joe lowered the phone from his ear and looked at it. He swallowed hard at the thought of this woman's final words being directed at him. Moving professionally past that thought, he was unable to conceal his disappointment at there being no definitive identification of the woman on the clip. He knew that Whindle would ignore whatever final statement this girl had made, instead seizing upon the lack of a categorical ID. Having stolen a few seconds to absorb this new information, Joe returned the phone to his ear and spoke quietly. "I know I'm asking a lot Jess, but please can you keep this latest find quiet until we can give the DCI a little more?" Reluctantly, Jessica agreed. Closing the phone, Joe strode purposefully towards Kevin's car, getting in and continuing to mull over his next move as Kevin accelerated away.

Upon arriving at Newcastle Central station, Kevin made his way to the rear of the car, and handed Joe his bag from the boot. He promised to go back through everything he had on the Sean Grant case. Kevin agreed to request further checks in the vicinity, and to keep Joe informed if any suspicious mail was received. Thankful for the help of an ally, Joe once again promised to keep Kevin in the loop, telling him he would be 'mentioned in dispatches' for what he had done. Joe watched Kevin get back in his car and pull away, before turning on his heels and making for the platforms.

Regardless of how Joe spun things around in his head though, he could not avoid the fact that he was returning to the station with nothing, save the piece of glass he had found, and he had decided to wait and see how that developed before informing DCI Whindle, hoping at the same time that the latest video clip would yield some fresh clues beyond the fact that the killer seemed to be taking an increasingly personal interest in him in terms of communicating a message.

-48-

The gentle rumble of the train's engines gradually pushed Joe towards some welcome sleep as he was jolted back to full consciousness by the rattling and banging of the catering trolley as it made its way through the carriage. Scowling at his reflection in the carriage window, Joe pulled out his wallet, deciding that coffee, as opposed to revenge, was the best course of action. The steward poured a large cup and flung three tiny milk cartons onto the table top. Handing Joe some napkins, he smiled falsely, snatching the five pound note from

Joe's hand and thrusting forth a few coins in return. Joe was still staring at the coins as his phone rang. It was DC Violet.

"Hey Sarge" he said, in cheerful yet hushed tones.

"What's up Glen?" Joe said, stirring the milk into the coffee, the details of the case still hurtling around in his head.

"We've been hitting a bit of a brick wall here if I'm honest" he said.

"I know the feeling" Joe replied, his face grimacing at the harshness of the coffee as he tentatively sipped the super-heated liquid.

"I decided to go over the Anna Brown evidence. Statements, physical evidence, anything and everything really" he said, his voice increasing in volume.

"And?" Joe asked, motioning to him to continue even though he couldn't be seen.

"Unfortunately I haven't found anything that is a case breaker" he said. The sudden rush of hope Joe had experienced was just as suddenly leaving him. "We did have a report from one of the deceased's neighbours saying that they had noticed a blue car a few times in the days leading up to the death. They haven't seen it since." Joe paused, mentally retracing everything that he could remember about the Brown death to see if the factoring in of a blue car would link any dots. To his dismay, he could only come up with another blank.

"What did the DCI make of it?" Joe asked

"Haven't told him yet" said Glen, the hushed tone returning. "I know he's had you under the cosh a bit of late Joe, so I thought I'd give you the inside line, see if you could steal a march by putting it together with something you may have got from Newcastle"

"Thanks for that Glen" Joe said, smiling at such a show of loyalty. "You'd best be careful though. You know how he can get. Watch your back mate"

"Always do Joe!" he said cheerily, the hushed tones once again thrown aside. Ending the phone call, Joe sat back in the chair, recoiling as he took an enthusiastic mouthful of the coffee in front of him, only to press his spine into the back of the seat as his taste buds screamed in protest. Closing his eyes, sleep finally washed over his body and he relaxed into the chair, the Yorkshire countryside flashing by the window.

-49-

DCI Whindle stood at the office door of Commander Hayley Carlton, his closed fist hovering an inch or so away from the surface of the door as he checked his watch again. Satisfied that he was neither early nor late, he rapped on the door three times.

"Come" bellowed the stern voice from within. DCI Whindle hated having to justify his actions, even to superiors, and he made no exception for the Commander. Carlton was known on the force as somewhat of a micro manager. She liked to have regular daily meetings with the senior investigating officers under her charge, and was infamous for her frustration at lack of progress in cases, especially major or high profile ones. Despite having risen sharply through the ranks, she was thirsty for more advancement, and as a graduate of the accelerated promotion scheme, and its successor, the high potential development scheme, Carlton was some dozen or so years Whindle's junior, with around eight years less service, yet she sat three ranks higher, and this irritated DCI Whindle. Grasping the door handle and opening it, DCI Whindle adopted his best diplomatic smile as he entered the room. Commander Carlton was stood by the window, her tailored tunic, skirt and shiny black shoes as immaculate as ever as she studied the car park. Her jet black hair was neatly styled into a short bob. A pair of angular, yet stylishly feminine designer spectacles adorned her face, and gave her a slight look of severity and intellect that many found even more intimidating than her usual demeanour.

"Sit down Evan" commanded Carlton, disguising it as a request with an almost mercurial wave of her hand. Whindle complied, lowering himself slowly into the chair. Carlton turned from the window, and walked across to her desk, sitting down in a deliberate and controlled gesture, her face serious. She made a point of ignoring DCI Whindle as she looked through a bundle of papers that were set out neatly in front of her. After a moment she glanced up, letting the papers rest back on the desk, and taking off her glasses.

"I'm hoping that you have some progress to report Evan" said Carlton, looking DCI Whindle directly in the eye.

"We are still following up on numerous leads Ma'am" replied DCI Whindle politically, deciding against mentioning the videos that Joe had received.

"Don't try to flannel me Chief Inspector" snapped Commander Carlton, her eyes still trained on DCI Whindle as she slowly and methodically cleaned the lenses of her spectacles. "I've spent the opening part of today's play fielding calls from three or four national newspapers, in addition to the Mayor, two local MPs, and the Commissioner" Whindle shifted uneasily in his chair. "I'm going to level with you Evan. I have been concerned at the lack of movement on these murders. The press are starting to get on my back, and so is the Commissioner. The lack of any tangible leads is putting me in a very difficult position" Quelling the sensation of fury that was building inside him, DCI Whindle forced a smile and spoke through strained lips.

"Are you pulling me off this case, Commander?" Carlton sat expressionless, her hands resting on the desk. After a few seconds she spoke, as if she had spent the last few seconds actually considering the option. Finally, she smiled.

"No Chief Inspector, I am not removing you from the case. I need something that I can take to the Commissioner, and I need it quick" Commander Carlton smiled again in an attempt to diffuse the obvious tension that was emitting from Whindle. It didn't work.

"Look Evan, I am not your enemy. I have a great respect for what you have achieved as a senior investigating officer. You're one of my best men!" DCI Whindle scowled as the blatant attempt to massage his ego bounced off him.

"All I want is the perpetrator of these heinous crimes brought to justice, and quickly" said Carlton.

"Bollocks" thought Whindle, turning his head towards the door as somebody knocked on it. "All you want is the quickest route to the top" though he wisely decided against putting that thought into words. "You know how it works Evan. Those higher up the chain need to see results. I cannot keep stalling them forever!" Commander Carlton said as she rose to her feet and opened the door, ushering in Dr Rothesay. Whindle nodded at Dr Rothesay, and then checked his watch in the hope that Carlton would take it as a hint and end the meeting early.

"I'm aware that Dr Rothesay is involved with the case on a forensic science level. He is also experienced in criminal profiling, so I have asked him to compile a profile of the suspect" said Commander Carlton, ignoring DCI Whindle's gesture completely. "Would you care to share with us your thoughts?"

"It appears to me that we certainly do have ourselves a peculiar set of circumstances here" he began. DCI Whindle rolled his eyes. Carlton scolded him with a stare. "Whereas, one can usually begin the process of garnering information and characteristics on the perpetrator of most crimes by using some kind of triangulation method, this chap seems to be operating without any clear reference to any sort of comfort zone, geographically speaking. Having said that, the attacks have so far taken place within the railway network boundaries, so it could well be assumed that the railway is the comfort zone, rather than any one locality"

"Fascinating!" snapped DCI Whindle "Owing to my countless years of experience in catching murderers, instead of studying the dead bodies they leave behind, I have already considered that possibility! I however, prefer to keep an open mind rather than cling onto the first tagline that I can construct. No offence!"

"Well, it isn't quite as straight forward as that Evan!" said Dr Rothesay, ignoring the obvious swipe. "There are aspects of these crimes, especially within the first attack that suggest that, whilst the perpetrator is indeed familiar with the railway network, his actions do indicate a certain nervousness within that environment, as if he is knowledgeable but not completely comfortable" Dr Rothesay paused for dramatic effect. "No offence taken, by the way." He smiled falsely, warming to the duel.

"Go on" said Commander Carlton, slowly taking her glasses off and gently taking the tip of one of the arms between her lips. Dr Rothesay continued as he consulted his papers.

"There are numerous directions in which this investigation could go. We could be looking at the relative of a railway worker, a worker who has been sacked, an aspiring Train Driver, the list goes on"

"Brilliant!" exclaimed DCI Whindle. "So you're saying it could be anybody who travels on trains, likes them, has been sacked from them, or even who was bought a Hornby train set as a kid!" Dr Rothesay's face flushed as anger started to grow inside him.

"The point is Inspector" said Dr Rothesay, a sudden harshness creeping into his words "That there are certain traits that are clearly indicated in the crimes that have been committed. All I am here to do is to highlight them to you. What you then do is entirely your choice!"

"For the love of god Hayley!" snarled Whindle. "Do I really have to listen to more of this mumbo-jumbo claptrap? I've already had a belly full of this from that upstart Tenby!" Commander Carlton motioned to rise from her chair, cautioning Whindle with an outstretched hand.

"Ah, the new chap!" remarked Dr Rothesay. Commander Carlton glanced across at Dr Rothesay as she replied.

"Indeed he is. Not great on paper, but very promising judging by performance. From memory I believe he has a degree in psychology. I'm sure you'd find a chat with him interesting!"

Dr Rothesay nodded. DCI Whindle bit his bottom lip and breathed heavily.

"Let's just hope that the new impetus can yield some prompt results, for all our sakes!" Commander Carlton said, looking directly at DCI Whindle.

"Will there be anything else Ma'am?" DCI Whindle asked through gritted teeth.

"That will be all, Detective Chief Inspector" She replied. The sentiment behind the meeting was crystal clear. Get results, or get out. Not being a fool, Whindle realised this, and once again fixed his best political smile on his face as he left the room. Closing the door behind him, he turned and glared at the nameplate. Suppressing his anger, he smiled as he slid his hand inside his pocket. Pulling out the piece of notepaper that Joe had thrust at him, DCI Whindle unscrewed it, studying the hastily scrawled car registration number as he smoothed the paper's edges. As his eyes scrutinised the text repeatedly, he felt unconcerned by the warning he had just received from Commander Carlton. DCI Whindle still had an ace up his sleeve, an ace that would solve his two biggest problems; Commander Carlton, and DS Joe Tenby in one glorious swoop.

He glanced across the street at Amelia Park Police Station, its modular construction and awkward dimensions accentuated by the two level car park adorning the flat roof. Bringing the car to a stand, Steven craned his neck, slipping the car into reverse gear and peering over the headrest as he began backing up. Suddenly he stopped. Something was telling him that it wasn't a great idea to park so close to the police station. It was obvious that they would be looking for him by now, even though they clearly had no idea who he was. Still, he had spent long periods of time parked in the same spot, studying the routines of those who must pay. The prospect of being noticed was a risk he was prepared to take. He was careful though. He made sure he had a method for every act. He considered his next prey. Luckily for him, people have a habit of building their life into distinct structures. Companies are especially guilty of this. So desperate are they to foil their employees chances of relaxing on the job, they timetable everything. If he were a politically motivated man, he would find this distasteful, unfair, or even abusive. But politics was not at the forefront of his thoughts today. Today he was a man of dark and ruthless intent. Scanning the horizon, Steven checked for any sign of his prey. Looking down briefly at the passenger seat, he smoothed out the corners of the piece of paper that sat there, its edges growing increasingly grubby. The harsh sound of a car horn behind him grabbed his attention. Glaring over his shoulder, the woman driving the car behind him was gesturing. Resisting the urge to raise his middle finger into the air, he instead smiled and raised his hand, changing gear from reverse to forward and driving away. He indicated right, and turned into a side street about 200yds further along the road. Pulling into the kerbside, he switched off the engine. Checking his mirrors, Steven reached down into the foot well behind his seat, carefully lifting the plastic tube from the dirty carpet. Slowly opening the lid, and gently stroking the smooth surface of the glass, he made his choice, selecting a chunky, serrated piece. Reaching across to the glove box, he opened it and carefully wrapped his fingers around the syringe box he had taken such care to store earlier. Holding it up to the light, Steven nervously looked around before opening the box and examining the cylinder of the syringe. He had deduced that the problems he had experienced with Sean Grant were down to air bubbles that had prevented all of the medicine getting into Sean's blood. Having satisfying himself that the problem was rectified, he returned the syringe to its box, placing it into the lining of his coat. Checking his mirrors once more, he got out of the car and crossed the road, reaching the end and turning left. Searching quickly for the best vantage point, Steven saw three bus stops. Looking at the second one, he saw that on its sign it read 'Special Events Only' He walked over to it and stood there, confident that no bus would complicate matters by stopping for him.

As he made a subtle show of checking the information board that was strapped to the pole of the bus stop, he trained his eyes on a small car park which occupied a corner plot of land next to the Police Station, occasionally becoming distracted as he watched the station's main entrance. Now and again a Police Officer, or a pair of officers came and went, usually deep in conversation. Steven smiled as he watched them. They were in their comfort zone. His confidence grew as he continued to observe. A number of buses had slowed near him, but thankfully none of the drivers had been concerned enough to stop and tell him he was waiting in the wrong place. Checking his watch, he was becoming mindful of the dangers of standing there for too long. Frowning, he considered his options.

"He's usually here by now" Steven thought as he peered across the road, scouring the car park once again for any sign of movement. He was just on the verge of turning to walk back to the car when he caught a glimpse of motorcycle helmet emerging from the mid-afternoon traffic. He stood perfectly still as he watched as a man on a small scooter indicating left, riding slowly into the car park and stopping next to the ticket machine. Steven gently shivered as the hairs on the back of his neck stood on end. Filtering out all other distractions, he studied the man. Although the front of the helmet was flipped up, it was impossible to see Russell Danton's face from this viewpoint. A motorist behind Russell approached him, asking what time the car park closed. He turned to answer them, his helmet emblazoned at the back with the words 'PARKING ENFORCEMENT'. Turning back to face the front of the scooter, Russell dismounted the scooter and wheeled it to the far corner of the car park. Breathing out slowly and deliberately, Steven calmed himself, looking at his task logically. There were simply too many potential witnesses for him to seriously consider doing anything here. Convincing himself of the need to observe, and observe only for now, Steven continued to look on as Russell completed checking the car park. Pushing his hands deep inside his pockets, Steven smiled menacingly as he readied himself to walk back to his car. Just then his view was blocked by a bus, his ears filled with the harsh squealing of its brakes as the doors flew open.

"Shit!" he said inwardly, putting his head down and staring at the floor as the driver leant out of his cab.

"You're at the wrong stop mate" he said, his voice rose above the rumble of the engine.

"I, err..wait for someone" he stammered in reply, shifting from foot to foot and disguising his voice with his best attempt at a polish accent.

"Fair enough!" said the driver cheerfully, before he closed his doors and moved the bus noisily into traffic. Craning his neck around the back of the bus, he was relieved to see that his prey had not moved. Russell's wrist flicked at the throttle and the scooter lurched forward as he crept up to the junction with the main street.

"Steven turned and jogged back to the side street where his car was parked. In a few seconds he was unlocking the driver's door and clambering into the seat, thrusting the key into the ignition and starting the engine. He gunned the accelerator, the wheels spinning slightly as he pulled away from the kerbside. Bringing the car to a rough stop at the give way sign he briefly looked left and right, forcing his way into the line of traffic at the expense of a heavily laden lorry whose driver was too slow to close the gap between him and the car in front. By now, Russell was sitting 3 vehicles ahead. That was just where Steven wanted him. The traffic was rolling at a steady pace, and he was gradually calming his breathing and slowing his heart rate from the unexpected run to the car. On his lap lay his treasured piece of paper, complete with creases, smudges, and a scrawled list with three names crossed out with straight, purposeful lines. His eyes switched almost constantly between the page, the brake lights of the car in front, and Russell's brilliant white crash helmet. Oblivious,

Russell leaned back as the traffic halted, looking left and right before checking his watch. What he didn't know was that he was being stalked. Back in the car, that tired, grubby piece of paper was being studied once more. Steven wasn't worried. He knew exactly where Russell was going. After all, he had routine on his side. Relaxing into his chair, he placed the paper back onto the passenger seat, drumming the steering wheel gently with his fingertips as the traffic began inching forward.

-51-

The amplified voice of the train's Conductor shook him from his temporary rest. The handful of people who were sharing the carriage with Joe were busying themselves gathering their belongings together in the hope of being able to make a sharp exit, probably toward the underground. Joe stretched dramatically, his knuckles touching the cold plastic on the underside of the overhead luggage racks. Looking out of the window, the weather looked gloomy. The sky seemingly even greyer than usual when set above the ageing brick walls that bordered the platforms of London's Kings Cross station. Joe was the last passenger to step from the carriage and onto the platform. A cold breeze whistled from north to south, its pace and coldness amplified by the yawning tunnels sitting just off the end of the platforms. Peering down the length of the station toward the concourse, Joe was undecided as to whether he should fish his ticket from his coat now, or take a chance on not needing to. His considerations were interrupted by his phone ringing. Joe managed to grab it before it went to answer phone. It was Glen.

"Hi Glen" Joe said, smiling yet slightly disappointed that it wasn't Jessica. "What is it?"

"We've all been called in for a special briefing!" Glen whispered. Joe guessed he was either in the canteen, or the corridor outside.

"I haven't received any message!" Joe sighed. His shoulders sagged. Relations were worse than even he'd imagined between himself and DCI Whindle, who was now clearly trying to freeze Joe out.

"When is this happening Glen?" Joe asked, pausing at the top of the stairs.

"2000hrs" he said.

"Okay Glen" said Joe, "I need you to help me here"

"What can I do?" asked Glen compliantly. Joe paused for a second. He really wasn't sure about whether it was right or fair to risk dragging DC Violet into the on-going feud with DCI Whindle. Glen had already put himself in the crosshairs by running background checks on victims and families that he knew were behind the DCI's back. "Then again" he reasoned. "There is a killer to catch, and it is a dog eat dog world" His mind was made up.

"I need you to go back to those checks you made for me about the victims and their families. I know it's going to be a drag of a job, but I need you to extend the parameters of the search and look at everyone." He could hear the sound of pencil on paper. "Cross reference them with any reports of grievances against the railway that have spilled into disturbances, breaches of peace, assaults, that sort of thing."

"Will do Sarge" said Glen, still scribbling. "How long am I going back?" he asked.

"The type of rage shown in these attacks suggests that whatever is motivating the killer is a grudge that has been fermenting for a fair while. I'd say 5 years as a starting point. We can work back from there as needed."

"5 years. Got it!" said Glen. "Sarge" he said, his voice half an octave lower and much quieter.

"Yes"

"Is this still below the radar?" Glen asked.

"I'd very much appreciate it if you kept it quiet Glen, yes"

"No problem" said Glen. "I'll get started as soon as the coast is clear!"

"I'll see you at eight o'clock DC Violet. Thank you." Joe replied, closing his phone and dropping it into his coat pocket as he changed direction and headed towards the staircase leading to the Underground, pointedly ignoring a Big Issue seller as he went.

Tiny fragments and shards of frosted glass lay on the kitchen floor glistening in the moonlight. Despite spending what seemed like an age checking to see if the house truly was empty as he slipped on his latex gloves, Steven still felt the need to freeze for a full minute after entering via the kitchen door. The back gate wasn't even bolted, and the aging door would have provided little resistance regardless of his chosen method of entry. It had taken seconds to breach the door, its window folding and crumbling from the force of a single, expertly aimed jab from a hammer wrapped in oily rags at the corner of the window pane. Satisfying himself that nobody was home, he allowed his eyes to adjust to the darkness, blinking repeatedly as he grasped for his night vision. Despite the darkness, he could see clearly that the cabinet he had destroyed in his fight with Robert only two days earlier was still heavily damaged, sitting forlornly in the corner of the lounge. Walking over and prizing the door open, Steven rifled through the seemingly random papers that lived within, the latex against his skin causing his fingers to sweat slightly. Swearing under his breath, he turned his attentions to the three drawers, yanking out their contents and leaving them strewn across the rug. Looking over his shoulder he remembered the cupboard that hid behind his Mum's chair, training the light of his torch on it. Shoving the armchair roughly to one side, he snatched the door open. The cupboard was extremely well organised, its four shelves filled with regimented contents. Plain white boxes were lined up in symmetrical formation, with four pristine photo albums stacked just as neatly on the top shelf. On the second shelf there were a couple of old ornaments, gifts from old friends long forgotten, and a glass figurine which was a wedding gift to his parents from his grandmother. He paused, thinking of his father's mum. The loss of her son had eaten away at her, the grief almost dissolving her like a cancer. Yet despite all the suffering that everyone felt, all the loss and anger, his mum and grandmother just seemed to drift apart. His grandmother seemed to strengthen her grip on the memories of her son more and more as they faded into time, and his mum seemed to cling to her own mother, the distance becoming greater as time passed. Snarling at the memory, Steven grabbed the figurine, placing it on the ground beside him and shining the torch at the remainder of the cupboard's contents. Turning his attentions to the photo albums, he scooped them from the shelf and laid them out on the floor. Opening each one in turn, he flicked through the plastic sleeves, making various faces of disgust at the pictures of Graham. Methodically he worked his way through the first three, quickly discarding them. Slowly, he opened the cover of the fourth photo album. He sat himself down on the carpet, crossing his legs as he studied the photograph of his father that looked back at him from within its sleeve. Forcing his tears back from his eyes, he flipped the photograph over and continued examining the contents of the album, stopping every now and again to study particular shots, running his forefinger over the face of his father now and then. As he adjusted his legs, he dropped the album onto the carpet, his attentions drawn to a photograph that had slipped from inside back cover. Picking it up, he turned it over.

"That bitch was going to hide him away completely!" he spluttered as he stared unblinking at an old army picture of his father that until the fight Steven had with Robert, had sat proudly on the wall above the cabinet that had been damaged in the fracas. Slipping the photograph back into the cover of the photo album and tucking it under his arm, he got to his feet and made for the door. Carefully, he gathered up the figurine, gripping it gently as he switched off his torch and returned it to his jacket pocket. Taking one last glance at the cupboard, he took a deep breath, pausing to run his hand along the back of his father's chair before exiting the room and disappearing out of the broken kitchen door.

The CID Office was a veritable hive of activity. Glen was making a show of busying himself, something that Joe had learned already was a sure sign that the DCI was nearby. Jessica was in a side office, away from the throng of to-ing and fro-ing that was taking place. Joe stood at the door for a second as he surveyed the chaos. Not wanting to announce his arrival just yet, Joe stared across the room at DC Violet, silently willing him to detect his presence. After a few more seconds, Glen looked up from his paperwork, smiling tensely as he acknowledged Joe. Joe gestured to him to get Jessica and come outside into the corridor. He stared back at Joe momentarily as his brain deciphered Joe's signals. Nodding his understanding, he rose casually from his seat and sauntered across to the side office where Jessica was busily working. Joe disappeared from the doorway and waited for the two of them out of sight and earshot of the CID office, almost loitering in the shadows of the half lit corridor.

Lost in his own thoughts, Joe was shaken back to reality by Glen's voice

"Alright then Sarge?" enquired Glen. Glen smiled and nodded.

"Welcome back Joe" Jessica's voice echoed gently off the walls and polished floor.

"Thanks" he replied. They both exchanged blushes.

"Any luck on those checks Glen?" Joe asked, his tone business like.

"If I'm honest Sarge, I'm struggling." said Glen. "You've asked me to go back 5 years, and I've found nothing. Because of budget cuts, all search requests have to be approved by the Senior Investigating Officer". Joe frowned.

"We need these background searches Glen" he said "There has to be something in the history of these people that has linked them to the killer"

"I knew you'd say that!" said Glen. "I took it upon myself to ask a girl in the intelligence department as nicely as I could if she could extend the search field instead of the time span, but she can't do it without an authorisation code from an Inspector." Joe leant back against the wall and put his hands on the top of his head. He was crestfallen at this setback, but desperate not to show it.

"Okay" he said thoughtfully "We'll just have to chew this one over for a bit." Suddenly, an idea popped into Joe's mind. He smiled as he slapped Glen on the shoulder. "Thanks Glen, its appreciated" he said. Glen smiled.

"Don't mention it sarge" he said.

Glen turned back to Jessica.

"Please tell me you have something positive" he said.

"Yes and no" she replied. "The glass pieces we have recovered are definitely from a railway mirror, manufactured during the time of British Rail. It was primarily fitted in train toilets and also in station's, office and first class compartments." Joe smiled

"But" she said, raising her hand. "It is of very similar composition to many other types of mirror manufactured for lots of differing uses. It's tenuous at best Joe" Joe's smile faded.

"How tenuous?" asked Joe. "Do you think that it strengthens the theory of a probable link between the victims via the railway? If the glass I found is from the same mirror as the glass used to attack Tina McBride, it would prove, even to

Whindle, that we have a link!"

"I'm not sure whether we'd be able to positively match two glass pieces definitively to the same mirror. Besides, it doesn't matter what I think Joe" said Jessica. "It's what DCI Whindle thinks that counts" Joe knew she was right. He was desperate to torpedo the DCI's constant attempts to make him look stupid. He knew that he needed to be patient if he were to be allowed the chance to be proven right. Taking a deep breath, he made a decision.

"Jessica" he said, his face serious. "I need you to do something for me that you probably aren't going to like" She looked at him, her face one of questioning, her large dark eyes wide and curious.

"I need you to keep these tests on the glass shards under your hat for the time being" he smiled awkwardly.

"Joe!" she replied, "He's the Senior Investigating Officer! I've already ran tests on that discs and the videos without him knowing!"

"I know, I know!" he said, his hands raised. "It's just that I'm up against it here. You know how hard he's looking for an excuse to get one over on me at every turn" She looked away. Glen shifted awkwardly from foot to foot, looking up and down the corridor for sign of interruptions. "I know that we're on the right track here. I think that you know it too! Look, the pathologist has found Medazolene in Sean Grant's blood. That's a link I can present to the DCI! I just need time to work on the rest because I know he's going to shoot me down, even though the blood results are solid! I need to be bulletproof Jessica. Just a few days"

"Joe!" she spluttered. "This isn't a game! There's a killer out there and it's our job to find him! My uncle is a very well connected man. I already told you how he could ruin your career. Mine too! He's at his worst when he thinks he's backed into a corner, which is why you have to be honest with him. Go in there and show him everything you have about the blood results, about the glass, about Newcastle, and the videos. You never know, he might change his view of you." She held his gaze, her eyes wide as they locked into his. Reluctantly he broke eye contact.

"No." he said looking down. "I can't. You know what he's like. He's made his mind up about me and there's no going back! Besides, he's not as connected as he may think! If I go in there now and put the evidence that we have in front of him, he'll shoot it down straight away and this whole investigation will be pushed in the wrong direction! He's already stopped me conducting vehicle checks!" After a pause, she nodded. "Thank you" he said. Without a further word they both turned on their heels and made their way back into the CID office with Glen following behind, his hands deep in his pockets.

Glen sat on the edge of a desk where a pretty brunette in uniform sat diligently working. Now and then she looked up at him and smiled, then returned to her typing. As Joe watched, he couldn't work out whether her smile was one of interest or one of sympathy. Glen glanced in Joe's direction. Joe smiled and raised his eyebrows. Glen's cheeks flushed a little and he shifted his body so as to face away. Joe glanced over at the side office that Jessica was using. She was hard at work. He picked up his pen and continued reading one of the many witness statements that had been collected since the first killing, guiding his eyes through the text by way of the pen's nib.

The sound of a door being roughly snatched open killed the hustle and bustle of the CID office instantly, transforming it into complete silence. All eyes turned to DCI Whindle. He stood at his office door, a tense frown on his face that quickly switched to a scowl as he saw that Joe was one of the many officers waiting for him. Joe allowed himself a smile of satisfaction. DCI Whindle looked down, shuffling a handful of paperwork in his hand, then looked up, readying himself to address the room.

"Right then" he said, eyeing Joe again. "I'm glad that you all managed to make it in at such short notice" Joe resisted the urge to laugh. "Despite our best efforts, it would appear that the great and good think that we are in need of assistance in apprehending the person or persons who carried out these crimes" He wiped his forehead with the back of his hand.

"Violet" he barked. Glen sat bolt upright.

"Guv?" he said, grabbing at the papers he had set down on the desk beside him.

"Progress, Mr Violet! Progress! His eyes fixed on Glen. Glen looked down; hurriedly searching though the papers for anything he could offer up.

"I've been concentrating on links between our first victim and anyone with a grudge against her, grievances, restraining orders etc. I have nothing so far. There seems to be no link to anyone that would explain the attacks. No debts, No enemies, no common links between victims"

"Except the fact that they were both employed to work on the railway" All eyes in the room switched from the DCI and onto Dr Rothesay who was emerging from inside Whindle's office. Whindle continued to glare at Glen. Dr Rothesay stood at DCI Whindle's shoulder. DCI Whindle breathed slowly and deeply in an attempt to curb his rising frustration.

"Tina McBride and Anna Brown" said Dr Rothesay. "Two women of differing ages, differing backgrounds, from different areas of the city. They do not share the same economic advantages, nor have they even studied to the same level, educationally speaking. Mrs McBride was in her forties, earning a salary at the lower end of the median scale, Miss Brown was within a career that was due to yield earnings of a much greater magnitude." He made a visual sweep of the room. The eyes of everybody were fixed securely upon him. He continued. "Experience tells us, along with significant bodies of academic studies and research, including candid interviews with the perpetrators of these types of crime that there is nearly ALWAYS a link between the victims, either in terms of their backgrounds, occupations, beliefs, family and social circles, lovers or activities elsewhere, or indeed the perception of them by the perpetrator". DCI Whindle was staring into the distance, his mind elsewhere. Joe had stopped what he was doing. He listened, suddenly enthused at this fresh approach to examining the murders. "The Commander has asked me to advise you as to the likely areas by which the killer is linking his victims, utilising all of this research and experience" Crossing his hands at his front, Dr Rothesay stepped back into the doorway, leaving DCI Whindle suddenly exposed and unaware of the fact that everybody had now fixed their stares upon him. Looking up, he loosened his tie and unbuttoned his collar.

"What are you all gawping at?" he hissed, "You heard what he said!" He jerked his thumb over his shoulder at Dr Rothesay.

"Sgt Tenby, did your outing to Newcastle produce anything other than a hang over?" DCI Whindle asked. Joe hesitated. He was getting used to the eyes of the room being upon him, but he was still of a mind to keep the latest developments to himself, at least for now. Jessica fixed him with a worried look. Resisting the urge to respond to the DCI's jibe directly, Joe placed his hands on the table in front of him.

"Having spoken to Dr Ross Marvell, a home office pathologist in Newcastle, I believe that we may have something to look at. A railway maintenance worker by the name of Sean Grant was killed by a train 2 nights ago. His body was ripped apart by the train's pantograph and the overhead power lines. Dr Marvell has conducted toxicology tests using tissue samples, and he has identified the presence of Medazolene in Sean Grant's tissue" DCI Whindle shrugged.

"So?" he said. Joe looked at him disbelievingly, restraining himself from the urge to shake his head.

"The same drug was found in Anna Brown's blood stream guv! Surely it's worth looking into?"

"So there are two idiots taking recreational drugs who have died on a railway line? Anything else that we can use, Mr Tenby?"

"I'm still looking into certain avenues of enquiry guv" he said cryptically, forcing his frustration to the back of his throat. "I've requested some further information from colleagues in Newcastle and I'm waiting for it to be sent through."

"Come on Tenby!" snarled Whindle. "I'm your boss! This isn't crime stoppers! If I'm financing you going on a jolly up to Newcastle then you're going to bloody well tell me what you did when you were there! Was the trip relevant to the investigation, or was it a waste of time?" Joe grasped for a suitable answer that would leave him with enough room for manoeuvre. Just as he was about to speak, Jessica interjected.

"I'm currently running some tests" Joe closed his eyes, his head dropping. DCI Whindle aimed his gaze squarely at Jessica who was almost wincing as she spoke. "DS Tenby has also identified a potential line of inquiry focussing on some shards of glass that may be linked with the glass used to stab Tina McBride" Whindle shot Joe a look of fury.

"Is this true Tenby?" Joe looked across at Jessica. She mouthed "Sorry" at him. Joe took a deep breath.

"I think I need to brief you fully guv, in private."

"I think that's probably one of your sharpest ideas Tenby!" snapped Whindle, motioning Joe and Jessica into his office with a violent jerk of the head.

-54-

With the traffic having cleared, he was able to smoothly increase his speed, always ensuring that he was close enough to keep a visual contact with Russell's scooter as it accelerated toward the next stop on his daily schedule. Despite the gruesome activities he had planned out to fill the evening, he felt relaxed, at ease, happy even. The sun was daring to break through the cloud base, and as he ventured further and further into the eastern end of the city, he had to admit that it didn't look half as grey and lifeless as it normally would.

Steven remained relaxed. He was well versed in the daily routine of this particular subject, and was certain that there would be little, if any deviation from it. He had checked the car park opposite the police station, a delicious slice of irony that Steven had revelled in! Following this, he always, without fail, made his way across the city to a multi-story car park near the docks. The car park had 6 floors in total, and provided a myriad of opportunity for Steven to make his move, as he was certain that there was no CCTV installed in the structure. Abruptly, Steven turned right down a narrow residential street. Speeding noisily down the road, his car complained grumpily as the chassis creaked and moaned over a succession of speed humps. Reaching the end of the street he turned left, gunning the accelerator and checking his rear view mirror as he went. Suddenly, the car park sprang into view, and he swung the car left into the entrance, pausing briefly to take a ticket from the automated machine, watching the barrier that spanned the entrance pivot lazily upward. Steven elected to park closer to the top, as these floors are usually emptier and therefore present a smaller risk of anyone disturbing him whilst he was at work. Having driven slowly around all six floors to make sure that there were no drivers readying to leave, he descended back to the fifth floor. There were only a handful of vehicles parked. Checking the staircase and listening for the sound of wheels climbing or descending the ramps, he ensured that he was alone before parking in a lonely corner. Getting out of his car, he immediately walked over to the side of the car park overlooking the main road, scanning the traffic for sign of the scooter. After a few seconds, Russell duly came into view, checking over his shoulder and indicating to pull in. Steven smiled to himself as he watched, then quickly set about checking the tickets displayed in the windows of the other vehicles. Two of the cars had been parked there for a week, and were displaying tickets valid for another four days. The other four displayed season tickets. Steven noted that he still had at least another 90 minutes or so before any commuters were likely to return to their vehicles. Knowing that Russell was still likely busying himself with the heavily used lower floors of the car park, Steven sprang into action. Jumping back into the car, he reversed it out of the space, and parked it across the thick white line which separated his space from the one next to it. Turning off the engine, he flicked on the radio, switching the volume up as far as it would go. Deciding to leave the driver's door wide open, he moved to the boot. Opening the lid, he laid a thick black hood and a length of rope carefully on the carpet, then reached inside his pocket and pulled out an envelope. From the envelope he took a single piece of paper, unfolding it and placing it carefully on top of the hood and the rope. Laying the paper face up, he aligned it to ensure that it sat perpendicular to the line of rope. On the paper was a simple caption written with a calligraphy pen. It read 'Justicia'. Satisfying himself that all was ready and in order, he returned to the driver's door and reached in, pulling out an iron bar wrapped in grimy bandages. Tapping the end of the bar gently against his thigh, he retreated behind a large pillar to await the arrival of his prey, readying himself as the sound of Russell's scooter echoed off the smooth concrete walls.

Steven watched as Russell dutifully checked the tickets on the first two cars. Taking his helmet off, Russell turned and stared at the car, the sounds of the radio filling the air. Looking around for any sign of the owner, Russell placed his helmet on the seat of his scooter, and cautiously approached the rear of the vehicle. His attention was drawn to the white piece of paper that had been so precisely positioned by Steven only minutes earlier. Stooping, he read the message, mouthing it to himself as he picked the hood up and examined it. Taking that as his cue to spring from the shadows, Steven lurched from behind the pillar, wielding the iron bar high above his head as he rushed towards the back of Russell's head. Spinning around, Russell came face to face with his attacker, managing to put up his left hand in defence as Steven brought the bar down on his temple. As he stumbled, Steven pushed him, causing him to stumble clumsily back against the car, sending the hood skidding across the dusty floor. Steven took aim once more with ruthless precision, swiping the end of the bar across Russell's cheek and knocking him unconscious. He reached down and scooped up the hood, stuffing it over Russell's head, and rolled him onto his front, binding his hands and feet before levering him into the boot of the car, slamming the lid closed. Steven walked around to the driver's door and leaned in, switching off the radio. Sliding a hand into his pocket, he fished out a pair of latex gloves and slipped them on as he walked towards Russell's scooter. Working his fingers fully into the gloves, he picked up the helmet and walked over to the car, opening the boot and throwing the helmet on top of the now captive Russell. Closing the boot lid, he went back to the scooter and swung his left leg over the seat, kicking the stand away. He started the engine and wound up the throttle, the scooter lurching forward as he sped up the ramp to the top floor, parking the scooter in the furthest corner, as far out of sight as possible, before walking calmly back down to the pay machine, inserting his ticket into the machine and slotting in the required coins. Returning to his waiting car, Steven reversed away from the scene of the attack, and eased the car down the succession of ramps, to the exit barrier, inserting his ticket into the machine and merging effortlessly with the passing afternoon bustle.

-55-

Joe studied the filing cabinet that the doctor was leaning against. He was sure it wasn't there previously. Leaning slightly leftward, he noticed that it was hiding a dent in the thin office wall, something that was undoubtedly caused during his physical altercation with Whindle a day or two previously. Peering to the right of Whindle's desk, he could see the pressure marks in the carpet from where the filing cabinet had previously stood.

Still standing in the office doorway, DCI Whindle leaned forward towards the staring eyes of the team, his face contorted with rage. "Get back to work!" he barked as he slammed the door closed, stomping around to his seat, and throwing himself down.

"I think it's time you filled me in properly on what exactly has been going on!" Whindle snapped.

"Nothing has been going on!" said Jessica.

"You've been going behind my back, running unauthorised tests, failing to keep me informed of developments on a major inquiry, and you think that constitutes nothing going on?"

Jessica's face reddened. "I could have your accreditation pulled for a stunt like this! You should fucking well know better!" Whindle consciously tried to calm himself, taking slow, deep breaths. "As it stands, I think it's fair to say that we can put this down to you being led astray by him!" he gestured towards Joe.

"How dare you?" spluttered Jessica.

"How dare I what?" replied Whindle.

"How dare you speak to me like that? I am not a little girl anymore! Don't you dare insult me like that!" Whindle sat there for a second, looking on in shock. He glanced at Dr Rothesay who was observing the exchange between Jessica and Whindle with a clinical interest.

"You still here Doctor?" said the DCI rhetorically. Dr Rothesay uncrossed his arms, his concentration broken. He looked at all three of them.

"I'm sorry?" said the doctor.

"Do one!" DCI Whindle hissed menacingly, motioning towards the door with his hand. Reluctantly, Dr Rothesay picked up his jacket and left the room. DCI Whindle watched him as he went, ensuring that he closed the door firmly behind him before turning his attention back to Joe and Jessica.

"I want to know everything!" he demanded.

"First thing is first" Joe said. "I have reason to believe that both of our active murders are linked to the incident in Newcastle." Whindle sat back in his chair.

"Go on" he said.

"At the scene of the second murder, some pieces of reflective glass were recovered. Admittedly these were recovered alongside quite a large volume of other items and miscellaneous litter, but I also found some on the bridge overlooking the incident in Newcastle. Chain of evidence is good, and all protocols are being followed."

"I've managed to ascertain that the glass from both scenes is of British Rail era manufacture, and has been used in mirrors made for first class compartments, station toilets etc. We think there is a good chance that it is from the same mirror or piece of glass that was recovered from Tina McBride's body. It's not much, but alongside the videos Joe has received, it's the only link we have." Jessica said, desperate to repair the damage she had done.

"Not much?" shouted DCI Whindle. "It's fuck all!" Joe and Jessica looked at each other. "So I send you off to Newcastle against my better judgement, and all you can show for it is a lot of bravado and a couple of pieces of mirror that could have been there for years?"

"As Jessica said, it's the only thing we have right now!" said Joe, leaning forward. "The checks you asked for and the background work I have been overseeing so far have failed to turn up anything! It's like the doctor said, there has to be a link!"

"You're as full of shit as he is Tenby!" spat the DCI. "This whole thing is a desperate attempt to not be shown up as the sham of a detective you truly are! Joe sat motionless for a second. He breathed in sharply, suppressing his anger.

"With all due respect, I resent that comment deeply!" DCI Whindle shrugged. "Look at the facts! Tina McBride, Station Staff. Anna Brown, Management Trainee for Network Rail. Sean Grant, fixes trains in a maintenance depot!" Whindle slammed his hand down on the desk. "You have no solid evidence to definitively say whether or not the Grant murder in Newcastle has any bearing on our case!" Joe threw his hands up in despair, sinking back into his chair.

"Come on!" he said, his frustration beginning to boil over. "All three victims are railway employees! All three were found on the railway line, mutilated by passing trains. What are the chances of three unconnected people being killed in such similar ways? I have received two video clips. They were sent directly to me! One of them even has my name in a caption! My first name!" The DCI sat with his arms folded, his head slowly shaking as he considered Joe's comments.

"You can't positively identify the girl in the second video!"

"What about the first? That is Tina McBride!" Joe spluttered. DCI Whindle ignored him.

"This Sean Grant character was way up in Newcastle! How many serial killers would kill two people, both women, and then suddenly switch their focus a few hundred miles north, and go and kill a man?"

"That depends on the causal link" said Joe.

"Causal link? You get a tin pot degree in psycho-babble from the Open fucking University and you think that means you can swan around like some half arsed guru spouting meaningless bollocks?" Whindle rose slowly from his chair, leaning further forward as he spoke, his face reddening. "I'm here to tell you right here and now Tenby, that isn't going to happen!"

"Where do you get off making judgements about me?" shouted Joe. He too was beginning to leave his seat and Jessica was becoming concerned at how the conversation was beginning to escalate. "You know nothing about me! You swan in and swan out of the office bullying junior officers, snapping your fingers and expecting people to drop everything, doing less than bugger all to lead this investigation, and then stamping your feet when no leads turn up! You won't even consider for a minute that the videos sent to me are relevant to these murders, despite it being obvious to anyone who cares to take a fucking second look! Wake up!" Whindle was almost snarling by now. His lip was slightly upturned, and he had started to sweat as Joe continued. "Any link between these victims is a link worth exploring. I still say that the railway is the key link! Why don't you see that?"

"You're forcing me to consider disciplinary proceedings against you for insubordination!" snapped DCI Whindle. "I have looked at your silly little theories, and I am telling you that they're nothing more than a trick! Accept my decision or I will report you! That wouldn't look so good on the record of a High Potential Development Candidate now, would it?" Smiling, DCI Whindle sat back in his chair, certain he had cornered Joe.

"Well if we're talking about official proceedings Chief Inspector, we can always start with a phone call to the Department for Professional Standards, and a complaint to Commander Carlton about your violent attack on me the other day!" Joe motioned to the filing cabinet. "I can see you've tried to hide the evidence!" DCI Whindle stood up slowly, his eyes never leaving Joe for a second. Jessica remained motionless, wanting to say something to engineer an exit from the confrontation, but being fairly sure that whatever she said would make things worse.

"If you can at least act like a semi competent Detective, and gather together some actual evidence of these supposed 'links' then your egotistical ramblings may be a touch more believable!" DCI Whindle said. "Until such a time as you deem it appropriate to do that, I suggest you concentrate on your job, and not your imagination! Now get out!" Joe and Jessica made for the door, Joe deliberately taking his time in rising from the chair and sliding it back under the desk.

"Tread carefully Tenby" hissed the DCI, placing his hand on Joe's chest. "I don't think you appreciate quite who you're dealing with"

"Neither do you!" Replied Joe, flatly.

"Just remember Tenby. Undermine me in front of my team again, and I will cut you off at the knees!" Joe held Whindle's gaze for a second, neither man willing to back down.

"Do you mind?" said Joe, looking down at Whindle's hand. Whindle stood back, allowing Joe to leave the office, slowly closing the door. Joe looked around the room. Jessica was stood by the window looking out over the car park. He walked over.

"Are you ok?" he said softly, his fingertips brushing her shoulder.

"Don't talk to me Joe!" she said, turning away and walking toward the door. "Leave me alone!" Joe watched as she marched into the corridor and disappeared, his hands falling to his side in a mixture of dejection and confusion.

"What have I done now?" he said to himself, suddenly conscious of everyone watching him.

Russell felt the sensation of slowing down. He slid gently away from the red lights that were dimming and brightening at random intervals, and in an instant his view was filled with a flashing orange.

"Brake lights! Indicators! I'm in a car!" he tried to say. He tried as hard as he could to review everything that he could remember in an attempt to work out how he got here and why. His brow furrowed as he recalled the dark blue car parked awkwardly. He remembered that the door and boot was open. "The note!" he thought, a vision of Steven's message appearing in his mind. "Justitia" he kept trying to say to himself, reciting the message written on the page in an attempt to provoke some sort of memory that might explain how he came to be lying here, and what the word meant. He tried desperately to separate his wrists, but they were bound tightly, the only result of his efforts being a burning sensation from where the rope had begun to cut into his flesh. Russell dropped his shoulders as low as he possible could in an attempt to remove the hood completely, and after a minute or so of concentrated wriggling, grinding and shuffling, the bottom of the hood finally rode up above his eyes. He blinked furiously. Without the filtering effect of the hood, the red light gave out almost a chic ambience as it reflected off the smooth surface of his motorcycle helmet. He looked desperately left and right, up and down in an effort to find a means of escape. Training his eyes on the source of the light, he noticed that the back of the lighting cluster was uncovered. He could just make out the wiring that fed the lights with power. "If I could just get to those wires" he thought, shuffling his body towards them. Wrenching at the bindings on his wrists, he winced in pain as the ropes dug deeper into the skin. It was obvious that there was no hope of working the bindings loose, no matter how hard he tried.

Russell found himself starting to cry, his shoulders softly heaving as he began to realise that, whatever the reason for him being here, it wasn't going to end well. "Who is doing this to me? "he thought, his eyes darting from place to place, drinking in every detail of his surroundings that were visible. "Why am I here? What do these people want from me?" With questions racing around in his head, sadness and confusion were being pushed aside by a rising tide of anger and injustice. Breathing deeply and slowly, he began to rage at what was happening. Eyes not moving from the wires in front of him and without further thought, he lurched at the grimy coverings that protected the wires, missing them and cutting his nose on the sharp metal that housed the lock to the boot. Grunting in pain, he squinted as blood ran down the bridge of his nose and onto the rag that filled his mouth. Again, he lurched forwards, managing this time to grab one of the wires between his teeth. Yanking back on it violently, the cable snapped, momentarily throwing him into darkness. Spurred on, he tried again, missing on his next two attempts before he finally managed to grab a second wire, this time disconnecting the right hand indicator. Determined to complete the job, he shuffled his body around, aiming for the reversing light and left hand indicator, managing to disconnect both within five attempts. Spitting the fragments of wire and insulation from his mouth, he drank in gulps of air, his body covered in sweat. All he could do now is hope that fortune would favour him by drawing the attention of a passing police car, of anyone, to the defective rear lights on the car. Exhausted, he lay still for a while and prayed.

The late evening was just starting to blend into early dusk, and the sun was slowly preparing to disappear, giving way to the inky darkness of night. Where the afternoon sun had camouflaged Russell's desperate bid for help, the encroaching dusk could only serve to amplify it. Steven was in a line of traffic moving at very slow speed, his eyes flicking between the rear view mirror, the car in front of him, and his watch. "This is taking far too long" he thought, his jumpiness increasing as each minute passed. Straining his neck, he peered past the car in front, sighing as he lost count of the endless lines of red lights that snaked into the distance. "I can't just sit here!" he said aloud, looking down the left hand side of the road. "I know there's an exit just up here" Mercifully, the traffic was moving. After a few minutes of stopping and starting, he could just see one edge of the traffic sign indicating that the turn off was imminent. Flicking his indicator on, Steven swung his wheel left and pushed the accelerator down hard. The car sprang forward, veering past the car in front and speeding down the inside lane, cutting into the path of a Ford Fiesta. Braking sharply to make the exit lane, Steven was just merging across the white lines when the car suddenly jolted forwards. Looking in his rear view mirror, he could see an angry face scowling at him from behind the windscreen of the car behind. Steam was rising from the front of the Fiesta, and the driver was now thrusting his door open and getting out. On the other side of the rear seats, Russell was curled up tightly in a ball, still trembling from the impact. Strangely, he was trying not to laugh as he peered through the gap in the cushions. Via the rear view mirror, he could see the panic on Steven's face, and he was enjoying it. He felt sure that help was only a short distance away. The driver of the Fiesta was studying the damage to his car, his hands on his head. Angrily he stomped over to Steven's window.

"What the fuck are you doing? He shouted, banging on the glass. Thinking that there may still be a way to talk his way out of this fix, Steven lowered the window slowly. A quick assessment of the lines of potential witnesses already sneaking guilty peeks in his direction however, soon made him realise that talking himself to a swift exit wasn't looking likely. Considering his options, he elected to thrust the car into gear and stamp on the accelerator, racing away from the scene. Glancing in his rear view mirror, he watched as the driver of the Fiesta stood in sheer disbelief, his mouth wide open as he looked at the rear of Steven's car, the unlit rear end exiting the carriageway.

-58-

Instinctively PC Andy Mills reached out to the control panel on the dashboard that activates the blue lights and sirens, his attention having been drawn to a minor accident in the queues of teatime commuters. Deciding after all that the lights were not needed, Andy reasoned that it was a minor rear end shunt, and the volume of traffic would ensure that there would be no shortage of willing contributors who were only too pleased to give a statement. Signalling right as he relayed the details of the incident to his control room, Andy made his way down the hard shoulder, immediately regretting the decision not to utilise the emergency lights as he waited patiently to merge into the traffic from the wrong side of the queue. Waving in appreciation to the driver of a large van, he eased into the traffic. Just then, he saw one of the drivers involved in the accident marching over to the car in front. Fearing a confrontation, he jabbed his finger on the activation button for the emergency lights, the darkening sky being filled with flashes of pale blue. In the same instant, the car at the front of the collision abruptly jerked forwards, its back wheels spinning as the driver made for the exit lane, his sudden move catching the driver standing next to his window unawares. He stabbed at the 'yelp' button, sending a shrill squeal of police siren into the air. Immediately, the motorists that had been blocking his way began trying to clear a path for him. Slowly he started to gain ground on the site of the collision, finding that he was able to make much faster progress by hugging the white line that separated the two lanes of the carriageway. The driver of the offending car had managed to gain quite a start on him, and usually he would have his right foot firmly on the floor by now, punishing the engine of his patrol car in a bid to catch up to the perpetrator ahead. Something told him however, that this was a situation that called for discretion. Flicking on his emergency sirens long enough to clear the exit from the carriageway, Andy carved his way through the rush hour queues efficiently enough to catch sight of the dark coloured car as it tried unsuccessfully to blend in.

Satisfied that he was close enough to keep pace without provoking a high speed chase, Andy killed his lights, merging back into the flow of traffic, which was moving easier, now that he was on the right side of the congestion. Clicking the 'transmit' button on his radio, Andy went to relay details of what had occurred to the control room, something which he should have done instantly. For some reason though, perhaps his hunger for action and recognition, he decided not to, releasing the radio from his grasp and instead devoting his entire focus to following and capturing the driver of the dark coloured car. Losing out on recent promotion had really got to Andy, and although it was only a minor accident and failure to stop, something was telling him that more was occurring here. He had a hunch, the famous 'gut feeling' that there was more to this than meets the eye. The driver of the car hadn't seen Andy behind him, one of the advantages of driving an unmarked patrol car. Andy stayed half a dozen vehicles back, not wanting to give the driver any idea that he was being followed by a police officer. He muttered the name of each land mark and speed change under his breath as if giving a commentary, finding himself on a gradually narrowing residential street. The road followed the edge of a railway line, and there was a busy junction with a level crossing just up ahead. Without warning, the dark car ahead veered into the lane for traffic turning right and Andy followed. indicating and checking his mirrors before easing into the same lane. Watching the traffic in the left hand lane speed gratefully past as they continued straight ahead, Andy edged towards the right turn along with his fellow motorists. Just as the dark car approached the crossing, the yellow warning light for the railway lines illuminated, and the traffic lights automatically turned red. Steven reacted instantly, nosing his car into the junction and just managing to cross the railway lines as the barriers began to fall.

"Shit!" said Andy, banging the top of the steering wheel with the palm of his hand as he watched Steven disappear from his view.

Russell's mind was still hurtling. His senses seemed to be getting keener with every turn and bump in the road.

"We're stopping!" he whispered to himself harshly. He craned his neck so as to peek between the back seats of the car, desperate to catch even a fleeting glimpse of a passing landmark. As evening set in, all he could see through the windows of the car was darkness, occasionally complimented by the briefest of light beams from a passing headlights, or intermittent streetlight. Try as he might, he could not stop his hands from trembling.

Having navigated the increasingly unstable and narrow road, Steven brought the car to an abrupt halt just out of sight of where the road continued further into the darkness. Reaching across to the glove compartment, Steven opened it and pulled out a well-worn copy of *Rail* magazine. Flipping it over, he ran his forefinger down the columns of writing, resting its tip on a short paragraph which he had circled hastily with a red marker pen. The paragraph contained details of maintenance work being carried out on the main route to London over which he sat. Hitchworth tunnel was in the middle of a major refurbishment and upgrade, involving the rebuilding of a Victorian airshaft that had become unstable over recent years.

He had made it his business to discreetly observe these works from a distance, taking note of the fact that the moss covered brick tower that usually protruded from the gentle brow of the hill, and kept mischievous youths, the curious and the suicidal safe from the sheer drop into the tunnel below, had been carefully dismantled and removed, the top of the shaft being covered by a rectangular wooden hatch. The old brick tower had stood proudly in the middle of a small clearing, and that clearing was now marked out clearly with security fencing bedecked with warning signs. Health and Safety regulations had decreed that the entire area was flooded with harsh, artificial light at all times during darkness, even though there were no workers around. This had caused Steven a big problem in terms of planning his latest escapade, and in response he had been fastidious in his research. He knew that the maintenance staff would not be back until tomorrow morning, and that the power to the floodlights came from a mobile generator that was positioned just within the perimeter of the fencing. Unbelievably, the fencing had an access point that was not padlocked. It was held shut by a heavy chain that wrapped around the top of the gate and the adjacent fence panel. Taking a deep breath, he licked his lips and sprang into action, throwing open the car door and getting out. During his research, he had planned for this eventuality, having spent a considerable time working out the best way to cut the lights without making himself visible, without damaging them, or leaving fingerprints. After much consideration he had settled on a simple plan. Crouching at the fence, he produced a slim metal pole from his inside pocket. Aiming it through the metal links of the security fence, he carefully slid it through until he was only holding it by his fingertips. Checking that he had lined up the tip of the pole, he thrust it as far forward as his minimal grip would allow, forcing the tip against the control panel on the bottom left hand corner of the generator's rear end, striking the emergency stop button firmly. Within an instant, the clearing was plunged into pitch darkness. Triumphantly, he stood up, cursing as the pole tumbled from his grasp and came to rest in the mud next to the generator. Steven made a mental note to pick the pole up once he had finished his work, and then strode back to the car to collect his waiting victim.

Straining to see through the gap in the seats, Russell had watched as the interior light came on, convinced that this was his time to die. As he heard the footsteps fade gradually, his attentions were drawn to his groin. Terror had seized control of Russell's bladder, and had chosen to empty its contents all over his trousers. Silently, he started to sob. He gazed sightlessly thought he gap in the back seats of the car.
"Oh god! Oh fuck!" grunted Russell through his gag as he listened. Steven's heavy footsteps were quickly returning, his boots crunching the mud and gravel. Russell's body stiffened as he stared at the lid of the car boot, almost as if he were trying to peer through the very metal itself. Outside, Steven paused. He had chosen this place carefully, having carried out countless scouting missions in the preceding weeks. Steven savoured the atmosphere, studying the piece of paper in his hand. Steeling himself for what was to come, he opened the boot lid, fixing Russell with an impassive glare.
"Come" he said, without emotion. "We must go now"

Grunting sounds spilled from Russell's mouth, filling the night air. Steven carefully folded the paper along well established lines before placing it in his pocket, his cold eyes never once leaving the face of his prey, bound, gagged and ready for the taking. Reaching down, he untied the restraints around Russell's legs and then grasped his bicep, hauling him roughly from the boot of the car and sending him crashing face first onto the sodden gravel. Wincing at the pain of being thrown so roughly to the floor, Russell choked back tears as he pressed his forehead into the mud, his skin becoming sore as the gravel and dirt mixed with his sweat, aggravating the cut on his nose. Without warning, Steven grasped his shoulder, spinning him over and placing his boot in the centre of his chest. Rummaging in his pocket, he produced a reel of surgical tape, kneeling on Russell's chest and forcing each eye open in turn, pressing the tape against each eyelid firmly as he ignored the gargles and muffled screams from Russell's mouth.

"Get up" said Steven coldly as he lifted himself to his feet. "Please" Russell screamed through the fabric. "I don't know who you are! What do you want? I'll do anything!!" As his muffled words spilled through his gag, he stared unwillingly into the darkness, his naked eyes pleading with his captor. Steven's gaze pinned him like an insect. Dejectedly, he dragged his aching body into the upright position, the wind stinging his eyeballs. In one smooth movement, Steven snatched the discarded hood from the boot of the car and shoved it over Russell's bowed head.

"Move!" commanded Steven, jabbing him in the back with his fist. Crying out, Russell stumbled forward, staggering from the impact of his captor's latest assault, struggling to breathe through the soaking material of his gag. Blind, disorientated and unable to cry for help, the feeling of being increasingly convinced that he would die tonight could not be shaken. And there was nothing he could do to save himself.

-60-

Whereas normally, Phil reserved a special volley of rugby-based banter and abuse for Joe, this evening he seemed to have sensed that now was not the time. Instead of engaging in the usual theatre, he had poured Joe's drink before he had ordered, placing it on the bar and looking eagerly in Glen's direction.

"I'll have the same please" Glen had said as he looked down at Joe's drink.

"It's one of the advantages of being predictable Glen" Joe said. Smiling, Glen nodded before turning his attention to the sepia photographs of rugby league players of the past. Squinting at them, it was clear that he had no idea who any of them where. Glen rapidly returned his attention to Phil, who was now lowering Glen's drink onto the bar. He was clean, with slight stubble, his clothes providing comfort over style. He exuded a middle aged scruffiness, and mischievous warmth that was typical of a much loved history teacher.

"Is this a colleague of yours Joe?" asked Phil as he took a ten pound note from Joe and punched the order into the till.

"DC Glen Violet, meet Phil." Joe said warmly. The two men shook hands. All three stood for an instant in awkward silence.

"Right then" said Phil, picking up a couple of dirty pint glasses from the opposite end of the bar. "I'll leave you two to your evening!"

"Thanks Phil" Joe said as the two men turned and made their way to a nearby table. DC Violet sat opposite him, swilling the dark brown liquid in his beer glass in a circular motion as he listened, nodding occasionally as Joe vented his frustrations. Although Joe hadn't said anything specifically, Glen was certain that much of the frustration his new superior was feeling was down to the fact that Jessica Hopewell wasn't returning his calls. Initially Glen couldn't help but feel slightly envious as he had watched the apparent spark between Joe and Jessica as it developed. As the last few days had passed however, he had found these feelings to be overtaken by a growing respect for DS Tenby. He saw Joe as a leader, someone to be admired and respected, and if he were being honest, he was slightly flattered that Joe felt that he could trust him enough to share his thoughts and frustrations over a pint. Glen continued to listen. The video clips, and the shards of glass were bothering Joe. The longer the investigation continued, the more he was convinced that both were to somehow pointing to the killer. They nagged at him, taunted him almost. Exhaling loudly, Joe sat back in his chair as he stared into space.

"Why would the killer use mirrored glass?" he said to himself absently.

"It could be more symbolic than using a knife" offered Glen. In one movement he swallowed the remainder of his drink and rose to his feet, gesturing to Joe with his glass. Joe nodded with a smile, picking up one of the beer mats from the table and fiddling with it as he considered Glen's suggestion.

"It's certainly possible" Joe said as Glen returned to the table. "Our first victim was so heavily injured by the impact of the train that a stab wound or laceration as a message, might easily have been disguised"

"Same with victim number 2 Joe" replied Glen eagerly. "After she came to grief she wouldn't have been much more than lumps of dog food!" Joe pulled a disapproving expression before taking a mouthful of beer.

"I don't know Glen" he said as he stared at an old portrait. This one was a panoramic view of King Edward Street in Hull, the vista crammed with gentlemen in hats and suits, poorer families in flat caps and ragged clothing, and grand trolley buses. He allowed himself to be distracted by the safety of the image for a second.

"I cannot, for the life of me understand why the DCI won't take the videos seriously! One of them actually shows the murder! I'm beginning to think he's an imposter who kidnapped the real DCI Whindle!"

"Do us all a favour Joe" interjected Glen. "Find some solid evidence of that before you present it to Whindle!" Both men laughed.

"I won't make that mistake again mate" said Joe, relaxing slightly as they remembered the stand-off between Joe and the DCI.

"What is that guy's problem?" said Joe as he picked up his glass.

"Don't ask me Joe" answered Glen "I gave up trying to work Whindle out a couple of years back"

"You've only been with him a couple of years" said Joe

"What can I say?" said Glen with a smile as he slouched into his chair "I've always been a quick learner" The two of them laughed once more before sliding gently into a tired silence.

"Seriously though Glen, we need a breakthrough! I need to get something to shut Whindle up" Adapting to the change in mood, Glen sat up slightly.

"We're all under pressure Joe" he said softly "We all realise what's at stake here"

"This bastard always seems to be one step ahead though" said Joe. "At the same time I've got Whindle breathing down my neck. It's as if he spends his time just waiting for an excuse to jump on me. I can't understand what it is that I've done to offend him so badly"

"He sees you as a threat Joe" said Glen. "Take it as a compliment. You are more than good enough a copper to hold your own in major crime. DCI Whindle doesn't know how to deal with you so he gets angry, what with that, and Jessica!" Glen was looking over Joe's shoulder as he saw Jessica come in through the side door.

"Don't get me started on Jessica!" Joe sighed, completely failing to understand that Jessica had just walked in and was approaching the table. "I've got Whindle playing the psycho boss, and now she's not talking to me and I don't have a fucking clue why!" Glen's face reddened as Jessica stood behind Joe, her expression darkening as she listened. "She thinks that because I talked to Carlton about the investigation I've betrayed the team, but she doesn't get it!"

"Joe" said Glen in a vain attempt to shut him up.

"I mean, it's not as if Whindle actually does anything is it? He gets paid for being grumpy and looking like shit, and all the while I get it in the neck! The guy's a dinosaur who needs putting in a museum. She needs to realise that I'm not a grass, that's not what I'm about!" Joe felt emboldened by the beer he was drinking, and took a healthy swig from his glass before continuing. Glen put his head in his hands as Jessica glared at the back of Joe's head. "She doesn't have the right to make snap judgements about me! Despite what she thinks, she doesn't know me!"

"Oh I know you Detective Sergeant Tenby!" Jessica hissed. Joe froze, his eyes fixed on Glen.

"I didn't.." he started to speak, but broke off midway through the sentence, realising that it was pointless trying to defend himself.

"Don't bother Joe!" scolded Jessica "I may not know you intimately, but I know enough!" Joe motioned to get up but Jessica stopped him, raising her hand. "To think that I actually came looking for you to apologise for flying off the handle!" she said "I didn't realise that I would be intruding on a meeting of the jolly boys club!"

"Jessica, please" said Joe

"No Joe!" snapped Jessica "If you came looking for someone to make peace with them only to overhear them insulting a member of your family, I think you might be a little pissed off too!" Joe looked across at Glen, who was busily studying the same portrait Joe had lost himself in moments before.

"I'll leave you boys to your little bitching session" said Jessica coldly. She turned on her heels and marched across the pub to the door, yanking it open and pausing before turning to face Joe once more. "I thought you were much better than that Joe"

As his ordeal went on, Russell sank deep into despair as his feet sank deeper into the freezing mud. His nostrils hurt as he inhaled as deeply as he could in a bid to compensate for the gag that disabled his mouth. The plummeting temperature seemed to be thickening the air, leaving a fine layer of moisture on everything and everyone, Russell's eyes stinging more and more, the further the temperature plummeted. Russell stumbled and groped in the enforced darkness, his breathing becoming heavier and more erratic.

"Keep moving!" barked Steven impatiently, jabbing him now and then with his fist. Russell's sobs began to soften and grow quieter, the pain he felt from each jab and strike was gradually decreasing. An eerie tranquillity seemed to be washing over Russell as he doubtless neared the place where his captor intended to kill him. The sheer horror of his predicament had dissolved his resignation, his feet moving on auto pilot as his brain debated whether to fight or to take flight. His feelings of defeat and despair gave way to clinical assessment, and a rising will to not go quietly. Russell's thoughts of determination were abruptly halted as Steven grabbed his shoulder, stopping him in his tracks and spinning him around.

"Where are we?" demanded Russell, his voice now deeper and slightly more assured.

Steven chuckled. "We're at the end of the line." He said menacingly.

Joe's mouth was still full of beer as he emerged from the pub.

He managed to pick out the sound of high heels, and immediately ran across to his car, unlocking it and jumping in. Starting the engine, he swung the car out into the street, gunning the accelerator in an attempt to catch Jessica up as quickly as he could. Following the road, he picked out her familiar walk. Pulling level with her, he opened the passenger side window and leant across.

"Jessica!" He called. Her eyes flicked toward him as her pace remained constant, her head facing resolutely constant.

"Drop dead Joe!" she retorted, walking quicker. Joe sighed, pressing his foot down slightly harder on the accelerator in an attempt to match her speed. Glancing out of the windscreen as the car rolled slowly forward, Joe tried again.

"Jessica, please!" he said. "We need to sort this out!" Jessica stopped.

"Why do we need to sort anything Joe?" She crossed her arms, waiting for Joe's answer. "I mean, it's not as if we know each other really, is it Joe?"

"I wasn't having a go at you!" Joe countered. The headlights of a car filled the rear view mirror as Joe remained still as he leant across the passenger seat. "I'm under attack here! I need results! Your uncle wants me out, and I can't let him win!" Joe glanced up at the rear view mirror. The driver of the car sitting behind him flicked his main beam on and off a couple of times, his patience clearly starting to wear thin. Joe reached across and opened the door. Jessica stepped back, her arms still crossed. "Get in!" he said. For a second, she still didn't move. The driver of the car behind sounded his horn. Jessica jumped, fixing the driver with a glare. Tightening the grip on her bag, she reluctantly stepped into the car, gently pulling the door closed. Joe raised his hand in apology to the driver behind and slowly pulled away as Jessica fastened her seatbelt.

-63-

Steven abruptly jabbed Russell in the back, sending him sprawling face first into the mud. As he tried to get back to his feet, Steven placed his foot in the centre of Russell's back, forcing him back down onto the sodden ground. Walking over to the metal fencing, Steven unhooked the chain that had been securing it, and slung it roughly over the top of the adjacent fence panel. Heaving the gate open, Steven stepped inside, walking straight across to a large wooden hatch. Stooping, he grabbed at the padlock he had earlier snapped, pulling it from the steel ring and flinging open the latch. Russell's laboured breathing grew sharper as his mind raced in a desperate attempt to decipher the noise that echoed in the still night. His fingers clenched, grabbing handfuls of dense, freezing mud. Not daring to move, he knew he was faced with a choice; fight for his life, or snatch whatever chance fate deemed fit to hand him. The calmness that had enveloped his body was leaving him. He now trembled gently and rhythmically as a dark, almost malevolent survival instinct took its place. He was no longer listening for noises to interpret. He was listening for weakness, for hesitation. He was listening for his chance to save his life.

-64-

Joe had pondered where to go, driving aimlessly as he stumbled towards making a decision. Desperate not to offend

Jessica still further, Joe finally started heading towards home. She had not voiced her disapproval, so he eventually decided to keep driving toward there until she did. He pulled the car smoothly to a stop outside the front door, switching off the lights and unclipping his seatbelt. Jessica remained still. He looked across at her, forcing himself to maintain his gaze until she looked at him. Unclipping her seat belt she opened the door and deftly exited the car. Joe got out, filled with a new confidence, as if getting her to his house and out of the car was a major achievement. He put his key in the front door before pausing and turning to her.

"Well come on." He said. "I can't do honesty without coffee"

She smiled, as she followed him inside, grateful for the chance to clear the air, as well as to claim sanctuary from the cold evening.

Following Joe into the kitchen, Jessica could not help but assess the décor and tidiness of the hall and lounge as she passed through. It was decorated a little too darkly for her taste, the lounge painted with an admittedly complimenting mix of coffee, and darker browns, with matching wooden blinds at the impressive bay window. The kitchen was much brighter and energetic, decorated with a combination of white and stainless steel. Joe stood at the sink looking out of the window as he filled the kettle. Jessica stood at the door. She smiled as they caught each other's gaze in the window's reflection. As he brought coffee to the table he motioned for her to sit. Gracefully she lowered herself into the chair. Joe placed her drink in front of her, dumping himself down, sitting at a right angle to her. They sat in awkward silence for a moment, each one waiting for the other to speak.

"I'm sorry if I offended you back there Jessica" Joe began. "I honestly didn't mean to make you think that I was disrespecting your family"

"Well you were being disrespectful, and I found it hurtful!" she said, her smile fading. Joe studied the dark liquid in the cup as he considered his reply.

"You've got to admit though, that your uncle has it in for me. I just find it frustrating that he won't give me a chance to prove myself, on a level playing field"

"Are you saying that my uncle is jeopardising a murder enquiry to score points against you Joe?" said Jessica, her delicate eyebrows rising sharply.

"What?" Joe stammered.

"You heard me" she said, her face now stern.

"Why would you think I was saying that?" he asked, genuinely confused.

"You obviously think that you're the centre of the universe as far as my uncle is concerned!" She pushed her chair back sharply.

"Hang on!" he said, his voice climbing in volume. "Where did that come from? I never said anything of the sort! All I meant was that I want to earn the right to be respected as a member of this team on my own merit! That's all!"

"Thanks for the coffee!" she said coldly. Standing up, she turned and made for the front door, slamming it behind her. Shaking his head, he hauled himself to his feet and followed her, throwing the front door open. She had her back to the door and was calling a cab.

"Get lost Joe!" she said over her shoulder as the taxi operator answered her call.

"You have got to be one of the most annoying people I have ever met!" he said, breaking into her conversation with the taxi operator. She stopped abruptly and turned to face him.

"I beg your pardon" she said.

"You heard me!" replied Joe. "You are one of the most staggeringly annoying, frustrating, confusing and unpredictable people I have ever encountered." He walked over to her. "Every time I think I'm starting to get an idea about how you feel, what you want, where you are, you throw up another wall! How am I meant to have even the remotest chance to know what's right and what's not?" She looked to the floor, sliding her mobile phone closed.

"Why are you wasting your time then?" she asked, lifting her gaze to meet his.

"Because, even though you annoy me, I can't stop thinking about you! When I'm near you, I turn into a clumsy idiot. You make me feel like a nervous wreck, and the most powerful man on the planet, all at the same time" Joe stopped. He could feel himself blushing. Jessica was looking at him, her expression blank. All of a sudden, Joe felt vulnerable, slowly turning away and walking back inside.

"I'm sorry Jessica" he said with a sigh as he re-entered the hallway. "I shouldn't have said that" Making his way back to the kitchen, Joe picked the coffee cups up from the table. Padding dejectedly over to the sink, he tipped the remnants of coffee out and placed them on the worktop. Glancing up at the window, he saw Jessica stood behind him.

"How can we work together now?" he said softly. She stood silently for a second, obviously still taking in everything he had told her. Joe couldn't help but stare into her deep brown eyes as they twinkled under the kitchen lights. His heart raced as he awaited her reply, certain that it would be one of rejection.

"Discretion is probably a good start" she said, her smile wide and mischievous. He looked at her, silent and dumfounded. She rolled her eyes theatrically as she stepped forward. They were almost touching. He could smell her subtle perfume and it was driving him crazy. "Joe. If you've gone to the trouble of bearing your soul to me, you may as well go ahead and kiss me!" He smiled, and leant into her, their lips meeting tentatively. As the gentle kiss parted, they stared into each other's eyes. He stroked her hair as he felt his arousal begin to rise. He slipped his hands around her waist and pulled her into him, kissing her passionately. She responded by pressing herself against him, her arms sliding across his back and shoulders and across his neck. After a few seconds, they paused for air.

"Wow!" he whispered. "Thirty seconds ago we were arguing!"

"We can carry on if you prefer" Jessica said with a smile

"I think I like this better!" Joe retorted, planting a kiss on Jessica's lips.

"Well that's promising!" she said, gently biting her bottom lip. She stepped coyly away from him. "You've shown me the kitchen and the lounge" she whispered. "Is there anywhere else in the house you'd like me to see?" He grinned as he took her by the hand, leading her across the kitchen toward the door, and the staircase to the upper level of the house. Pausing at the foot of the stairs, he turned to her.

"Step this way madam. I promise you'll not be disappointed!"

He took her hand and raised it to his mouth, kissing it gently, revelling in the foreplay. Joe led Jessica slowly up the stairs, the pair of them giggling as they went. Guiding her into his bedroom, he turned to her and kissed her again, holding her hips and pulling her onto him as he stepped back into the room. As she roughly snatched at the buttons of his shirt, forcing the material apart, he reciprocated, sliding his hands under the silky material of her top. She gasped as his lips teased the sensitive skin of her neck, and with a kick, the door swung closed behind them as they fell breathlessly onto the bed.

-65-

Andy thrust the gearstick forward then back as he raced along the road, which was now bordered with a much more rural surrounding. Bushes, trees and obscured styles peppered his peripheral vision as he sped along the country lanes that led away from the towns and into the rolling Surrey countryside. "Come on!" he shouted, the realisation dawning upon him that he had lost the subject of the chase. Not only that, but that he was now also miles away from where he should be. He was on in the territory of another police force, and was out of radio contact. As Andy looked for somewhere to turn the car around and head back towards the operational safety of London, he saw a large iron gate as the car rounded a bend. It was open. Stopping abruptly, he studied the gate in the rear-view mirror. There was a railway sign on the fence warning trespassers to stay away, and a well-worn muddy track heading down the embankment towards the railway line that snaked gradually away to towards the coast. Something told Andy that this gate was not meant to be open. Taking the car out of gear, he sat for a moment, considering the best course of action. He had just allowed himself to embark on a wild goose chase that would inevitably earn him a bollocking from the relief sergeant. It wasn't a good idea to make things worse by annoying the railway authorities by interrupting maintenance work, or whatever was going on down near the track. Despite the small voice of sense though, he just could not ignore the feeling that was sitting in the pit of his stomach. It was a feeling that he really should drive down the track, and find out what is going on for himself. It was the instinct of an experienced Police Officer. Closing his eyes and telling himself he was an idiot, he yielded to the compulsion, and reversed the car back past the gateway, swinging the nose into the narrow track and driving carefully down toward the railway line, cursing himself as he went.

The winding track seemed to go on forever. He was now certain that he had driven down here for no good reason, and would now have to try and find a place to turn the car around without damaging it still further. He drove on, grimacing as yet more bushes and thorns scraped paint from the car's wings. Suddenly, the narrow track widened out into a small turning circle. Breathing a sigh of relief, Andy allowed himself a smile as he duly began working out whether he could safely swing the car around in a single movement without having to reverse. Beyond the turning circle, the muddy track continued, Andy guessed that it led to the side of the railway line. He yanked the wheel as far to the right as it would go, and the nose of the car lurched obediently. As he began to turn, the glare of the headlights picked up a reflection. Stopping quickly, he frowned. He slowly put the car into reverse and held the steering wheel hard to the right as the car crept backward, the beam of the headlight searching the undergrowth until it highlighted the grubby licence plate of a dark blue car.

"I'll be damned!" whispered Andy, his mouth running dry. He drove slowly down the muddy track a few more yards and manoeuvred the car behind the suspect vehicle, turning off the engine and headlights. This time, his hand went straight to the transmit button on the radio. He knew he had to call for help. He would explain himself later, hopefully once a criminal had been arrested and a crime solved or prevented.

"Bravo India 743 to control" he said, his eyes never leaving the vehicle for a second. He released the transmit button. His only reply was loud static. He repeated himself, twice more. Still nothing. "Shit!" he hissed, clipping the radio to his shirt. He really was on his own. Now he was feeling vulnerable. He grabbed his mobile phone, stabbing at the touchpad. The screen simply read; 'No Service' Sliding the phone back into his pocket, he carefully opened his car door, he had a good look around, closing the door as quietly as he could. Taking out his torch, he motioned to turn it on, before thinking better of it. Approaching the car, he studied it. The boot lid was partially open. Flicking it upward with his fingertip, the boot lid gave way. The inside of the boot, Russell's crash helmet, along with a few scant items were instantly illuminated. Ignoring the items, he concentrated on the crash helmet, frowning as he read the large lettering on the back of it before his attention was drawn to two plastic panels which were lying in the middle of the boot. Looking down at the back of the car's lights, he saw the exposed wires.

"Definitely the same car" Andy whispered to himself. His eyes were then drawn to a muddy boot print on the underside of the boot lid.

"No wonder he didn't want to be caught!" said Andy. "He had someone in the boot!" Once more, he reached for his phone. Still, he had no reception. The feeling that something was not right just wouldn't leave him alone, if anything it was getting worse. Despite this, he knew that he could not simply get back in the car and drive away, even if it were only to summon help. Out there in the darkness, there was somebody who had been brought here against their will. Taking a deep breath, Andy steeled himself and strode forward, sweeping the floor with slow movements of his torch, studying the ground in front of him for any sign of the unknown victim and their attacker.

Listening keenly, he was certain that he could hear movement up ahead. Aiming his torch straight down at the floor so as to minimise the chances of the light being seen, he inched forward, gulping at the cold air as his mouth seemed incapable suddenly of finding moisture. As he followed the route of the muddy track, it angled away to the left slightly, giving way to a small clearing. To the right was an embankment which presented a sheer drop onto the railway line that disappeared into the yawning mouth of an imposing tunnel. Pausing, he turned off the torch. Stepping slowly forward, he could just make out the sharp angles of metal fencing. The access gate in the fencing was open. Beyond the gate, his eyes picked up what seemed to be a hooded figure, standing next to a large wooden access hatch. The hatch was open, and the mystery figure was peering into it. Inches from the mystery figure lay what looked like a roll of carpet or a duffle bag. Andy edged over to where there were a few scant bushes, grateful for at least some protection. Was he witnessing someone about to dispose of a body? Was he watching someone attempting vandalism or theft? He painstakingly worked his way around the perimeter of the clearing, stalking the mystery figure from behind the scattered bushes and shrubs as his mind raced, grasping for a plan of action.

Steven peered into the inky blackness of the air shaft, that familiar wave of excitement beginning to course through his veins. His hands trembled slightly as he looked down at the prone figure lying face down in the cold, wet mud.

"The time for justice is near" he said to himself, as he took his cherished paper from his pocket and unfolded it. It was far too dark for him to read it, but he traced his thumb along the top edge of the page as his mind wandered for a second in anticipation of the release that would soon follow. The wind was getting stronger, whistling across the clearing and rattling through the branches and bushes. Steven was sure that Russell had been sobbing quietly, but could no longer hear him. Prizing Russell from the muddy floor by his arm, Steven forced him to stand. Unlike when he was first flung from the boot of the car though, Russell did not plead or beg for survival.

"Has he given up?" mused Steven. For some strange reason,

the thought of Russell surrendering to his fate mentally, accepting what was to come had aroused Steven. He still felt a deep unease at his impulsive raping of Sean Grant. Unlike the other videos, he had been unable to watch it so far, and as such, he tried his best to ignore the pulsing in his crotch. Reaching inside his jacket, he produced the plastic tube from within, opening the lid and grabbing the syringe. He grabbed Russell's jacket at the neck, standing him upright, pulling a torch from his pocket and shining it into Russell's face. Steven felt the need to lean over and peer inside the yawning chasm that gave way to the tunnel below, but was too busy revelling in the moment.

Behind the branches and bushes at the edge of the clearing, Andy peered through the links of the security fence with an increasing horror as the prone figure was hauled to his feet. He knew that whatever it was that was going on, it wasn't looking good for the victim. Just then, the still night air was pierced with the unmistakable sound of a speeding train. He glanced down at the railway line falling away below, catching a glimpse of the express train as it disappeared into the tunnel. The rushing air and shrill sound of the train seemed to erupt from the floor.

"Shit!" he whispered, swallowing hard. "This maniac was about to throw someone down the shaft and onto the railway line!" He had to act, and now. Reasoning that he had the shroud of darkness, and the element of surprise on his side, he decided to go for it, making a grab for the perpetrator clearly on the cusp of a heinous act. Cautiously and deliberately, he readied himself to pounce, his eyes flicking between the silhouettes of his target, the floodlight masts, and his boots, which were noisily sinking into the mud.

"Stand up straight!" barked Steven. Russell didn't respond, instead focussing on his breathing, and nothing else. Without warning Steven yanked hard on Russell's coat, forcing his head back, brandishing the syringe in readiness to sink it into Russell Danton's body. As he cried out, Russell heard footsteps. Instinctively, he turned his head toward the source of the sound, bracing himself. Steven's grip on Russell's coat tightened.

"This is it!" Russell said to himself as he clenched his fists. This was his moment. Fight for life, or die with a whimper.

Having been able to move around the perimeter fencing, and access the gate silently, Andy was almost within touching distance of both attacker and victim. Quickening his pace a little, he readied himself to pounce. Suddenly Andy's phone burst into life, the screen spilling a harsh light into the darkness, and the speaker transmitting the opening chords to Thin Lizzy's *Whiskey in the Jar*. Andy looked down at the phone, grabbing at it in an attempt to cancel the call. As the music stopped abruptly, he threw himself toward Steven's lower legs.

"What the fuck!" Exclaimed Steven, hesitating for a second as an unexpected figure lurched from the darkness.

"Stop! Police!" yelled Andy, making a grab for Steven in an attempt to restrain him and pull him clear of his intended victim. Staggering backward, Steven released his grip on

Russell's coat. Russell's body was trembling. He was still blind to his surroundings, but his ears were filled with the sound of imminent attack. He let out an instinctive, primal cry as he span to confront the approaching threat, his mind racing.

"Fuck you!" he shrieked, thrusting his arms out in front of him in a bid to charge his way to freedom. His hands struck Andy squarely in the chest, throwing him wildly off balance and causing him to fall backwards.

"No! I'm a Police Officer!" cried Andy, desperately trying to right himself. As he stumbled, his left knee impacted with the wooden hatch, up ending him. Letting out a scream, he clawed at the smooth, wet surface of the wood as he bravely fought a losing battle with gravity, falling into the shaft and disappearing into the darkness, his final breaths bouncing off the dirty bricks as he slammed into the track below.

Both men froze. In the struggle, Russell's blindfold had been ripped from his face. He tried to blink as his eyes reacted to the stiff breeze, but the surgical tape fixing his eyelids held firm.

"No, please, no!" he whispered under his breath as he stared at the wooden hatch. His lips trembled as the dawning realisation overran his racing mind, that he had just caused the death of another human being.

"So not only are you a problem to be dealt with, you're a cop killer as well!" Steven's voice was calm and low as he fixed Russell with the glare of his torch. The anger within him boiled over as tossed the syringe to the floor. Almost growling, Steven sprang toward Russell, grasping him by the neck.

"Please!" said Russell as Steven thrust him aggressively

towards the wooden hatch and threw down the torch. He grabbed Russell by the hair with his free hand, spinning him around and whipping his head back violently so that Russell's ear was next to his mouth.

"There's only one way to deal with cop killers" he hissed, releasing his hold on Russell. Picking up the torch, he smashed it into Russell's kidney, barging him into the tunnel shaft as his body folded up in reaction. The thud from his body smashing into the prone remains of PC Andy Mills, and the steel and stone of the railway echoed through the tunnel and up the shaft, softly announcing another death to the clearing above. Steven peered into the shaft, shining his torch downward as his heart pounded like a bass drum. He could see the spread-eagled remains of the Police Officer, partially covered by Russell. Andy's phone was still attached to his police vest, its screen illuminated as someone made a call that would never be answered. Not caring who the caller was, Steven turned away, closing the hatch and wiping the lock clean. He shivered slightly as his eyes darted from left to right, his body turning rapidly so as to gain as panoramic a view as possible in the search to ensure that there was nobody else waiting to thwart him from the shadows. Taking the list from his pocket, he put the torch in his mouth so he could hold the paper and his pen. He slowly ran his shaking fingertip along a line of text, pausing, before writing something hurriedly in the margin. Despite the unexpected addition to his success this evening, he could not taste victory. He had been unable to record the administering of justice, and it was for this reason mainly that he felt no remorse for the death of the Police Officer. As Steven stood indecisively at the wooden hatch, he found it infuriatingly ironic that he had been forced to tolerate his justice being obstructed by an officer of the law, of all people! Now, he faced a dilemma. He had his justice, but he had no proof! Memories fade and minds cloud with time, but video knows no lies!. Looking around in all directions, he made a decision. Past the fences of the clearing, there was a steep staircase giving access to the track and the tunnels below. Breathing deeply, he switched the torch on, scanning the muddy ground in search of the discarded syringe. Locating it, he picked it up, cursing the fact that it had remained unused. Patting his jacket, he comforted himself by confirming the presence of the camera. Slipping out of the fences, he jogged toward the top of the staircase, descending the first half dozen steps, and reassuring his own worried mind that no trains were scheduled to pass through the tunnel until morning. He could only think of capturing the proof he needed as he neared the level of the track with each careful step. Disappearing into the tunnel, he switched on his torch, sticking to the middle of the track so as to minimise the risk of slipping over and being trapped inside. It didn't take long to locate the bodies. Ignoring PC Mills, Steven crouched at Russell's, shining his torch into the face of a dead man, his eyes still firmly taped open. Looking left and right, Steven grabbed at the camera, swiftly turning it on. He focused on Russell Danton's face, zooming in on a trail of blood that seeped from the corner of his victim's mouth. Pointedly, he steered the camera away from the nearby Police Officer until he had recorded fully the bloodied details of Russell's demise. As he was about to walk away, he turned, filming Andy Mills' lifeless form, the blood that coated the side of his face shining in the light of the camera. Not even allowing himself time to revel in his work, he walking away as quickly as the treacherous floor of the tunnel would permit, gratefully emerging from its huge portal and briskly scaling the steps back to the clearing above. Looking around nervously, he secured the clearing gate and walked back to his car, getting in and taking a moment to slow his breathing before putting the car carefully into gear and driving away, leaving the chaos and death of the last few minutes to fade into silence.

-66-

Joe smiled to himself as he watched Jessica sleep. Unable to take his eyes from her, he marvelled at how soft and flawless her skin seemed. Even now he wanted to touch it, to feel her against the tips of his fingers. Despite his yearning for contact, he remained motionless, opting instead to merely look at her. He still didn't quite understand how they had moved from arguing in the street, to making love within the space of an hour. He allowed his eyes to travel along her feminine curves. Even though her body was covered by the duvet, she still looked perfect. Her gentle breathing sounded like the subtlest of waves massaging a sun kissed shore, a melody his ears drank thirstily. Just as he was thinking to himself that life wasn't going to get much better than this, the calm and peace was shattered by the shrill ringing of his phone. Jumping, he scrambled for the phone and the light simultaneously, missing both and instead sending them spinning onto the floor, his phone landing face down before coming to rest on Jessica's side of the bed.

"What are you doing?" murmured Jessica grumpily as she

groped in the darkness for her bedside lamp, not realising initially that she was not in her own bed. Joe finally managed to turn on the light, both of them blinked furiously as they scrambled for the elusive phone as it continued to ring.

"It's on your side" grunted Joe, rubbing his eyes. He couldn't help but look as she threw back the covers and stooped to pick up the phone. The cool air had made her nipples erect, and Joe's body was reacting. Squinting at the phone, she tossed it to him.

"It's Glen" she said, running her hand through her hair. Joe frowned at the screen.

"This had better be a matter of life and death Glen!" snapped Joe as Jessica pulled the covers over her naked body, much to Joe's disappointment. He playfully tugged at the corner of the duvet as DC Violet began to speak. Jessica giggled, clutching it tightly to her, making an exaggerated show of covering her modesty as she held a finger to her lips.

"Sorry to wake you up at such an hour Joe" Glen's voice was sober and flat. Joe's demeanour immediately changed to reflect the mood. Jessica had been teasing him by sliding her leg from under the quilt in a provocative pose and pointing her toes as if being photographed for a centrefold, her smile mischievous as she saw the effect she was having on him. His reaction to the phone call told her this was bad news, and she quickly covered herself up.

"What's going on?" said Joe, his facial expression now causing real concern for Jessica as she silently questioned him.

"He's struck again Joe" said Glen. "It's one of us this time!"

Joe took a deep breath as he processed Glen's words.

"What happened?"

"Andy Mills from response" said Glen "They found him in a railway tunnel. From the looks of it he either fell, or was pushed down an air shaft! Andy and another guy. A parking attendant by the name of Russell Danton. By the looks of it, Andy got caught up in a murder, which is now a double killing." Joe's heart was racing as his blood began to boil. Andy Mills was the first uniformed officer Joe had met upon arriving at Amelia Park. No Police Officer likes the thought of a colleague being targeted. Clearing his mind of all other thoughts, Joe jotted down the location. Just as he was about to end the call, a thought popped into his mind.

"Glen, not that it's the most important issue right now, but how come you're informing me? My phone's been switched on all evening." Glen paused before he replied.

"It was on orders of the DCI Joe" he said. "He rang me five minutes ago, told me I had to inform you."

"Fucking mind games!" Joe hissed, before reprimanding himself for allowing his mind to become distracted from the burning issue at hand.

"Did you sort things out with Jessica?" asked Glen casually.

"Jessica?" said Joe defensively. The two of them exchanged worried glances.

"Err, yeah, all sorted mate, managed to square everything off"

"Good stuff" said Glen. "I'll see you at the scene" Joe closed his phone. Jessica was sat up now, her head on his shoulder.

"What is it?" she said softly.

Joe's shoulders sagged as a lump grew in his throat.

"There's been another one" he said, swallowing hard. "A copper" She lifted her head from his shoulder, her eyes meeting his as they shared a feeling of shock and despair.

Slowly getting up from the bed, Joe began getting dressed.

"I'd expect a phone call" he said, stepping into his boxer shorts, and fishing a sock from behind the drawers next to the bed.

"I'll get a taxi" she said, sliding out of bed and picking up her panties before slipping them on and grabbing her for her bra.

"Last thing we need whilst all this is being dealt with is gossip" He nodded as he grabbed his shirt from the floor, shivering slightly as he began fastening the buttons. Joe decided not to tell Jessica about DCI Whindle and his latest power play. He refused to allow her uncle to become his priority. As he slipped on his trousers, Jessica's phone rang. He smiled awkwardly, backing out of the room and waiting for her downstairs.

A tall, thin police officer approached the car and asked Joe for identification. Flashing his warrant card, Joe watched as the officer undid the tape that stretched across the road and allowed him to pass. Slowly, he drove up the muddy track that snaked up hill, the already narrow path obstructed every few yards by officers, forensic staff and their equipment. Eventually, he made it to the circular clearing that was the focus of all the attention. Having parked his car a few yards down the track, he was taken aback by the viciousness of the icy wind, pulling his coat around himself as he made his way toward DC Violet, who had acknowledged his arrival from within the perimeter fencing with a business-like nod of the head. He was busily speaking into his mobile phone as he stood next to Dr Rothesay. At the edge of the clearing, directly above the tunnel, there was a secured staircase just visible that lead straight down to the track. Trains had been stopped for obvious reasons, and a large secondment of uniformed officers from neighbouring forces were busily staffing a cordon spanning the neighbouring fields and vantage points, doing their best to repel the efforts of the more inventive members of the press who were desperately trying to gain a view of the track. Predictably, Amber Rawson was among them, desperately trying to attract Joe's attention. Ignoring her, he turned towards Dr Rothesay.

"Where's the crime scene?" Joe asked delicately.

Straightening up, Dr Rothesay motioned toward the wooden hatch that stood proudly in the centre of the clearing. Joe looked past him, swallowing hard as he studied it from a distance. The lid had been removed and was being placed in a protective covering so as not to compromise any evidence that may remain on it. Two forensic technicians were busily photographing the area, and a third was carefully making a plaster cast of footprints around the opening. A few yards away two grim faced constables were hastily erecting a plastic barrier around the now gaping hole in the top of the hill.

"He's..it..I take it..down at track level" Joe stumbled over his words.

"DCI Whindle is in the tunnel as we speak" said Dr Rothesay.

"Have you been down yet?" asked Joe.

"Briefly" replied the doctor. "I'm just preparing myself to go down and do a more comprehensive examination, then prepare for removal"

"Is it..." Joe's voice trailed off. Glen looked away.

"It's always like that when one of our own crosses my table

Joe" Dr Rothesay sighed. He placed his hand on Joe's shoulder, leaving it there for a second before he picked up his forensic case, and headed for the staircase down to the trackside. Watching him disappear from view, Joe turned to Glen.

"Do we know anything yet?"

"All we know is that PC Mills was monitoring traffic on the dual carriageway near to the A2. He contacted control about a minor traffic collision, and that was the last anybody heard from him" said Glen as she shook himself from deep thought and pulled out his notebook, flicking the pages over until he found the information he had been scribbling a few moments before as Joe drove into the clearing.

"All we have are basic identifications" said Joe, stabbing the page with the tip of his pen.

"The Borough Commander is on her way though!" Glen said wearily.

"Commander Carlton, that's all we need!" sighed Joe as he saw the Commander's black Audi cruising up the hill toward the outer cordon, stopping by the tall officer who had let Joe in minutes previously.

"We need to get this wrapped up now Joe!" snapped Glen.

"He's got one of us now! This is out of hand!" Joe nodded. He stepped forward, placing a hand on Glen's shoulder.

"That is why I need your support" said Joe quietly, glancing over his shoulder before he spoke.

"I've had enough of the power games Joe!" said Glen as he pushed Joe's hand away. "Yes, the guv has treated you like shit, and I don't know why either, but I trained with Andy, we were at Hendon together! I just want to nail the bastard who did this!"

"So do I mate!" countered Joe. "We're on the right track. I know we are! We are all on the same team too! The guv is just as committed to solving the case as you, me or anyone else on the team, but he's going in the wrong direction! I just need to know that I can trust you" Glen looked away, and then nodded.

"Right, let's push on and catch this killer!" said Joe, mindful of the need to avoid Commander Carlton until he at least had some basic facts to present her with. He marshalled Glen toward the staircase, both men heading down to the trackside to join DCI Whindle.

Looking up at the yawning mouth of Hitchworth tunnel as he stepped off the staircase, Joe was struck by the sheer scale of the construction that made up this impressive portal. Its face was made up of cast concrete sections, moulded at the curve of the tunnel roof into an elegant lip, the top edge of the portal façade angled toward the centrepiece, which was an intricately carved gargoyle, seemingly keeping a sinister watch over the tunnel mouth as trains hurtled into and out of the stagnant darkness below. The rails seemed to snake out of the tunnel like a tongue, which gave the whole scene a dark quality that fitted the scenario perfectly.

The two men paused at the entrance, both picking up forensic suits from the muster point that had been set up in the open air. They both ripped open the protective packaging, sliding the suits awkwardly on over their clothes and fastening them securely with zips. They both carried shoe protectors to put on when they entered the inner cordon of the crime scene in a bid to avoid compromising any evidence with dirty shoes. As they stepped inside the tunnel, an officer handed them both torches. Joe shuddered as he felt the stark decrease in temperature. Glen was shining his torch at the roof lining of the tunnel, its beam of light exposing the chaotic brick work, and patched repairs from previous leaks. The whole place smelt of damp. Everything echoed. They could hear voices up ahead, undoubtedly coming from the crime scene, which they still were unable to see, thanks to a bend in the tunnel. Joe swept his torch from side to side, pointing it diagonally downward towards the track. This whole area was equipped with conductor rails to power the trains. Joe was mindful of the fact that conductor rails didn't always run along the same side of the track. He felt uncomfortable being so close to electricity in a place so dark, and so full of hazard, and was therefore keeping a close eye on Glen, whose mind seemed to be elsewhere.

"Glen!" said Joe. Squinting in the light, Joe gave Glen a stern look, before pointing calmly downward.

Glen looked down, taking in a sharp breath as he realised that his foot was inches from a conductor rail. Stepping clear of the danger, he held a hand up in apology.

"It alright Joe" said Glen. "I'm sure the electric will have been turned off by now!"

"Doesn't matter Glen!" said Joe. "Even when they're switched off, they still retain enough electricity to knock you out!"

"I said I'm sorry!" said Glen, looking down distastefully at the metal rail.

"Come on then!" said Joe, striding into the darkness, the

ballast crunching beneath this feet.

Rushing to catch up with Joe, Glen cursed as he saw in the torchlight the damage that was being done to his shoes by the sharp stones underfoot.

"I'm sorry Joe" Glen said, again. "I just can't stop thinking about Andy. We weren't best mates, but we kept in touch over the years, went out for the odd drink now and again. I just can't believe that he's dead!" The pair had just reached the curve in the line where the tunnel wall obscured what was beyond. The clinical lights erected at the crime scene threw random shadows along the floor, and the light shimmered off the moisture that clung to the filthy brickwork. Joe stopped abruptly and Glen followed suit as they spied the tape marking the beginning of the inner cordon that had been stretched across the tunnel and secured on metal poles. Joe looked at the bend in the tunnel for a second as he considered his words, opening the shoe protectors and sliding them on. "Glen, if you're too close to this victim, you need to take a back seat." Glen swallowed hard, choosing not to answer and instead concentrating on putting the protectors on his shoes without marking or damaging them any more than the ballast had. "I'm sure the guv would give you other things to do" "I'll be fine" said Glen. "It's just a bit weird having known the victim, that's all."

"You sure?" Joe asked. Glen nodded. "Okay then! Let's get down there before the guv has kittens!" Both men ducked under the tape then made their way carefully round the bend, their eyes narrowing instinctively as they neared the crime scene. The forensic operation was in full swing, although it was being executed by a far smaller team of scientists. They were scattered along a length of tunnel spanning around 50 metres, busily scrutinising various areas of interest for any clues or leads. Sitting atop the bodies of the deceased, the familiar angled walls of a forensics tent obscured the remains and provided the vicinity of the bodies with a defined perimeter. Its interior was illuminated just as starkly as the tunnel, Dr Rothesay's silhouette projecting itself onto the side of the tent as he knelt slowly beside the deceased. Joe looked up and down the illuminated section of the tunnel, searching for DCI Whindle. As he squinted in the glare of the bright lights and white forensic suits, Joe's nostrils were filled with a familiar scent.

"Morning Guys" Jessica's voice was low and mournful.

"Hi Jessica" said Glen. Joe hesitated for a moment. His heart had jumped when he heard Jessica's voice. Despite all that was around them, the death, the dank bricks, the invasive coldness, the sober, forensic activity of the small army of technicians and scientists, he wanted to scoop her up in his arms and kiss her, and hold her body tightly against his as he stared into her eyes and told her how much last night meant to him, and how he dared himself to dream that it wasn't just a one-time occurrence. But he couldn't. Now was not the time, or the place. A police officer was dead, and the number of victims was mounting up quickly. He stared into the darkness as he struggled to find appropriate words. Focussing on the oily metal of the conductor rail, his attention was drawn to it. Narrowing his eyes slightly, he turned his right ear towards it, studying the air.

"Can you hear that Glen?" he said, his back still turned to Jessica. Glen's eyes flicked between Joe and Jessica a few times in confusion.

"Hear what?" he asked. He leaned in, but heard nothing, except the background noise generated by the crime scene investigations going on behind them. Glen looked at Joe, shaking his head. Spinning round, Joe held up his hands.

"People, please!" He shouted. Everyone stopped what they were doing and looked up. "I just need a moment of quiet, thank you" Turning around, he said to Glen "Now listen again" Once more, Glen leaned in slightly. His brow furrowed.

"I can definitely hear something!" he said. "A hum, maybe?"

"That's what I thought it was" said Joe. He knelt down, tilting his head almost to 90 degrees as he listened intently, still ignoring Jessica's presence. By this time, Dr Rothesay had emerged from the tent, and everyone was still looking at the three of them in confusion.

Springing to his feet, he called to a uniformed officer who was standing at the inner cordon tape at the opposite end of the crime scene to where Joe and Glen had entered.

"Does your radio work down here?" The officer looked at him startled.

"We've got separate radio sets for down here Sarge" he said, offering the radio forward as Joe walked briskly toward him.

"Thanks! Joe said. "I need you to get back to the tunnel portal as quickly as you can and make sure that nobody comes down here until I say so!" The officer nodded. Joe snatched the radio from his hand, turning back to everyone working within the crime scene.

"Ladies and gentlemen, I need you to stop whatever it is you are doing and move to a place that is well clear of all conductor rails. Please make sure your equipment is clear too!" They all paused, looking at each other questioningly before moving all equipment away from the conductor rails and gathering in a gap between the rails at the far end of the inner cordon.

"Joe, what are you doing?" said Jessica, stepping forward.

"I'm doing what your idiot uncle should have been doing before anyone came in here!" said Joe, before he could moderate his obvious rudeness. Everybody who had gathered at the other end of the cordon stood silently listening. Joe could almost feel their eyebrows rising collectively. Jessica stood looking at him, the shock on her face evident for all to see. He hadn't intended to be so stern in his reply, he was just so angry at the fact that another two people had needless been killed. Try as he might, he could not stop blaming DCI Whindle. Before Jessica could answer, he keyed the microphone on the radio.

"This is Detective Sergeant Tenby calling Bravo India"

The radio bleeped, then fell into silence for a few seconds, before crackling into life as the operator replied. "Go ahead DS Tenby" The reception in the tunnel was awful, the voice of the middle aged woman on the other end of the line only just intelligible.

"I'm down at the crime scene inner cordon at Hitchworth tunnel. Has anyone isolated the electrical supply to the conductor rails?, Over."

Again, a few seconds of silence.

"DS Tenby, we have not requested any electrical isolation. The railway authority has confirmed that the line is closed to trains so you are safe. Joe was grimacing almost as he listened hard to the speaker.

"Yes, I receive that control, but I wasn't asking if you had requested an isolation! Is the electricity turned off down here?"

"Not sure what you mean DS Tenby" replied the control operator. "I will refer this to the railway authority for clarification. Please stand by" The radio made a squealing type sound before falling into silence. Joe didn't wait for an answer, instead he thrust the radio into his jacket pocket, spinning around and holding up his arms once more.

"Attention please everybody! You need to quickly make sure that you and all of your equipment and evidence are secured, and make your way out of the tunnel. We have to stop the examination until.."

"Until what Tenby?" demanded DCI Whindle as he approached Joe from behind. His suit was dishevelled, and his hair lank and greasy. The DCI's face was a depiction of unshaven fury. "Just who do you think you are, coming down here and disrupting my crime scene? A copper was killed down here, his uniform is still warm! You think this is the time or place for your parlour tricks?" Everybody in the tunnel froze. Joe could not hide his anger. Spinning round, he thrust an accusing finger toward the DCI.

"How dare you?" he snarled. DCI Whindle looked at him blankly. "I have done what I have done for the safety of the people I work with, and the safety of those who will bring PC Mills' killer to justice!" DCI Whindle rolled his eyes dismissively. Shining his torch on the conductor rail, Joe continued. "Do you see that, Detective Chief Inspector? That is a conductor rail. It carries between 650 and 750 volts of Direct Current electricity. It's still humming, which means that nobody has seen fit to have it switched off! There's more than enough current in that rail to kill someone!" The DCI looked down at the rail. Joe didn't give him chance to speak. "You swan around here, making out that I am incompetent, that I'm out of my depth. What have you done to find the killer?" Jessica, who had been quietly walking away following Joe's harsh comment to her, had made her way back, curious as to what the fuss was about. She was standing to his right and stepped forward, placing a cautionary hand on his shoulder. Joe raised his hand without looking, signalling for her to back off. "All you have done since I joined this team is crash around kicking doors and threatening people who are just trying to do their job! If anyone is out of their depth, DCI Whindle, it's you!" A few people took in sharp breaths at this comment. The officers, technicians and forensic scientists gathered in the tunnel were shocked, and equally curious as to what the DCI would do or say in return. His eyes remained fixed on Joe, almost as if trying to burn through his skin. His chest was rising and falling rapidly as he breathed deeply, probably in an attempt to contain his temper, Joe reasoned. Glancing around at the faces encircling him, DCI Whindle paused, before straightening himself up.

"Detective Sergeant Tenby, I think it would be more appropriate if this issue were concluded at the station. Shall we continue with the job at hand people" He paused for a second, nodding towards Joe. "Once these conductor rails have been switched off, obviously!" Without another word, he turned on his heels, marching purposefully toward the tape marking the edge of the inner cordon. Thrusting it skyward, he ducked underneath it, disappearing around the bend and into the darkness.

Outside in the open air, DCI Whindle was pacing back and forth as he bubbled with a mixture of fury and acute embarrassment. He glanced over at Commander Carlton, her uniform immaculate as usual as she fended off questions from eager journalists. He knew that she wanted him out. She saw him as a problem to be dealt with, a dinosaur to be placed in a museum. No doubt she would see this as an opportunity to make out that he wasn't up to the job.

"Uptight little bitch!" he murmured to himself. Turning away from her, he watched Joe, Glen, Jessica and Dr Rothesay emerge from the tunnel, deep in conversation. He knew that he was in danger of being upstaged by DS Tenby. The four of them stood in a huddle, oblivious to all else around them. Suddenly, the familiar figure of Amber Rawson skipped across to the huddle, elbowing her way in. Taking a deep breath, he walked over to them.

The four of them were, up until the intrusion from Amber Dawson, deep in discussion. DCI Whindle was unsure as to how much was a show for the benefit of Commander Carlton, but either way, there was more than a little part of him that saw it as mutiny. His initial priority though was dealing with the unwanted attentions of this nosey reporter. As he walked up, he could hear Joe talking to her, his words as ever smooth and diplomatic.

"Arrogant prick!" he muttered.

"I'm sorry Ms Dawson, this is a restricted area, and you are not getting any comment from me or anyone else, so you need to leave!" Before she could respond, she noticed DCI Whindle, and turned her attention fully toward him, blanking the others.

"Come on Chief Inspector!" she said coyly. "Surely you can tell me something?"

DCI Whindle puffed out his cheeks, exhaling loudly, his breath forming transient vapour trails in the morning air.

"What did he tell you?" Whindle asked, nodding towards Joe.

"All he said was no comment!" she replied, crossing her arms.

"I'll go one better!" Whindle said, leaning forward, beckoning her towards him. She leaned in.

"Fuck off!" he said, flatly.

"I'm sorry?" she said, looking at him with a confused expression.

"I said, Fuck off!" he hissed, jabbing his finger towards the perimeter tape. She looked at the rest of the group. They returned her gaze with blank expressions. Whindle motioned with his head towards the tape once more, smiling falsely. Accepting defeat, she turned and walked back towards the perimeter, shooting an angry look at Whindle as she went.

"So, it looks as if your little theory is dead in the water Detective Sergeant" said DCI Whindle smugly, rubbing his hands. The group swapped questioning glances and looked at him.

"How so?" said Joe, deliberately averting his gaze from the DCI.

"Well, this is clearly an escalation in the killer's activities" said DCI Whindle, stepping into the circle of the group. He continued speaking before anyone had the chance to reply.

"It's obvious that whoever is carrying out these attacks has a grudge against the Police, against authority." Now it was Joe who was rolling his eyes. "Come on Joe!" said DCI Whindle with mock pity. "Just admit that you got it wrong."

"So you're saying that these killings were carried out as revenge?" said Joe through gritted teeth, his anger barely contained. DCI Whindle shrugged.

"Dr Rothesay, did you observe anything at the crime scene that may suggest that the bodies were deliberately arranged? Perhaps they were staged in a particular configuration so as to send us a message? Was PC Mills the first to have been pushed down the shaft, or was our friend the parking attendant first and the bodies re-arranged?" Both Joe and DCI Whindle stared intensely at the increasingly uncomfortable Dr Rothesay. He stared back at them, blinking rapidly.

"Ah, no." he said thoughtfully. "There were no obvious signs of the bodies being arranged, although it is far too early to say at this stage, obviously."

"What about lividity doctor?" asked Joe. The doctor shook his head as DCI Whindle cut into the exchange.

"What about you saving your forensic report for the Senior Investigating Officer, Dr Rothesay?" said DCI Whindle dryly. He turned to Joe, his voice low and calm as he began to speak, the volume rising steadily.

"What about you leaving me to do my job, as incompetent as I clearly am at it, and kindly getting on with your own?" DCI Whindle promptly turned away to face the rest of the group, before turning back and fixing Joe with an icy glare.

"Why are you still here, Detective Sergeant?" Joe electing not to reply, instead stepping backwards away from the group and heading for his car, slowing as Commander Carlton crossed his path, her phone to her ear as she fought desperately to pacify the angry Commissioner. She nodded at Joe as they passed each other.

"Ma'am" said Joe as he fished his car keys from his pocket. Opening the door, he slid into the driver's seat and took a deep breath. His mind wandered onto the DCI's theory about a 'grudge' against authority. He felt his frustration rising as he considered the merits of the theory. There were none. Moreover, there was no previous communications between the suspect and anybody in the police except Joe himself, and the DCI seemed willing to go to any length to dismiss the prospect of the killer wanting to speak directly to Joe!.

"He's leading us down the wrong path" Joe said to himself, hitting the top of the steering wheel with the heel of his hand. Suddenly, the passenger side door opened. It was Glen.

"Talking to yourself Joe!" he said with a smile. Behind him, Joe heard the sound of the driver side rear door opening. He craned his neck as Jessica lowered herself into the car without speaking. He tried to hold her gaze but she looked away. Turning his attention back to Glen, Joe put his head back against the headrest.

"So what's this then?" he said, watching the window slowly steam up.

"I, err..we, thought it would be a good idea to put our heads together" said Glen.

"And?" said Joe, still watching the rising condensation on the windscreen.

"Well, maybe we have to examine the possibility that DCI Whindle is right" said Glen. Joe folded his arms.

"You seriously think that Whindle is onto something by thinking that because a copper and a parking attendant were killed, it's obviously a grudge? Show me the link! Show me the evidence that speaks to any form of escalation from previous behaviours. There are none!" Glen and Jessica smiled at each other as Joe continued. "Are you seriously telling me that the connections to the railway industry that we have been finding are just coincidental? What about the videos?" Glen sat back in the chair, still smiling as he glanced in the passenger side wing mirror. Jessica leant forward, her voice gentle, her lips just inches from Joe's ear. He could feel her breath.

"In that case, perhaps we should prove it!" Joe looked at her, those deep brown eyes wide and alluring. "You won't outgun DCI Whindle Joe. Get into a shouting match with him and you will lose. He's been around for too long and has too many friends. Back up your hunches with facts, and he'll have to accept what you say" Joe smiled as he contemplated her words. She looked down at her lap. Suddenly, Joe grabbed his seatbelt and fastened it, twisting the ignition key and turning on the engine.

"Where are we going?" asked Glen. Joe thrust the gear stick into reverse and started to manoeuvre the car away from the clearing.

"We're going to do what the DCI told us to do DC Violet" said Joe. Jessica and Glen looked at him questioningly. Joe smiled as he took the car out of reverse and started moving slowly forwards. "We're going to find him a cross to nail the killer to. It'll just be a different cross" As he eased the car towards the outer cordon he glanced in the rear view mirror. "Thank you" he mouthed, catching Jessica's gaze.

"Let's just get the job done" she whispered. Gesturing his gratitude, Joe carefully turned onto the road, smoothly accelerating towards town.

68

Reaching down, Steven threw the cupboard door below the worktop open, pulling from the filthy depths a half full bottle of vodka. Twisting the cap, he threw it onto the floor and snatched up a dirty glass, filling it and gasping at the burning sensation of cheap vodka on vocal chords as he took a large mouthful. He stood for a moment catching his breath as he stared at a smear of grime at the top of the kitchen window, his mind transporting him back in time.

Suddenly, he was a boy again. Everywhere he looked there were adults; all dressed in black, and looking at him with pity. The church looked like some vast gothic house of horrors, its pointed roof, sinister carvings, and stone arched road entrance almost sounding a death knell in the onlooker's mind. The immaculate lawns stretched out towards a crumbling wall overgrown with discoloured ivy, the lush green of the grass interrupted at the far end by rows of seemingly ancient gravestones that cast shadows on the boundary wall. A sea of flowers formed a guard of honour for the mourners as they walked solemnly to the church doors. The vicar hovered dutifully, shaking hands and passing condolences as people filed in and took their seats.

"Are you ok little man?" Steven froze. It was him! He felt his body run cold, and his skin turn to goose bumps as a heavy hand settled on his shoulder blade.

"Get off me" he whispered, his eyes scanning the hordes of black suits and dresses in search of his mother. The hand slid across his back and onto the opposite shoulder, pulling him in. He found himself clutched into the waist of a familiar, yet unwelcome adult. Struggling against the strength of the arm that held him, his nostrils filled with the smell of dated aftershave.

"Come on!" soothed the voice from above. "It's okay to be upset. Be brave. Remember. You're a special boy" Steven's stomach lurched. The alarm bells were ringing in his head, and they were warning him of danger. Slowly, the visual memory began to blur and fade, the sound of alarm bells piercing his ears, those in turn being replaced by the shrill tones of a phone ringing.

Walking across the kitchen, he snatched up the phone. It was Robert. For a brief second he considered not answering, but quickly relented.

"What do you want?" he snapped as he wrenched the phone open.

"I know it was you!" hissed Robert. "You broke into Mum's!" Steven chose not to answer, instead smiling to himself, breaking his misery just long enough to appreciate his small victory.

"You know nothing! It was probably some low life looking to score drug money!" Steven spat.

"Come on!" said Robert. "Only photographs were taken you idiot! Why would anyone else only take photographs? You're the only one living in the past! Who else would it be?"

"Go away Robert." Steven said flatly. "Leave me alone and go back to being a yes man for that slag of a mother of ours and her shit head boyfriend!"

"Why did you do it?" shouted Robert.

"More to the point, why did YOU do it?" screamed Steven in response.

"What did I do?" asked Robert, confused.

"Think about it!" he hissed, snapping the phone shut and staring furiously at the screen, before slamming the face of the phone into the filthy work surface repeatedly, then throwing it at the wall, its screen, battery, and several small plastic fragments exploding from the handset and spreading themselves in all directions as he stomped out of the kitchen, an angry growl rumbling from his mouth as he went.

69

Joe sat at his desk, desperately trying to focus his mind on the task at hand as he shuffled papers across his desk. He was still kicking himself for the way he spoke to Jessica in the tunnel, and he could see that it had hurt her to be humiliated by him so publically. He was desperate to make her see that he was sorry, but also was equally desperate to find some evidence that would convince DCI Whindle that he was wrong about the link between the murders. Trying as hard as he could to remove Jessica from his thoughts, he ran through everything that he could remember about each killing in terms of common features. All of them, except these last two were railway employees. All of them were killed on railway property. The behaviour of the killer would suggest some level of railway knowledge, although to what level is a matter for debate. Pausing for a second, he mused over DCI Whindle's logic.

"Why is the DCI so convinced that this is some kind of grudge against the force?" he muttered under his breath as a female constable pushed open the office doors, a bundle of mail under her arm.

"A copper and a traffic warden. It's an easy leap to make Joe" said Glen, his chin balanced on the heel of his palm as he flicked robotically through photos on the computer screen.

"Yeah, but what about the others?" said Joe. "It's as if he is desperate to push the investigation away from any link involving the railway, and I just don't understand why. It's the best link we have." Glen shifted his gaze away from the screen and across to Joe, his tone conspiratorial.

"Perhaps he's the one we're after!" he whispered. Joe raised his eyebrows.

"Idiot!" Joe said, as the constable placed an envelope in front of him, smiling professionally. Glen chuckled as he turned his attention back to the computer screen. Joe's stomach lurched as he examined the envelope. It was identical to the ones he had received previously, and had been delivered by hand.

"I think you'll find it's probably just a case of not wanting to admit that he's wrong" Glen said as he robotically clicked the mouse as he scanned more pictures for evidence. "You know what these senior officers are like Joe. Like to make out they're invincible"

Before Joe could respond, or open the envelope, both men were startled by DCI Whindle behind them. Slamming his hands down on Glen's desk, he leaned in towards him, scowling.

"I've got news for you Violet!" he snarled. Glen leant back in his chair, swallowing hard. "We fucking well ARE invincible!" In an instant his snarl of anger had switched to a smile. Straightening himself up, he stepped away from Glen. "Now, whatever it is you're doing, do it better, and do it faster!" Pausing mid-stride, he span around, and walked over to Joe's desk, a wide smile on his face.

Joe noticed immediately that DCI Whindle had been freshly shaved. He was wearing a different suit and his shoes were highly polished. His hair was immaculate, and he projected the scent of expensive after shave in his wake. Whindle produced a folded piece of paper from his suit jacket, placing it on top of the envelope. "Once you get the hang of the basics, you'll realise that detective work isn't done just off the back of wild hunches!" Joe looked down at the page, unfolding it and studying its contents.

"What's this?" said Joe as he digested the information.

"That, Detective Sergeant, is a summary of the personal details of one, Edward McBride" Joe looked up at DCI Whindle questioningly. "Mr McBride was a special constable in Grantham. He died in a house fire. The coroner returned an open verdict."

"So?" Joe was puzzled.

"So" said DCI Whindle, enjoying the chance to play to the gallery at Joe's expense "Edward McBride was the uncle of a certain Tina McBride. He was a copper!" Joe glanced quickly around the room.

"What does this prove, other than the fact that our first victim has an uncle who at one time was a volunteer police officer, and at one time died in a fire? What about Sean Grant? Is there a link there? Was he drugged too?"

"It proves that there is a link in this case, and I have people looking over Sean Grant's life, as well as Anna Brown as we speak!" snapped Whindle, thrusting the paper back at Joe.

Joe calmly took the paper and laid it on his desk, his posture and facial expression making it clear to all watching, including the DCI that he remained completely unconvinced of the theory's validity.

"I'm just saying that we have limited information to proceed with. Further to that, it's almost as if the last two killings hold an entirely different motivation to the preceding three. I just can't buy into the idea that there are two killers operating with such similar MO's, and I see no link between the victims and the force, other than the last incident" The entire team waited anxiously for the DCI's response. They were as unused to his authority being questioned, as the DCI was himself. Much to their surprise, he didn't explode into rage.

"I'm not paid to justify my decisions to junior officers Tenby!" DCI Whindle said. "I'm paid to catch killers! Edward McBride may yield important clues that will unlock the origin of this grudge against the force. So the team will follow it up. That is what they are paid to do." The phrasing of that last sentence began to ring alarm bells in Joe's mind as he spoke.

"Surely Edward McBride would have been killed because he failed to save someone from a fire, not because he died in one?" DCI Whindle crossed his arms, his facial expression darkening rapidly. "As for a grudge against the force, we're Metropolitan Police. Edward McBride was Lincolnshire Constabulary"

"I know who I work for, thank you very much!" hissed Whindle.

"So that's it then?" asked Joe. "We're ditching all the work and concentrating on this?" DCI Whindle didn't reply. He just stared menacingly. "Can we not at least run tandem lines of enquiry?" asked Joe, although knowing what the answer would be.

"This team run what lines of enquiry I tell them to run Tenby!" DCI Whindle said sternly. Joe sighed. DCI Whindle turned to walk away, heading to his office door.

"So that is it" he said under his breath, hurriedly opening the envelope.

"Oh no!" said DCI Whindle as he stopped in his tracks. "I've always believed in saving the best for last Joseph!" Producing a second piece of paper from his jacket, he unfolded it, holding up a page containing pictures of a blue Volvo, and the man Joe had seen at two of the murder scenes. Joe studied the page open mouthed as he absentmindedly tipped the contents of the envelope onto the desk. We have Edward McBride's son in custody!"

"What?" spluttered Joe. He felt sick. Replaying the incident in his mind, he watched a mental image of DCI Whindle stuffing the piece of paper into his pocket from Joe's notebook into his jacket pocket that had the registration number of the blue Volvo on it! The DCI had even blocked Joe from making further background checks and had flagged this vehicle so that nobody else could check it! "I gave you the registration number for that car! You stopped me from checking it!"

"Simply not true, DS Tenby" Whindle replied coolly. "I received this registration from a confidential informant. As for me stopping you checking this vehicle, all I did was make sure I knew what spurious theories you were wasting taxpayers' money on!" Joe's chest heaved as he blinked rapidly. "About an hour ago, I attended the registered address of Vincent Bridges." As DCI Whindle continued, he pointed to the photograph. "He was arrested on suspicion of murdering Tina Phillips and Anna Brown. He is a collector of historic railway pieces, has a brilliant working knowledge of the railway timetable, has no alibi, and has been captured on video and CCTV in the vicinity of the murders" Joe looked across at Glen, who was equally as amazed. "Best of all" said DCI Whindle "Vincent Bridges claimed at the inquest into his father's death that the house was burned down by a local gang in retaliation for his father arresting one of them! He tried and failed to take out a private prosecution!" Shell shocked, Joe didn't know what to say. Glancing down at the objects that had escaped from the envelope, he was wrenched momentarily from the fury that was building inside him. He picked up the CD that sat on the desk. Like previous ones, there was also a note. The message read;

"ANOTHER INSTALLMENT PAID. THANK YOU FOR THE BONUS!"

"Perhaps you'd care to join me in my office, DS Tenby?" DCI Whindle called over his shoulder as he breezed confidently into his office, closing the door behind him. Swiftly realising that somehow, DCI Whindle had hijacked his suspect from the blue Volvo, Joe was furious! He glanced across at Glen as he slipped the picture and note back into the envelope and put it in his inside pocket. Rising from his chair, Joe once again found himself feeling the burn of his colleagues' collective stare as he crossed the office and knocked on the DCI's door.

Joe entered the DCI's office, closing the door discreetly behind him. Not only had he been double crossed by his own commanding officer, h was also playing catch up to a dramatic change in the DCI's demeanour and standards of personal hygiene. Joe felt positively under-dressed in comparison. Perhaps Commander Carlton had spoken with him about setting a professional example? Whatever the reason, Joe was quickly learning that the DCI had the eternal ability to surprise. He watched DCI Whindle making a show of reading some files on his desk. He considered showing the latest disc to DCI Whindle, but swiftly decided against it. He knew that everyone would be best served by sending it straight to Jessica for analysis, and besides, given what had just happened in the main office, Joe was now weary that the discs would be hijacked by Whindle as well. The DCI looked at Joe briefly, motioning loosely with his hand for Joe to sit, pausing for dramatic effect before speaking.

"Joe, I have to be honest. You concern me." Joe sat back in the chair, his expression deliberately neutral as he listened.

"The step up from traffic is a big one. Nobody would find it easy. I think it's time we have to be frank and open"

"If we're being frank and open DCI Whindle, you just double crossed me out there!" snapped Joe. Whindle smiled, keeping his gaze fixed on Joe as he unbuttoned his shirt sleeves, folding the cuffs of each arm carefully over.

"I'm not here for tribal war Joe. I just want the perpetrator of these heinous crimes to be brought to Justice!" Joe smiled thinly as Whindle dropped his silver cufflinks carefully onto the desk in front of him.

"Come off it!" replied Joe. "You poured cold water on a lead I produced, stopped me from following it up, and then used it to claim an arrest for yourself! Is that how you got the bump to Chief Inspector?" DCI Whindle shifted in his chair.

"Come now Joe!" said Whindle mockingly. "Sour grapes are most unbecoming! Don't take it personally! There is a world of difference between issuing speeding tickets and solving murders! If you did come across Vincent Bridges hanging around at the crime scenes, and you failed to check him out, that isn't my fault! That is you being a poor investigator!" Joe's lip curled slightly as he suppressed his anger.

"You and I both know that you're going in the wrong direction on this investigation!" he spat.

"Are you saying that Mr Bridges is not a person of interest Joe? DCI Whindle asked. He was enjoying himself immensely as he watched Joe grasp for a winning line in the argument. They both knew there were none. "If he's not connected with these murders, why is his arrest such a big deal?"

"I am saying that you are overlooking the obvious!" Joe hissed, struggling to stop himself from raising his voice. "These killings are the result of a grudge against the railway, not the police! You're forgetting the letters and CDs I have received! Why do you insist on ignoring them? I know there is a connection to the railway!"

"I know that I'm the one in charge Tenby!" he said smugly. "Joe, the pressure of a big investigation is clearly getting to you." His tone changed to one of concern. "I think it's best for all concerned if you take a break." Joe glared, his fists clenched. Whindle tapped a couple of buttons on his computer, and the printer whirred into life, spitting out a piece of paper with an official heading on it. Leaning over, he snatched up the page and scribbled a signature at the bottom, before handing it to Joe. Joe studied the content of the page, his eyes widening.

"You're transferring me?" Joe spluttered. "You can't do that!"

"Oh, I can Joe" said Whindle calmly. "I've arranged for your lateral transfer into the Motoring Prosecutions and Enforcement Directorate. It comes into force with immediate effect." Joe sat staring into space, his mouth hanging open. DCI Whindle continued. "It's one thing to drive really fast in a traffic car, but when it comes to proper police work, you have to stand aside and leave it to the real detectives!" Joe didn't react. He was too shocked to speak, his eyes kept scanning the text on the letter over and over again. "Oh, and don't even think of going running to anyone over this. I think you'll find I've done nothing outside of your conditions of service Detective Sergeant! Don't forget that you're on probation following your transfer! If you want to pick a fight over it, I'm happy to square up. Don't forget though, that you failed to follow up on a vital lead, if Commander Carlton were to believe your version of events! You might even win the scrap over being reassigned, but I guarantee you I'm connected well enough in the right places to make sure you get bounced straight off the High Potential Development scheme!" As if on auto pilot, Joe stood slowly, his body trembling with anger. He knew that Whindle was right. He was well connected, and he was vindictive enough to wreck Joe's career. DCI Whindle had turned his attention back to the folder on the desk. He waited a few seconds before looking up at Joe. "Is there a reason you're still here, Sergeant Tenby?" Joe turned and left DCI Whindle's office. He walked over to his desk, pausing only to pick up the CD, and his briefcase. Without saying a word, he silently padded out of the office, walking straight past Glen who was looking up from his computer questioningly, watching as Joe approached the double door at the far end of the room. Joe gently closed the door behind him before heading towards the stairs.

70

Recent events had underlined the importance of prior preparation. In the hours following his last kill, Steven had felt his confidence shaken to its core. Part of him was happy about the fact that he had secured an unexpected bonus whilst 'collecting the debt'. Another part of him was angry that such a casual act of carelessness had almost led to his arrest. Evading the Police was a discipline that he was more than familiar with. Steven had repeatedly scolded himself for allowing arrogance to creep in and blur his judgement. The payment of outstanding justice was one that had to be taken with a cold, calculating head. He had almost failed in his mission, a mistake he would not repeat. He had chosen a side street positioned diagonally across from the old Victorian terraced building. The scars and imperfections dealt to the structure by the passage of time had been covered up with repeated coats of white masonry paint. Rust from the ancient guttering pipes had contaminated the cleanliness of the walls, causing the building to look hideous, standing out from its neighbours like the topping to an outdated blancmange. As he watched, Steven kept a careful eye on the people and vehicles around him. He didn't want to position himself anywhere that was too busy, in case somebody remembered him for whatever reason, but on the other hand, he didn't want to leave the car exposed by being the only vehicle left in a particular place. He looked down at his watch, sighing as a drop of water formed at the top edge of the window pane and ran earthwards, carving out abstract landscapes in its wake. Although he still raged at the world for the cruelty he had received, he felt that he was now more ordered, more balanced in his plans. The debt he was owed was nearly collected in full, and he anticipated justice.

The slamming of a door across the street wrenched his concentration back onto his subject. On the stairs of the garish building opposite, two men stood talking. One was older and scruffy, the other slightly younger, but still in advanced middle age. A dog which was sniffed around the shoes of his grey haired target as the two men talked. With his index finger trembling, Steven ran its tip down a list of phone numbers that were scribbled in a notepad. He already knew the answer to the question that he had asked himself, but he squinted through the window in an effort to compare the number in the notepad to the number illuminated on the large sign above the door. Taking another look in the mirrors of the car, he reached inside his jacket pocket and produced a photograph. He studied the photograph intensely for a moment, its image burning itself into his brain. Putting the photograph on the dashboard, Steven reached behind his seat and grabbed the box of glass shards, choosing a stumpy, chaotic piece. Placing it on top of the photograph, Steven closed the lid and concealed it once more as uncertainty filled his mind. He had nearly paid a dear price for not sticking fastidiously to the plan. Was it really a good idea to add to the list? "Those who owe will be made to pay" he whispered to himself as he deliberated "Does this man owe?" "Will his payment mean that a debtor will pay twice?" his fingers drummed the steering wheel as he considered his options. Moving the glass shard tenderly from the surface of the photograph, he picked it up, studying it as he struggled to make a firm decision. Absent-mindedly he chewed his bottom lip, his eyes gazing blankly at the photograph.

"What would you do, Detective Sergeant Tenby?" he asked aloud, placing the photograph back down on the dashboard and reluctantly tearing his vision away from Joe's photograph. Pursing his lips, Steven watched as his intended target walk slowly down the steps and along the footpath towards the nearby bus stop.

-71-

Joe slouched in his plastic chair, his head bowed as if he were trying to hide behind the screen of his laptop, the chair's back rest turning a lighter shade of greyish blue under the strain of his weight as he read the confirmation details of his 'secondment' back to traffic. It was an office job, and Joe felt as if the pit of his stomach was laden with sludge. He had been backed into a cul-de-sac, and there was nothing he could do about it. Out of the corner of his eye he checked his phone, sighing forlornly at the black screen. It had been black since he had driven Jessica to the forensics lab. She had coolly gotten out of the car, taking from him the latest CD and note, and refusing steadfastly to share any kind of eye contact. That understandable rejection, alongside his removal from the investigation had given him a thorough understanding of what humiliation felt like, and he sat there, almost willing the phone to ring, or a message to come through so that he could tell her how sorry he was for talking down to her so publically. After thirty seconds of staring at it, Joe forced himself to concentrate on the fact that he was being side lined. Taking a deep breath, Joe snapped the lid of his laptop closed. He knew that there was only one way to turn this setback into an opportunity. Unexpectedly, the words of his father filled his mind "There's only one way to get the job you want Joe." His father had repeatedly told him as he progressed through the junior ranks of the police force. "That's to do the job you've got as well as you can!" Joe's father hadn't been a police officer, nor had he been a manager. He was a leader though. He exuded an authority that people seemed to subconsciously recognise, even if they didn't obey. Joe had been aware of this elusive quality as he had grown up, finding it infuriating as a rebellious teenager, those feelings transforming into respect and even envy as he grew to be a man. He had always discounted the advice of his father, believing that the traditional socialist views of a lifelong trade unionist were simply not relevant to an ambitious young member of the police force's High Potential Development scheme. Suddenly though, the flawless logic of his father's words became clear. Knowing what he had to do, he grabbed his phone, scrolling through his contacts until he found the number of his new Chief Inspector. Pressing the call button, Joe picked up the briefcase and headed purposefully for the door. "Jessica will have to wait" he said to himself. "Getting myself out of this hole can't"

Phil took a long, harsh drag on his cigarette. Squinting at the small print of the *Racing Post*, he groped for a pen as he stared at the name of the horse he had spotted.

"Samba's Shadow" he muttered to himself. "3:45 at Beverley" He circled the name of the horse, and threw the pen triumphantly back onto the desk. Satisfied with his afternoon's work, he put his hands behind his head, blowing a long plume of smoke toward the heavily stained ceiling. The office was even more dilapidated than the bar area and function rooms. Once upon a time the walls were a crisp white, the office furniture a deep scarlet. Now, both colours had faded to a point where they simply looked dirty. Phil, like the furniture and the club itself, had seen better days, his beard and hair chaotic at best. On one side of the desk was a diary. Phil kept it handy in the event of someone phoning to make a booking for the function rooms, but business was so slow that this had been almost forgotten in the burgeoning chaos. Luckily, Phil's overheads were low, and his clientele small but loyal, mostly being retired railway workers, old socialists, and drunks looking for the cheapest mouthful of ale in town. Suddenly, the phone rang. So unusual was this, Phil initially stared at the receiver for a second, his brow furrowed in suspicion. After a few rings, he snatched up the receiver. "Milward Club" he said in his best business –like tone. As he listened, a wide smile began to occupy his face as he picked up the pen and grabbed the nearest magazine, cursing silently as coffee stains prevented him from scribbling down the details of his conversation. Throwing it onto the floor, he snatched up the *Racing Post*. "So you want to hold a reunion here next Friday?" said Phil as he tried to hide his excitement. Scribbling the caller's name, he continued to grin as he listened. "The reunion is for forty people? Well, it is slightly short notice Mr Anderson, but I'm sure we can deal with that!" Phil laughed falsely, the professional edge to his voice lapsing briefly as he noted down the final few details. "Well, you're more than welcome to come in to finalise the details and make payment anytime!" Phil nodded as he scribbled a few more notes. "Well, thank you." He said, adopting that business-like tone once more. Before he could exchange pleasantries to close the conversation, the line went dead. Phil looked questioningly at the receiver before returning it to its cradle. He re-read the scrawled notes he had made on the newspaper once more. The caller, a Mr Anderson, wanted to stage a railway staff reunion next Friday for around forty people, and was prepared to pay for catering as well! Feeling as if he had just won the lottery, Phil briefly re-opened the paper, looking once more at the race and horse which he had circled moments earlier. He was only planning to put a £20 bet on the race, but he was now feeling lucky. "What the hell! I'll whack £50 on it!" Phil then reached across for the long neglected diary, flipping through the pages to the relevant date, before copying in the details he had so hurriedly scribbled on his newspaper.

"Why am I here?" Vincent Bridges asked the question as he held DCI Whindle in a challenging glare without blinking. "Let's establish the order of service" DCI Whindle replied, returning the stare and pausing for a full ten seconds before speaking. Glen looked on, flicking his gaze between the two men as he became increasingly anxious at the approach of his senior officer. Bridges sat directly opposite Glen, his posture upright and demeanour neutral. To his right was an empty chair, his solicitor was stood just outside of the door making a particularly animated phone call. Glancing towards the door, Whindle leant on the desk, craning his neck towards the suspect. "I ask the fucking questions here pal!" Vincent's expression remained unchanged. Whindle took off his jacket and sat down, adjusting his chair and opening a folder of papers in front of him. With an apologetic smile, Bridge's solicitor bustled into the room, his long black coat draped carefully over his arm. Glen busied himself with the tape recorder, switching it on and prompting Whindle, and then Vincent's solicitor to declare their identities for the tape. Following suit himself, he sat back as DCI Whindle slowly read the first two pages in the folder.

"Mr Bridges, you've been arrested and informed of your rights, because you have been observed in the immediate vicinity of two murders driving a suspect vehicle. Do you understand those rights?" Glen said, as officiously as he could. Vincent fixed him with a glare, nodding slowly as he chewed gum. "For the tape!" DCI Whindle huffed grumpily, continuing to read.

"Yes. I know why I'm here!" Vincent sighed. Bridges solicitor opened a notepad and brandished a silver fountain pan, scrawling hieroglyphics across the page at an unnatural angle. Whindle's gaze left his papers and followed the sweep of the solicitor's hand. He frowned as he failed to decipher what was being written.

"Let's cut to the chase Vincent!" snapped Whindle. "I am a busy man who has other things to attend to today!" He produced a photograph and slid it across the desk. "Is this is a photograph of your vehicle? The photograph is recorded in evidence as EW01" Vincent looked at the photograph and nodded, crossing his arms. "Why was your car in the area of Upper Charleston railway station on the day this image was captured?" Vincent shrugged.

"That was the day you lot were crawling all over the station!" Vincent said. "I like trains. I was just being nosey!" Whindle smiled falsely.

"There were no trains Vincent!" he snapped. "As you well know, the line was closed because somebody murdered a woman and dumped her on the track!" Bridge's expression changed instantly. He looked at his solicitor. The solicitor stopped scribbling.

"Look!" spluttered Vincent. "I don't know what you're trying to fit me up with here, but I am telling you that I haven't killed anyone!"

"I don't believe you Vincent!" DCI Whindle hissed as he leant forward, holding Vincent's gaze. Pausing, Whindle licked his lips. "I think you managed to trick your way inside the ticket office at Upper Charleston station, I think that you drugged Tina McBride, and I think that you raped and murdered her Vincent!" Vincent Bridges recoiled in shock. He glared at his solicitor, who in turn stared at DCI Whindle.

"I do hope you have more than just an attitude problem to back that accusation up, Detective Chief Inspector!" he said, placing a hand on Vincent's shoulder. Whindle switched his stare from Vincent to the solicitor.

"Did it feel good Vincent?" Whindle asked. Vincent looked at him questioningly. "Did it feel good to violate Tina McBride? Did you like getting that pathetic little dick wet? I'll bet it was a new experience, eh Vincent?" Vincent's solicitor slammed his hand on the desk in protest.

"Detective Chief Inspector!" he bellowed. "Either you retract that baseless and vulgar remark, or I will be making a complaint to your superiors!"

"Stow your outrage!" snapped DCI Whindle. "Your client has a bit of a track record when it comes to violence, don't you Vincent?" DCI Whindle flipped over a page from the folder in front of him. "According to this file here, Mr Bridges, you were formerly employed as a Postman. You were dismissed, and arrested after threatening one of your colleagues with a ceremonial sword!" Vincent sat motionless. He stared straight ahead, pointedly ignoring his solicitor. "Which brings me nicely to the subject of you being seen at the location of another murder!"

"This is bullshit!" sighed Vincent, finally looking across at his solicitor.

"Oh no!" chuckled Whindle. "You were seen hanging around near the location of the murder of Anna Brown by two police officers!" Vincent shifted in his seat.

"I haven't killed anyone! I'm no rapist!" he shouted.

"What was it Vincent?" spat Whindle. "Did you fancy something a little tighter? I bet she felt good!"

"What is wrong with you?" asked Vincent, his brow furrowed.

"Well, Tina McBride was middle aged. Anna Brown was a teen. I'm just wondering if you decided that you wanted to upgrade to a nice, tight, newer model? Maybe you were seen hanging around because you wanted to relive that feeling of power, that tight sensation!"

"You're sick!" said Vincent as he shook his head slowly. Glen had been busily scribbling notes as the interview went on. He looked up in disbelief.

"I have you at two crime scenes Vincent!" said Whindle. "My detectives are searching for any sign of you or your car in the vicinity of the third and fourth!"

"DCI Whindle, you still haven't produced any evidence that isn't circumstantial!" said the solicitor. Whindle sat back in his chair and smiled. He crossed his arms.

"You don't like the police, do you Vincent?" he said.

"Can't say I'm that fond of you!" Vincent shrugged.

"You tried to sue Lincolnshire Constabulary over the death of your father. According to the court records, you accused them of leaving your father to be hunted like a fox on new year's day!" Whindle spread three sheets of paper across the table, tracing his finger along lines of text as he spoke.

"I was upset. Looking back I can see that they weren't to blame. He took the risk by being working for you lot!" Vincent eyed the papers nervously.

"That just doesn't work for me!" said Whindle. "I have a string of murders, you're hanging around them like a bad stink! I now have a dead copper to add to the body count! You can polish history all you like Mr Bridges, but we both know that you're talented when it comes to holding a grudge! You held a grudge against your colleague in the Post Office, and you hold a grudge against the police for the death of your father!"

"That dickhead at the post office was a bully! He wouldn't leave me alone! The managers wouldn't listen! As for the police, I told you! My dad took a risk and he got killed! I blame the bastards who burned him alive, not the police, and I am certainly not a cop killer!" Bridges was almost pleading in his response. Whindle was unmoved.

"Mr Bridges, where were you three nights ago?" he asked.

"I was at a friend's house all evening." Bridges replied.

"Does this friend live anywhere near Newcastle?" asked Whindle. Bridges frowned.

"Newcastle? No. They live in Clerkenwell!"

"Can you prove this?" asked Whindle, his smile fading. Vincent paused for a moment, chewing his lip as he considered his options. He lent into his solicitor's ear and whispered. His solicitor cleared his throat.

"Chief Inspector, my client spent the evening with a prostitute" he said, matter of factly.

"Do you expect me to believe that you spent all night with her?" Whindle spat. "More likely ten minutes!"

"I was there from around 7 until 10pm" Vincent whispered, his face flushing with embarrassment.

"You'll need to prove it, stud!" Whindle said sarcastically. He snatched a piece of paper from the folder and slid it across to Vincent. "Wrote her name here" he ordered. Obediently, Vincent scribbled a name on the sheet and slid it back to Whindle. Without looking at it, Whindle pushed it across to Glen.

"Go and check this out. Now" he said. Silently, Glen got up and slipped on his jacket, confirming for the tape that he was leaving the room. As he left, Whindle checked his watch.

"You want to hope and pray that this whore backs you up Mr Bridges" he said. "Interview suspended at 17:22"

74

Joe watched two traffic officers walk up to the staff entrance. One of them removed his white cap as they chatted, fiddling with a stray thread on the inside of the hatband as his colleague swiped his access card through a reader. The imposing steel gate that protected the building from the car park protested noisily as it slid backwards along a rail, coming to an unceremonious rest against the giant frame that held it in place. As both officers casually walked through and disappeared behind the grey steel expanse of metal fencing, Joe couldn't help but compare the gate to that of a prison. He felt like an inmate with no chance of parole, and no possibility of escape. Checking his watch, he realised that it was time he started preparing to meet his new senior officer for the first time. He hadn't heard the name of his new boss before, but then again, the department he had been 'transferred laterally' to was somewhat of an enigmatic one. Their offices were separate to the rest of the division, as were their rest facilities. Every door was controlled by swipe card entry, and covered by what seemed like legions of CCTV cameras. Joe had received written details of his departmental move, along with an access card and directions to the part of the building where he would be working. Even so, he felt as if he were awaiting dispatch into a foreign world from which there would be no return. Reaching for his phone, he picked it up from the dashboard. Checking it for messages, his shoulders sagged once more as he saw that Jessica had still not replied to his numerous calls. The lack of any reply from Jessica was beginning to make him think that he had lost her before he even had her, and it made him angry with himself.

"This is stupid!" he said as he scrolled through the contacts in his phone. Locating Jessica's number, he stabbed the 'call' button with his thumb, checking his mirrors as he waited for the phone to connect. The phone rang once before being abruptly sent to answer phone, Jessica's light, smooth voice instructing the caller to "Go ahead and leave a message" Joe sighed, stopping himself from leaving a rambling, agitated monologue, instead trying his best to conceal his frustration by leaving a polite reminder that he had called a few times, that he really needed to speak with her, and can she please "Call soon" as they both had issues to sort out. Looking at himself in the rear view mirror, Joe breathed out loudly and reached behind him, grabbing his jacket from the back seat. Opening the car door, he stepped out, slipping the jacket on as he looked at the opposite row of cars. Spying the bright red 'SAAB' belonging to the Inspector he had been assigned to, Joe felt pleased that he had taken the initiative by phoning his new boss and breaking the ice, his father's advice still ringing loudly in his ears. Inspector Lynch certainly seemed nice enough. He was definitely much easier to handle than DCI Whindle.

"Yep, you've really stitched me up Whindle" he whispered to himself as he crossed the car park. "You might have won this battle, but I will win the war, and you will not keep me down!" Walking over to the large gate, he swiped the card through the reader and waited for the gate to slide open, keeping that positive train of thoughts at the front of his mind as he strode toward the main doors, forcing a professional smile onto his face.

75

"The DCI is not going to like this!" hissed Glen under his breath as he stared down at the papers in front of him. Glen was alone in the main office, having just arrived as everybody else was going home. Glen was uneasy about the fact that he had chosen to take the side of DS Tenby in the on-going struggle that existed between Joe and DCI Whindle. He knew deep down that Joe was right to say that the guv's theory of a vendetta against the police was clearly a wrong one. He had checked out the prostitute who Vincent Brides claimed to have spent the evening with. Initially, she had denied all knowledge of Bridges, but after some gentle coaxing, and a thinly veiled threat to check her immigration status, she had reluctantly corroborated his story. The interview, and DCI Whindle's haranguing of the suspect hadn't convinced Glen of Bridges' guilt, and he knew enough to realise quickly that it wouldn't convince Commander Carlton, never mind a jury. It appeared that Vincent liked her company as well as her body. He paid her for the full evening to spend time together. He was a regular customer, and she had taken pity on him and invited him to stay at her flat. She confirmed that they had sex, and that they had spent the remainder of the evening watching television programmes in silence. In response, Glen had spent the rest of the day searching every possible connection between the victims in a search for even the most tenuous link that may give credence to Whindle's hunch. As he searched, he thought of Joe. It wasn't that he wanted to prove Joe wrong, he just wanted to avoid doing anything that might provoke more outbursts from his boss. Looking up over the top of his computer monitor, he could see Whindle hunched over his desk, muttering to himself as he scribbled notes. He had been acting more strangely in the last day or two, his temper becoming more volatile and his actions more bizarre. Glen looked at the picture of the prostitute he had been interviewing. Vladimira was an undeniably pretty woman, of slight build with pale skin, blonde hair and bright green eyes. Her looks made it obvious that she would have no shortage of clients, but despite this she had been categorical in confirming that Vincent Bridges was at her flat in North London for the majority of the evening when Sean Grant had been murdered 350 miles away. As he read the data on the papers for the ninth time, Glen couldn't deny to himself anymore that the DCI was leading the investigation in completely the wrong direction.

"There's nothing for it" he said under his breath as he slid the pages back into their folder and stood up. Smoothing down his shirt and straightening his tie, he scooped up the folder and walked across to DCI Whindle's office, pausing at the door before knocking firmly.

"What do you want Violet?" snarled Whindle from behind the door. DCI Whindle was still hunched over his desk, scribbling furiously on a notepad, his top lips curled slightly in anger as he wrote. Glen coughed politely. Whindle didn't react. Glen stood there silently, becoming increasingly aware of the aroma of whiskey that hung in the air. He was unsure of what to say. It was obvious that the guv was not in a good mood. It was more than likely that he was hung over. Glen had seen him twisting the cap off whiskey bottles and taking large mouthfuls whenever he thought that nobody could see him.

Inspecting the office, it was apparent that Joe was right about the DCI.

"What is it?" spat Whindle as he continued taking notes.

"The prostitute" stammered Glen, holding up the folder. Whindle still didn't look up.

"The one who entertained Vincent Bridges? What about her?" he asked.

"She confirmed his story sir!" Glen said quietly.

"What?" spluttered DCI Whindle. "He was there all evening?" He picked up a coffee cup from the desk and swilled the contents as he glared at Glen.

"She says he was there from just before 7 until after 10pm. They had sex and then watched TV"

"Is he a punter or her boyfriend?" asked Whindle.

"He pays her for her time!" replied Glen. "She said he is a regular. He has sex with her and then pays her to spend the evening with him so he's not lonely!"

"So he couldn't have been in Newcastle at the time of the murder?" Whindle muttered to himself, the contents of the cup still swirling.

"Who is she anyway? Whindle asked. "Does she have a record?"

"Yes guv!" replied Glen as he produced the photograph and held it up for DCI Whindle to see. As Whindle glanced at the picture, the cup slipped from his grasp, bouncing across the desk and flooding it with tepid brown liquid. Glen froze momentarily, before grabbing for some paper towels and offering them to his boss.

"Never mind my clumsiness! Just carry on the background checks as I asked!" hissed Whindle, continuing to stare at the picture

"I've been over everything guv. Looked at every victim, their relatives, work mates, friends, lovers, bosses. I've even looked at their school records and teachers. I can't find anything to suggest a connection to the police service"

Whindle threw the sodden paper towels on the table, his fingers trembling slightly.

"You'll have missed something. Go back! Try looking at Police Cadet Records, and also look at juvenile reports and records. It's not rocket science Violet!"

"I've already checked the police cadet archives, and I've checked each victim. The only one to have any record was Sean Grant. That was for drunk and disorderly when he was 15. He was given a conditional discharge. No basis for a dispute, no record or suggestion of a grudge. I'm really sorry guv!"

Whindle breathed deeply, clearly trying to contain his temper as a constant stream of coffee spilled noisily onto the floor.

"First that idiot Tenby, and now I have a snotty nosed DC trying to tell me how to do my job!" Glen froze. "Don't you dare tell me where this investigation is going! I decide what, for how long, and when you investigate leads Violet! You do as you're told! I'm telling you that there is a link between these victims and the police! Now fuck off out of my office and find it!"

Glen flinched at DCI Whindle's words. Steeling himself, he spoke.

"Sir, I have prepared a detailed report on each avenue of investigation I have undertaken, if you care to have a look, I'm sure you'll see I've been quite thorough" Cautiously, he held the folder at arm's length, offering it to DCI Whindle. Whindle looked at the folder as he spoke, his voice increasing in volume.

"I don't want reports full of bullshit excuses Violet! I want results! I want that link! Take that report and shove it in the bin. Write me one telling me what the fucking link is that will break this case!"

Glen's arm remained outstretched for a fraction of a second too long. Whindle sprang forward and grabbed the folder. Glen recoiled in surprise.

"Get out!" shouted Whindle. Glen paused like a rabbit caught in the headlights.

"Go on!" screamed Whindle. "Get the fuck out!"

Glen didn't need further direction. He grabbed at the door handle, managing to wrench it open and pull himself through the doorway into the relative safety of the main office. As he turned to look at the door, his report hurtled through the air, narrowly missing his left ear before it crashed to the carpet in a violent heap. Instinctively, Glen ducked and turned away, staring disbelievingly at the pile of papers that were strewn across the floor. As he stooped to pick them up, he heard heavy footsteps approaching him from the direction of the office. Before he could react, DCI Whindle had stomped past him, slowing his pace long enough to glare furiously as he approached the open doors.

Glen carried on scooping up the loose sheets of paper as he tried and failed to make sense of what had just happened.

Fishing his mobile from his pocket, Joe looked at the screen as it vibrated. It was Amber Rawson again. Taking a deep breath, Joe answered the call.

"Tenby." He said.

"Joe!" Amber replied with false glee "How lovely of you to answer my call!"

"What do you want Amber?" Joe asked. He was due to meet with Inspector Lynch, and certainly did not want Rawson knowing that Whindle had bounced him from the investigation.

"Why are you so cagey Joe? Amber asked. "All I want is to know what's happening with the investigation. The public are rightly concerned about these murders. Now that Vincent Bridges has been cleared of all involvement, they want to know that you're close to catching a suspect!" Joe stared disbelievingly at the phone.

"Bridges has been cleared!" he thought to himself. "This throws the case wide open!" Keeping his attention firmly on the phone call, Joe hesitated for a second before replying, choosing his words carefully.

"Amber, you know that investigations are on-going. You know also that I can't tell you any more than that. Goodbye."

"Hang on Joe!" she said before he could end the call. "I still have a couple of questions"

"Go on then!" Joe sighed, checking his watch. "It's not as if I'm going to tell you anything anyway, but ask away!"

"Okay, well first of all, what's the deal with you and the brunette who works in your forensics lab?"

"The deal, Ms Rawson, is none of your business! She and I are friends and colleagues. Will there be anything else?"

"Yes. Why are you now working from the Road Policing Headquarters, Detective Sergeant Tenby?"

"I beg your pardon?" Joe spluttered.

"It's a simple question" she said, her voice almost purring. "I heard you were stationed in the enforcement section Joe. Rumour has it you've been bounced from the team!"

"Listen!" Joe spat, struggling to maintain his calm. "Nobody has bounced me from any team! I am working with colleagues in other policing sections as part of an active investigation. It's quite routine, and all part of pursuing various lines of inquiry. So stop wasting everybody's time by trying to make a fairy story up to get yourself attention!" Before she could say anymore, Joe finished the call and stuffed his phone back into his pocket. Just at that moment, Inspector Lynch appeared across the office, beckoning Joe with a smile. Joe raised his hand in acknowledgment and made his way across the room, still inwardly furious at Amber Rawson.

"It's all really quite straight forward Joe" said Inspector Lynch, Joe's new supervising officer as he guided Joe through the workings of his new departmental home. Lynch's voice was a nasal monotone which grated on Joe as he persevered with the Inspector's continued attempts to make his department sound more exciting than it possible ever could be. Clearly he was trying to engage in modern management techniques, having ditched his tie in favour of an open neck with a white t-shirt beneath, but it was plain to see that he was far from comfortable. Not that Joe particularly cared. He was struggling to maintain his level of concentration and composure as he battled to block out the memory of his heated exchange with Amber Rawson.

Joe stared as hard as he could at the coated window opposite him, but could only just make out the branches of a tree as it swayed rhythmically in the breeze, its blossom floating majestically through the air, unbridled by boundaries, fading offices, or over-zealous DCI's. Suffering suddenly from claustrophobia and blossom envy, Joe wrestled his thoughts back to what Inspector Lynch was saying.

"We have a regular shift progression between Speed Camera Verification, where we double check the particulars of vehicles which have set off a camera and which have a problem with the vehicle details or owner registration, and our Litigation Referral section, where we pass those who refuse to pay on to the legal eagles" He smiled broadly at Joe as he enjoyed the wordplay of that last sentence, inviting Joe into the conspiracy of the comedy. Joe didn't take up the invitation. Looking around him, he couldn't help but feel that everything was somehow dry, lifeless, bereft of passion or energy. As he made occasional notes about procedure, Joe's mind found itself puzzling over the glass shards.

"That cannot be a coincidence!" he thought to himself as he smiled at another lame joke from Inspector Lynch. "It simply has to mean something! I'll bet he's pissing himself with laughter at how stupid we've been by not picking up on his messages!" Glancing up at Lynch, he satisfied himself that the Inspector was still indulging a love of his own voice, which left him free to continue. He stared at a computer image of a green BMW that had triggered one of the permanent speed cameras on the A2. Passing in the opposite direction was a dark blue Toyota Carina, the driver's face partially obscured. It only served to deepen his distraction from Inspector Lynch. Vincent Bridges had been cleared, so that surely meant that his car couldn't be the same car seen in the vicinity of Anna Brown's house. At first glance the vehicle seemed not to be out of place, but with a second look it was clear that the blue car had some kind of damage to the rear. He flipped over a page in his notebook, noting down the major points of procedure he was being told. Lynch was explaining how to import the images from the database to an official notification form to be sent to the alleged keeper of the vehicle. Clearly, he was enjoying himself. Trying not to lose track of what the inspector was telling him, Joe found that his attention was being drawn to the rear damage to the car on the screen. He searched his mind frantically.

"Andy Mills chased a blue car with rear end damage!" his mind whispered as he stared intently. "Oh my god!" he hissed. Inspector Lynch stopped talking and stared at Joe.

"Sorry" said Joe. The inspector blinked four or five times as he considered Joe's seemingly random statement before electing not to respond. He smiled politely and continued his briefing, the words melting into a strange echo as Joe simply stopped listening. He felt as if he had walked into his bedroom and spied a venomous snake skulking beneath the duvet. "Could this be the blue car that was described by witnesses in the Anna Brown murder?" he thought to himself. "Could it really be the car that Andy Mills chased out to Hitchworth Tunnel?" Remembering to nod in the right places so as not to give Inspector Lynch the impression that he was not listening, Joe resumed his scribbling. Now though, the notes he was scribbling so intently were revolving around the vehicle on the screen in front of him. He made a note of the licence plate details, and the time, date and location of the photograph, along with the identification details of the traffic camera. Chewing on the end of the pen, he considered as many different questions needing urgent investigation as he could think of "Who is the driver? Was this vehicle involved?" Most importantly, Joe recognised that he had to engineer a way of feeding this new information into the investigation, whilst at the same time keeping it clear of the poisonous influence of DCI Whindle. Jessica seemed to be growing in confidence, and seemed willing to stand against her uncle, but at the same time she failed to keep to herself previous attempts by Joe to make more discreet investigations of his theories. As he realised that Inspector Lynch had been waiting for a response from him for almost 30 seconds, Joe became aware also of the fact that the room seemed to be getting hotter.

"You'll have to excuse me Inspector" said Joe as he pushed his chair away from the desk and made for the fire escape.

"Are you okay Joe?" asked Lynch

"I'm fine thanks" Joe replied with a forced smile. "I just need a breath of fresh air, that's all. "Your briefing has been very in depth, I just need to digest everything you've told me so far. I hope you don't mind" Before Inspector Lynch could answer, Joe pushed the bar on the fire door and disappeared onto the fire escape, grateful for the steady breeze as he searched for the swaying tree, smiling to himself as he watched yet more blossom making it's escape, his smile fading as he wished forlornly that he could do the same.

Joe clawed at his tie, yanking it away from his collar. Undoing the top button, he breathed deeply as the cool air soothed the skin of his neck that had previously been hidden. He leant forward, his arms gripping the hand rail of the fire escape as he stared across the car park, past the security fences and over the open countryside that seemed to roll endlessly toward a nest of towering wind turbines. Joe closed his eyes as he tried to place his hurtling thoughts into some kind of order. He was reminded of the lyrics to the chorus of *Bullet with the Butterfly Wings* by Smashing Pumpkins.

"Despite all my rage I am still just a rat in a cage" he sang under his breath. With each glimpse he took, that rolling countryside, and the cantering blades of the wind farms seemed farther away. The walls of the office seemed to be closing in, his new colleagues seeming to be turning ever more faceless and grey as they laboured at their desks. He felt as though he had at last seen the weak, glimmer of light radiating from the far portal of this long and very black tunnel, but had come across a locked gate in his attempts to escape into the warmth of the sun. The chaotic spinning of his mind was slowed by a vibration from his phone. It was Glen.

"JUST BEEN IN WITH DCI. UR RIGHT. HE'S LOSING IT! BRIDGES WAS WITH A PROSTITUTE AT TIME OF SEAN GRANT MURDER. WHINDLE NEARLY ATTACKED ME WHEN I TOLD HIM, THEN STORMED OUT. NOT SURE WHAT TO DO NEXT. G"

Joe read the message a further three times. It was clear that he was needed. DCI Whindle was either on the edge of a massive breakdown, or a spectacular strategic error that could well seal his fate as a senior investigator. Reading the last part of Glen's text, Joe chewed his lip as he tried to come up with a plan to rescue the investigation.

"I know the feeling Glen" he said to himself as he called Jessica. Joe heard four shrill rings before the call was sent on to the answer phone.

"Jessica, please pick up! I need to talk to you! Please, for the sake of the investigation, get back to me!" Joe slowly closed the phone, and glanced over his shoulder, seeing that Inspector Lynch was hovering. It was time to return to the reality that sat before him. As he trudged back inside, the sound of Jessica's voice from her answer phone greeting played in a loop in his head. As he sat down at his desk, once again listening patiently and smiling at intervals as Inspector Lynch droned on, he came to a decision. He had felt sorry for himself for far too long. The victims he had seen as part of the investigation were not afforded the luxury of self-pity. He had a duty to them to not allow this investigation to run off course. He knew that he had the key to unlocking it; he just had to figure out which lock that key belonged in. His new resolve drowned out the intoxicating, addictive sounds of Jessica's voice, and replaced them with the deep, authoritative tones of his father's.

"Remember son, you get your next job off the back of doing the one you have as well as you can"

"You're right Dad!" Joe thought to himself as he re-fastened his top button and straightened his tie. "The time for talk is over. I have to make things happen!"

Robert sat in the armchair opposite Joyce, his eyes switching between Graham's bruising and the damaged cabinet as he nursed a cup of coffee. His brother's outburst, and the revelations that had come to light at his father's grave had brought him even closer to Graham, and his mother, and he felt a duty to be happy for them. As he took a sip of coffee, Graham caught his gaze.

"It'll heal, eventually" he said with a smile, his hand automatically rising to the purple skin covering his left cheek.

"Sorry about that Graham" said Robert as he breathed out in reaction to the hot liquid.

"Why are you apologising?" said Graham. "You haven't done anything!"

Joyce sighed as her eyes looked skyward in search of inspiration.

"He's a very angry man Robert" said Graham softly. "Don't take this the wrong way lad, but I don't think you'd be able to cool him off. He needs two things to sort him out. The first thing is a dose of home truths, and the second thing is enough time to come to terms with them!"

"I do worry about him though!" said Joyce as she fiddled with her wedding ring, an expression of worry etched upon her face. "He's just so eaten up with anger and hatred. He can't carry on like this forever!"

"Don't go holding your breath!" said Graham. An uneasy silence befell the three of them as they sat in awkward reflection.

"Did your Mam tell you Robert? I've been invited to a reunion?" Graham smiled in an attempt to break the mood. Robert reciprocated.

"Are you going?" he asked, spreading his gaze between Graham and his mother.

"I don't know about that!" said Joyce as she rose from her chair and walked toward the kitchen with her empty cup in her hand. She paused in the doorway. "A room full of drunken old railwaymen, swapping stories about locomotives and broken signals? I never used to go to those reunions when they actually invited me, never mind as a gate crasher!" Graham shook his head as the three of them laughed.

"It'll do you good to get out for a change!" said Robert as Joyce disappeared into the kitchen.

"Besides" interjected Graham with a mischievous smile. "They're sending two tickets, so I'll have none of this talk about you being a gate crasher!"

"Hmm!" replied Joyce from the kitchen. Graham and Robert exchanged hopeful grins. "We'll see" she said as she opened the refrigerator. Neither Graham nor her son could see, but she was smiling as she reached inside and took out a Victoria sponge.

"Got her!" whispered Graham. Both men nodded as they chuckled.

"Should be a good night by the sounds of it!" said Robert, his eyes being drawn to the cake as Joyce brought it in from the kitchen and placed it on the table.

"Yes well I haven't decided whether I'm going yet!" hissed Joyce as she cut the first slice. "Now eat your cake!" she said as she placed the slice on a small plate and put it in her son's lap.

"Course you'll go!" snorted Robert. "We'll see means yes!" Joyce hesitated as she looked at Robert and Graham, who were trying their best to avoid laughter as they looked back at her, smiling.

"We'll see!" she said, her voice cracking with laughter. The three of them exchanged broad smiles as she shared out the cake.

78

As soon as she had sat down, Jessica was standing again, waspishly flitting around the table to double check a particular evidence bag or container. She was angry, partly at Joe, but also at herself for allowing even the tiniest semblance of pettiness to infiltrate her usually flawless professionalism. She had felt so humiliated and hurt by the way he spoke to her in the railway tunnel, but no matter how hard she tried, she was drawn heavily to him. He wasn't an Adonis, and he certainly had shown her that he was at times anything but charming, but there was a raw honesty to him, an inner passion for exposing the truth and righting wrongs. Biting her bottom lip, she stared across at one of the many evidence containers awaiting processing, desperately seeking distraction as she scrutinised the video clips that Joe had been sent. The edge of a glass shard was catching the harsh light of the laboratory, almost as if it were winking at her. Making an effort to ignore the glass, Jessica focused on the video analysis. She had played the clip almost on a constant loop, and yet had never once failed to wince, despite knowing advance what was about to happen on the screen. The footage was less chaotic than the previous clip they had received, though no less disturbing. A young woman presumed to be Anna Brown was staring from the screen, her face so close to the camera that the perimeters of her features were lost. Her eyes seemed somehow pleading, as if she were looking for something or someone. She spoke directly to the screen, her voice flat and bereft of emotion.

"Joe. I'm here because of you. You could have saved me! Goodnight Joe!" she said, not blinking once. Abruptly, the screen filled with a harsh light, the speakers screaming with the unmistakeable sound of a train horn as the front of a locomotive appeared menacingly over Anna's shoulder. Jessica resisted the urge once more to scream at Anna to get out of the way, the sound of a violent impact, probably the camera being propelled through the air, filled the room as the screen went black. After a second or two, the screen came back to life. The camera zoomed in gently on a severed hand carefully laid on the wooden lengths of a railway crossing. The hand was clutching a piece of mirror. The top of the cameraman's head was fleetingly visible in the mirror as the camera rocked and trembled. From the rhythmic shaking, and sound of laboured breathing, it was clear that the cameraman was finding this sight highly arousing. After a minute or so, the heavy breathing calmed and the footage steadied, the distorted sound of laughter rolling into a fade as a caption appeared underneath the amputated limb.

"GIVE YOURSELF A HAND JOE! EGO SUM JUSTICIUM"

She had been disturbed at the personal way in which the killer seemed intent on speaking to Joe. She knew that if someone was trying to communicate with her on such a deranged level, she would struggle to deal with it, and despite the recent animosity, she felt the need to make sure he was ok. So far though, her resolve had held firm. Rewinding the clip to the point where the killer was visible in the reflective glass, she paused it and positioned the cursor over the glass. Just as she steadied her hand, her phone rang. It was Joe.

"Shit!" she whispered. For a brief second, she debated whether now would be a good time to tackle Joe, but before she could talk herself out of it she pressed the 'accept' button on the screen and gently positioned the phone at her ear.

"Joe" she said flatly

"Jessica, look. This need to be sorted out!" said Joe as gently as he could.

"Now is not the time to be discussing personal issues" she said as she reached for the computer mouse and opened up a fresh window on the screen.

"I'm not ringing to talk about us" replied Joe. "Well, I am, but not initially"

"What do you want Joe?" she sighed as she enlarged the partial image of the killer and copied it to the new screen. Joe hesitated, taken aback by her coldness. "What else can you want?" she said. "I mean, it's not as if you're on the investigation anymore, is it? DCI Whindle has been telling everyone you've been transferred at your request!"

"Yes, well your uncle hasn't been a paragon of honesty lately!" hissed Joe as his temper spiked for a second.

"My uncle is an experienced detective who is under a lot of pressure!" replied Jessica sternly. Pushing the computer mouse away, she had already decided to stop until after she had finished her conversation with Joe.

"I can't argue with Whindle's experience" said Joe "but I can't stand by and watch him ruin this investigation!"

"Ruin your reputation more like!" she snapped, immediately

regretting her outburst. She winced as she listened to Joe breath in sharply on the other end of the line. With each blow she landed on him, it was becoming harder to withhold Joe's new potential lead, but he stowed his frustration, knowing that the time for sharing would come soon, although now was definitely not it.

"Let me tell you something about your precious uncle" said Joe, his voice calm and his speech carefully enunciated. "He's told everybody that I requested a transfer because I can't do the job. I'm telling you that I made no such request. Why would I? You know how much I love that job!" Jessica listened silently as she considered his words, acknowledging inwardly that, given Joe's enthusiasm for his new job, asking for a transfer simply didn't make sense. She knew in her heart that Joe was right, and continued to listen as he spoke. "At the same time as he's trying to torpedo my career for his own ridiculous personal reasons, he's torpedoing this investigation! Your uncle doesn't want to examine my theory because it's my theory! He's allergic to my help Jessica! The killer isn't as picky as your uncle! He will accept whatever breaks come his way to avoid being arrested!" Finally, Jessica was conceding that Joe was right. She had been battling the realisation for a while now. She simply didn't want to imagine that her uncle were capable of allowing a personal vendetta to impede the hunt for a serial killer.

"So what do you want me to do?" she said softly as she grabbed the pen and notepad that were sitting on her desk. "Go back over all the evidence recovered from every crime scene" he said. He could hear her scribbling. "Look for any trace, no matter how small of similar glass shards or pieces. It could be just a shattered little square in amongst dust, leaves and ballast, but it might give us something solid."

"Okay" she said. "Then what do we do?"

"Then, providing we catch a break on the theory, we take it to Commander Carlton."

"I don't know Joe" she said, "That could ruin Whindle's career"

"We need to act!" said Joe. "We can't take it to Whindle because he'll discount it all regardless of the strength of evidence! He damn near smacked Glen because he couldn't find any evidence of a link to the police for god's sake!"

"Oh my God!" she exclaimed. "Is he okay?"

"He's fine!" spluttered Joe as her question threw him from his train of thought. "Glen's a big lad! Judging by the size of him, he'd be able to handle Whindle with no problem."

"That's what he wants you to think" she said. "The only reason he's bulked up is because he can't talk his way out of trouble. Unlike some people I can think of!" Joe smiled. "I couldn't possibly imagine what you mean Miss Hopewell!" he said playfully. "Besides, we're getting off subject! Are we okay with examining the glass evidence, taking another look at everything recovered from all crime scenes, and then presenting whatever we find directly to Commander Carlton?" Joe took a deep breath as Jessica paused. "Okay" she said finally, her defences coming down once more and the familiar softness of her voice returning. "I'll examine all the evidence, but it's going to take a little time. I've got to do this all below the radar, you need to fly below the radar too!"

"I know" said Joe. "Jessica"

"Yes?" she asked.

"I'm not doing this to ruin your uncle. I just want to find the killer and get my job back. That's all."

Jessica smiled. "I know"

"So now we've got that sorted" Joe said cheekily "What about us?"

Jessica laughed.

"One thing at a time tiger!" she said playfully before hanging up the phone and turning her attentions back to the glass inside the container.

79

DCI Whindle didn't even have time to react to the stern knocking at his office door before the door was thrust open as Commander Carlton paraded in.

"Do come in Ma'am" he said dryly as he forced a smile.

"Sarcasm is most unbecoming of you Evan!" snapped the Commander as she sat down, smoothing her skirt against the backs of her thighs as she lowered herself into the chair. As much as he detested the woman, Whindle couldn't resist grabbing a small glimpse of her smooth, toned legs as they disappeared beneath the material of her uniform. Commander Carlton knew that she was attractive and intimidating in equal measure, and she used both qualities to their maximum effect.

"Can I help you with something Ma'am?" he asked.

The commander smiled.

"As a matter of fact Detective Chief Inspector, you can. I'm here for a progress report. I need results on this case Evan! After your false dawn with regard to Vincent Bridges, the Commissioner is getting restless, and worse still, the press are getting restless!"

DCI Whindle shrugged.

"At the present time there isn't really anything significant that I can tell you" he said. Commander Carlton pursed her lips, shaking her head slightly. DCI Whindle knew that what he had to say would simply not be good enough, bracing himself for the expected lecture, he sat back in his chair.

"We're following up on a number of leads as we speak Ma'am. We still believe that the killer has a grudge against the police, which directly manifested itself in the last two killings, and we're back tracking through the histories of the other victims in an attempt to substantiate the theory with hard facts" Commander Carlton raised her eyebrows.

"Is that really the best you can do Evan?" she asked.

"I beg your pardon Ma'am?" he said as he leaned forward, his facial expression one of puzzlement. The commander waved his question away with a sweep of her hand.

"What's this I hear about DS Tenby?" she said. "All of a sudden I have people telling me that he has requested a transfer?"

"What can I say Ma'am?" said DCI Whindle with mock concern. "Sometimes people seem to be ready for a step up until the reality bites"

"So DS Tenby requested to be moved to Road Policing?" asked the commander. DCI Whindle nodded.

"What with the pressure that we're all under to get a result here Ma'am, it was my considered judgement that overall, it was the best thing to agree to his request" He shot her a broad smile that she did not return.

"You'd better come up with some leads on this case Detective Chief Inspector! I'm afraid that glib promises simply will not do!" DCI Whindle's smile faded. Commander Carlton uncrossed her legs, before crossing them the other way. DCI Whindle made a point of not looking. "What people like you need to realise Evan, is that there comes a time when you cannot trade anymore on your past glories!" She was staring straight at him as she spoke. "The clock is at five to midnight Evan. Get moving on this!" Before he could respond, she had stood up. She turned away from him and opened the office door, turning back to face him for a second. "I want you to understand that I see no value whatsoever in getting rid of you, Detective Chief Inspector Whindle. You're one of the most experienced investigators I have. But make no mistake, I will pull you from this case in a heartbeat if I think it is the best thing for this force!" Whindle gritted his teeth and nodded. Commander Carlton turned back to the door and stepped out of the office.

"Don't force me into making that decision Evan" she said ominously as she walked away.

Jessica stood motionless. She had not moved in several minutes. Before her were each of the glass pieces which had been found so far. She had fingerprinted them, checked the edges for trace evidence, transfer or other deposit, catalogued, photographed them, and had now laid them out in sequence of crime scene. Meticulously, she recorded their dimensions in her notebook, ensuring that each piece was measured whilst lying on each side. To the right of the glass pieces were the CDs Joe had received, and a series of papers laid out in regimented rows, listing batch numbers of mirrors installed on trains built in the 1950s and 60s. She was just about to go to the evidence store to being out the remainder of the evidence recovered from each scene when the door to her laboratory swung violently open. It was DCI Whindle, and he was not happy. She took a step back as he marched toward her.

"Jessica, you had better have some encouraging news for me!" He barked. She took another step back in an attempt to shield from his view the glass shards, picking up her notebook as casually as she could, whilst at the same time trying to act naturally. She failed.

"Look, as I keep telling DC Violet, forensic examinations aren't the same as having a quick look under the bed for an odd sock! You have to give me time to make sure that everything has been done properly!"

"Whatever Jessica!" he said dismissively, his attention being caught by the items and papers spread across the table. Jessica put her head down as he motioned her out of the way, stepping past and glaring at the table. As he moved toward the table, she was almost certain she could smell alcohol on his breath.

"If you're so busy" he said, his hands resting on his hips as he span around to fix her with an icy glare "What is all this?" She rallied desperately for an answer, but was unable to manufacture one.

"I'm sorry!" she said. "It's just that, DS Tenby is onto something with his theory on the railway link! I was just seeing whether he was backed up by science! If I found anything I would have brought it straight to you!"

"Bollocks!" he spat. "You'd have gone straight to lover boy! You need to recognise your priorities! We have some maniac running around harbouring a grudge against anyone in a uniform! This is not the time to be mooning over some overgrown traffic warden who thought it would be fun to have a go at playing detective! Guess what Jessica? He's gone! I'm still here! That's because he's good at issuing parking tickets, and I'm good at catching criminals. It's called natural order! Deal with it!" Jessica's gaze shot up from the floor and met Whindle's stare.

"Now who's talking bollocks?" she said. Whindle took a step backward, genuinely shocked at Jessica's tone and language.

"You and I both know that Joe was the one who first saw Vincent Bridges, and when he came to you with the details you dismissed it, just like you dismissed the CDs! Is it any wonder people are saying you've lost control?" As intimidated as she was feeling, she didn't dare blink. He stared back at her intensely, his facial muscles twitched slightly. Without warning, he turned on his heels and marched back out of the laboratory, almost slamming head on into Commander Carlton.

"Evan" she said in a business like voice as they both stopped in their tracks.

"Ma'am" he said, his face flushed with anger.

"Everything okay Chief Inspector?" she said. DCI Whindle turned back and glared at Jessica, who was now desperately holding back a torrent of tears as the adrenaline was slowing in its journey around her body, her hands trembling gently.

"Everything is just peachy Ma'am!" he said with a sarcastic smile. Before the commander could comment further, he stepped around her, shoulder charging the half-open the door and sending it slamming against the wall with an echoing crash as he left it rebounding in his wake.

Catching the commander's gaze, Jessica could not hold back
her emotion a minute longer. Putting her hand to her mouth,
she turned and made for the sluice room, her chest heaving
heavily as she sobbed, her tears landing noisily in the
stainless steel sink. Pinching the bridge of her nose,
Commander Carlton took a deep breath.

"I don't know what on earth has been going on, but I think it's
time you told me everything Jessica" she said, walking over to
the sluice and placing a hand on Jessica's shoulder.

Jessica dabbed delicately at the area beneath her eyelids as
she collected her thoughts. Commander Carlton had made two
cups of tea and had placed one in front of Jessica.

It's the DCI Ma'am" said Jessica. "He's losing control!"

Commander Carlton frowned at that statement.

"That's quite a thing to say!" said the Commander.

"I don't quite know what has caused it, but it's this case"
continued Jessica. "Take what's just happened! I received a
phone call from Joe about these shards of glass" Jessica
motioned to the table where the glass pieces still lay, all in
order, awaiting further examination. "He has a theory that the
killings are connected to the railway rather than the police. I
had the idea of trying to match them with the batch numbers
of mirrors used by British Rail. The DCI came in and went
crazy when he found out" Commander Carlton looked
genuinely confused. Jessica picked up her mug.

"I'll admit that Whindle is behaving oddly" she said. "But why
on earth would DS Tenby be in communication with you over

this investigation? He requested to be re-assigned to Road Policing!" Jessica looked up from her tea.

"He didn't ask to be reassigned Ma'am" said Jessica. "DCI Whindle arranged for him to be transferred!"

"I see!" said Commander Carlton as she took another sip of her tea.

"Joe was the officer who discovered the Vincent Bridges lead. He took it to the DCI, and he dismissed it as a dead end!" Commander Carlton glanced down at the table as she placed her cup on the table. Frowning, she picked up one of the CDs, studying it closely. "What's this?" she asked, holding it out to Jessica.

"It's one of a series that were sent to Joe Ma'am!" Jessica replied as she continued dabbing gently at her swollen eyelids. "He's received one shortly after each death!"

"What CDs?" Commander Carlton spluttered. "Why wasn't I aware of this?"

"DCI Whindle dismissed them too! He said they were pranks from Joe's colleagues in traffic! When Joe questioned his decision, DCI Whindle threatened to get Joe bounced from the High Potential Development scheme!"

"So DCI Whindle has been focussing on ruining the career of a junior officer whilst a serial killer is running around free?" Commander Carlton hissed. Jessica looked at the floor. "This charade has gone on long enough!" she snapped. "I thought I was running a policing division, however, it turns out that I was wrong! I appear to be running a uniformed crèche for dysfunctional children!" Abruptly, she got to her feet, picking up the mug of tea, and taking one last mouthful before placing it back down on the table.

"Where are you going Ma'am?" asked Jessica.

"To sort this ridiculous mess out!" replied the Commander as she snatched up the other CDs. "Thank you for the tea, Miss Hopewell!"

"Pleasure Ma'am!" called Jessica after her as she disappeared along the corridor, her purposeful footsteps echoing behind her as she walked.

"This is crazy!" DC Violet whispered under his breath as he studied the lines of data on his computer screen. He had been badgering the police force's technical support department almost constantly for the downloaded information from PC Mills' police car, and it had finally arrived, but the arrival of the data had not brought positive developments. Glen ran his hands through his hair, grabbing handfuls of it and tugging gently as he stared at his desk.

"What's the matter with you?" barked DCI Whindle as he barged past Glen's desk, spinning around and standing behind him.

"I'm examining the data from the vehicle that PC Mills was driving on the night of his death" said Glen. "I thought that if we get hold of the camera footage from the on board recorder, along with the GPS and satellite navigation information, we may be able to find a lead that we can use to try and find whoever killed him" Glen looked up at DCI Whindle who was nodding thoughtfully as he squinted at the data on the screen.

"So what's the problem?" asked DCI Whindle.

"The problem is guv, that the car PC Mills was driving that night was one of three vehicles the force still has that doesn't carry an on-board video camera, or Satellite Navigation programmed into the GPS unit. It means that we can only track the vehicle's speed, direction and co-ordinates" Glen pointed to a line of numbers half way down the screen. "See here? It shows that the car was stationary for 47 minutes. Then it's moving at an average speed in a north-easterly direction for 8 minutes. Then it's stationary for a further 6 minutes before continuing forward for 23 minutes." DCI Whindle shrugged. "There is no data that bears any relation whatsoever to local landmarks, street names or anything we can use without spending hours cross referencing the co-ordinates with street map or something similar. Ironic thing is guv, that technical services were saying that the system on board the vehicle was due for upgrade next month!" Suddenly, and without warning, DCI Whindle had switched from being relatively relaxed to being increasingly angry, his voice turning into a shout. "Don't sit there whinging about what the car hasn't been fitted with, use what you have, and get me some progress! "Before Glen could answer, DCI Whindle stomped into his office, slamming the door closed. Glen remained perfectly still, not daring to move as he listened to the battered venetian blinds swinging wildly and banging against the glass.

Joe was surprised by the sheer variety of vehicles that had broken the law. No matter how unusual the vehicles and the violations of their owners were proving to be however, every car, bus, truck and motorcycle that appeared on the screen looked initially like that blue Toyota Carina that looked so menacing in the grainy image that stole his attention so effectively. Now was the time to lay the groundwork. Even the task of sorting through his work emails, something which he had not done since before he was transferred could not make him feel depressed right now. Opening up his email account, he punched in his password, tapping out a tune on the side of his cup with a pen as a long list of unopened emails filled the screen. Ignoring two newsletters from the police federation, Joe's eyes were drawn to an email from Kevin McDonnell. He opened it in earnest, quickly scanning the first half dozen lines of text, which talked mainly of the rugby match they had both attended, and then mentioned some procedural paperwork that needed to be completed with regard to the evidence Joe had recovered from the crime scene in Newcastle. Suddenly, his concentration was broken by the sound of footsteps approaching his desk. Glancing up, his heart missed a beat as he saw Commander Carlton standing next to him. "Don't get up Joe" she said. Glancing from the screen to the commander and back again, Joe hesitated, before hammering out a response as quickly as he could. Closing the web page, he smiled professionally at Commander Carlton who had waited patiently.

"How can I help you Ma'am?" he said, his dad's voice ringing loudly in his mind once more.

"You can start by telling me what on earth has been going on!" said the Commander. Joe hesitated. Sensing his concern, Commander Carlton spoke before Joe could formulate an appropriately political answer.

"Before you say anything DS Tenby" she said, placing her hand on Joe's desk "I am aware of what has happened with regard to Vincent Bridges, and your, shall we say, unexpected lateral move, as well as DCI Whindle's dismissal of these CDs you were sent!" Joe nodded, the relief he felt at being free to speak the truth was plain to see.

"Well ma'am" he replied. "DCI Whindle has problems. I believe that he is drinking heavily, and his behaviour is increasingly erratic." Commander Carlton nodded slowly as she listened to Joe, expressing shock when Joe told her of the physical confrontation he had endured with the DCI, and the damage to the office wall. "Further to that Ma'am, he seems hell bent on ignoring valid and promising lines of enquiry with regard to the case. It's as if he has tunnel vision! To be perfectly frank, I think he is heading for some type of breakdown." The Commander raised her eyebrows in surprise.

"I never realised things had gotten this bad" she said. "Whindle has always been loose cannon, but from the looks of things he has gone way too far!" Joe remained silent. He had already flagged up the failure to investigate the CDs, but had elected not to share the possible breakthrough concerning the blue car. Wanting to make sure that he had something backed up with hard fact to stake his claim with, Joe felt he had said enough for now.

"Ma'am. You should also be aware that Ms Rawson has been sniffing around again. I had a phone call from her asking why I was working from Road Policing HQ! There has to be somebody feeding her information!" Commander Carlton paused as she considered Joe's words.

"Leave it with me Joe" she said. "Whatever you do, don't discuss the leak with anyone! If we're to find the source, we can't go letting them know that we're looking for them"

"Absolutely Ma'am! I'll keep it to myself" He turned his attention back to the computer screen and slowly began typing, unconsciously lounging back in the chair as his fingers found their rhythm once more.

"One more thing Joe" said Commander Carlton with a slight smile. "Don't get too comfortable in that chair" Joe looked up at her questioningly. "That is unless you intend bringing it back to CID with you!" He stared at her for a split second as his mind processed her words.

"You mean?" he asked, not managing to finish the sentence.

"I do." she said. "I suggest you finish up the report you are in the middle of, and make your way back to CID." Joe couldn't believe it. His heart rate was racing so fast, he could feel his pulse in his fingertips.

"What about the DCI Ma'am?" Joe enquired as she turned to leave.

"Leave him to me Detective Sergeant! Just get yourself sorted and get back to CID. Keep it under your hat for now though Joe. Give me chance to clarify things." As she spoke, she hadn't even stopped walking. Raising her hand in the direction of Inspector Lynch, she motioned towards his office, no doubt to inform him that his new Sergeant would be leaving much sooner than planned.

The white border of the photograph had long since lost its crispness, the sun, and the ravages of time causing it, and the detail of the picture itself to fade slightly. Steven studied the scene. Raymond Kilkis was looking straight at the camera, a smile of genuine happiness spread across his face. Steven was looking up at his father adoringly. That picture was taken on a camping trip, and was one of the happiest times in Steven's life. Stroking the surface of the photograph, he placed the photograph down with the rest of his collection, spreading them out to look at them all. He reached for the phone as it started to ring.

"Yes!" he said impatiently.

"Hi Steve" Robert replied. "We need to talk!"

"I thought we'd said everything already!" Steve said as his fingers traced the outline of his father's face on another photograph, this time one of all three of them outside his Grandma's house.

"You said a lot of things that can't just be forgotten!" Steve rolled his eyes.

"Look, none of us are angels here Rob!" He held the phone away from his ear as he took deep, calming breaths.

"I was just saying to them that things are worth sorting out one last time, surely?" Robert said. "I know it'll take time, but I suggested we all meet up for a dinner and take things from there. How does that sound?"

"That sounds like a brilliant idea!" Steven said, much to Robert's amazement. He saw an opportunity, and grabbed it, hurriedly doing some mental arithmetic.

"How about Friday the 16th?" asked Steven, knowing full well that Graham and his Mum already had plans.

Robert paused. "I don't think that would be any good Steve. Graham has been invited to some railway reunion party. He's convinced Mum to go with him. Maybe the following Friday?"

"The following Friday is great!" said Steven enthusiastically. He nodded his head in satisfaction, a smug smile occupying his face. He now knew that his Mum and Graham would be present at the party.

"Lovely!" Robert said. "I'll make the arrangements and ring you in the week!"

"Okay bro!" said Steve cheerfully.

"I'm really glad you've realised what's important Steve!" Robert said.

"Just lately Rob, things have become so much clearer!" Steven replied. Ending the call, he slouched back on the sofa, smiling contentedly at the continuing advancement of his plans.

-84-

Joe felt as if it were his first day all over again, only this time he was commencing the journey with the benefit of his recent experiences. He had remained in the offices of the Roads Policing Unit for a further few hours following his impromptu meeting with the Commander yesterday, carrying out vehicle checks on the blue car. It was registered to a Gavin Kilkis. He had no criminal record, no outstanding warrants, summons or fines, and was registered as living at an address a few miles across London in Gordon Hill. Joe had hoped to be able to put a face to the name, but checks with the DVLA were frustrated by the fact that Gavin Kilkis was the holder of an old style non-photographic licence. Enquiries with the Passport Agency had yielded no luck. Nevertheless, Joe would not be discouraged. This was progress! Finally he could produce someone other than a neighbour who they could search for, then interview! Slipping his jacket on, Joe strode purposefully over to the main door, entering the building and throwing a cheerful "Morning Sir!" through Inspector Goodman's open door as he breezed past the office and up the stairs.

Reaching the corridor leading to the main CID office, Joe felt a vibrating in his pocket. Taking out his phone as he turned right from the staircase, he unlocked the screen. It was a text message from Commander Carlton. Joe stopped as he read.

"JOE. I NEED TO SPEAK TO YOU. MY OFFICE. ASAP."

Frowning, Joe changed direction and headed back past the top of the stairs and towards the offices occupied by senior officers, an area of the station known as 'The Exec Deck' by the rank and file. It was immediately noticeable how the décor improved, the closer you got to the Exec Deck. Along the standard corridors were seldom polished hard tiled floors, the walls dressed in tired shades of grey or blue, their expanse only interrupted periodically by notice boards or random pictures of old borough police forces, the forerunners to the constabularies of today. In the Exec Deck however, the colour scheme changed from ageing blues and greys to pastille based turquoise, feature wallpaper with bold geometric patterns, chic up-lighting, and tranquil watercolours of the sunrise over the Thames at Battersea, and a cubist interpretation of Vauxhall Bridge by night.

"Sir!" said Joe quietly as the Chief Superintendent passed him in the corridor, smiling ominously as he nodded. Commander Carlton's office door was open, and Joe was suddenly nervous. The Chief Superintendent had just left the Commander, and Joe had the feeling that the Chief Superintendent knew something that Joe did not. Taking a deep breath, he straightened his tie and smoothed his suit jacket, then knocked on the door.

"Come in Joe" said Commander Carlton sternly. Upon entering, Joe saw that he and the Commander were not alone. There were two seats arranged in a slight arc to the front of the grand desk that dominated the room. The seat farthest from the door were occupied by Dr Rothesay He was calmly and carefully writing notes in a large notebook, whilst intermittently studying a sepia portrait of children in cloth caps and pinafores playing on Hampstead Heath. Obediently, Joe entered. The Commander motioned to the seat opposite her. Sitting himself down, Joe exchanged awkward smiles with Dr Rothesay.

"Gentlemen, shall we cut straight to it?" said Commander Carlton as she slipped on her glasses and began reading a loose sheet of paper. Without waiting for a reply she continued, addressing herself toward Joe.

"Detective Sergeant Tenby, following our conversation yesterday, you left me with a great deal to think about, and a large amount of remedial action to undertake. You made some very serious allegations which could not go unchecked." Joe's mouth dried as he listened.

"I decided to speak to Dr Rothesay about your concerns, and to my astonishment, he seems to agree almost entirely with what you have said Joe. He believes that DCI Whindle has problems with conflict, and with stress management, and is becoming overly emotional." Commander Carlton paused, studying Joe as he raised his eyebrows, nodding solemnly. "He also believes that you are right to feel aggrieved by DCI Whindle's actions, as you have become the focus of Whindle's malice. You seem to be the only officer on this case who has made any real headway in terms of police work Joe! Why don't you bring me up to date on all of the lines of inquiry you have highlighted as potential leads?" Clearing his throat, Joe proceeded to inform the Commander Carlton of his thoughts regarding the glass shards, the CDs, and the developments surrounding the dark blue car caught on the traffic camera.

"You have a name for the driver?" asked Commander Carlton eagerly.

"The car is registered to Gavin Kilkis" Joe said, not needing to refer to his notebook. Preliminary inquiries have shown that he has no prior record, no outstanding warrants, and no fines. There's no photograph on record because he has an old style driving licence. This guy doesn't even have a passport!"

Commander Carlton looked thoughtful as she contemplated Joe's comments.

"If this Gavin Kilkis has no priors, I would be surprised if he were the perpetrator of these crimes!"

"Well, I have to say ma'am, I really think we have something here. Joe countered. "I fancy this Kilkis character! I don't know why exactly, and I need to look into him further, but something is telling me that he is somebody who I need to be bothering! I take on board fully, your observations regarding the profile of a likely perpetrator Doctor, but I see this slightly differently. I see Kilkis as a man who has conspicuously crawled along under the radar, managed to rub along within society at a low level without the need to leave a trail. You may think that I am reading too much into a small amount of information, but my opinion is that we have a man who has made a point of evading the everyday records that we all generate. I want to know why, and I feel that he should be our focus, at least initially Ma'am" As he spoke, a thought occurred to Joe. Gavin Kilkis hadn't appeared on ANY database, except for his driving licence. He had an NHS number, but that was it. The familiar sound of alarm bells were making themselves heard once more. Joe knew that there were an awful lot more databases and points of contact to approach in order to carry out the depth of checks required to satisfy the inquiry, and Joe's curiosity

."Anything further Joe?" asked the Commander.

"Yes ma'am. I think that we need to review the particulars of each killing from a fresh angle. Given the fact that we are all agreed that the DCI has failed to lead the investigation thoroughly enough, there could well be leads that have been missed. I feel that the killer has had a big enough head start, and that lead needs to be reeled back in by whoever you appoint as Senior Investigating Officer before someone dies or the press break the case before we do!" Commander Carlton had been making some brief notes as Joe spoke. Looking up from her papers, she fixed him with a steely expression, which warmed to a slight smile as she spoke.

"I couldn't agree more Joe" she said. "You have made some excellent and very salient points, and I'm sure that you'll do an excellent job"

Joe reeled as he took in what she had said.

"Ma'am?" he asked.

"I'm placing you in charge of the investigation DS Tenby" Commander Carlton said. "My colleagues in the executive team believe I'm making a mistake given your lack of experience, but you have so far shown an impeccable instinct, not to mention a belief in your theories!"

"Yes Ma'am! Thank you Ma'am!" he spluttered.

"DS Tenby, I suggest you use the meeting room next door to prepare some notes. You will have to speak to your team today. I will accompany you to the CID office where we will explain that DCI Whindle has been placed on leave and that you are assuming control of the investigation. You need to hit the ground running!"

"Absolutely Ma'am!" Joe said, adopting a confident, business-like tone as he rose from his seat. Picking up his briefcase, he strode from the Commander's office and made the short walk down the office to the meeting room. Commander Carlton and Dr's Rothesay stood also. The Commander picked up her phone as they walked to the office door.

"Don't make me regret this Joe!" Commander Carlton said under her breath. Unlocking her phone, she dialled DCI Whindle's number, staring at the closed door of the meeting room as the phone rang. Abruptly, DCI Whindle answered.

"We need to talk Evan" she said coldly.

"Joe!" Jessica exclaimed, dropping her papers onto the desk and rushing over. Glen looked up, the shock on his face clear to see.

"What are you doing here?" asked Jessica, her face flushing as she became slightly embarrassed by her reaction. Before Joe could answer, the door to DCI Whindle's office slammed violently open. All eyes turned to the DCI as he stood in the office doorway, a cardboard box with a collection of personal items tucked under his arm. His face was flushed, and his expression angry as he stepped forward, glaring at Joe. Commander Carlton stepped discreetly from the doorway a few steps behind.

"I was just telling Commander Carlton that she is making one huge mistake!" DCI Whindle jerked his thumb aggressively over his shoulder. Joe didn't reply.

"This isn't speeding tickets and dodgy MOTs Commander!" Joe bit his lip, choosing to ignore the insult.

"Detective Chief Inspector, please!" Commander Carlton said softly, motioning him towards the exit. Stepping forward, Joe offered DCI Whindle his hand.

"No hard feelings?" he said. Looking down at Joe's hand, DCI Whindle sneered.

"Fuck you Tenby!" he spat, pushing past Joe and storming out of the door. For a split second, everyone in the office looked around at each other, unsure as to what was going on. Commander Carlton stepped into the centre of the room, her expression sober.

"Ladies and Gentlemen, I am advising you that, with immediate effect, Detective Chief Inspector Whindle will be stepping back from his role as Senior Investigating Officer. Detective Sergeant Tenby will assume the role of Senior Investigating Officer forthwith" The assembled officers exchanged looks of sheer amazement, although nobody dared utter a word. Joe too remained silent, his attention staying with Jessica, who was clearly reeling at the demise of her uncle. He wanted her to look at him so he could show his regret, so he could prove that he had not manufactured this situation for his own career advancement. Jessica stared intensely at the floor. Finally, Glen was the one to break the silence. Coughing gently, he attracted Commander Carlton's attention.

"Ma'am" he said cautiously.

"Yes DC Violet" Commander Carlton responded.

"May I ask why DCI Whindle was removed?" Commander Carlton chose her words carefully.

"Well Detective Constable, DCI Whindle lost his perspective. He is a committed, dedicated and valued senior officer, but he needed to take a break, and I need a fresh approach if we're to move forward." She scanned the room once more looking for any sign of dissatisfaction with her response.

"Does anybody have any issues with the appointment of DS Tenby as your interim SIO?" Joe knew that the question was not one that was intended to be answered, but nevertheless he breathed a sigh of relief as he noted that nobody had offered any objection. "Good" said Commander Carlton. "The executive team have complete confidence in Detective Sergeant Tenby, and we have complete confidence in all of you. Know this though." She paused for effect, the forefinger of her right hand raised skyward. "We need progress on this. It has been 5 days since our first victim, and all we have to show for our efforts is a former suspect threatening to sue, and a metric tonne of press hysteria! The press are hunting for scapegoats; the Commissioner is getting tired of stalling MP's and the families of the deceased. I don't want shortcuts, I want you all to do your jobs, and find me something to calm everything down." Turning on her heels, she paused briefly at Joe's shoulder, speaking in a whisper.

"This could make or break you Joe. I urge you to seize this opportunity"

"I understand Ma'am" Joe replied.

"I do hope so DS Tenby." The Commander said, before disappearing into the office and collecting her hat and bag. Reappearing, she slipped the strap of her bag onto her shoulder as she walked across the room, nodding at the assembled officers as she headed for the door, her steely gaze fixed on the corridor.

86

Looking over his glasses in the direction of the door, Graham rose stiffly from his chair, cursing as his joints clenched under his weight. Placing his newspaper on the table, he walked gingerly down the hall, groaning to himself as he stooped to pick up the mail, turning and making his way back to the kitchen table. Lowering himself back into his chair, he sighed under the sheer effort of his short journey, before sorting through the small collection of letters. Putting two of them to one side, having identified them already as bills, Graham studied the typewritten address on the front of a third envelope. Turning it over, he tore open the flap, sliding his thumb inside and forcing it along the breadth of the envelope before he slipped the contents onto the table. Inside was a short letter, together with four small tickets. They were for the railway reunion. Picking up the letter, he read it carefully;

Brother Crosbie.

I have pleasure in enclosing your tickets, as requested, for the reunion function this Friday at The Milward Club. We welcome the attendance of family and partners at our functions, and wish to see as large an attendance as possible.

Therefore, we enclose a further two tickets with our compliments for you to pass on to your family, and/or any colleagues or retired persons you know who may wish to join us. We look forward to seeing you on the night.

Yours Fraternally

Retired Members Committee.

Rising to his feet again, Graham walked across to Joyce who was busying herself at the cooker. She had been oblivious to the arrival of the post, lovingly nursing a pan full porridge as she hummed gently to herself.

"I've just received the tickets for Friday night Joyce" Graham said, holding them in front of her as she stirred the contents of an ageing saucepan. Joyce frowned as she struggled to focus, tilting her head back slightly as she tried to decipher the small writing on the tickets.

"You know how useless I am without my glasses Graham" she said, her right arm moving in a subconscious circular motion. Graham pulled the tickets from her view, returning to his seat. He dropped them onto the table as he sat down.

"They've sent us 4 tickets" he said.

"Well why did you ask for that many?" she asked, still stirring the porridge.

"I didn't" he replied. "They sent a letter saying that they've given another two tickets to give to family or friends"

"That'll be nice then!" Joyce said as she lifted the saucepan from the hob.

"Who are we going to ask?" said Graham as he watched Joyce sharing the porridge between two bowls. "Everyone I know will probably be already going. Everyone else is dead!" Joyce laughed as she scraped the last spoonful from the bottom of the pan.

She lowered herself gracefully into her seat, slowly lifting her spoon from the table and positioning it over her breakfast as she watched Graham snatch up his spoon and thrust it into his porridge, brandishing an overloaded spoonful and shovelling it into his mouth. The two of them continued their breakfast in silence for a moment, before she placed her spoon back down.

"Why don't we ask Robert?" Joyce asked. Graham paused as he considered the idea.

"We could do" he said, looking thoughtful. "It would be nice to introduce Robert to some of the old gang!" Joyce smiled. She knew that Graham was not the perfect man. Even when younger, he was unkempt, brash, and sometimes downright rude. Despite his failings, he had a good heart. She had endless admiration for how he never appeared territorial on the subject of her late husband. Graham had always been accepting of the legacy of Raymond's death. He had even taken a second job as a truck driver when they had moved into a larger house, and had taken both boys away with him at various times in on long journeys an attempt to build relationships, despite the turbulence between Graham and Steven. Perhaps it was because he felt guilty at being present when Raymond was killed. Whatever the reason, Joyce genuinely loved Graham, his honesty, eccentricity, humour, and his willingness to allow her to grieve as and when she felt the need, had gradually drawn her in. His readiness to introduce her youngest son to his circle of friends, to those who had known Raymond was a testament to his worth as a man. She watched, smiling warmly as he continued to eat. "I'm sure he'd love that" she said. He looked up from his breakfast, returning her smile as his hand stopped in mid-air, another batch of delicious porridge suspended between dish and mouth.

"That's settled then" he said. "I'll ring him a little later on. I'll ask him if Lisa wants to come too!" Graham's attention returned to his porridge.

"Thank you" Joyce mouthed silently as she rested her chin on her clasped fingers. That said, the pair of them resumed breakfast, the monotonous conversation from the radio once more assuming aural dominance over the gentle clinking of spoon on dish.

87

The sound of detectives at work was proving somewhat distracting to Joe. He sat inside what had until recently been DCI Whindle's office, and despite his best efforts, it still felt like enemy territory. In the short time he had been using the office, he had been toying with how to leave the door. Open or closed? He had initially closed it, but then worried about whether he would be seen to be separating himself from his team. He wanted to be approachable, but at the same time he needed to concentrate. Having reopened the door, he was increasingly unable to focus on his work. Throwing the biro onto the desk, he picked up the paper that was lying on top of the pile in front of him. It was the picture generated from the traffic camera being activated by the mysterious Gavin Kilkis. Joe stared intently at the picture. Little of the physical characteristics of the driver could be made out, largely due to the picture having been taken whist the image was captured at speed, and the camera was angled so as to photograph vehicles travelling in the opposite direction. It was frustrating that there was still no firm link to move forward with, but even so, Joe was certain that this was a promising lead. He had instructed the team to review the entire investigation to date. Officers had been sent to re-canvass the areas close to where victims had lived, worked and socialised, and every interview record was being pored over in an attempt to ensure that nothing was overlooked. Joe had contacted the local hospitals to see if they had any such drugs missing from their stocks, as well as the Department of Health to ask for records of all privately practising Doctors who were authorised to buy Medazolene. In the meantime, Joe had instructed Glen to contact the parking enforcement company who had employed the parking attendant who had died alongside PC Mills, and was eagerly awaiting contact from the background check on Gavin Kilkis. The Driving Licence database had only yielded an address which had been demolished 18 months previously. Clearly, Gavin Kilkis was a man who was accustomed to working in the shadows. Having found no record with the passport agency, Joe had contacted HM Revenue & Customs, and the Association of British Insurers database, credit referencing agencies, and had made searches using the electoral roll. Despite the frenetic activity in his brain, his eyes had not left the image on the page.

"Who are you Kilkis?" he said to himself. Before the picture could offer an answer, Joe's attention was drawn to Glen Violet who was standing in the doorway. Joe smiled, motioning for Glen to sit.

"Sarge" Glen said as he looked around the room. He had no need to verbalise how strange it was for Joe to be sitting in the DCI's former office.

"What's up Glen?" Joe asked as he gathered up the papers in front of him and returned them to their folder. "You can't have got those checks back already, surely?"

"I know you're busy Joe, but I'm still having real trouble getting all the data I need for the GPS system on PC Mills' police car. So far it's just a meaningless load of numbers and letters! Traffic are taking ages in getting back to me." Joe held out his hand. Glen obediently handed over the paperwork he had compiled to date. Opening the folder, Joe scanned the first three pages before closing the cover and handing them back.

"You've got what you need to do a basic reconstruction Glen!" he said leaning back in the chair. The role of SIO was becoming increasingly natural surprisingly quickly, and he found himself revelling in it. Glen looked on questioningly.

"These are co-ordinates using latitude and longitude. Get the co-ordinates of the traffic camera, cross reference it with the data you have in there, and use it as an anchor point to work out where the vehicle went!"

"Okay sarge!" Glen said, clearly annoyed with himself for not thinking of that himself.

"In the meantime I'll get onto traffic and hurry them along. I'll make a call to technical support as well and see if there are any computer programmes we can use that will overlay this data onto ordnance survey maps."

"Thanks!" Glen said, his shoulders back and posture slightly more confident as he stood.

"You know where I am if you get any more problems!" Joe said confidently as he made his way back to his desk. No sooner had Joe allowed himself a second to be pleased with his handling of Glen's dilemma than his phone started ringing.

"Detective Sergeant Tenby" he said coolly into the mouthpiece. The caller was from the insurance database. Excitedly, Joe grabbed a piece of paper and his pen, scribbling the details chaotically. At that moment, Jessica appeared at the door. Joe waved her in as he finished his phone call. Putting the phone slowly down onto the desk, Joe sat for a moment as he read the scrawled details he had just put on the paper, his breathing slow and heavy.

"Are you okay Joe?" Jessica asked as she sat down.

"Yeah, I'm fine. What do you have?" Jessica smiled at him mischievously, causing him to momentarily blush.

"Don't we sound every bit the boss man?"

"I'm sorry" Joe said. "I know it must be awkward for you. I'm glad you're okay with this." Jessica held up her hand slightly, motioning Joe to stop.

"Joe it's all good. I know you didn't make my uncle behave the way he did. I'm just glad that you're coping with the pressure. It must be a bit scary" Joe looked past Jessica and into the bustling CID room, then back at her.

"Truth be told Jessica, it's terrifying, but it feels sort of natural too!" Jessica nodded.

"Well you'll be glad then, oh glorious leader, when I tell you that I have some positive news on the forensic front!" Joe smiled broadly.

"In that case Miss Hopewell, please continue!" As Joe looked into her deep brown eyes, it was now her turn to blush.

"On the subject of the shards of glass" Jessica said, "I know that I told you before that the glass was pretty generic. I have managed to narrow it down. It was used in the manufacture of mirrors installed in some really old trains." Shuffling her papers, she produced a small document wallet. Slipping two sheets of paper from it, she examined them and placed them in front of Joe. Studying the picture on the top page, Joe leant back in the chair.

"British Rail Southern Region 1963 Electric stock" he said.

"That is still really quite generic! That train was the staple unit used in the south of England for about 40 years! It's all history now though! Most of those units have been broken up for scrap with the exception of a few. They were hived off to museums and preserved railways"

"Wow Joe!" Jessica said. "I never pinned you as a train spotter!"

"I'm not!" Joe replied. "I am the product of one though! I spent quite a few weekends with my dad at railway festivals and steam fairs. He's got books and pictures on just about every type of train ever built!"

"Ouch!" Jessica said with a laugh.

"Well, he worked on the railways all his life. He loved his job. Can't help but admire someone getting paid for their hobby!" Returning to the subject at hand, Joe leaned forward.

"Are there any records of batch numbers that we can trace the glass to?"

"I'm not sure what good that'll do us" Jessica said with a frown. "You said yourself that the most of these trains have been scrapped!"

"That is true, but if we can somehow pinpoint which train, or which batch of trains this mirror came from, or which maintenance depot it was sent to before it was fitted to a unit, we may be able to get some kind of idea of the geography of the killer in terms of his background. A search area for us to start looking at the railway industry might lead us somewhere, and from there, we can build a picture to either prove me wrong or, confirm my suspicions" Joe finished the sentence with a sly smile. Jessica's mind was so busy processing the possibility of hunting down batch lists of mirrors made for a defunct state operation dating back five decades or so, that Joe was certain she hadn't picked up on his last comment. "Well, I can see what I can do" she said with a shrug. "I'll make a call to the transport police, see if they have any idea on where I should start looking.." Her voice trailed off. Frowning, she looked at him. "What do you mean, prove you wrong or confirm your suspicions?" Grinning to himself, he picked up the folder containing the details of Gavin Kilkis. Sliding it across the desk, he paused to savour the moment. "Do you remember that we were told about a man in a dark blue car being seen in the vicinity of Anna Brown's house?" Anna opened the folder and studied its contents. "Yes, I do recall something being said, though from what you and Glen were saying at the time. Anyway, that turned out to be Vincent Bridges didn't it? I thought you'd managed to discount him as a suspect?"

"Vincent Bridges? You mean the DCI's cast iron lead?" snapped Joe, raising his hand in apology as he spoke. Jessica smiled awkwardly. "Well, I got to wondering whether there was actually a second blue car that had been spotted, unconnected to Mr Bridges. As it turns out, fate has as misguided a sense of humour! Our mystery driver was photographed driving in the other direction when a BMW triggered a traffic camera on the A2! I picked up the activation during my spell in enforcement! We've got an address for the owner!"Jessica looked up from the folder.

"How do we know that this is the same guy?" she asked.

"We don't!" Joe said. "I've made some initial enquiries and he isn't showing up! He isn't on the passport database, the electoral roll, and he has no credit profile!"

"That's strange!" Jessica said. "Don't we have a photograph of him?" Joe shook his head.

"He's got an old style licence and it hasn't been upgraded, and the address was demolished a few years back"

"That's not just strange, that's ringing alarm bells!" Jessica replied as she studied the hazy image from the camera.

"So now you see why I'm fancying him as a solid lead?"

"Absolutely!" Jessica exclaimed. "So what are you going to do now?"

"Well, seeing as the address on the licence isn't valid, I think I'll pay a visit to the address listed on the insurance database, and on the DVLA records for the car!"

"Good work Joe!" Jessica said. Joe stood up and grabbed his jacket.

"Thanks. It's what I do!" he said with mock modesty.

The address that they were visiting was around 45 minutes from the station, and despite his desire to remind Glen of the importance of keeping pressure on the parking enforcement company for the records of Russell Danton, Joe was firmly of the opinion that it was best to give him as few distractions as possible if they were to arrive in any fit state to conduct an interview. Despite his misgivings at the standard of Glen's driving, Joe could not help but feel excited. He was deliberate in maintaining a sober demeanour, but inwardly he was almost drunk on the anticipation of finally moving the investigation forward. Glancing across at Glen, Joe sensed that he too was hungry for progress. Not only was he a member of the team, he had lost a friend, and Joe had taken the conscious decision to ensure that he was closely involved, so long as he proved he was able to be professional in his approach. Joe's mind had been racing for the entire journey, and the two were only minutes from their destination when Glen finally broke the silence.

"So, what's the plan?" he asked as he moved into the outside lane without indicating. Joe could only hope that he had bothered to check his mirror before moving.

"Well, that depends on what we find when we get there Glen" Joe replied. "He's already using a false address on his driving licence, so I'm not expecting to find a pillar of society waiting for us!" Glen smiled in reply. Making a right turn, Glen accelerated to the bottom of a quiet suburban street, turning the car around, and returning at a much slower pace toward the main road, the two of them scouring the opposing rows of houses in search of number 27.

"Here we are!" Joe exclaimed, pointing across the road at an anonymous bungalow with two cars in the drive. Glen brought the car to a stop on the other side of the road and the two men got out. Joe walked ahead as Glen locked the car. When Glen caught up, Joe was studying the house.

"What's up?" Glen asked.

"They've got two cars." Joe replied. "A red Ford and a black Vauxhall. I can't see any blue Toyota"

"Perhaps they have three cars. Kilkis could have taken his car to work" Glen offered with a shrug.

"He doesn't work!" Joe snapped. "He's never paid tax or national insurance! Something is seriously wrong here!"

"So what do we do?" Glen asked.

"What we do best, as professional Police Officers, DC Violet! We wing it!" Joe answered with a grin. He then opened the garden gate and walked down the driveway, reaching inside his jacket pocket and preparing his warrant card for whoever answered the door.

Stepping forward, Joe knocked firmly on the door twice. Through the frosted glass he could see a blurred outline approaching. The lady on the other side of the door was obviously security conscious, unlocked the door and opened it as far as the chain would allow.

"Detective Sergeant Joe Tenby Madam, Metropolitan Police" Joe produced his warrant card and held it forward for her to scrutinise. "This is my colleague Detective Constable Violet" Joe motioned toward Glen who smiled professionally. The old woman unfastened the door chain and opened the door fully, glancing back and forth between the two with a confused expression.

"May I ask what this is about?" she said.

"We're making enquiries about some motoring offences. May

we speak with Gavin Kilkis please?" Joe asked. The woman reacted as if Joe had punched her in the stomach, the air in her lungs noisily leaving her as she reeled in shock.

"Madam! Are you okay?" Joe asked, rushing forward and steadying her as she grasped at the wood of the doorway. From inside the house a man shouted as he hobbled briskly down the hall toward the door.

"What on earth is going on? Are you okay?" he said, his hands resting on the woman's waist. Fixing Joe and Glen with an angry stare, he stepped forward, moving the woman gently aside. "Who are you and what do you want?" he asked.

"We're Police Officers" replied Joe as he produced his warrant card once more. "We're here in connection with Gavin Kilkis. We need to speak with him as a matter of urgency"

"Is this some kind of sick joke?" the old man hissed. The woman collapsed into a heap on the floor, her hands over her face as she sobbed hysterically.

"I am so sorry" Joe said as he looked over at Glen. Glen shrugged. "May I ask who you are sir?"

"I'm Graham Crosbie." He replied.

"I'm Joyce Kilkis" the woman on the floor sighed through her tears. Wiping her eyes she looked up at Joe.

"You can't speak with Gavin Kilkis I'm afraid. He's dead Detective Sergeant!"

As it was early evening, Steven brought his car to a smooth stop in one of the pay and display parking spaces just around the corner from the club. Having observed the club at length, he was aware of the fact that the doors were closed and locked, and the usual lights were not switched on. He had prepared for a lengthy wait until after the normal closing time, but was pleased when he saw that justice would be delivered much faster than expected. Congratulating himself for managing to plan ahead and tamper with the lock to the door on the upper fire escape at the rear of the club, he allowed himself a tense smile as he anticipated the release that swift vengeance would surely bring. His approach to resolving matters had changed markedly since he his work had begun. Initially, his sense of retribution had decreed that it would only be those on his list, those who deserved to be punished who would face his justice. Now though, he was willing to entertain the possibility of 'collateral damage' in order to achieve his ends.

As much as he was doing his best, Steven was struggling tonight to maintain his usual calm. The events of a few days ago had spooked him. His initial reaction to the death of the Police Officer had been that it was an unexpected bonus. With the cloud of adrenaline lifted from his view however, Steven was beginning to appreciate that he was very nearly stopped from completing his task. It also underlined to him the importance of utilising the opportunities that presented themselves. Lifting the plastic box from behind his seat, his fingers trembled slightly as he opened the lid. There were only three pieces of glass remaining. Sensually, he brushed the surface of the remaining pieces with his finger before seizing one at random and examining it closely

"You'll not be needed tonight" Steven whispered under his breath. Placing the glass back inside, he closed the lid, stowing the box in its hiding place. Keeping a constant watch in the car's mirrors for signs of any unwitting observers, he satisfied himself that he was alone. Opening the car door, he slipped out, crossing the deserted street and disappearing down the side of the Milward club, his orange overalls tucked under his arm as he ducked into the alleyway, silently opening the gate to the rear yard.

Phil was hunched over the desk, his fingers working quickly and haphazardly through a deep pile of invoices, scrawled notes and fading betting slips. He had been busily organising the food, music and other final arrangements for the retirement reunion that was due to take place at the club the next day. Muttering whispered profanities under his breath, he was becoming increasingly panicked as he hunted for the contact details and order confirmation from the caterer he had hired.

"That fucking gate!" he hissed, in reaction to the dull thud of wood against stone as he continued rifling through the array of paperwork that covered his filthy desk. The club was in darkness. It had been a very quiet night, and Phil had decided to cut his losses and close early. He was in a foul mood, and it was only worsening with each minute that passed. Finally, he laid his hands on the contact details he needed, grunting through the effort of bending sharply to one side in order to rescue it from beneath the desk. Picking up the telephone, he slowly dialled the number he had scribbled on the crumpled paper before him, tapping the fingers of his free hand impatiently as he waited for an answer.

As he slipped into his overalls, Steven took a look around him. The yard was bare, save for a few empty lager barrels. The shed in the far corner appeared to be on the verge of collapse. Steven placed his foot on the first step of the fire escape, grimacing slightly as it gave out a dull creak. Adjusting his foot, he slid it across from the centre of the step to the inside edge, slowly increasing the pressure until his entire body weight was loaded onto it. Satisfied that he had navigated his first problem of the night, he carefully ascended the rickety staircase, quickly arriving at the balcony that led into the main corridor. Before climbing the stairs, he had checked to see whether the curtains to the office were open or not. Seeing that they had been drawn, he knew that his journey inside the building would now go unchecked. He could see through the material of the curtains that Phil was most likely asleep in his office, or getting off on some grubby website after hours. Whatever he was doing behind those curtains, Steven knew that he would be too distracted to detect his intrusion before it was too late.

It was only just noticeable in the fact that the door was not entirely aligned with the door frame. Late the previous evening, Steven had scaled the steps to the balcony, having assumed correctly that Phil would still be in a deep, after hours, drunken sleep either in his office, or his bedroom, which was situated on the other side of the building. He knew that Phil quite often neglected to check the fire escapes and windows before stumbling into bed, and was unsurprised when he arrived on the balcony to find the fire door slightly open. Peering down the dark hallway, Steven had reassured himself that there was minimal chance of him being disturbed, the only audience to his arrival being an overly friendly dog, who Steven had befriended by dumping a bag full of pork scratching on the floor and ruffling his ears as he snaffled them enthusiastically. Holding the door between his knees, he reached inside his jacket, producing a small clamp. Applying it to the lock, he gradually tightened it, pulling the ageing lock towards him until it no longer lined up with the recess in the door frame. Looking towards the far end of the hallway once more, he repelled a temptation to make his move a day early, backing quietly out of the door as the dog waddled happily to his bed and disappearing down the stairs, knowing that he had guaranteed himself entry for when he returned with the equipment he needed.

It was now almost exactly 24 hours later. Managing to prize the door open with the tips of his fingers, he stepped inside. From where he stood he could hear muffled words. It sounded as if Phil was engrossed in a telephone conversation, something that would only solidify the element of surprise that Steven was intending to use to his advantage. The dog approached from the darkness once more, and Steven was ready with a tasty treat. This time, it had been laced with sedatives. Watching as the dog swallowed three biscuits whole, he observed him wandering back down the corridor. Within minutes he was fast asleep, snoring loudly from his musty bed. Resolving to deal permanently with the dog at a more discreet time, Steven reached inside his jacket and withdrew his iron bar, still wrapped in the bandage and cloth that had dulled its unmistakable sound during his previous work. His fingers squeezed the smooth, cold surface. Taking a deep breath, he stepped forward into the darkness, pausing a few steps from the office door. He could now hear Phil clearly.

"My client, Mr Anderson is extremely fussy, and it is imperative that he is impressed by the food!" Phil said in a business-like tone. Steven stifled a laugh as he listened to Phil discussing the imaginary 'Mr Anderson'. After exchanging a couple of pleasantries, Phil ended the call. Opting to entice Phil from the office, Steven looked around him. Against the opposite wall sat an old wooden chair. Reaching across the corridor, Steven picked it up and tossed it a few feet down the hallway. From inside the office he heard Phil get out of his seat and walk across the office. The door opened abruptly, filling the hallway with light.

"Hello?" Phil said into the empty corridor, his back to Steven as he stepped away from the wall.

"Hello" Steven replied warmly. Phil span around to confront the intruder, but before he could utter a word, Steven had smashed him in the mouth with the iron bar, sending his yellowing teeth flying through the air. Phil was hurled to the floor under the sheer force of the impact, his hands clamping to his bleeding mouth as he screamed an unintelligible scream, his eyes shut tight in agony. Steven's heart was pounding as he stood over Phil's prone figure, the bar raised high in the air.

"Don't take this personally" said Steven as he brought the bar crashing down onto Phil's nose. His body went limp as more blood and tissue sprayed the floor, walls and Steven's overalls. Mercifully, Phil passed quickly into deep unconsciousness. Unable to control himself, Steven descended into a primal rage, his arms swinging wildly as he reined blow after blow down onto Phil's body, the air of the hallway filled with the sickening thud of the iron bar on aging skin and collapsing bone, and the vicious grunts of a man revelling in the dispensing of unadulterated and gratuitous violence, the onslaught only stopping when the ragged carpet was sodden with the seeping blood of a viciously murdered corpse.

Deciding to leave the body where it was, he walked to the other end of the hallway, satisfying himself that he had the freedom to make his preparations. Flicking the hallway lights on, he stared for a moment at the full detail of his exertions. A mist of blood coated the walls, skirting boards and even the ceiling in the area where Phil's body was lying, the carpet glistening under the lights. Turning his attention to the office, he walked inside.

"Time to prepare for the big day" he said to himself as he closed the office door behind him, leaving his latest victim to suffer the indignity of his brutal passing alone. Walking over to the desk, he picked up the paper with the details of the false booking he had made.

"Time to put on a reunion those bastards will never forget!" he hissed as he sat down. "Not before I raise the stakes with one last message to Mr Tenby!" He stretched his legs out underneath the desk, the cushioned chair still warm from where Phil had occupied it during the last moments of his life.

"May we come in and discuss this further?" Joe asked tentatively.

"I don't think that's a very good idea son!" Graham said.

"Joyce is very upset, I think it best if we let things settle down a little"

"Can I make an appointment with you to come to the station and speak to us there?" Joe was desperate, pleading almost. Graham did not answer. He was kneeling beside Joyce, his arms thrown around her shoulders. "Mrs Kilkis" Joe said softly. She peered around Graham's shoulder. Her tears had ceased, but streams of moisture still clung to her cheeks. "Believe me when I say that if I had any idea that your son had passed away I would have never have upset you like this, but I am here in connection with a matter of the gravest importance. I'm investigating a series of serious incidents and I need your help, if you can find it within yourself to forgive our intrusion" Joe smiled softly, his eyes wide and sincere. She stared into his eyes, searching them for confirmation that he meant what he had said. Looking at Graham, she offered her hand.

"Help me up Graham" she said. Graham looked backwards at Joe, grudgingly heaving her to her feet.

"You don't have to help them!" he said in a loud whisper. "The disrespect they've shown you! Tell them to sort their own bloody problems!" Readjusting her skirt, she patted Graham's arm.

"Oh come now! Helping the Police is the right thing to do! Sergeant Tenby is only doing his job!" Joe looked nervously at Glen.

"Are you sure you're okay Mrs Kilkis?" Joe asked softly. Joyce nodded sagely, reaching behind the front door and producing her coat. Slipping it on, she stepped back into the hall and checked her reflection in the mirror, dabbing at her reddened eyes with a handkerchief and smoothing her hair with the palm of her trembling hand.

"We can do this here if you'd prefer" Joe offered.

"Sergeant Tenby, I would rather keep the sadness that your questions will bring, away from my home!" As she spoke, Graham was unhooking his coat from the rack behind the door, gingerly slipping his arm into the sleeve as Joyce stepped out of the door. "Besides" said Joyce with a thin smile, "We have a rare chance to go out and have a nice time tomorrow. I have shed gallons of tears Detective Sergeant, and I am determined not to allow sadness to hold me back!"

"That's understandable Mrs Kilkis" Joe said, seizing on the opportunity to break the negative mood. "Is it a special occasion?"

"It's a reunion!" Graham snapped. "I'm retired, used to work on the railway tracks!" Realising that his attempt was unsuccessful, Joe nodded at Graham before turning and following Glen who was slowly walking down the path toward the gate. As they walked, Glen's phone rang. Showing it to Joe, he walked further ahead, exiting the garden through the gate and standing across the road near the car as he took the call. Joe waited at the gate for the elderly couple as they took a few minutes to turn off the TV and secure the house before walking slowly down the path. Without saying a word, Joe marshalled them to the rear doors of the car, standing back and looking on impassively as they got in. Glen was already sitting in the driving seat. Joe got in and looked across at Glen.

"Any news?" he asked as Glen slowly moved the car away from

the kerb.

"We've got some details back from the parking company. I'll follow it up when we get back"

"Good stuff!" Joe replied. Turning to Joyce and Graham, he smiled.

"Bear with us, we'll be at the station soon enough" Joyce nodded, smiling tensely. Graham scowled as he looked out of the window at the passing traffic. Turning back to face the front, Joe decided it was best to allow the journey to continue in silence, noting how Glen's style of driving seemed much more measured and careful as he indicated right, merging into the evening traffic.

91

Throughout the journey, Jessica had been able to think of nothing else other than Joe, the case, and her uncle. Part of her felt the need to find out how DCI Whindle was, but another part couldn't help but feel that he had gotten everything he had deserved. As regards Joe, she was scared for him. He seemed to be coping well, but being put in charge of a big investigation like this one was fraught with dangers, both emotionally and in terms of Joe's career. She felt her attraction to him grow stronger as time went on, although all this had managed to do though was muddy the waters still further. Her phone began to ring. She could see it was her mother calling, and with a sigh, she rejected the call and walked over to the evidence table, reaching underneath the leading edge and flicking a switch, causing the surface of the table to illuminate with a brilliant white light. Following Joe's instructions, she had been reviewing all of the physical evidence from the previous killings, but had taken the decision to switch her focus onto the most recent crime scene. She had never been one to strike out on her own, but she could not let lie the murder of a police officer, and she was certain that Joe would not mind her prioritising PC Mills. There were the usual heavy quantities of physical evidence recovered from the scene; wood, decaying paper, old safety vests, helmets and the like. None of these were expected to be of any use, such was the regularity with which track crews discard of broken and faulty equipment as they walk. Opening the first box, she checked the manifest, and lifted the contents on to the surface of the table one by one. As expected, the majority of the evidence recovered was typical of what you would expect to find on and about the railway line. She meticulously examined each piece of evidence. After ten minutes, Jessica decided to move on to the second box, choosing not to dismiss the contents of the first, but instead look for items which were obviously out of place, and then work back from there.

Having tidied away the first group of objects, and opened the second box, Jessica swiftly took care of the paperwork. This box contained items recovered from the clearing above the tunnel. A broken armlet with the word 'PILOTMAN' printed on the plate, some off cuts of wood of varying lengths, and a cylindrical length of aluminium, similar in dimension to a tent pole. At first glance, she didn't think too much of the pole. Placing it gently on the table she studied it for a second before moving on to the wood pieces. Sorting them into size order, Jessica decided to document the lengths and widths of the wood to ensure that no detail was left unrecorded. Reaching for her camera though, her eyes kept being drawn to the pole that lay across the brightly lit surface. The more she looked at it, the more out of place it became. It just didn't seem robust enough to be where it was found. Pressing the tips of her fingers against each end of the pole, she lifted it gently from the table, turning it as much as she could in order to look closely at it from all angles.

"What were you doing there?" Jessica asked rhetorically as she continued to turn the pole slowly under the harsh light. She picked up a knife and carefully cut through the evidence seal, sliding the pole from its sheath, and walking over to a neighbouring table. Placing the pole into a clamp, Jessica picked up her camera and photographed the pole from every conceivable angle, being sure to capture as much visual information within the pictures as she could, already thinking in terms of the impact such pictures could have on a jury. Next, she dusted the pole for fingerprints, liberally covering every centimetre of the metal with forensic powder, before working her away around the dimensions of the pole with fingerprinting tape. After the first few attempts, she had failed to pick up even a partial print, and was beginning to think that perhaps her optimism that the metal length was significant had been premature. Jessica Hopewell however, was not a woman to give up easily, and dutifully continued. It was after a further seven attempts that she stumbled across what initially looked like a scuff in the powder. Stopping and examining the scuff closer, she soon became convinced it was a print!

"Yes!" she said, punching the air as she steadied her nerves.

Grabbing her camera, she zoomed the lens in as far as she could in an attempt to capture all the detail that was present. Having comprehensively photographed the fingerprint, she gently opened the tape and placed it over the print. Resisting the urge to rip the tape from the bar, she instead peeled it away at an agonisingly slow pace, carefully closing the tape against the display card within and making sure that the adhesive was sealed with no bumps or ripples.

Jessica deliberately walked slowly across the laboratory, sitting down in front of the computer and scanning the fingerprint in preparation to conduct a search of the computerised database. Her hand reached for her mobile. Abruptly, it stopped mid-air, hovering just above the phone. She had immediately wanted to telephone Joe, but decided it would be better to wait until she completed the search of the numerous databases for the owner of the fingerprint. After a solid ten minutes of watching the search bar slowly travel across the foot of the screen, she decided to continue cataloguing the other evidence. Picking up the camera again, she was just composing the first picture of the pieces of wood recovered from the clearing, when the computer beeped. Looking up, she threw the camera back onto the table, running around to the screen as the owner of the fingerprint appeared before her.

"Oh my god!" Jessica whispered, the breath leaving her body as her slender fingers clamped across her lips. Grasping behind her for a chair, she stumbled back, her eyes locked firmly on the photograph displayed prominently on the screen. "There has to be some mistake!" Jessica sighed, re-inserting the fingerprint into the database and repeating the checking procedure. Within moments, the same picture had appeared on the screen. "I'm sure there's a rational reason for it!" she said in an attempt to convince herself. Blinking back a tear, she reached for her phone.

"I need to speak to Joe!" Jessica said to herself as she dialled his number, closing her eyes and shaking her head slowly as she waited for an answer.

Joyce and Graham seemed grateful for the respect Joe was paying them, despite being stoically eager to get this over and done with as quickly as possible.

"Please accept my apologies for us talking in an interview room. I would've liked to have used somewhere less formal, but time and space are against us!" Joe gave a warm smile, which was returned politely by Joyce. Graham crossed his arms and stared at the notice board behind Joe, his face deadpan. "Okay then!" Joe said as opened his notebook to a fresh page. He had decided to conduct the interview alone, directing Glen to follow up on the information from Russell Danton's employer. Having summoned a constable to sit in on the interview, Joe was eager to hear what Joyce and Graham had to say, and return them home as soon as he could. Reaching inside his pocket, he pulled out two tape cassettes, breaking the plastic seal on both and inserting them into the tape recorder. "Don't worry" Joe said with a smile. "I thought it best to record our conversation so that I can minimise any need to trouble you again in the event that my notes don't capture everything. If you'd rather we didn't that's fine."

Graham motioned to speak, but before he could, Joyce spoke across him.

"Whatever you find most convenient Sergeant Tenby!" Graham looked at her, only to be confronted with a stern glare. Reluctantly, he returned his gaze to the notice board.

"If you're sure" Joe said, unfastening the top button of his shirt and loosening his tie slightly. After stating the required particulars for the benefit of the tape, Joe took a deep breath.

"First of all, I want you to know that your help is appreciated. I can only imagine how difficult this is for you, but we can pause for a break whenever you want to." Joyce nodded.

"I'd like you tell me Mrs Kilkis, about Gavin. Please do take your time" Joe said as gently as he could. Joyce took a deep breath and exhaled slowly before answering.

"Gavin was, is my son!" replied Joyce flatly. "He was born as a twin. Both boys were fine, healthy. Then one morning I went into their room to get them up, and only one of them was crying." Joe looked to the floor. He could see the pain she still felt as it manifested itself in the muscles of her face, in her eyes.

"I knew straight away something was wrong" she whispered. Graham placed his hand on hers. Without looking at him, she turned her hand over and locked her fingers into his. "Steven was chattering away in his cot, grasping for me. Gavin wasn't moving." A solitary tear streamed down her cheek.

"I braced myself as I looked into his cot. I think I already knew he was gone! He looked so still and so content, as if he was in a deep sleep. I placed my hand on him, but he was so cold!" as she completed the last sentence, her last few words fell into unintelligible sobs as she leant against Graham. Throughout everything she said, he stared intently forward, his eyes glistening with moisture, his heart breaking as he witnessed her raw sadness laid bare for the very first time.

"Mrs Kilkis, I am so sorry for putting you through this! Joe said as he gulped firmly against a rising lump in his throat. "What, may I ask, was the cause of death?"

"Cot death Sergeant" Joyce replied. "My son just went to sleep one night, and never woke up!" Joe's attention suddenly turned to Joyce's earlier comments.

"Forgive me." Joe said softly. "You said earlier that Gavin was 'your' son? I assume Mr Crosbie that you're not Gavin's natural father?" Joyce closed her eyes and breathed deeply.

"No, Detective Sergeant." Graham replied. "Gavin's father was killed in an industrial accident years ago. We worked together" Joe nodded his understanding.

"What line of work were you both in Mr Crosbie?" Joe asked as he took a note of Graham's answers.

"We worked on the railways!" Graham snapped. Joe sat immediately upright, the possibility of proving his theory making the hair on his neck started to stand on end. "Gavin's father, Joyce's late husband was hit by a train!" Graham's voice softened as he glanced nervously at Joyce. "Why are you asking all of these questions Sergeant?"

"Well sir" Joe said delicately as he tried his hardest to remain business-like. "As part of our enquiries, we have identified a particular vehicle which has been seen in the vicinity of where some serious incidents have taken place. Initial checks of various databases have indicated, and I appreciate that this will be hard for you to understand, that this vehicle is registered to Gavin Kilkis." Joe sat back, crossing his hands on the desk in front of him as the elderly couple across the table stared at him unblinking. After what seemed like minutes of awkward silence, Graham coughed.

"That's impossible!" he spluttered. Joyce remained still and wide eyed, her brain struggling to process the words Joe had spoken.

"Believe me when I say that these databases have been double checked!" said Joe. "The vehicle itself is registered to an address which was demolished around a year and a half ago, but the name is not in doubt I'm afraid!"

"How can this be?" Joyce muttered.

"Surely this could be someone with the same name?" Graham interjected.

"It certainly is possible" Joe conceded. "What I need from you Mrs Kilkis is as much information regarding Gavin as you can give. Date of Birth, National Health number, things like that. Any personal data you have will help us confirm whether the Gavin Kilkis on the database is a different one. Although, I have to caution you, that it would be one hell of a coincidence if a Gavin Kilkis who holds no connection to you was found to be fraudulently residing at your address!"

Taking Joe's words on board, Joyce reached down under the table and picked up her handbag. Opening the clip, she reached inside. There were two large sized purses, both black. Plucking one of them from within, she opened it and carefully slipped her hand inside, producing an aged rectangular card, a folded piece of official looking paper, and a hospital band. Placing them on the table in front of her, she fixed Joe with a mournful expression.

"There you are Sergeant." Joe looked at her with a sober

expression. "These are things that go everywhere with me. I have Gavin's hospital band from when he was born. I have his birth and death certificates, and I have his NHS card."Joe moved to pick up the NHS card, mindful of the presence of an NHS number on one of the checks he requested. Stopping short of picking the card up, he looked up at Joyce.

"May I? Joe asked.

"Please do" Joyce replied quietly. Gently, he lifted the card from the table, picking up his pen and noting down the national health number on the front, along with the date of birth. Moving on to the birth certificate, and the death certificate, he made notes of all the relevant information before folding them carefully and sliding them back across the table to Joyce, who placed them back inside the purse.

"Sergeant, you still haven't answered our question" Graham said as he watched Joyce pick up her bag and place the purse back inside. "How could this happen? It just doesn't make any sense!" Joe smiled awkwardly, resisting the urge to pull his tie still further away from his collar.

"What do you know about identity theft?" he asked. Joyce and Graham looked at each other before replying with blank expressions.

"As police officers, we come across the scenario often, where criminals steal the identity of those who have passed away in order to escape detection when committing crime. It might well be the case that this has happened with the identity of your late son"

"How can they just steal someone's identity?" asked Joyce.

"It's surprisingly simple!" Joe replied. "All it takes is for someone to attend a register office and request a duplicate birth certificate. There are all sorts of checks in place now to try and stop this happening, but up until really recently you could request a copy of a birth certificate, pay cash, and then effectively use it to build a credit profile, take a driving test, even buy property or get a passport!"

"So my son has a passport?" Joyce snapped.

"Actually, no." Joe said. Whoever has been using your late son's identity has taken a driving test, and has been using the licence, but the licence was issued before the law required drivers to carry photo cards" Joyce nodded her understanding. "It would have to be someone who could pass as being the same age as what your late son would've been in order for the fraud to be believable. He would be using Gavin's date of birth. Do you associate with anyone who would be of a similar age at all?" Joyce and Graham both shook their heads.

"We keep ourselves to ourselves Sergeant!" Graham said. "The only person I can even think of who would fit that would be.." His voice trailed off as he looked into Joyce's eyes.

"Don't be ridiculous Graham!" Joyce hissed. Joe's eyes switched back and forth between the pair of them, silently requesting an answer.

"Mrs Kilkis" Joe said. "Even if this person isn't involved, it will help us tremendously if we can exclude them straight away!" Joyce bit her lip as head filled with conflicting thoughts.

"Graham is talking about my son Steven, Gavin's twin!" Joyce rolled her eyes as she spoke.

"Steven has never really been one that fits in Sergeant" Graham said. "I'm not saying that he's the man you're looking for, I'm just saying he would be the right age, so it would be useful to get him off your radar!" Joe looked on thoughtfully.

"Do you have a photograph of Steven?" Joe asked. Joyce reached for her handbag once again.

"Of course!" she said, opening it and producing the purse full of mementos. Sorting through the various pieces of paper, she selected a small photograph and pulled it out, handing it to Joe. It was face down. Joe took the picture from Joyce, his eyes straying to the clock on the wall as he turned it over. As his gaze came to rest on the photograph, his heart almost stopped. With eyes as wide as they have ever been, he studied the photograph, desperate not to appear as panic stricken as he felt. Quickly gathering his thoughts, he looked up, mustering a casual smile.

"Would you mind if I took a copy of this photograph? The documents as well?" Joe asked, rising slowly from his seat.

"Of course not" Joyce replied, taking the documents she had shown Joe earlier and handing them to him. Taking them from her, he turned and walked to the door.

"I won't be long!" he said, opening the door and disappearing into the corridor beyond.

Having quietly closed the door to the interview room, he briskly walked along the corridor, almost skipping with a mixture of anticipation, dread and outright shock. Standing at the foot of the stairwell, he was unsure as to what to do. Pacing around in a circle, his mind raced. Try as he might, he just could not draw his eyes away from the photograph. Making his way to a nearby office to take copies of all the documents he held in his hand, Joe fished his mobile phone from his pocket, his thumb instinctively searching through the contact directory and seeking out the number of Commander

Carlton. Punching the dial button, he slid the birth certificate of Gavin Kilkis onto the glass surface of the scanner and closed the lid, pressing the copy button. Commander Carlton answered the phone on the third ring.

"Ma'am, it's Tenby" Joe said, as coolly as he could. "You need to come down here, straight away."

"How ironic" snapped Commander Carlton. "I'm on my way to see you, Detective Sergeant!" Joe hesitated.

"May I be so bold as to ask why Ma'am?" he asked

"You clearly have not seen the latest communication from our friend, The Trackman!" Without another word, the line went dead. Putting the phone down on the desk, Joe concentrated his thoughts on the scanning machine, his heart still pounding furiously as he tried to make sense of the Commander's words, as well as the unexpected storm he would now have to navigate.

-93-

Staring at his computer screen through the gaps between his splayed fingers, Glen's eyes were watering as a consequence of his intense concentration. He was flicking through CCTV footage taken from the front of the central police station. Russell Danton's employer had been relatively quick in providing details of his schedule, and Glen had noted almost immediately that he had been tasked to check the car park next to the station. His enquiries with the parking company had yielded some good news and some bad news. The good news was that Russell Danton's motorcycle was fitted with GPS technology, which meant that Glen could easily pinpoint his time and location relative to his schedule at any given point. The motorcycle had also been located. The bad news was that the company had already recovered it in the time between them realising it was missing, and being informed that it was connected to a murder, thus compromising any forensic evidence the killer may have left on it. Having identified the time that he was checking the car park next to the station, he had requested the CCTV footage from the front of the station. He had already picked out Danton's motorcycle, taking notes of the relevant details. So far however, he had seen no sign of any blue car. Watching the camera footage of Danton merging into the passing traffic and disappearing from view, Glen's shoulders sagged. Switching the footage to double speed, he focussed his mind on the road beyond the grounds of the station. There seemed to be an endless stream of buses, alongside vans, push bikes and legions of hackney cabs. After fifteen minutes of scanning the time-lapsed movements of afternoon traffic, Glen found a glimpse of what he was so desperately looking for. Running the camera footage back and forth over a time period of around thirty seconds, he was certain that he had captured a dark blue car attempting to reverse into a parking space on the opposite side of the road. Unsure as to the exact make and model of the car, and unable to get a clear look at the driver, Glen recorded the exact time that the car appeared on the footage, noting that the driver had decided not to take the space, despite having more than ample room to park. He was just getting ready to stop the footage, when he spied a lonely figure walking slowly up to the bus stops on the other side of the road. Not being sure why it was that he found the figure so intriguing, he froze the image, taking notes and studying the pixels. As he restarted the footage, his view of the figure was obscured by a bus stopping abruptly. Suddenly, Glen realised what was so strange about what he was watching.

"No buses have stopped for him!" he said to himself. "Why?" Licking his lips, he rewound the footage and studied the bus as it stopped once more, noting that it was slightly different in colour to the rest of the buses that were speeding up and down the road, with its mandatory red body colour disturbed by a blue jagged diagonal line. Being a regular bus user, Glen knew instantly which company the bus belonged to, remembering that all buses certified to operate in the metropolitan area had to be equipped with GPS and CCTV. It didn't take long for him to perform a quick internet search and obtain the number of the bus company. Within minutes he had telephoned them and requested the CCTV details of the vehicle captured on camera.

"You're one lucky bugger!" the Operations Manager at the bus depot snorted as he looked through the vehicle log on his computer.

We've only got three buses that are detailed to that service, and the one that was running the service at the time you requested is in for service and repair right now!"

"How quickly can you get the CCTV footage to me?" asked Glen excitedly.

"Give me twenty minutes Detective Constable!" the Operations Manager replied.

As promised, an email promptly appeared with a media file attached. Clicking open the file, Glen scrolled through the footage, searching for the corresponding time to the CCTV from the police station. Ignoring the constant stream of passengers alighting and leaving the bus, he forwarded the file to the exact point where the figure appeared on the camera footage he had studied earlier. The file showed the driver stopping the bus and leaning out of his cab, the figure captured on the station cameras clearly in view. Glen was amazed at the clarity of the camera footage, focussing his attention on the door. As the leaves of the bus doors folded back, Glen recoiled in shock.

"Fuck!" he said. "Fuck! Fuck! Fuck!" The image was clear and unambiguous. The identity of the figure standing at the bus stop was only visible for a brief second, but there was no mistaking who it was. Saving the file to his computer, Glen jumped up from his seat, hurriedly dialling Joe's number, cursing as he listened to the busy tone. "Shit!" he said, pulling on his jacket and running for the door.

"Come on Commander!" Joe whispered as he once again began pacing the corridor in a repeating, circular route. After what appeared to be an age of waiting, he heard the familiar harsh, staccato sounds of heel upon polished floor. Turning to face the source of the sound, he almost laughed with relief as he saw the Commander power walking towards him.

"Ma'am, I'm afraid you're not going to like what I have to tell you" Joe said soberly, stepping toward a side office and opening the door, inviting the Commander to walk into the room. Commander Carlton calmly followed, her eyes trained firmly on the collection of documents in Joe's hand.

"Nor I you!" she retorted, crossing her hands in front of her. Joe suddenly felt the need to let Commander Carlton speak first. With pursed lips, she pulled her phone from her bag. Stabbing at the screen with a slender finger, she swivelled the phone around so that Joe could see the screen. The Commander had logged onto YouTube. The screen went dark for a second before blinking into life, a video clip beginning to play. It was undoubtedly from the same hand as the previous CDs Joe had received. The shot was dominated by the face of a young man, his eyes betraying his neutral expression, almost screaming in abject terror as his mouth fell open.

"Is that Sean Grant?" Joe asked. Commander Carlton didn't answer. Joe knew that it was. The sound was distorted by the sound of what seemed to be repeated impacts. Marginally visible at the top of the shot was the head of another man. He was leant over Sean, grunting and swearing as the shot jerked and moved in perfect synchronicity with the thrusts his body was so obviously making. Joe swallowed hard.

"He's filmed himself raping Sean Grant! The sick bastard!" Joe whispered.

"That's not the worst of it!" Commander Carlton sighed.

"Oh bollocks!" Joe said as covered his face with his hands. The realisation that the video had been posted online had hit him.

"I think you've summed things up quite nicely!" Commander Carlton said flatly as she stopped the video clip. "I've already been fielding constant phone calls from the Commissioner! We're talking to the website to get the video removed but, it's already been viewed thousands of times" She placed her hand on Joe's shoulder. "You'd better have something to offer in the way of progress"

"I'm looking into the blue car Ma'am" Joe responded as he

gathered himself. "I've managed to visit the address at which the car is registered, and I have the occupants of the house in an interview room now" Commander Carlton's expression changed from stern to satisfied.

"Good work Detective Sergeant!" she said. "I take it that we're making good headway?" Joe held up a hand. The Commander's expression reverted to sternness in the blink of an eye.

"Commander, neither occupant of the house is guilty of any crime! They are an elderly couple!"

"I don't understand" said Commander Carlton.

"Mrs Kilkis gave birth to twin sons, one of whom died from cot death. It would now appear that the other twin has possibly stolen his late brother's identity, and has registered the car under that name" Commander Carlton's eyes flicked back and forth as she took in what Joe had said.

"I'm assuming that we have the identity of the living sibling? Do we have a location or a true address for him?" Joe took a deep breath.

"We're still searching for his location, as he is estranged it would seem from his mum, but we do have an ID, and this is where it gets weird"

"Weird? We're a long way past weird!" Commander Carlton chided.

"Mrs Kilkis has given us a photograph of the living sibling Ma'am. I think you'll want to take a good look at it!" Joe shuffled the papers in his hand and produced the photograph. Just as he moved to pass Commander Carlton the photograph, he and the Commander were distracted by the sound of hurried footsteps from the corridor outside. Stowing the photograph back within the papers he was holding, Joe looked nervously towards the door. Breathing deeply, Jessica appeared, her left hand supporting her body as it clutched the door frame, her face flushed through unplanned exercise.

"Joe! Commander!" she managed to hiss as she recovered her breath.

"What's the matter Jessica?" Joe asked.

"I need to show you both something, and you're not going to like it!" Joe and the Commander swapped confused glances. As Jessica approached them, their attention diverted to another set of running feet, this time coming from the opposite direction.

"Thank god I found you! I've been looking all over!" Glen spluttered as he unceremoniously stopped in the middle of the side office, his hands on his knees as he looked at the three of them.

"Ma'am! Jessica!" he hissed, wiping a bead of sweat from his brow.

"What on earth is going on here?" said Commander Carlton, her frustration obvious..

"That is a very good question Ma'am!" Joe said.

"I've got some developments on the case Joe!" Glen said.

"Ma'am, you need to see this too!"

"Joe, Commander Carlton." Jessica said firmly. "I have no idea what Glen has come up with, but I doubt it will trump this!"

"Oh really?" Glen replied.

"Cut it out, the pair of you!" Joe snapped. They both looked at him, slightly shocked at his tone.

"As it happens guys, I have some monumental news of my own, but as Jessica was here first, I shall let you go first" Glen rolled his eyes as Jessica smiled at him smugly.

"I've been going over the physical evidence recovered from the PC Mills murder" Jessica said. "A length of aluminium pole was recovered from the clearing on the top of the tunnel, and it just didn't look as if it belonged. So I examined it, and tested it for fingerprints."

And?" Commander Carlton asked as her patience began wearing thin.

"I only recovered one usable print from it, and I've tested it a few times to confirm it. It's come back as belonging to Detective Chief Inspector Evan Whindle" Jessica almost grimaced as she uttered her uncle's name. The Commander paused. Joe's heart jumped in his chest. This confirmed his very worst fears.

"There is no way this can be a coincidence!" Joe said softly.

"Coincidence, Joe?" Commander Carlton asked.

"The photograph I was about to show you Ma'am" Joe said mournfully. "This is Mrs Kilkis' surviving twin son!" Joe handed Commander Carlton the photograph, studying her face as her eyes studied the photograph of a young DCI Whindle, her expression transforming from bemusement to horror as she turned it over, reading the lightly scribbled note in pencil reading "Steven Kilkis, Summer 1989".

"That's not all Ma'am!" Glen said quietly. The Commander looked at him disbelievingly. "DS Tenby asked me to follow up on the parking attendant, Russell Danton. I received his schedule from the parking company, and worked out that he was responsible for checking the car park next door to central station."

"Go on" she said.

"By cross referencing the CCTV footage with his visit, I managed to find a grainy image of a dark blue car attempting to park across the road from the station, but the driver changed his mind and drove away. A short while later, the camera shows a single figure standing at a bus stop. Only one bus stopped at that bus stop but he didn't get on it. I contacted the bus company, and managed to get the CCTV footage rushed over to me."

"DC Violet, please tell me this is leading somewhere!" Commander Carlton scolded, her arms resting across her stomach.

"Ma'am, the footage from the bus shows the face of the man at the bus stop, only for a brief second, but there's no mistaking who it is." Without saying another word, he handed Joe a printed still taken from the camera, clearly showing the face of DCI Whindle partially hidden under a grimy baseball cap. Joe passed it to Commander Carlton, who studied it before closing her eyes and massaging the bridge of her nose.

"This removes any doubt Commander" Joe said quietly, his head swimming. "Steven Kilkis is DCI Whindle!"

Phil's badly beaten corpse was beginning to decompose. Rigor mortis had come and gone, and the body was surrendering to discolouration and slight swelling. The smell was escalating, and Steven knew that it wouldn't be long before the stench would attract flies. Disappearing inside the office, he retrieved a grubby duvet and threw it over Phil's body, concealing the bloody horror, at least for now. Thrusting his hands into his pockets, he ambled down the stairs towards the main function room on the first floor. The caterer had just delivered the food, and Steven had carefully laid it out on the tables in the function room. He had dressed the room in preparation for tonight, wanting nothing to be out of place. Deciding against going so far as selecting a menu of music, he reasoned that he would lie in wait for his 'guests' and play the nearest CD to hand. Standing in the middle of the floor, he surveyed his work, admiring the banners and decorations he had hung, revelling in the silent drama of the coloured lights he had sequenced. Striding back down the corridor, he stepped over the duvet and its grisly secret, walking into the office and throwing himself down into the chair behind the desk. Flicking on the TV screen in front of him, he settled into the chair as he watched the CCTV images of the front door.

"All I have to do is wait!" he whispered as he stared at the screen, waiting for early evening to arrive.

96

"Did Mrs Kilkis and her partner suspect that anything was amiss when you took the photographs Detective Sergeant?" Commander Carlton asked. Joe shook his head.

"No Ma'am. I told them it would be best for me to take copies of each document and photograph so I wouldn't have to bother them again. I did say I may be a while. I thought it best to buy myself as much time as I could"

"Good thinking!" Commander Carlton said.

"If I may Ma'am?" Joe asked, stepping forward. "The pattern of these crimes bothers me. I think we are dealing with a rising intensity of activity, possibly leading up to a crescendo of some kind! I think we may need to consider asking Dr

Rothesay to perform a psychological profile!"

"I don't know Joe!" Commander Carlton replied. "I really want to keep this as quiet as we can! The less people know, the better!"

"But we do not have time on our side!" Joe said. "I feel that we're going to be investigating more murders in quicker succession unless we can move forward rapidly! I think we need some basic profiling so we can best shape our investigation and deploy resources" The Commander looked thoughtful as she considered Joe's request. Suddenly, Glen's phone began to ring. Throwing out a sheepish look, he plucked it from his shirt pocket. Commander Carlton ignored him. "Arrange it please Joe" she said before turning to Jessica. "Miss Hopewell. I am going to give you complete authorisation to access DCI Whindle's Human Resources files. I need every bit of information we have on him. I know he is your uncle, but there are times when you simply have to distance yourself from personal influences. I'm sure you can handle it." As she finished her sentence, Glen looked apologetically at Joe, motioning with his head and backing quietly out of the room. Joe nodded, turning his attention back to Commander Carlton and Jessica.

"Yes Commander" Jessica replied, unblinking. "Though I have to say I'm just so confused!" Joe and Commander Carlton looked at her. Neither of them interrupted. "I don't know anyone by the name of Kilkis! I've never met this woman who claims to be his mother!" Joe stepped forward, gingerly placing his hand upon her shoulder.

"Jess, I know this is throwing up questions left, right and centre for you, and I can only imagine what it must feel like, but we need you to focus! Once this is all sorted, I promise I will help you to answer all the questions your mind comes up with. But until then, we have a job to do." Jessica smiled, placing her hand on the top of his. Without making further comment, she walked to the door and quietly exited the office.

"Well played Joe!" Commander Carlton smiled approvingly.

Joe looked at the Commander, ignoring his ringing phone, his eyes telling her that, far from making false promises as a professional ploy, he meant every word.

97

Having excused himself from the Commander, he had answered his phone and made his way down to Glen who had made the panicked phone call.

"What's the matter?" Joe asked, looking over Glen's shoulder and waving a courteous greeting towards Sergeant Gordon.

"I just got called down to speak to someone who has made a complaint of assault. I tried to pass it over because of the investigation, but bodies are a bit thin on the ground." Glen was clearly rattled.

"Go on" Joe said.

"I haven't spoken to her yet, but apparently she says that she was assaulted in the house of one of her clients." Joe raised his eyebrows. "From what the desk sergeant was saying about the bruising on her neck and the lacerations on her nose, I'd say it was serious!"

"I don't mean to be cold Glen, but I do have priorities!" Joe said.

"The thing is, she is saying that her attacker is called Steven. His general description fits.." Glen's voice trailed off as an officer walked past them, nodding his head in greeting. Both men acknowledged him before resuming their hushed conversation.

"We could be talking about a coincidence here Glen" Joe cautioned. "Steven isn't the rarest name after all!" Glen couldn't help but agree with that sentiment.

"Go and talk to her. See if you can get any more information" Joe said. "But make sure everything stays routine Glen! We can't have anyone getting wind of this whilst we still have no proof!" Glen nodded.

"Her English isn't that great though" Glen said.

"Get an interpreter if you have to!" Joe snapped as he turned to walk away, unlocking his phone and retrieving Dr Rothesay's number from the phone book. "Do whatever needs to be done! And arrange for some transport to take Mr and Mrs Kilkis home!"

"Yes Sarge!" Glen said, opening the interview room door and disappearing inside.

"What can I do for you Detective Sergeant?" Dr Rothesay asked as he leant casually against the open door to Joe's office. Joe had been engrossed in the list of approved private practice buyers of Medazolene he had requested from the Department of Health, desperately looking for any clue or connection to the case, or his new prime suspect. Looking up, the confusion at Dr Rothesay's question was plain to see.

"You asked me to pop in and see you Joe!" he prompted, still leaning against the door.

"Ah, yes! Come in!" Joe replied, his mind catching up with the conversation. He motioned for Dr Rothesay to sit, and the doctor duly lowered himself into the chair directly opposite Joe.

"Problems?" Dr Rothesay asked.

"Yes and no" Joe replied, sitting back in the chair. Dr Rothesay noted to himself how Joe had grown in confidence beyond recognition since command was thrust upon him. "I need your assistance doctor" Joe said. "I have the distinct feeling that we are trying to catch a killer who is escalating in terms of his hunger to kill. Can we use some kind of triangulation to build a profile?" Dr Rothesay looked thoughtfully at the side wall. "So I see you decided to remove DCI Whindle's mirror from the office? You need to make this your own territory if you're to lead effectively!" Joe didn't reply. He waited for the doctor's opinion on the value of triangulating the information they had. "These offences are spread over a wide geographical area. My experience of triangulation usually encompasses a city or small county at the most. This series of attacks stretch nearly the length of England!"

"What if we were not looking to triangulate over a general geographical area, but over a specific modal system? Joe asked. The doctor looked at him blankly. "Like the railway system"

"That's brilliant Joe!" he exclaimed. "If you give me a suspect, I am pretty sure the principles of triangulation would apply to any commonalities in his movements with regard to the railway!" Dr Rothesay's face suddenly lost its smile. "But you don't have a suspect Joe!" he said. Joe cleared his throat, crossing his hands on the desk in front of him.

"Well Dr Rothesay, this is where it all gets complicated!" The doctor looked on questioningly. "I need an assurance of your absolute discretion doctor!" Joe said sternly. Dr Rothesay nodded. "You'll understand once I've explained everything!"

"Are you okay Miss Hopewell?" The deep, almost mournful Geordie accent wrenched Jessica from her thoughts. She had been walking purposefully, her head down clutching a large white envelope tightly to her chest. So oblivious was she to her surroundings that she hadn't even realised that she had entered the main doors of the police station with tears still clinging to her cheeks.

"I'm sorry?" Jessica said, spinning around, her left hand instinctively moving to the moisture on her face.

"I was just wondering if everything was alright Jessica"

Looking up, she saw it was Inspector Goodman. Blushing, she slowly wiped her tears with the tip of her finger.

"I'm fine thanks Inspector" she said. "Nothing to worry about!"

"Good!" he said, clearly relieved that he wouldn't have to lend her a sympathetic shoulder. "Actually Jessica, you may be able to do me a favour!"

"Oh really?" she said, clearing her throat and checking her eyes in the glass of the office door. Inspector Goodman disappeared inside the office and returned carrying a large document folder from the archives.

"Would there be any chance you could pass this on to DS Tenby?"

"Of course!" Jessica said, taking hold of the folder and immediately being caught off guard by its weight. "I'm going up there now!"

"Thanks for that!" Inspector Goodman said. With an awkward smile, he disappeared back into his office. Hesitating for a second, Jessica lowly turned and headed for the staircase.

"Jessica!" Inspector Goodman called after her.

"Yes?" she replied, pausing at the foot of the stairs.

"Can you give DS Tenby a message too?"

"Go on" Jessica said.

"Tell him please, that I am expecting him to deliver. He'll know what you mean!"

"Oh, okay!" Jessica replied, digesting the message and shaking her head as she turned around and slowly ascended the stairs.

Joe had just finished explaining the intricacies of the situation surrounding DCI Whindle to Dr Rothesay, when the two men were disturbed by a knock at the door. Looking up, he saw that it was Glen. With a wave of his hand, Joe signalled Glen to enter. Dr Rothesay looked up at Glen, smiling cordially. Glen glanced between the two men repeatedly.

"What's up Glen?" Joe asked.

"I've spoken to our assault victim" Glen replied.

"Did you get any information out of her?"

"I did better than that!" Glen said with a smile. "I managed to get an address! She said the assault took place in the attacker's living room! She remembered where it was!" Before Joe could say a word, Glen placed a piece of paper in front of him with the address written on it, along with a photograph.

"That's some seriously good work Glen!" Joe said, smiling.

"Well done!" Joe looked down at the paper, studying the

address and the photograph. "Isn't this the prostitute who corroborated Vincent Bridges' alibi?" asked Joe with a frown. "No. Things keep getting weirder!" replied Glen. "This is Rula Katjestska. Her twin sister Vladimira was the prostitute who corroborated Bridges' alibi!" Joe and Dr Rothesay exchanged disbelieving glances. Glen leant in towards the two men. "Joe, I may be reading into things, but when I showed DCI Whindle the picture of Vladimira he dropped his cup!" Joe considered this new piece of information. For days they had found nothing, and now suddenly information was tumbling toward them like an avalanche. "Glen, this is all circumstantial! We need to focus on what we can prove! Can you run a check on the address? I'll finish up here and we'll arrange someone to pay the household a visit!"

"Sure thing Sarge!" Glen replied as he made his way to the office door, smiling at Dr Rothesay as he left the room. Before Joe could say anything further, the door opened, and in walked Jessica, struggling to carry the two folders she was carrying as well as her bag.

"Joe!" Jessica said, stopping herself mid-flow as she saw Dr Rothesay sitting in one of the chairs opposite the desk, smiling at her as he studied her blushing face. "Doctor" she said. Dr Rothesay nodded in silent greeting.

"Everything okay Jessica?" Joe asked.

"I have a copy of my uncle's, I mean, DCI Whindle's personnel file for you" She reached over and placed it in front of Joe, the awkwardness she was feeling was starkly evident.

"Thanks Jessica" Joe said softly. She stepped back, hugging the oversized archive file and looking on as Joe opened the cover of the personnel file.

"Oh! Inspector Goodman asked me to give you this!" she said, dropping the file onto the desk, "He also asked me to give you a message" Joe looked up from the file.

"Really? What was it?" he asked.

"He asked me to tell you that he expects you to deliver" Jessica said. Joe laughed, shaking his head gently as he slid the folder across the desk towards him and placed it to one side, returning his attention to the personnel file in front of him.

"So what was with the cryptic message then?" Jessica asked.

"It's nothing to worry about" Joe replied with a smile, glancing up at Dr Rothesay. "Let's just say I've been working at improving co-operation with other departments" Joe said with a smile. Jessica laughed.

As he read the content of the opening page however, the smile on his face faded. Frantically, he slid the folder to one side, grabbing the paper that Glen had left on the desk before Jessica had arrived. Seizing it, he held it in his left hand, grasping DCI Whindle's file and comparing the details on the two papers.

"No fucking way!" Joe exclaimed. Flicking through the folder, he found a photograph of DCI Whindle and ripped it from the page, lurching from his seat and charging out of the office, leaving Jessica and Dr Rothesay standing in his wake.

Thrusting the door to the interview room open, Joe burst into the room. Rula Katjestska let out a shriek as she threw herself back in her chair, her eyes wide with fear as Joe bore down on her. Holding the picture at arm's length, he pushed it at her. The constable who had been sitting against the back wall when Joe entered had just about managed to retain her composure at his sudden entrance.

"Is this the man who hurt you Rula?" he asked forcefully. Just at that moment, Glen caught up with Joe, and was immediately taken aback with the venom in his voice.

"Sarge!" he cautioned, stepping forward, gesturing to Rula that it was ok. Turning to the constable at the back wall, he motioned for her to leave them alone. Smiling gratefully, she promptly and quietly left, closing the door behind her. Joe fixed Glen with a look before returning his gaze to the woman sat in front of him.

"Rula!" he hissed, jabbing the photograph with his forefinger. "Is he the one who attacked you?" She stared at the image of DCI Whindle, her hands trembling.

"Joe! Calm down!" Glen said, his voice raised. Joe looked at Glen.

"I don't have time for calm DC Violet! I need to know! Now!" he barked.

"Yes! That him!" she said softly, before breaking down into hysterical sobs.

"Thank you Rula!" Joe said, turning and leaving the room, the door swinging wildly behind him. "Glen! With me please" Joe commanded as he strode down the corridor.

-101-

"You're completely certain on this Joe?" Commander Carlton asked as she sat at her desk. The pen she had been holding had dropped onto the papers in front of her, such was her disbelief at her worst fears being confirmed. As she listened, she was already beginning to plan the media response operation she would inevitably have to oversee. She had learned early on in her command experience that the press love nothing more than grisly murders and corrupt police officers. "Put the two together and you've got a journalist's orgasm!" she whispered to herself as she began making few notes. At the other end of the line, Joe pulled the phone away from his ear and looked at it questioningly. Glen was sat at the other side of Joe's desk, waiting eagerly for his next orders.

"I'm sorry Ma'am, I didn't quite catch that!" he said.

Commander Carlton blushed slightly as she realised that she had said what she had been thinking.

"Never mind Joe, just thinking aloud!" she replied briskly. "Not only do we have the circumstantial evidence from the traffic camera, and the CCTV from the bus, we also have the fingerprint on the metal bar!"

"It's hardly a smoking gun Joe! I agree that you have mounting evidence, but I want you to come to me with something more if we're going to make an arrest! This is a serving, high profile police officer for goodness sake!"

"Well Ma'am, DC Violet has just conducted an interview with a prostitute who has made a complaint of assault" Joe paused for a second. The commander chose not to speak. "She had gone to the assailant's home with him to have sex with him, but he became violent and nearly strangled her into unconsciousness. She remembered the address she was taken to. It matches the address on DCI Whindle's personnel file" As Commander Carlton took a deep breath on the other end of the line it was audible. Joe remained silent as he awaited her reaction.

"This is a mess Joe!" the commander said quietly.

"I know Ma'am!" he said, bracing himself for the commander's reaction. "The girl has been shown a picture of DCI Whindle, and she confirmed it was him! Commander Carlton slammed her pen down onto the desk.

"Are you insane Joe?" she bellowed. Joe closed his eyes and took a deep breath. He knew that he had no defence.

"Ma'am, I can only apologise! We needed to strike fast! I needed it confirming instantly!"

"What we need, Detective Sergeant Tenby, is a cool head in charge when there are times of crisis! You do realise don't you that if you had to pin your case on the photo identification, the prosecution wouldn't have a leg to stand on?"

"I do Ma'am!" Joe whispered, mentally kicking himself for getting so carried away at a vital time. "It was a mistake made with the best of intentions Ma'am"

"I think that the priority is finding DCI Whindle, or Steven Kilkis, or whatever the hell he's calling himself this week!" Commander Carlton hissed. "We need to search his address now before realises we're on to him! We don't even have time for a warrant application Tenby!" Joe looked at the floor.

"In that case Ma'am, I'm not sure as how is best to proceed" Commander Carlton sighed.

"Leave the warrant to me Joe. I can pull a favour in from a Magistrate. I can hopefully convince him that the burden of proof has been met and that he will be presented with the evidence in the morning if he issues it now. You'd best get a search team sorted ASAP, and pray that you haven't torpedoed this investigation! "If it sinks, I promise you, your career will be going down with it!"

Ending the call, Joe reached for his desk phone, calling the switchboard. "Inspector George Sargeson please" he said to the operator.

"You're an idiot Tenby!" he whispered to himself as he waited to be connected.

Graham's health was not improving. He was becoming breathless at completing even the most everyday task now, and Joyce couldn't help but worry about him. Calming his breathing, he took his coffee cup in hand and helped himself to a large mouthful, his face portraying his satisfaction as the liquid slid down his throat. Putting the coffee down, he looked across at Joyce.

"Are you sure you want to go?" he asked.

"Of course I do!" Joyce replied. "The police have told us that there's probably nothing to worry about!" She smiled reassuringly.

"Well just don't think you have to put a brave face on for my benefit, that's all I'm saying!" Graham replied.

"Graham dear" Joyce said softly. "We all put brave faces on. It's called life. It's something we have to just get on with! We can't allow every day to be haunted by the past!" He nodded thoughtfully as he took another mouthful of coffee.

"So has Robert let you know whether he and Lisa can make it?" he asked.

"They left a message this morning saying they're looking forward to it. Robert's booked a taxi so we can all go together"

"Lovely!" Graham sighed. "I can't wait to introduce him to everyone" Graham said.

"It certainly will be a night to remember" Joyce replied with a smile. "Right, I think I'm going to get ready!" She got up from her chair and crossed the room, pausing whilst she lowered her lips to his forehead, kissing it tenderly. He smiled and gently cradled her hand before she walked into the hallway and across towards the bedroom.

Closing the door to Commander Carlton's office, Joe stepped into the centre of the corridor, appreciating the gentle breeze that was blowing across his moist skin. He had gone to great lengths to illustrate everything he was doing to redress the situation he had created. Commander Carlton seemed pleased at the fact that he had organised a search team from outside the station, and had even agreed to authorise the payment of the overtime from the investigation budget, although Joe was certain she swore under her breath as she signed the form. Being as good as her word, she had managed to arrange the search warrant, sliding it across the desk towards Joe as soon as he had entered the room. Overall, he was feeling optimistic that he had managed to deal with a crisis of his own making. As he had made to leave the office, the commander had called him back.

"I must congratulate you Detective Sergeant on redeeming yourself! I was beginning to think that I had overestimated your ability to step up and handle the pressure of a big investigation like this! I'm glad you've persuaded me to grant you a stay of execution!" Joe could only a muster a grateful nod of the head as he excused himself from her presence, the back of his neck beginning to get sticky with anxiety and perspiration. The cool air was calming him down, and lowering his body temperature, and it was heavenly. The vibrating of his phone wrenched him from the moment. Taking it from his pocket, he saw that he had received a text message and opened it. The message was from Inspector Sargeson:

"TROOPS WILL BE WITH YOU IN FIVE MINS JOE. HOPE THEY CAN BE OF HELP. GOOD TO SEE YOU GETTING ON WELL. ALL THE BEST. GEORGE"

Joe smiled as he read the message, closing the phone and striding down the hall towards CID.

Striding into the office, he saw that Glen was talking to Jessica. They both looked up and smiled. Joe smiled back as he continued walking, disappearing into his office, and reappearing seconds later with a handful of paperwork and his suit jacket.

"Glen, I need you with me please" Glen duly rose from his seat and slipped his jacket on too. Jessica looked up at Joe.

"Am I needed?" she asked. Joe mulled her question over for a second. He was certain that a keen forensic eye like Jessica' would be needed, and he was sure that she would be called into the address anyway to carry out a full forensic examination. However, the house was the home of her uncle. Deciding that for now at least, she should be spared the ordeal, Joe made his decision.

"Not for now Jessica" he replied. "We may need you soon enough though, so keep your phone on!" That said, he turned on his heels and made for the door with Glen following closely.

"Is there anything you do want me to do?" Jessica called after him, suddenly feeling a little surplus to requirements.

Spinning around to face her, Joe continued to walk backwards as he spoke.

"There are some files on my desk from Inspector Goodman. Could you make a start on sorting through those? They're the checks into all of the victims we requested"

"I thought we couldn't get them authorised?" Glen said.

"Trust me Glen, it cost me dearly to get round that one!" Joe replied, still looking at Jessica.

"Ok, no problem!" Jessica said, getting up from her chair and walking to Joe's office. She looked back to the main door to say something, but Joe and Glen had gone.

"Bye guys!" she said to the empty room as she walked into the office and sat down at the desk.

It's a bit odd though Joe, don't you think? Getting traffic to do a house search?" Glen was trying his best to keep up with Joe as they raced down the steps and out into the yard.

"Not really!" Joe replied. "My take on it is that we need to keep this search away from the gossip of the station! Can you imagine what would be going around of we took officers from this nick and had them turn the DCI's house over?"

"That's a fair point!" Glen conceded.

"This way, the search is done by officers who are based a few miles away! It's bound to get out eventually, but at least we'll have a bit of time to try and get things sorted before the jungle drums begin beating!!" Joe said as they approached the van. Joe walked up to the side door and banged on it, the door sliding immediately open.

"Hello Joe!" said a familiar voice from within. Squinting as he looked at the back row of seats, Joe could see the unmistakable features of Sgt Bob Davis.

"Hello Bob!" replied Joe as he climbed in. Glen hesitated for a second before deciding to follow suit. "How's things?"

"Not as good as they are for you from what I've been hearing, Detective Sergeant!" Bob said with a grin. Joe smiled awkwardly, before introducing Glen to the assembled officers, all immaculate in navy blue police coveralls; their public order equipment was stowed neatly at the back of the van. Looking at the other officers, Joe had seen two or three of them around, but didn't know any names. Sensing this, Bob introduced them. As he was the only Sergeant present except for Joe, Bob had assumed command of the PC's.

"So why are we here then Joe?" Bob asked.

"Well, it's a bit delicate really." Joe said. Looking at each of the officers in the van, he went to speak, but hesitated, reaching over and closing the van door so as to prevent anyone from overhearing accidently. "We're investigating the spate of deaths that have been going on, and we have a suspect! We have an address that has been supplied by a prostitute who has alleged that the suspect assaulted her and nearly choked her to death after he took her back to his house for sex"

"Nice work!" said Bob.

"Guys, we need to get something straight!" Joe said slowly. "It is vital that nobody finds out what is going on today. If it comes out, it could only have been from someone in this van, or Commander Carlton, and I think we all know where the shit would land if there were a choice between us and her!"

The assembled officers looked at each other, all nodding and muttering their agreement.

"So what's the big secret?" asked Bob.

"This is the name and address of the suspect." Joe leant across and handed Bob a copy of the paper. Bob glanced at it and shrugged, handing it back to Joe.

"Steven Kilkis. So?" he said. "I'm not seeing the connection"

Joe shuffled the papers in his hand and produced a copy of the photograph he had shown to Rula Katjestska.

"What's this?" he asked, looking at it, and then looking up at Joe, frowning.

"That, Bob, is a verified photograph of Mr Steven Kilkis!"

"But this is DCI Whindle!" said Bob.

"I know." Joe replied flatly. "Steven Kilkis, and DCI Whindle are one and the same person!" The officers in the van swapped astonished glances. Most of them had never heard of DCI Whindle let alone met him; nevertheless they understood only too well the gravity of what Joe was saying.

"Bloody hell!" Bob exclaimed as he sagged back in his seat.

"Exactly!" Joe said, his expression grim.

Bob looked at Joe. "Are you sure this is right? I don't want to stitch up a copper if he's innocent!"

"We've got at least five pieces of separate evidence that confirm it! Commander Carlton would never have authorised me to assemble a search team otherwise" Bob didn't hesitate in his reply.

"That's good enough for me! What do you need from us?"

Joe and his makeshift team gathered at the end of the road. They stood in a tight circle, having parked well out of sight of the property they were here to search. The area looked a little bit scruffy, if Joe were being honest. He had always assumed that senior officers lived in large houses, but the homes on this road seemed to be more like council houses. The grass verges were overgrown but not wild, the cars tired and dated, not unlike their owners. "Keep a look out for railway memorabilia, magazines, timetables and clothing!" Joe had said to the team as the driver of the van negotiated a series of steep speed humps. "Also, I want you to keep an eye out for heavy tools, the type that would be too big to use on a car or around the house. In addition, please be alert to any sign that the property contains controlled drugs. I'm not talking about the traditional drugs, like heroin and cocaine; I'm talking legally manufactured pharmaceuticals that come in small vials. In particular we are looking for a drug called Medazolene." The policemen exchanged glances and the odd whispered comment as a few of them scribbled down notes. Joe produced the hastily obtained warrant, showing it without further word to Sergeant Davis, who nodded his verification of the details.

Curtains were twitching as the team ventured further down the road, and Joe found himself worrying about Whindle getting advanced warning of their presence. Holding his hand up, he turned to face the officers as they stopped in unison. "Bob! Take two of your lads and head around the back would you?" With a nod, Bob turned to the nearest two officers to him and gestured towards the alleyway which disappeared between two houses a few yards further down on their left. Arriving at the front gate, Joe paused as he considered what to do. Without referring to anyone on the team, he opened the garden gate and stepped inside the boundary of the fence. The garden had seen many better days by the look of it. The grass was at least knee-length, and against the wall rested a pile of rubbish bags containing decomposing household waste, judging by the smell. The walls were painted in a depressing coat of gun-metal grey, and the drainpipe lent at a worrying angle away from the structure of the house. Joe really was shocked.

"Looks like he's let himself go!" Joe turned around, the unexpected voice shaking him from his assessment of the building. It was Glen.

"I know!" Joe said. "I'd never have expected a senior officer to live in a dump like this!"

"It wasn't always a dump young man!" Both of them jumped at the intrusion, turning to face the direction from which the voice originated. A small, aging woman stood at the fence. On her side of the boundary, the grass was neat and flawlessly green. The border of her lawn was peppered with gnomes, miniature windmills, and stone ornaments featuring frogs, fairies, and dog's fishing from the bank of an imaginary pond. She too, was neat and tidy, her grey hair precisely curled and styled, and her navy blue dress spotless.

"I take it you're after Evan?" she asked. Joe hesitated.

"its okay" she said, offering her hand over the fence. Joe accepted, reciprocating. "I've known him for years!" the old woman said. "He's not here though! He hasn't been home for a couple of days!" Joe and Glen exchanged worried glances.

"Are you certain, Mrs..?" Joe said.

"Walker" the old woman said with a smile. "Yes, I am quite

certain!"

"Detective Sergeant Joe Tenby" Joe said smiling. "This is Detective Constable Glen Violet" the old woman smiled warmly at the pair of them.

"We're trying to trace Evan because we need to speak with him urgently" Joe said.

"Good luck with that!" she replied. "He doesn't even answer the door to the postman anymore! He used to have all the time in the world to stop and chat, but now he won't even look you in the eye, that's on the odd occasion that you see him at a normal hour!"

"Well, thank you for your time Mrs Walker" Joe said in an attempt to bring the conversation to an end, and get on with the purpose of the visit.

"I'll tell you what, it wouldn't surprise me if there was all sorts of crime, and unspeakable things going on in that house, what with the girls and strange people I've seen leaving there all times of the day and night!" She said, ignoring Joe's last comment.

"Mrs Walker, do you know what Evan does for a living?" The old woman looked at Joe as if he had spoken in a foreign language.

"Of course I do! You don't live next door to someone for all this time and not know what they do for a job! He's a track worker! On the railways!" Joe struggled to react naturally to what Mrs Walker had said. Taking a steadying breath, Joe keyed the microphone on his radio

"DS Tenby to Sergeant Davis, are you receiving?"

Putting the radio back into his pocket, Joe produced the warrant. Striding to the door, he paused for a second and took a deep breath. This wasn't the first time that Joe had served a warrant on premises that were to be searched, but it was the first time he had ever done so on the home of a fellow police officer! He collected his thoughts before clenching his fist and banging loudly on the centre panel of the door.

"Evan Whindle! Steven Kilkis! This is the Metropolitan Police! Open the door! We have a warrant to search these premises!"

From behind him he could hear the sound of tubular steel on concrete as one of the officers positioned himself to make use of 'the enforcer' a reinforced steel battering ram used by the police to forcibly enter buildings and to break locks. Joe counted to ten. Looking down at his pocket, he plucked the radio out and called Sergeant Davis.

"Any movement Bob?" Joe asked.

"Not a thing I'm afraid!" came the reply.

Clenching his fist one more time, he again hammered on the door.

"Open up!" he shouted. By this time, a number of doors on the street were open. People were stood in their gardens looking on at the spectacle that was unfolding. Joe and Glen looked at each other as they listened for any sounds coming from inside the house.

"Okay!" Joe said as he stepped back. He looked to the police officer patiently waiting with the enforcer. "In you go constable!" he said. The constable lifted the giant steel tube from its resting position against his thigh and levelled it at the area of the door where the lock was situated. Stepping forward, he tightened his grip on the handles, and swung both arms forward simultaneously, smashing the butt of the tube squarely against the wood. Joe half turned away in reaction to the loud 'crack' that filled the air. Splinters of wood that flew in all directions. Unbelievably, the door held firm, despite the damage to it. Again, the constable took aim with the enforcer and rammed it against the door. This time, the wood was no match for the force with which he swung the steel tube, flinging the door violently away from its lock, and sending it smashing against the wall. The officers rushed through the door, shouting loudly as they disappeared into the hallway, the old woman from next door looked on disapprovingly, having retreated to the safety of her front doorstep.

"What on earth is going on?" she shouted above the racket.

"Clear downstairs DS Tenby!" one of the officers shouted as two others pounded up the staircase. Seconds later, that declaration was followed with "Clear upstairs!" from the same officer. Ignoring her, Joe stepped inside the door. Glen followed behind, pausing to speak to the old woman.

"We have a warrant issued by the crown court Mrs Walker." He said gently. "We need to be inside this house. It's in connection with a quite serious matter."

"What kind of serious matter?" she asked, her curiosity spiked by the prospect of juicy gossip to share.

"I'm afraid I really can't discuss that, Mrs Walker" Glen said diplomatically. She tutted in disappointment, and marched back inside her house, closing the door firmly behind her.

Inside the house, Joe was strolling around the downstairs. Everything inside seemed just as grimy and forlorn as the outside of the property. The dark blue sofa in the living room looked as if it were ready for collapse. The air hung heavy with the smell of neglect. Mouldy food trays littered the work surfaces of the kitchen, and empty drinks bottles of all types were positioned randomly in each room. Joe was keeping a keen eye for the kind of things he had outlined to the team. All he could see so far however, was dirt. Sergeant Davis and his officers made their way into the garden via the back gate. Joe unlocked the door and let them in.

"Can you head upstairs and help with the search Bob?" Joe asked.

"Of course!" Sergeant Davis said, beckoning the other two officers who had entered with him to follow. Joe looked at Glen, who was obviously thinking along similar lines as Joe.

"How can anyone live like this?" Glen asked, the toe of his shoe pushing a half-eaten tray of Chinese food away from the side of an old armchair. Joe shrugged as he slid his hands clumsily into a pair of latex gloves.

"Take the living room Glen" he directed. "I'll take the kitchen" Standing at the junction between the two rooms, Joe was confused. He had expected to find railway memorabilia strewn around the house. He had convinced himself that the DCI was living a double life, whereby this house was in some way his sanctuary. All it seemed to be was a murky little house where Steven Kilkis indulged in darker pastimes, and from where Evan Kilkis put on a false façade for the rest of the world to hide his crimes. On the worktop sat a cardboard box. Joe opened it. Inside were piles of photographs. Steven Kilkis, Joyce Kilkis, and other people Joe had not seen before who had been pictured at family gatherings and days out. Quickly sorting through them, he was just about to put them back in the box when he saw a picture that made him do a double-take. In the picture stood a young boy with his arm wrapped around the leg of a man. The two of them were obviously related, so similar were they in features. The man was wearing an all in one orange coverall with a British Rail logo on the breast. Turning the picture over, Joe saw that there was a scribbled note on the back. It simply read "Me and Dad"

Before he had chance to examine anything else, his attention was drawn to heavy footsteps descending the stairs. Standing up, Joe turned to the doorway, where a breathless Sergeant Davis appeared at the foot of the staircase.

"You need to see this Joe!" he said.

Having finally plucked up the courage to open the file, Jessica had taken out the contents, and spread them across Joe's desk. The file contained something that Jessica's lecturer at university had referred to as a 'bunny check'. This was a slang term, used to describe an in-depth check on a closed group of people. Every person connected to the original group then underwent a similar level of scrutiny, with their acquaintances subsequently checked as well, with the resultant chain of information resembling a rabbit warren. Searching through the histories, love lives and work records of these people was beginning to prove tiresome, and Jessica could appreciate how easy one could become lost in the labyrinth of papers and data. Looking around the office brought her mixed emotions. The very fact that this was no longer her uncle's office had made her feel uncomfortable. In many ways, the sight of Joe sitting at this desk was offensive, but in another way, it signalled the beginning of a new freedom. She had every faith in Joe's ability to lead the team, and more importantly, bring the killer to justice. Like a vicious circle, her train of thought promptly brought her back to her uncle again.

"He couldn't really be the killer, could he?" she asked herself as she stared blankly at the sea of papers. Jessica knew only too well that she had no choice other than to allow the evidence to lead her to the truth, however painful that truth may prove to be. It was becoming clear that she was becoming more and more lost, the longer she tried to wade through these files. She had to think of a way to filter the data she was handling. As she considered her options, she had an idea.

"Joe's theory is that the common factor in all of this is the railway" Jessica said to herself, rising from the seat and walking out into the main office. Grabbing the white board cleaner, she wiped the board until all the writing had been erased. Returning to the office, she gathered up the papers and took them into the main room, spreading them out across two desks, pausing momentarily to ensure that the papers had not become mixed, and that each victim's profile was separated. Immediately, she started searching through them for any connection to the railway, noting down the names and job titles of each of the victims to date, with the exception of Russell Danton and Andy Mills.

Moving those two piles of papers to one side, she began her search at the pile topped with an A4 sized picture of Tina McBride which had been copied from her staff identification. It didn't take Jessica long to realise that Tina's occupation was not her only connection to the railways. She had an uncle who had worked as a track worker. A cursory examination revealed that Ian Ellington had worked for the railways for a total of 39 years before retiring, and subsequently passing away from pancreatic cancer. Dutifully, Jessica wrote Ian Ellington's name on the whiteboard, circling it and drawing a line connecting it to Tina.

Jessica swiftly moved on to Anna Brown. Anna's father had been employed as a trainee train driver years previously, but had his employment terminated after being involved in a car crash which had resulted in the loss of his right eye. Jessica made a note of this, searching Anna's father's record for any sign that he may harbour a grudge. He had not even had a parking ticket, and had filed tax and VAT returns for a business he had started with his brother which had proved to be quite successful. Continuing her journey through the lives of the victims, she rapidly came across a further link originating from Anna Brown. Gary Fenley, her uncle on her mother's side of the family had also worked for British Rail. He had been a Signaller, and a manager for 31 years before retiring to a small village just outside of Dawlish. Scribbling his name down, and connecting it to Anna Brown, she quickly completed the search of that pile of papers before moving on.

As she waded through page after page of addresses, records, employment lists and so on, she became increasingly alarmed, as well as excited. With each victim came fresh connections to the railway, and Jessica felt a mixture of anticipation at establishing a further pattern to be investigated, as well as anger toward her uncle for preventing the team from uncovering this link. Jessica made a note of the fact that Sean Grant was the son of a Train Driver by the name of Stuart

Mallon. Writing the details on the board, she could already see that there were far too many connections for this to be a mere coincidence. Reaching for Russell Danton's file, she was already prepared to find another link, and she wasn't disappointed. His father had worked as a Signaller. He was called John Tierney. Writing his name on the board, she shook her head at how crowded the whiteboard had already become. For the sake of thoroughness she had examined Andy Bell's file, happily confirming that he was not connected to the railway, and truly was just trying to do his job when he lost his life. Walking over to Glen's desk, she lowered herself into the seat facing the computer, and opened the log in page for the intranet. Starting with Tina McBride, she typed the names of every victim, and everybody else who was connected through the lines on the whiteboard into an online search, in an attempt to glean any further information that may have been missed in the files. It didn't take her long to realise that one person alone would simply take too long to sift through all of the template advertisements and links to commercial sites that were displayed on the screen every time she made a new search.

"This is ridiculous!" Jessica hissed. Putting her hands on the top of her head, she gently span Glen's chair in a slow rotation as she wracked her brain for a way to uncover another piece of information that might just link everything together and hand Joe the smoking gun that would definitively solve the case. Instantly, like lightning cutting through storm clouds, she had an idea.

"That's it!" she shouted, jumping up from the chair, and sheepishly looking around the room as her voice rebounded off the smooth surfaces of the floor and walls. "If I can't find anything about this lot" Jessica said, motioning towards the names on the whiteboard with a gesture aimed at nobody in particular "I'll search for Steven Kilkis!" Excitedly, her fingers pounded the keyboard, the ring finger of her right hand thumping the enter button. Within seconds, a link to a website dedicated to railway incidents appeared with a section of text including the words "fatality" "incident" "board of inquiry" and "Raymond Kilkis" As she scrolled through the text, it quickly became apparent that Raymond Kilkis had been struck by a train whilst working on the line near a town called Mallington. Her eyes widened as she read aloud from the screen. "The report into the incident concluded that the death was a result of the maintenance crew being given incorrect information. This had caused them to examine the wrong set of points. Arrangements had been made for their protection from trains, but due to the misunderstanding regarding the location of the fault, the crew had inadvertently exposed themselves to mortal danger by working on a line open to trains running at full speed. Trackman Raymond Kilkis was killed instantly as a consequence of being struck by the 21:14 southbound express from London Victoria." Her voice trailed off as she continued to read, her silence interrupted by her taking such a sharp intake of breath it sounded like a shriek.

"I think I've got our connection!" she whispered. Squinting into the screen, Jessica scrutinised the text to make sure that she had understood completely what she was reading. The site went on to recall the investigation, and the fact that a board of inquiry was convened to examine the incident. It was the name of the driver that caught her attention. It was Stuart Mallon. Looking up at the board, her mouth went dry. Scrolling frantically further down, she also saw the names of Jerry Pickford, John Tierney, Gary Fenley, and Ian Ellington. Not being able to believe what she was seeing, she stared motionlessly at the screen, streams of tears spilling over her eyelids and cascading down her cheeks.

"I don't believe it!" Jessica sobbed. "My Uncle Evan is the killer! My uncle is the trackman!"

Once she was satisfied that she was calm enough to control the pitch of her voice at least, she reached for her phone and rang Joe. His phone rang five or six times before he answered. Taking a deep breath, she went for it.

"Joe. I need to tell you something! I've found a connection in the case!" Jessica said.

"Before you do" Joe replied. "I need to tell you something. I think it's important so I'm just going to say it." Before Jessica could protest, Joe continued, stepping out of the bedroom and onto the landing. "There's no easy way of saying this Jessica, but your Uncle is our killer. I'm looking at the proof right now. Steven Kilkis is the trackman!" Jessica pulled the phone away from her ear and looked at it disbelievingly

"How do you know?" she asked. "What proof? Joe paused.

"We're searching his house as we speak!" Jessica took another deep breath. "What was your development on the case?" Joe asked.

"Well" Jessica said, fighting back the urge to cry once more.

"You have proved the who, I think I can prove the why"

"What do you mean?" Joe said.

"I've been looking at the background checks of everyone

connected to the victims. Every single one, apart from Andy Bell had at least one connection to the railway industry, other than their job. Jessica paused, forcing herself to remain professional. Joe remained silent. "When I entered all of the names of the relatives of the victims into an online search, I was directed to a website dedicated to railway accidents"

"This is sounding ominous" Joe said.

"They were all summoned to give testimony at a board of inquiry into the death of a track worker Joe. He was killed by a train. His name was Raymond Kilkis. He is survived by his wife, Joyce, and their two children Steven and Robert" Joe took in a deep breath and whistled.

"What are we going to do now Joe?" asked Jessica

"We're going to find him!" Joe replied. "He's not finished yet. I know it! Thinking about it Jess, can you run a background check on Graham Crosbie please? I'm sure he mentioned something about working on the railways too!"

"I'm on it!" Jessica said, ending the phone call and tapping Graham Crosbie's name furiously into the computer. As Joe put his phone back into his pocket, Bob Davis approached him.

"Joe. I've found something!" Silently, Joe followed Bob into the bedroom. The room was rectangular, with a chimney breast dominating the left hand wall. One of the recesses either side of the chimney breast had been filled with a home-made cupboard, its wooden doors covered in thick black paint. Bob walked over to the cupboard and opened both doors. Joe analysed the content and cleanliness of the cupboard's interior. It was spotlessly clean, and meticulously organised. On the bottom of the cupboard lay a large pile of Polaroid photographs, and in two rows on the back wall there were A5 sized pictures of numerous men. Joe snatched up the Polaroids, studying the images of reddening eyes and agonised faces.

"That explains him rubbishing my theory!" he muttered, turning his attentions to the photographs that faced him in meticulous rows. Judging by the style of their hair, clothes and the composition of the photographs themselves, Joe estimated that the pictures had to be at least twenty years old. Next to each main picture was a smaller picture of one of the victims. It was clear from the inside of this cupboard that Steven Kilkis had been linking the victims to an event that had happened involving the people in these photographs.

On the floor of the cupboard was a large lump hammer wrapped in grubby rags. A cursory glance at the head of the hammer revealed that it was heavily stained in blood and matted hair. It wasn't a giant leapt to assume that the hair was from Tina McBride. Puffing out his cheeks, he resisted the urge to smile at this breakthrough, instead looking to Bob and raising his eyebrows. Without uttering a word, Bob pointed at the inside of the cupboard door nearest to Joe. Joe looked down at the door, his facial expression transforming instantly from one of study to one of shock. There, in front of him was a picture of his father, and next to the photograph was a picture of Joe. It must have been taken from his service file. Joe's throat went dry.

"Isn't your dad dead Joe?" Bob asked softly. Joe nodded, his eyes still glued to the picture.

"I must be next on his list!" Joe said to himself as he shifted his gaze and stared unblinkingly at an image of his own face.

Walking to the top of the stairs, Joe called Glen's name.

Almost instantly, Glen appeared from the hallway below.

"Sarge!" he said dutifully.

"Glen. I need you to go and find Joyce Kilkis and Graham Crosbie. Find them and take them back to the station!"

"What's happened?" Glen asked.

"Just do it Glen! Go now! Find them and make sure they're safe! I'll explain later! Go!"

Without a further word, Glen disappeared. Joe heard the door close firmly behind him as he left, the dull rumble of the car being started confirming that Glen was on his way. Sighing as he returned to the room, Joe examined the cupboard once more.

"He's building up to a big finale Bob!" Joe said. Bob Davis didn't reply. He had only agreed to execute the warrant for some easy overtime. Despite his experience, he hadn't been prepared for this, and was still struggling to take it all in. "I just hope we can find him before he finishes his list!"

"I'm glad you called!" Amber whispered softly into the mouthpiece of the phone. She had just emerged from the shower, and was cradling the phone between her shoulder and ear as she secured the towel around her head. Taking the phone in her hand, with the other one she held the upper edge of the towel that was covering her modesty as she padded softly across the bedroom and sat in the chair that faced her dressing table and mirror. "I haven't heard anything from you since you were so mean to me at that crime scene!" Amber giggled as she began arranging the bottle of foundation, nail varnish remover and her lips stick, eye shadow, cotton wool and other make up into a row as the voice on the end of the phone reassured her that the rudeness was purely for show. "Yes, I am all damp and naked" she said softly. "I am not having phone sex with you now! I don't care if you're rock hard! That's just naughty mister!" she whispered playfully. The voice at the end of the line had told her to get a pen and paper. Reaching down to the drawer, she snatched it open, obediently taking out a jotting pad and a pen as she listened. She admired herself in the mirror as he spoke. "Oh really! You think I'd want to feel your lips on my body do you?" She giggled as the man at the other end of the phone delved into explicit detail. Suddenly, the voice at the other end of the line made her breathe in sharply, her eyes wide. "No way! You can't say that! Stop it!" she said as she pretended to be bashful, her excitement lifting her voice a couple of octaves. "You're sure?" She gently rubbed her teeth against her bottom lip as she returned her gaze to the mirror, her smile a mix of excitement and self-adoration. "Okay Mr Horny! I get the idea! So the police will be raiding the Milward Club tonight" she said as she made slow, graceful notes on the pad. "Eight O'clock! Sure I'll be there! This is the kind of ringside seat I need!" Cradling the phone once more between her ear and shoulder, she reached for the bottle of nail varnish remover and unscrewed the lid. Grabbing a large piece of cotton wool, she soaked it with the blue liquid and began firmly wiping the blood red thumb nail of her left hand, her face still illuminated with the smile of a woman who had gotten exactly what she wanted. "Okay then! I cannot thank you enough!" she said into the mouthpiece. "Well, maybe I can thank you enough then!" she giggled, maintaining the pretence of mutual attraction. "I'll speak to you soon!"

"Wait!" said the voice on the other end of the line. "I'm telling you this on the strict condition that you never reveal the source of your information! Fucking a reporter is one thing, but leaking the details of a murder inquiry is more than my career is worth!"

"Don't worry baby!" she soothed. "I won't tell a soul!"

"Good!" he said, pretending to be reassured by her guarantee, but not caring particularly whether she told anybody or not. It wouldn't matter soon. "I can trust you, can't I Amber?" he asked.

"Of course you can!" she insisted as she continued to rub the varnish from her finger nails, her mind already working overtime on tonight's unexpected exclusive. "I'll see you soon horny man!" she said playfully. "I suppose I really should thank you in person!" She examined her freshly naked fingernails as she spoke, knowing full well that she had no intention of following through with her words.

"I'll be looking forward to that!" he said breathlessly. "I have to go now"

"Me too!" Amber said, and ended the call, throwing the phone onto the dressing table and continuing to scrub at the finger nails of her other hand.

Steven locked his phone and sat back in the chair, smiling to himself.

"Like a sweet lamb to the slaughter!" he whispered, and then pressed the top of the phone to his mouth as he performed a mental review of everything he needed to organise for tonight. "I've got my arena, I've got my audience, now I only need the guests of honour!" he said to himself, licking his lips at the thought of what was to come.

"Can we help you young man?" asked the elderly gentleman with an authoritative tone. "This is a hawker free zone!" Glen reached inside his jacket pocket and produced his warrant card.

"I'm Detective Constable Violet sir, Metropolitan Police" Glen walked towards the fence and extended the warrant card in order to give the man an opportunity to scrutinise it. Having squinted for a few seconds at the particulars on the card, he looked at his wife and nodded. She looked across the fence at Glen with a warm smile, quite a transformation from the look of deep suspicion she had been eyeing him with until only seconds previously.

"Malcolm and Harriet Simpson, Detective Constable" The woman said cordially. She nodded towards her husband who smiled thinly.

"I'm looking for Mrs Kilkis and Mr Crosbie" Glen said, returning the smile and nod. "It is a matter of some urgency"

"I'm afraid they've gone out Detective Constable" Malcolm Simpson said.

"It must've been about half an hour ago" added Harriet.

"Well, 25 minutes perhaps" corrected Malcolm. Harriet smiled awkwardly as she looked briefly at the floor.

"I don't suppose you know where they've gone at all?" Glen asked hopefully. Malcolm shook his head slowly.

"I'm afraid not. We tend to keep ourselves to ourselves you see." He said.

"They were looking rather smart!" Harriet said. "A special occasion perhaps?"

"You definitely saw them leave?" Glen pressed the elderly couple, allowing himself to step towards the fence. Harriet looked unsure. She thought long and hard. "I saw them come out into the front garden, but then they went back inside, as if they'd forgotten something" Glen looked at Malcolm.

"I didn't see anything I'm afraid, Detective Constable. I was tending to my hydrangeas." Malcolm half turned towards the back fence, motioning with his hand. Glen nodded, none the wiser as to which plant exactly Malcolm was referring to.

"Well, thank you both very much indeed for your assistance" Glen said, stepping to the fence and offering his hand to the couple, each in turn accepting it and exchanging handshakes in a cordial fashion. Glen smiled once more before turning away from the fence and calling Joe.

"Are they with you Glen?" Joe said before Glen had chance to speak.

"I'm afraid not!" he said. "Nobody's answering the door and there's no sign of movement inside the house"

"Has anybody seen them leave?" Joe asked.

"I've just spoken with the next door neighbours" Glen replied. "They said they saw them walking out into the front garden, both dressed smartly. It looks to be honest, as if they've already gone out Joe!" Joe paused for a minute, thinking things through as rationally as he could.

"Did the neighbours actually see them leave the house Glen?" Joe asked. Glen could almost hear him pacing. "They never actually said they saw them leave Joe" Joe took a deep breath.

"

"Break in." he said calmly.

"What?" said Glen. "I can't do that! I need a warrant!"

"Yes you can!" Joe countered. "There's a very real chance that Joyce Kilkis and Graham Crosbie are in real danger Glen! They're on a list of people who have been targeted by Steven Kilkis, and we need to make sure they're not lying in a pool of blood!" Glen breathed deeply, his heart pounding.

"I'm not sure Joe" Glen said. He too was pacing.

"I didn't ask you if you were sure DC Violet, I gave you a direct order. Any comeback will stay with me Glen. Just do it!" Ending the call, Glen returned his phone to the inside pocket of his suit jacket. He walked over to the back door and examined it. He pulled out his gloves and wriggled his fingers into them, then unclipped his night stick from his belt and expertly extended it with a flick of his wrist. Resting the tip of the night stick against the bottom right hand corner of the pane, he brought his arm back in readiness to swipe at the glass. Just as he was about to swing his arm forward, he was interrupted by a voice.

"Detective Constable! What on earth are you doing?" Glen looked up at the fence. It was Malcolm Simpson.

"I'm going to have to ask you to go back inside sir!" Glen said diplomatically.

"There's no need to wreck the bloody door!" Malcolm said, ignoring Glen's request.

"I'm afraid there is sir!" Glen replied. "I have to reason to believe that Mrs Kilkis and Mr Crosbie may be in serious danger, and I need to get inside! This is serious police business sir! Please step back!"

Malcolm sighed in obvious frustration.

"You misunderstand me Detective Constable!" he said as he produced a set of keys. "You don't have to break in because we keep Joyce's spare keys for her!" Malcolm threw them gently over the fence. Catching them, Glen sought out the door key and nodded his thanks, his face reddening as he snapped his night stick closed, and returned it to his belt. Loudly identifying himself as a Police Officer, Glen unlocked the door and carefully slipped inside.

Walking to the top of the stairs, Joe called out "Up here Jess!" Stepping back to the bedroom doorway, Joe waited for Jessica to scale the stairs as he continued to stare at the screen of his phone. Jessica's flushed face suddenly appeared in his view, her breathing laboured as she struggled with three boxes of equipment.

"A hand would be nice Detective Sergeant!" Jessica said.

"Sorry!" Joe said as he met her halfway, taking two of the boxes from her and awkwardly climbing back to the landing, his phone wedged in his mouth. Putting the boxes down, he recovered his phone and put it in his shirt pocket. Joe and Jessica stood facing each other, her eyes travelling along the dimensions of the landing, and the connected rooms that she could see. Joe frowned as he watched her.

"You've not been here before!" he exclaimed. She answered his question with an awkward smile, clearly groping for an appropriate response. "Just let me know if you want to leave" he said. "If this gets too much for you, please tell me"

Joe motioned her into the bedroom. The black cupboard dominated the space. Its doors were still open, the rows of photographs and papers clearly in view.

"What's this?" she asked. Joe stepped forward.

"It's a list" he said simply. "Each victim is on here. They seem to be linked to some kind of common event from years ago, judging by the age of the photographs." Joe reached inside his pocket, producing the evidence bag with the photograph in that he had recovered from downstairs and handed it to Jessica. "I also found this" Jessica looked at the photograph for a few seconds, instantly recognising her uncle. "Do you recognise the man in the picture?" Joe asked her. She shook her head, her eyes still fixed on the image.

"I've never seen him before Joe, sorry." Joe smiled and put the evidence bag back inside his jacket pocket.

"I hope you don't mind me saying Jess, but I had the impression that you were close to your uncle" Joe said. Jessica looked him straight in the eye.

"He's always been protective of me, but he's my uncle by marriage. He married my aunt, but she died when I was a toddler."

"It makes you wonder whether the trauma of losing his wife was what started this!" Joe mused. Jessica didn't answer, and instead switched her attention to the photographs pinned to the back wall of the cupboard. "Hang on!" she said, turning to one of her equipment cases and flicking open the lock.

"What is it?" Joe asked. She produced a large bundle of paperwork and placed it on top of the other case. After a few seconds she produced a handful of loose papers and offered them to Joe. Joe took them and looked over the contents.

"Look at the highlighted names Joe" Jessica said. "Do any of them look familiar?" Joe studied the parts of the text where Jessica had made discreet oblong blocks with a bright yellow marker pen. He looked up at the board in disbelief.

"It's them!" he said. "This is what it's all been about!" He looked at Jessica for a moment, before suddenly started sifting through the pages he was holding.

"What's the matter?" asked Jessica.

"Where is he?" Joe asked, comparing each name to the names and photographs on the wall of the cupboard once more.

"Who?" Jessica replied as she scoured the photographs in the cupboard for a clue as to who Joe was talking about.

"My Dad!" Joe snapped. He flicked the right hand cupboard door with his fingertip, extending it fully and revealing to Jessica the pictures of his father, and himself.

"Oh my god Joe!" Jessica exclaimed, her hand over her mouth. "Why?"

"I don't know!" Joe said with a shrug. In all the excitement, Joe had not realised that Glen had sent the message that he had been waiting for so desperately when Jessica had arrived. Scooping his phone from his shirt pocket, he unlocked the screen and opened the message. It read simply;

"NO SIGN OF THEM HERE JOE. WHAT NOW? G"

Joe closed the message and thrust the phone back into his pocket. He needed to think calmly. Suddenly, he had an idea, planting the phone firmly to his ear.

"Who are you ringing now?" Jessica asked.

"Who do you talk to when nobody else in the world

understands the problem Jess, apart from your best friend?"

"My mum I suppose!" Jessica replied. "Why?" Joe silenced her with a raised finger.

"Mam!" Joe said warmly as he turned away from Jessica. "I need to pick your brains, and I don't have much time!"

Approaching the neglected exterior of the Milward Club, Amber tried her best to quell a rising tide of suspicion within her mind. The place seemed to be in darkness, and there were none of the usual retired or listless old men that frequented these kinds of places. Further to that, her heels seemed to be doing their very best to announce her presence with every step she took, the sound of stiletto on pavement bouncing around the empty street. She was dressed in a black military style coat, with an oversized burgundy scarf, skin tight navy blue jeans, and patented stilettos of the deepest red. Over one shoulder she carried a black canvas bag, containing her camera and Dictaphone, along with a note pad, pens, pencils, and a can of pepper spray she had bought from the internet. Her flowing, Scandinavian locks were tied neatly into a blonde ponytail that lay across the nape of her neck and down her left shoulder blade. What had seemed like a sensible yet stylish wardrobe choice was rapidly appearing impractical, at least in terms of the shoes.

"Whindle had better not be fucking me around!" she hissed under her breath as she stopped a few feet from the doors. They were closed, and judging by the lack of any light or movement inside, she was almost certain that they would be locked as well. Her shoulders sagged, and she placed her hands on her hips as she considered her next move.

Suddenly, her attention was drawn to a shadow moving across the window on the first floor, directly above the main doors. Instinctively she thrust herself against the wall beneath the window, out of the line of sight of whoever was inside. Feeling slightly ridiculous, she looked up and down the empty street.

"What am I doing?" Amber asked herself out loud. "It's a club for drunks and train drivers! It's not a restricted area!" Nevertheless, something was telling her that it was a good idea to stay out of sight for now, at least until she had a better idea of what was going on. As much as she tried to reason with herself, she couldn't escape from the real possibility that the killer was either inside the building, nearby, or would be here very soon. At the very least, the fact that this place was the chosen drinking hole of a certain Detective Sergeant was of interest enough! The fact that the Police were planning on raiding it only served to make it even more interesting! She would never admit it to anyone, but she was feeling a little vulnerable. Without warning, the main door rattled under the efforts of somebody inside trying to unfasten the bolt at the top of the doorframe.

"Shit!" Amber hissed, and managed to totter around the corner of the building, hiding in the alleyway and cursing her choice of footwear as she listened to the sound of doors being opened and secured. Daring to peep around the corner, she just caught sight of the back of a man's head as he disappeared back inside. Waiting a couple of seconds before moving, she stooped, slipping her feet from her high heels and padding carefully back towards the door, gasping at the cold concrete on her soles. In front of the doors, stood a large wooden sign which simply read 'CLOSED FOR PRIVATE PARTY'

"Nothing unusual there" Amber muttered to herself as she considered her next move. Her deliberations were rudely interrupted by the glare of headlights swinging into the street. Again, she retreated to the side of the building, peeking around the corner of the brickwork as she watched a taxi pull gently to a stand outside the main door and four people get out. Amber studied the four from the shadows. There was an elderly couple, along with a younger couple. The younger woman was heavily pregnant, and her partner was carefully helping her from the taxi, much in the same way as the older man was helping his partner. Putting the symmetry of the foursome aside, Amber was confused as she slowly drew her camera from her shoulder bag. Switching it on without looking down, Amber levelled the camera at the four people and efficiently took around half a dozen pictures before stuffing it back into the bag before they had chance to realise she was there. They all stood in front of the doors, looking at each other with unsure expressions. Amber's eyes darted from person to person as she observed and listened.

"Are you sure you got the right date Graham?" Joyce asked as she straightened her dress.
"Of course I got the right bloody date!" Graham snapped.
"Look! The place is closed for a private party!" Graham reached inside his jacket pocket. "The date's on the tickets, I've got them right"
"Silly old fool!" scolded Joyce. "You've forgotten the bloody tickets! Graham's cheeks flushed.

"Looks like its closed full stop!" Robert said, his arm slipping protectively around the waist of his heavily pregnant wife as he changed the subject.

"Well we may as well go in!" Graham said as he walked ahead of the rest, pushing the door open and waiting for the rest to join him. "I'll go and find one of the committee members! They all know me! The tickets won't be a problem! "They swapped uncertain glances for a second before joining him and disappearing inside. Amber remained where she was. She had an urge to follow them in and find out what was going on, but she could not ignore the feeling that she would be best served by going around the back of the building and seeing if she could find a vantage point from which she could watch the promised drama unfold. Deciding on the latter, she silently turned and stepped gingerly into the darkness, biting her lip as her bare feet impaled themselves on a series of sharp stones, decomposing litter and other things that she was relieved not to be able to see. Exhaling in an attempt to tolerate the sharp pain in her heel, Amber groped slowly at the gate to the rear yard of the club, sighing in relief as it opened as she pushed against it gently. Taking a quick look around the gate, she stepped into the yard, grateful for the smooth concrete as she disappeared inside.

-110-

Jessica was confident in stating that she had never attended a scene of crime where the lead detective had taken time out to phone his Mum! Smiling to herself, she switched on her camera, checking the batteries and the flash settings as she did her best to ignore Joe's conversation. He had phoned to ask his mother if she had any contacts of his father's, who were still active in the retired members committees of the union, as well as any knowledge of his late father's involvement in the high profile incident involving the death of Raymond Kilkis. After rifling through the notebook next to the phone, his mum had passed to him three numbers which he scribbled on the back of his free hand. Amazingly, given the amount of union cases Joe's father had worked on, she remembered Raymond Kilkis' name.

"That's a name that sticks in the mind Joe!" she said. "It was all over the news! One of your dad's biggest cases!"

"Why was he involved?" Joe asked, feeling slightly awkward as he stood in the middle of the room, mindful of Jessica's presence.

"From what I can remember, the railway were trying to pin the blame on the signaller, and the man who in charge of the maintenance team" Joe nodded. Ian Ellington was in charge of the P-Way gang on that night, and Jerry Pickford was the signaller, it was a matter of record. "Your dad was the union official looking after them. He did the TV interviews and all that type of thing. From what I recall, he managed to convince the inquiry that the systems of work were at fault, not just the staff. He prevented criminal charges being brought!" Joe took a moment to consider his mother's words. "Why are you asking about your dad anyway?" Joe's Mum asked.

"Oh it's nothing!" Joe lied in response. "It's a planning exercise as part of my study programme for promotion. We were given a choice of two investigations to examine and dad came up in this one! Small old world eh?"

"I'd say!" she replied with a laugh. "What are the chances?"

"I've got to go, I'll speak to you soon. Bye" Joe ended the call and turned immediately to Jessica who by now was standing, her expression one of enquiry.

"Tut tut Detective Sergeant Tenby!" she said mockingly. "Lying to your mother! I'm shocked! I've learned something there!"

"Well if it's education you want, I've learnt something as well!" Joe replied as he turned back to face the cupboard, once more scrutinising the faces pinned to the back wall.

"What is it?" Jessica asked as she joined him in front of the parade of victims.

"I know why your uncle wants to kill me!" Joe looked her straight in the eye as he spoke. Jessica swallowed hard. Thankfully for her Joe's phone rang before she had to produce a response. Joe raised his forefinger as he answered the phone.

"Glen! What have you got?" he said into the mouthpiece as he turned away

-111-

Standing in the hallway of Joyce and Graham's house, Glen could not feel more like an intruder if he had dressed specifically for the occasion. Although heartily relieved that the neighbour had provided him with the spare key, he felt a deep unease at being stood alone on someone else's home, despite the fact that he was a Police Officer with good cause. The walls were a calm shade of ocean blue, contrasted by the crisp white of the woodwork, and the tiling that lined the back wall near the sink. The pine table and chairs looked as if they had recently been bought, so flawless was the wood, the surface of the table free from even the slightest hint of clutter.

Walking through the open door into the hall, Glen found that the solitary shelf in the hall was empty and dust free, save for four tickets which had been placed face up, presumably whilst the owner put their coat and shoes on. Seizing them and scrutinising the writing, Glen was overjoyed!

"Got you!!" he exclaimed as he produced his phone from his pocket and phoned Joe. It was obvious that Joe was waiting for Glen to find some information for the team to act on. Judging by the tone of Joe's voice, the adrenaline was pumping through his veins, a sensation Glen was beginning to share.

"Joe, I know where they're going!"

"Where?" Joe snapped.

"Retirement Committee Reunion at Milward Street Trades Club" As he spoke the words, Glen realised that he knew that place. Joe too, was struck by yet another coincidence. He knew that it was most likely that her uncle was going to be either at the club, or on his way, and that he was seemingly intent on yet more brutal killing. All of a sudden, he realised that this also meant that Phil would be in danger too!

"Meet me there!" Joe barked down the phone. Ending the call abruptly, he turned and ran for the stairs. Jessica jumped back in shock.

"Where are you going?" she called after him, his footsteps echoing heavily off the walls as he pounded down the staircase.

"Let me know how it goes processing the scene Jess! I'll call you later!" Staring at the empty doorway in wait for a further answer, she was only rewarded by the slamming of the front door.

The internal doors from the foyer were pinned open, and Graham swore under his breath as he accidentally kicked a fire extinguisher that held one of the doors in place. The bar also was in complete darkness, the beer fridges, pumps and shelf lighting all unlit, and stools still upturned on the bar top. The entire place seemed shrouded in an eerie silence, except for the dark rumbling of what sounded like distant music.

"What on earth is going on?" asked Lisa, her right hand sitting protectively on the top of her bump as she squinted blindly towards the source of the mysterious sound.

"I really think we should go home Graham! I don't like this!" Joyce said, her hand discreetly sliding around his arm and gripping firmly.

"Come on!" soothed Graham. "The party is probably upstairs!" Graham walked slowly over to the doors at the other end of the room and opened them, the strange and distant music suddenly appearing much closer. The four of them looked at each other, still unsure as to whether to leave and go home, or to scale the steps and see what awaited them on the first floor. Taking a deep breath, Lisa was the first one to make a decisive move. Breathing heavily, she turned to the others.

"Curiosity is getting the better of me now!" she said. "I need a change from rubbish TV!"

"Yeah!" agreed Graham with a smile. "What's the worst that could happen?"

"I'll tell you what's the worst that could happen shall I?" Joyce said in a serious voice. The others looked on. "You'll get a belly full of ale and start telling us all the same stories you've been telling us for decades!" They all laughed as they slowly climbed the staircase, making their way towards a reception they could never have anticipated.

Standing in the yard of the club, using the cover of the shadow of the building, Amber observed the structure as best she could, planning her route inside, via the fire escape and either the main door on the balcony, provided that fortune was to be kind enough for the owner to have left something unlocked. Noting almost instantly that the yard wasn't overlooked, she concluded that she could get inside the building undetected. Making sure that the strap to her bag was safely on her shoulder, she motioned to step onto the first step of the fire escape, the cold, aggressive grip of the metal surface reminding her that she was barefoot. Looking down at the shoes she carried in her right hand, she sighed to herself as she eased her weight onto her naked soles, gasping in discomfort as she scaled the metal staircase. What had seemed like a stylish mainstay of her wardrobe all of a sudden appeared to be a liability. Reasoning that she could just slip them back on once she was inside and safely hidden away, she stepped gingerly onto the balcony. She made conscious efforts to control the volume of her breathing as she edged closer to the door. It was unlocked! Better still, it wasn't even closed properly! Looking upwards into the night sky, she mouthed the words "Thank You!" to an imaginary guardian angel before taking a slightly more confident step forwards and reaching out for the door handle. Suddenly, she saw what she thought was a figure moving in the shadows of the corridor. She scuttled across to the far side of the balcony, grasping for the cover of shadow as her heart pounded in her chest. As she had lurched away from the view of the door, her fingers had lost grip of her prized footwear, the shoes tumbling from her grasp and falling noisily onto the yard below.

"Shit!" she hissed as she glanced forlornly at the balcony wall. Amber knew that she simply could not afford to go back and retrieve her shoes, and she was angry at herself for considering the option. Resolving to carry on without them, and promising herself that she would collect them after she had secured a career-making exclusive, she focussed her attention on the door and the windows once more. They were still in darkness. Slowly and tentatively, she stepped back towards the door, reaching forward, and wrapping her slender fingers around the door handle. Opening the door wide enough to slip her body inside, she pulled the door closed just with just as much care as she had opened it. Once inside, she stared intensely into the gloom in an attempt to accustom her eyesight to the all-encompassing darkness. Turning on the lights would be out of the question, so she would just have to navigate blindly, and carefully, in the hope that she could reach whatever part of the building was of so much interest to the police before the action took place. She groped through the darkness as deftly as she could, placing one foot in front of the other as if she were a gymnast on a beam. After her first few minutes of lightless navigation, her heart rate began to ease. Little did she know however, that her every move was being hungrily observed from only feet away.

From behind the office door, Steven watched the unmistakable outline of Amber Rawson as she inched past. Even in such a state of pitched darkness, there was no doubting who this unswervingly feminine figure was. He felt the urge to grab her right now, pull her through this door, throw her forward onto the desk and have her. The primal forces which were building pressure in his loins were urging him to her, urging him to give her what she so clearly wanted. The fact that she was navigating the floors of the building barefoot seemed to make her seem more vulnerable somehow, and he licked his lips as his arousal increased. The fabric of his jeans were straining as he indulged himself in the fantasy of what it would feel like to penetrate her. Reasoning with his primal self, Steven managed to calm himself down, his left hand pressing firmly against his crotch as he watched her slender outline disappear into the darkness of the corridor. He had planned since they had first met, that she would witness his prowess as a killer, and as an arbiter of justice. Her disdain for his carnal advances however, and his sudden arousal at the thought of making her his own, had persuaded him of the need to show her his prowess in other ways too. Forcing the manufactured imagery of Amber's most intimate places from his mind, he focussed instead on the immediate task ahead. Amber was in the building, and so were his Mother, Brother, Sister-in-law, and Graham. Now, he only needed to await the arrival of Joe Tenby, and everything would finally be in place.

"All in good time!" he whispered to himself as he silently made his way out into the corridor. "I will have my revenge, and then I'll get my trophy!"

114

Looking down the corridor, the double doors at the far end seemed to be hiding the source of the muffled sounds that had attracted them. Without anyone exchanging a word, they all began walking towards the doors in unison. The fact that they had not seen any other people since they had entered the building was worrying to all four of them. Nobody had said it explicitly, but the whole evening just did not feel right. It was Graham who reached the double doors first. The music was louder now. The track playing was a version of *Summertime* by Sam Cooke. Graham frowned. He couldn't hear any chatter from beyond the door. He felt ridiculous for even thinking it, but he could not help but feel as if the whole scene was somehow staged. Pushing open the doors, he entered the room, followed by the other three. Against the back wall and across the blemished dance floor, a sound system pumped out the music, and a dated lighting system cast oblique shapes and faded interpretations of green, red, violet, and yellow across the ceiling and walls. Above the dance floor there was a small balcony overlooking the room, its seating area shrouded in darkness. It had long since been forgotten, and was used only for storage. A grubby sheet hung scruffily over the hand rail. Over to the right hand side, two tables stood adorned with sandwiches sealed in plastic wrap. All of a sudden, the music stopped. They looked around frantically, each of them beginning to surrender to the more sinister interpretations of their minds.

"I really don't like this! Where is everybody?" hissed Joyce as she grabbed Graham's arm once more. Looking back at her, he could only muster a puzzled frown, followed by a shrug. "I don't know about you three, but I'm going home!" Joyce said. Suddenly, the lighting machine stopped producing its multi-coloured spheres, its ambience replaced by the harsh glare of the ceiling strip lights.

"Come now mother, there's no time for that!" Steven said coldly, as he closed both of the doors and locked them.

"What the hell is going on?" said Robert, his voice rising as he stepped forward.

"I wouldn't do that if I were you Robert!" Steven said, as he produced a pistol from his inside pocket. "I have dreamed about this for far too long! That scumbag will pay for what he has done to me!" Steven jabbed the pistol in the direction of Graham, who flinched instinctively. "She will get to make her choices all over again!" He hissed, repeating the gesture in his mother's direction. She however, did not flinch. She did not react at all, other than for a slow stream of tears that cascaded down her cheek, along her jaw line, and down onto the floor.

-115-

The streets flashed by as the car sped faster and faster toward the club. Joe had an uneasy feeling that he was also hurrying towards the final showdown. Scanning the horizon as he rounded a gentle left hand curve in the road, he switched his gaze to the rear view mirror and the wing mirrors in rapid sequence, the evening shadows being penetrated by pulsating beams of blue light as they shone harshly from the beacon positioned haphazardly on the car's roof. Gunning the accelerator, Joe watched the speedometer as the needle passed sixty miles per hour. Bearing down on a grubby white van, Joe peered past it before smoothly overtaking and veering back into lane. Having set his phone up on his hands free system, Joe had been calling Phil repeatedly, but had still received no answer and was becoming increasingly worried. His finger had also hovered over the call button on more than one occasion after programming in Jessica's number. He felt that she deserved to know what was going on with regard to her uncle, but at the same time he was only too well aware of the fact that she would jump in her car and head across the city to the club. The last thing he wanted was to put Jessica in any kind of danger. As he approached a crossroads, a bus driver paused mid-turn to allow Joe to pass. Waving in gratitude, Joe checked that he was clear of the junction before accelerating away once more. Suddenly, Joe's phone blinked into life. It was Kevin. Wondering what it was that Kevin wanted, he muttered under his breath, rejecting the call as he swung violently right and into the street where the Milward Club stood eerily in darkness. Pulling sharply to the kerbside, Joe jumped out of the car and ran to the doors of the club. Rattling the doors harshly, he swore as he looked through the glass and saw that they had been chained shut. Joe looked up and down the street, wondering where Glen was. Spying the alleyway at the side of the building, Joe took a final look at the empty road before disappearing into the shadows and pushing open the gate to the yard.

-116-

"What the fuck is this Steven?" Robert hissed as Lisa closed her eyes and breathed hard, her left hand gently massaging her stomach in a circular motion. Ignoring Robert's question,

Steven lurched forward without warning and pressed the barrel of the pistol against Graham's forehead.

"Choices Robert!" Steven said as he pushed Graham back. Joyce shrieked as Graham stumbled. Steven spun around and pointed the gun at Lisa's belly. "It's all about choices!" Robert pulled Lisa behind him as she gasped, whispering a plea for the life of her baby. Noticing movement in his peripheral vision, Steven glanced upward, his attention being drawn by the gradual pulling of the grimy sheet that hung from the balcony above. He smiled to himself as he realised that Amber Rawson had found her way inside the room. Now he was waiting only for the arrival of Joe Tenby. Knowing that he would not be waiting long, he chuckled to himself as Lisa cried hysterically.

Up in the dingy shadows of the neglected balcony, Amber silently cursed as she realised that her crouched movement was causing the faded sheet that she had been kneeling on to gather and slip. Staying perfectly still, she watched tensely as the sheet eventually stopped moving. Glancing down at her jeans, she stifled a groan as she saw that they were covered with dirt, dust and grime. Her feet were coated in black muck and felt uncomfortable and sticky. She had managed to blunder her way through the pitched darkness of the corridors and walkways, and had found herself kneeling on this balcony as a result of taking the decision to follow the muffled sound of music. Carefully, she unzipped the bag and pulled out her camera and Dictaphone, checking the batteries, she switched them both, placing them on the floor next to her. Satisfying herself that all sounds were being properly captured by the

Dictaphone, she focussed on the dance floor below. Daring herself to kneel up far enough to peer over the hand rail of the balcony, Amber could hardly believe what she was witnessing. The same four people that she had seen entering the building earlier were stood below, along with Detective Chief Inspector Evan Whindle!

"What on earth is going on?" she whispered to herself, forgetting momentarily that the Dictaphone was running. "Whindle isn't armed police! Why does he have a gun?" Looking down at the camera, she debated whether to risk taking a photograph. She was, after all, only here to capture a scoop. Nevertheless, there was a man on the dance floor below who was brandishing a gun, and despite him being a police officer, and indeed the source who had been keeping her informed of developments on the investigation, she felt unsafe. Picking up her camera, Amber turned off the flash and gently raised it above the hand rail. Kneeling up as far as she dare, she aimed the camera and took her first picture, snatching it briskly behind the cover of the balcony and flipping it over to inspect the picture on the camera's screen. The picture clearly showed DCI Whindle aiming a small pistol at the stomach of a pregnant woman. Instantly, she started formulating the framework of an article detailing the actions of 'an unrelenting and experienced Detective who brought a killer to book at gunpoint'. Tearing herself from that thought process, reality rapidly overtook her creative distractions. Amber tried her best to think of a context within which DCI Whindle would be able to explain his carrying a firearm, and worse still, aiming that firearm at the stomach of a pregnant woman. There was no such context. Suddenly, the realisation dawned on her.

"What if they're not in custody?" Amber asked herself. "What if they're hostages?" Amber's mind raced as she computed possible reasons why a serving police officer would take hostages. There was only one possible answer. "Whindle is the Trackman!" she said to herself in disbelief. With a shaking hand, she checked that the Dictaphone was still recording, before leaning back against the balcony wall, desperately trying to formulate a plan for escape.

Slowly opening the gate to the yard at the rear of the club, Joe peered around it in an attempt to ensure that nobody awaited his entrance. Looking up at the first floor fire escape, Joe saw straight away that the door was slightly open. Anxious to ensure that Phil was safe, Joe considered whether to wait for Glen, or to go inside the building straight away. Looking down at the floor, Joe's eye was drawn to a glinting light. It was a shoe. Stooping to pick up the shoe, Joe also saw that the matching shoe was only a yard or so away. They looked familiar.

"I've seen those heels before somewhere!" Joe said to himself as he examined them intensely in the poor light in an attempt to establish the colour. Instantly, his mind replayed his meeting in the pub with Jessica. "Amber Rawson!" Joe exclaimed. Looking up once more at the rear of the building, it was obvious that she was inside. Grabbing his radio, he keyed the microphone. "DS Tenby to Bravo India"

"Go ahead DS Tenby" came the reply.

"I'm at the Milward Club. DC Violet is en route. I need further assistance, we have an armed suspect in there and a civilian has gone inside. I'm going in!"

"That's a negative DS Tenby!" replied the radio operator. "Wait for assistance please!"

"Sorry Bravo India. I can't wait any longer. Inform Commander Carlton of our location. Tenby out." Before the radio operator could protest, Joe switched the radio off and thrust it into his inside pocket. Taking a final look around the yard, Joe stepped onto the fire escape and scaled the ladder as quickly and silently as he could.

"Put the gun down and stop being an idiot!" Robert barked. Steven snarled in anger.

"Idiot? You think I'm an idiot? Seeing as we're dealing in labels, why don't we at least be accurate about it?" Lisa still stood behind her husband, her eyes closed tightly. "There are lots of names that you could call me; Hunter, Defender, Leader" Steven distributed his cold stare evenly between the three of them. "I suppose you could even call me a killer, taking into account recent events" He stroked the underside of his chin with his free hand as he added the last comment as casually as he could.

"Oh my goodness!" Joyce shrieked as she recoiled in horror. "My own son? A killer? Who have you killed?"

"He hasn't killed anyone!" spluttered Graham. "He's full of his own hot air!" Steven's eyes flickered with rage, his fingers tightening their grip around the pistol. "You're a joke lad! Nobody in this family has ever taken you seriously, and nobody ever will!" Joyce placed her hand on Graham's arm in an unspoken warning to stop taunting her son. He chose to ignore that warning. "I bet that's not even a real gun!" As he

spoke, his face was filled with scorn. Without another word,

Steven swivelled his aim around to Graham, the barrel of the

pistol aimed towards his kneecap. With a cold detachment,

Steven pulled the trigger, discharging a bullet that smashed

into the shrivelled flesh encapsulating the old man's knee.

Squealing in agony, Graham reeled backwards, hitting the

wall and sliding down it as pained grunts escaped from behind

his clamped teeth. Walking over to him, Steven crouched over

him. His voice was low in volume, and cold in tone.

"Are you taking me seriously now? He hissed. Graham ignored

Steven as he struggled for breath. Steven stood up, staring

down at the semi-prone figure before him. Joyce ran over to

Graham and knelt at his side, cradling him as she stared

furiously at her son. Steven pressed his foot firmly down onto

Graham's kneecap, causing him to cry out. Joyce went to

speak, but before she could, Steven aimed the gun at her.

"Stay out of it Mother!" she gulped hard as he cocked the

pistol, his hand remarkably steady. "At least for now, anyway!"

he said.

"Please Steven!" Graham gasped, his hands shaking violently

as they clawed at the torn material of his blood-soaked

trousers. "Please! I'm begging you! Stop this!"

"Ironic isn't it? How the tables have turned Graham?" Steven

spat, the gun still aimed steadily at his mother's forehead.

"What are you talking about Steven?" cried Joyce as she took

off her coat and wrapped it around Graham.

"I'm talking about all the times I begged your precious

Graham to stop!"

"Son, you're not making sense!" Joyce said. "You said that you could be called a killer. Who have you killed? What have you done?" Steven stared down at Joyce expressionlessly.

"Have you been reading the local newspaper Mother?" Steven asked. Joyce nodded.

"We have it delivered every day"

"So you will have read the excellent pieces about the serial killer the police have been hunting for who has been nicknamed 'The Trackman'?"

"Yes I have, but what has this got to do with why we're here? Graham needs help!" Joyce said as she undid Graham's tie and fastened it around his lower thigh in a bid to stem his blood loss. Steven spoke in a calm and flat tone. "Mother, there really is no easy way of telling you this, but I am The Trackman!" Joyce's mouth dropped open in disbelief. Steven turned away from his mother and looked up towards the balcony, a wicked smile spreading across his face as he did so. "Did you get all of that Amber?" he yelled. "I wouldn't want you to miss anything for your next front page splash!" Up on the balcony, Amber cowered at the mention of her name.

"Oh shit!" she whispered. "How did he know I was here?" Amber remained motionless in one last vain attempt to fool Steven into thinking that he was mistaken, although she knew that the game was up. Before she could decide what to do next, Steven had fired the pistol up at the balcony, causing the aging strip light suspended from a chain to shatter. Instinctively, Amber screamed as she flinched away from the sound of the firing gun.

"Give it up!" Steven said in a patronising tone. "Save me the time and the bullets Amber!" Even now, Amber sat perfectly still, though it was more from the shock of being fired at rather than a conscious attempt to fool her armed captor. Again, Steven fired upwards in the direction of the balcony, this time the bullet dug violently into the ceiling. With great reluctance, Amber got herself to her feet, gathering her Dictaphone and camera and slipping them into her bag before she tentatively peered over the top of the balcony wall, both hands held up in a gesture of surrender. She had left the Dictaphone running, and was praying that it could still record all that was said despite lying at the bottom of her bag.

"Please don't kill me Evan!" she pleaded as she moved slowly towards the stairs leading to the main dance floor below. "I don't want to die!"

"Who is that woman and why is she calling you Evan?" asked Joyce as she stroked Graham's forehead.

"We all have to die Amber!" Steven replied coldly as he flatly ignored his mother. "We have no choice over it. We do, however, have a choice of when and how, don't we Graham?" he said as he aimed a swift kick at the bloodied kneecap of the old man. Graham howled in pain as Lisa sank to her knees and began to sob. Amber began descending the staircase, slipping her hand into the side pocket of her bag as she did so. Producing her 'press' identification badge, she remembered that the door out into the private corridor to the offices was left slightly open when she had made her way up the stairs towards the balcony. Checking that she was not yet in view of the others, she unclipped the strap of her bag and jammed it into the void between the doorframe and the door, forcing it further open. Reaching through into the cool air of the corridor, Amber debated whether she could escape the building before Evan had a chance to catch her. Swiftly, she realised that the chance was a slim one, and decided that it was better for her survival chances to comply with his demands. She carefully dropped her identification badge into the middle of the corridor in the hope that it would be found by any help that may arrive. Back on the dance floor, Steven stood dispassionately studying Lisa. Without shifting his gaze, Steven addressed himself to his family.

"We're here for justice!" Robert was knelt next to his wife, desperately trying to calm her.

"What are you talking about?" Robert snapped. "You're not making any sense!"

"I brought you here to expose some home truths, and to put right the wrongs that have ruined my life!" Steven snapped as he turned to Amber, who had just emerged from the balcony stairs, and was slowly padding across the dance floor to where Steven had called her. "And you, Miss Rawson, will record it in all its judicious glory!"

Once satisfied that there was nobody lurking in the vicinity, Joe produced a folded latex glove from his pocket and eased the fire door open. The fact that it was ajar had immediately caused Joe concern. Stepping inside, Joe crept forwards a few paces. To his right, he saw that the office door was also slightly open. Joe opened the office door and slipped inside, groping the wall with his folded glove for the light switch. A swift look around the office made it all too obvious that Phil hadn't been in here for quite some time. The air was thick with stale body odour and cigarettes, and the desk was covered in stained paperwork, overfilled ashtrays and filthy coffee cups. Returning to the corridor, Joe pulled out his phone and called Phil, craning his neck as he heard a muffled ring tone. Looking up the corridor, Joe followed the sound. Pausing outside one of the bedrooms, Joe looked down at his phone as he listened through the door. Just as he placed his hand on the doorknob, the unmistakable sound of a gunshot bounced off the walls from further down the corridor. Instinctively, Joe threw the door open and ducked inside. Leaning back against the closed door, Joe was drawn to what looked like a pile of coats that lay beside a single bed. It was from here that the sound of the ringing phone was coming. Snatching his radio from his pocket, Joe switched it on and jabbed the emergency button, speaking into the microphone as calmly as he could.

"Bravo India, this is DS Tenby requesting urgent assistance and armed response to this location. Shots fired!" Joe returned his attention to the pile of coats, and dialled Phil's phone number once more. Within seconds, the muffled ringtone of a cheap and aging mobile filled the room. Stooping over the pile of coats that sat in the corner, Joe hesitated for a second before carefully pulling aside an old waterproof jacket. As he dropped the jacket onto the floor he became aware of a moist substance on his fingertips. The light wasn't strong enough for him to properly identify what the moistness was, but Joe instinctively knew that it was blood. Moreover, he had a sinking feeling that he knew whose blood it was. Moving another jacket, Joe stepped back as the unmistakable aroma of decomposing flesh hit him head on. Groping backwards in a half-stumbling motion, Joe managed to flick the lights on. As his eyes adjusted to the sudden switch from darkness, he reached down and pulled a discarded curtain away that was keeping the source of the stench a mystery. Steadily sliding the material to one side, Joe covered his mouth with his free hand as Phil's badly beaten face was revealed. Phil had obviously been dead for at least 24 hours, given the putrefaction that was beginning to take hold of his stubbly features. Joe knelt slowly beside his friend, silently praying that his death had been mercifully quick, whilst knowing only too well from the extent of the injuries Phil had endured, that his passing was brutal, and most likely excruciating. Reaching once more for his radio, Joe relayed to control, the details of the body, including its location and a brief overview of the horrific injuries suffered. Once the details had been logged and confirmed, Joe returned the radio to his pocket, then positioned his head as closely to Phil's ear as the stench emanating from his corpse would allow.

"Sorry Phil" Joe whispered. "I'm so sorry you got caught up in this" Solemnly, Joe placed the curtain back over Phil's swollen and disfigured form, before getting up off his knees and dusting down his suit and jacket. His experience and training as a Police Officer were telling him in unison to get out of the building and wait for the armed back-up he had requested only moments before. Despite it going against every aspect of training he had received, Joe knew that he could not simply walk back up the corridor and out of that fire escape. DCI Whindle, or Steven Kilkis, or whatever his rightful name was, had gone out of his way to make this personal with Joe from the very beginning. Taking a moment to collect his thoughts, Joe turned the lights back off before carefully opening the bedroom door and edging out from behind it, taking one last, longing look in the direction of the fire escape, before turning towards the thickening darkness of the far end of the corridor, and slowly working his way towards the direction of the gun shots.

120

"Can I help you?" Jessica asked as she emerged, deep in contemplation from one of the small side offices. She had repeatedly been trying to reach Joe on his mobile, but had only succeeded in contacting his answer phone. Glen too, was failing to pick up. Jessica had been trying as hard as she could to concentrate on correctly logging all of the items she had recovered from her uncle's house onto the computer system. It was inevitable that, in the event of arrests being made, and charges being brought, that any half-competent defence barrister would try to make plenty of mischief with her biological relationship to the prime suspect, as well as her connection with the officer who had taken over her uncle's role on the investigation. Despite her best efforts though, she could not help but wonder where Joe was, and whether everything was okay. The fact that he had been out of reach for so long was only heightening her anxiety. Deciding to take some research files home to look at over a late dinner, Jessica was caught unawares by the burly, suited figure standing in the doorway. It was DC Kevin McDonnell.

"I'm looking for Joe Tenby" Kevin said. "I hope I'm not disturbing you, I'm not sure whether I'm in the right place!"

"It's no problem!" Jessica replied with a polite smile. "You're not the only one wondering about DS Tenby's whereabouts!"

Kevin's eyebrows raised in a silent question.

"DC Kevin McDonnell" he said as he offered Jessica his hand. "Jessica Hopewell" replied Jessica as she accepted the handshake. "If you're the same Kevin that tolerated Joe in Newcastle, I've heard a lot about you!" Kevin smiled.

"If you're the same Jessica that, er.." Kevin's voice trailed off as his cheeks flushed slightly. He had realised that he was giving away too easily the fact that Joe had mentioned Jessica to him in more than a professional context. "You get the picture anyway!" Kevin said with an awkward grin. Hearing heavy footsteps pounding the polished corridor outside, Kevin gladly accepted the distraction from his faux pas as he instinctively stepped away from the door, just seconds before it swung wildly open, announcing the arrival of a sweaty and breathless Glen Violet.

"Jess!" Glen spluttered, ignoring Kevin McDonnell. "Joe's at the Milward Club now! Control is sending armed response as back-up!" Jessica blinked rapidly as she took in Glen's words. Her mind went into overdrive as she struggled to remain calm at the thought of Joe being at the mercy of a gun. Her eyes darted between Glen and Kevin, whom Glen had still failed to acknowledge. Glen looked across at Kevin and smiled nervously. "Sorry mate!" Glen said nervously. "I didn't see you there! I'm DC Glen Violet" Kevin offered a handshake. "I'm not interrupting anything am I?" Glen asked Jessica as he shook Kevin's hand.

"I'm here to see DS Tenby" Kevin replied in his deep Geordie tones "Did you say there've been shots fired? Joe's mentioned that club a few times to me! Mind if I tag along?" Glen and Jessica looked at each other. Jessica shrugged.

"It's fine by me Kevin" Glen said. "But we have to go now!"

Kevin nodded and pushed the door open, waiting for the other two to take the lead in the dash to the car. "There's something you should know Jess" Glen said. Kevin looked in the opposite direction. Jessica's face dropped. "The gunman" whispered Glen. "It's your uncle!"

121

Amber stood with trembling hands as Steven pointed the gun at her temple. She was trying her best to pull her Dictaphone from her bag, but the shaking of her fingers was making it difficult to maintain a grip on it.

"Don't panic yourself" Steven soothed with mock concern. "We've got all night!" Graham was grunting with each breath as the pain coursing through his body increased almost by the second. A thin sheen of sweat coated his brow and he was starting to shiver slightly as Joyce held onto him as tightly as she could, whispering softly in his ear as she held back tears. Finally, Amber managed to produce the Dictaphone and her camera, setting them both down on the floor in front of her.

"What do you want me to do?" Amber asked meekly, her head almost bowed.

"I want you to do your job Amber!" Steven said, the gun still levelled at her head. "As a journalist, you're meant to report the truth, are you not?" Amber nodded quickly. "Things have to be put right!" Steven continued. "I want you to record and document them. If you do that, you get to leave here with that pretty face of yours intact!" Steven cocked the pistol for dramatic effect. "If you try any stupid stunts, or if you try to escape, I'll have no option but to do to you what I've done to so many others" Suddenly he reached inside his jacket with his free hand. Amber let out a stifled cry. Giggling to himself, Steven produced a folded bunch of papers. Nonchalantly he threw them on the floor in front of Amber. She didn't dare move. "Pick them up!" Steven commanded. Amber hesitated. "Pick them up and read them!" he said. Slowly, she reached down and scooped up the papers, trying her best to read them as they shook and rattled in time with her fingers. As she scanned each page, her expression changed from one of fear to one of amazement.

"My god!" Amber exclaimed. "It's been you all along? All this time you've been giving me inside information, and you've been responsible for these deaths?" Steven shrugged. "But you're a Policeman!" she said indignantly.

"What?" Robert said. "You're a Policeman? Since when?" Steven smiled as he replied.

"Oh Robert! There are so many things you don't know! The silence that hung in the air beyond those four walls was suddenly shattered by the harsh tones of police sirens, the night being pierced by the accompanying blue lights. Steven looked skywards as he listened to the approaching Police vehicles as their sirens grew louder. "Speaking of the police!" Steven said. "I think it's safe to assume that my final guest for the evening has arrived!" Amber was still engrossed in the papers Steven had thrown to her. The others looked at each other nervously. "Come on Detective Sergeant Tenby!" Steven said. "Hurry up! I do so want you to be in time for the main event!"

Joe edged slowly and meticulously along the corridor, clinging to the wall in an attempt to safeguard himself as best he could. The darkness seemed to double the length of the corridors, and multiply any possible threats infinitely. Carefully treading as gently as he could, it seemed to be taking an age for him to get precisely nowhere. As his eyes fully adjusted, he was able to pick out more details of his surroundings which enabled him to move slightly faster. Gradually, his ears began to pick out little pieces of distant conversation. He had no way of knowing what was being said, or where exactly the conversation was coming from, but he knew that confrontation with an armed killer was growing nearer with each step. Continuing to inch along the corridor, the voice was growing slowly louder. Joe saw a door with a small frosted glass window, through which, a diffuse light was spilling onto the linoleum covered floor. Edging nearer to the door, he saw that it was wedged slightly open. Fearing some kind of armed ambush or booby-trap, Joe paused, assessing the door as best he could. Pressing his ear against it, he could hear the familiar voice of Steven Kilkis. Nobody else was speaking, but Joe assumed that Kilkis was not alone. A careful examination of the partially closed door swiftly revealed that there was nothing leaning on it, or connected to it that could work as a booby-trap. Joe stepped back for a second as he considered his next move. As he did so, his heel caught something that was lying in the shadows, sending it skidding into one of the skirting boards. Stooping down to pick it up, Joe held it to the light. It was a 'press' identification card, complete with a photograph and the credentials of Amber Rawson.

"She must've dropped it here as a signal! She's in there with him!" Joe whispered to himself. His mouth ran dry. Now he was looking at a best case scenario of three live witnesses and a crazed gunman! Pushing the door slightly open, he managed to catch sight of Steven Kilkis. Joe concentrated hard in an attempt to listen for any other sound or voice that could give away or confirm the identities of any hostages. All he could hear was Steven Kilkis' voice. Studying Amber, Joe couldn't help but notice how vulnerable she looked as her hands shook. Reaching for his radio, Joe stopped as he realised that he ran the risk of being discovered if he was overheard making a radio call. Instead, he pulled out his phone and turned it back on, managing to switch it to silent before the inevitable flurry of messages came through. Flicking through the phone's menu, he hurriedly tapped out a text message;

"I'M INSIDE THE CLUB. KILKIS IS HERE. AMBER RAWSON HOSTAGE. PHIL IS DEAD. POSSIBLY MORE HOSTAGES. AM TRYING TO ESTABLISH NUMBERS. DO NOT CALL. WILL RELAY VIA TEXT. J"

Without stopping to check its contents, Joe hit 'send'. Closing the phone and dumping it in his pocket, Joe dared himself to open the door a little further. In the far corner he could see Joyce. She was knelt beside Graham, who looked to be seriously injured. A few feet away stood a man and a woman. They had their back to Joe, but the fact that they were a couple, and their fear, was only too easy to perceive. "That makes five hostage and one dead" Joe said grimly to himself as he produced his phone to send an update to Glen's phone. As he began writing the message, the couple turned in the direction of the door. Joe's mouth dropped open as he observed from his concealed viewpoint. "Shit!" he hissed. "She's pregnant! This is all I need!" Sending the message, Joe opened the door as quietly as he could and slipped inside, closing it carefully behind him.

123

"Tell me Robert, do you still think that Graham is a great guy now that you know he destroyed Mum and Dad's marriage?" Steven asked as Robert spoke softly into Lisa's ear, his hand protectively on the small of her back. Looking up from his wife, Robert fixed Steven with a cold stare.

"Steven, please!" Joyce cried. "Enough is enough! You've ruined your life! You've allowed this to turn you into a killer!" Steven's face twisted with rage.

"I didn't allow this to turn me into anything! That perverted old bastard did that for me!" He jabbed the gun in Graham's direction.

"For god's sake Steven!" Lisa screamed. "Stop talking in pointless fucking riddles! If you've got something to say, just get on with it!" Steven returned the aim of his pistol back at Lisa's distended stomach, glancing at Amber and motioning for her to pick up the camera. Robert stepped in front of his wife. Steven's voice was emotionless as Amber hesitantly began taking pictures.

"I suggest strongly Lisa, that if you ever plan on holding that baby of yours, you learn to keep your mouth shut!"

"Come one then!" Robert said, as Lisa began to sob quietly.

"Put us out of our misery! How is Graham a pervert?"

"Oh, I think that Graham should be the one to tell you all

about what he did to me. I wouldn't want you to think I was making anything up just to gain attention!"

"What is he talking about Graham?" Joyce said, looking down at Graham who was still cradled in her arms, his breathing becoming more erratic as more of his blood oozed relentlessly onto the floor.

"He's crazy Joyce!" Graham said unconvincingly. "I always said that boy wasn't quite right! He's a liar!"

"I'm a liar?" shouted Steven as he stepped towards Graham. Joyce leant across the old man as she thrust her palm out towards her son. Steven shivered slightly as he stood over the elderly couple. Normally this might have been put down to raw adrenaline, but he knew that Joe had arrived. Glancing over his shoulder briefly, he saw that the curtain concealing the staircase at the far end of the room was swaying slightly. Joe was clearly hiding in the shadows back there. Steven was certain that Joe would be able to see everything that was happening. Smiling to himself, he turned his attention back to Graham. "So you didn't put your hands on me, your mouth on me? All the times we went away in your truck?" Graham's heart rate noticeably quickened, as did his breathing. His face flushed as he scrambled for an answer as Joyce looked down at him searchingly. Suddenly Robert was furious.

"You're a fucking liar Steven!" he raged. "You're forgetting that Graham took me away too! Never once did he place a finger on me!" Joyce was still looking down at Graham, waiting for an answer. "If he was a kiddie-fiddler, he'd have been messing around with me too surely?" Robert added.

"Maybe you just didn't float his boat Rob!" Steven said as he raised the pistol once more, taking aim at Graham.

"Graham!" said Joyce, her gaze unblinking. "Are you going to deny this?"

"I don't have to!" Graham snapped. "Listen to your other son! The one who hasn't made your life a living hell! The one who hasn't laid blame on your shoulders for everything he's failed to achieve!" Joyce continued to look down at him, the doubt that lingered in her mind beginning to assume control of her face.

"Finally!" shouted Steven, the gun still steadily aimed at Graham's prone body.

"Pardon?" Joyce asked.

"You don't believe him do you?" Steven said triumphantly. Joyce didn't answer. She kept looking from Graham to Robert, and back again.

"Mum! You can't believe this!" Robert said. "Steven's sick in the head! He'll say anything to make you hate Graham like he does!" Still, she didn't answer. Steven never said anything. He knew he didn't have to. Graham had immediately looked like a guilty man the instant Steven had accused him.

"Tell me it's not true!" Joyce demanded.

"Go on Graham!" snarled Steven "Tell her it isn't true! Tell her you didn't take me away so you could lock me in your cab and put your disgusting hands on my body! Tell her you didn't abuse me!" Graham stared into Joe's eyes, tears cascading down his harrowed cheeks.

"Graham! Please!" Joyce pleaded.

"Are you getting this?" Steven said to Amber. She nodded nervously, pointing to the Dictaphone as she shifted from foot to foot.

"I don't believe this!" Robert whispered. "Mum doesn't either, not if she's honest!" Joyce chewed the nail of her left forefinger as she stared absently into the distance.

"I don't know! I just don't know what to think!" Joyce stammered.

"I never thought for one minute you would believe me Rob!" Steven said. "By the way, next time you step in front of your wife, you'd best be prepared to take a bullet for her!"

"I am Steven, every time!" Robert replied, subconsciously stepping across his wife again.

"Good for you!" Steven said with mock admiration. Lifting his arm, he aimed the gun at Robert's knee and fired, felling him instantly. Both Lisa and Joyce screamed as Robert curled up into a ball, rolling from side to side as he clutched his lower leg. Amber cried out as she stumbled backwards, falling to the floor and covering her face as her whole body shook in terror. Steven spun around to face Amber, towering over her with a menacing air as his lip curled in abject disgust. "Get up!" he barked. Frantically, Amber hauled herself to her feet, scrambling for her camera. "You'd better not miss a heartbeat of this!" Steven snarled. "The only reason you're not dead is because I want everyone to know the truth!" Amber nodded as she struggled to avoid crying hysterically. Sensing this, Steven stepped over to her and leaned in, pressing the barrel of the gun against the underside of her chin. "No crying either!" he hissed. She recoiled slightly as his hot, pungent breath filled her ear. "We don't want your blubbering interfering with the recording now, do we?" Taking deep breaths, Amber managed to calm her breathing and suppress her sobs. "Good girl!" Steven whispered before stepping back. Looking down at his brother, he watched as Joyce and Lisa busied themselves about his prone form. Graham was sat up against the wall, his shoulders sagged and his spirit broken as he watched Amber photographing Robert. Joyce kept glancing across at him, her mind racing as she struggled to choose whose version of history she could believe. Steven smiled contentedly to himself as he watched her obvious turmoil, a feeling of joy and achievement dancing through his veins as he tasted the first succulent morsels of justice.

.

Behind the curtain, Joe was barely concealing his desperation as he watched Steven shoot his own brother in cold blood. Every part of his being was screaming out to be allowed to rush across to the two casualties and help to stem their bleeding and ease their pain. He was no paramedic, but was trained in advanced emergency aid. Alongside his desperation to help was the shock at what he had heard Steven accuse Graham of doing.

"Shame you can't prove it Kilkis!" Joe murmured. "If you could, I'd happily let the bastard bleed to death!" Scrambling for his phone, he rapidly typed a message to Glen.

" UPDATE; FURTHER SHOTS FIRED. TWO GUN SHOT VICTIMS. TOTAL HOSTAGES; 5. 1 HEAVILY PREGNANT. MULTIPLE AMBULANCES REQUIRED. HOSTAGES INCLUDE JOYCE KILKIS & GRAHAM CROSBIE.CONFIRM GUNMAN IS STEVEN KILKIS. J"

Hurriedly completing the message and making sure it was sent, Joe put the phone in his pocket as he pondered his options. If he were to blow his cover now, he would almost certainly risk being shot.

"What can I do anyway?" Joe asked himself as he watched. "One unarmed man against a nutter with a firearm! I don't like those odds!" Joe knew that his police training had taught him that the best course of action was to remain in a place of safety and cover, and try and provide intelligence for the firearms teams that he hoped were already outside and forming a plan to gain entry to the club. Resigning himself to the task of avoiding posthumous heroism, Joe concentrated on remembering as many details as he could, shifting his position as silently as he worried about how long the two gunshot victims could avoid unconsciousness and death without medical assistance. As he looked on, Steven turned slowly in the direction of the curtain behind which Joe was hiding. He stared intensely, almost as if his gaze were cutting through the fabric of the curtain.

"Keep calm!" Joe whispered as Steven continued to stare. Taking careful and deliberate steps, Steven began walking across to the curtain.

"Shit!" Joe hissed as he quickly looked around for a new place to conceal himself. There was nowhere. Eyeing the stairs, Joe knew that he would make too much noise and give away his location if he were to make a rush for them. "If I'm going to be found, I'm sure as hell not going to give him the satisfaction of finding me trying to run from him!" Joe said to himself, realising that he had no choice, but to stay as still as he could in the hope that Steven was walking towards him for another reason. In a handful of purposeful strides, Steven was upon the curtain, throwing it back dramatically and aiming the gun at Joe's forehead.

"So good of you to join us Joe!" Steven said. Joe stared as calmly as he could at the barrel of Steven's gun. The light was diffuse as it reflected off the matt surface of the metal. The gun was still giving off the strong smell of gunpowder, and Joe breathed it in deeply as he worked hard to appear not intimidated by Steven. In a strange way it helped to soothe him as he slowly raised his hands. Steven motioned with the pistol for Joe to come out from behind the curtained area and join the rest of the group. Joe did so without complaint or sudden movement. His mind had diligently analysed his options as he had faced the gun for the first time, and his strategy now centred on buying as much time as possible and stalling Steven so as to afford the firearms officers ample opportunity to put whatever plan they had come up with into effect. As he stepped into the light, Joyce looked up in shock.

"Detective Sergeant Tenby!" she said. Joe smiled awkwardly.

"Mrs Kilkis" he said. Looking across at Graham, he could barely conceal his disgust at the allegations made against the old man. "Mr Crosbie" Joe said with an expression of obvious disapproval. Looking at the other two, Joe knelt down next to Robert and took off his tie.

"What are you doing Tenby?" Steven snapped, the gun once more pointing at Joe.

"These two will die if they aren't helped!" Joe said. "They'll bleed to death!" Mulling over Joe's words, Steven lowered the gun.

"I suppose it serves a purpose" he shrugged. Looping the tie around Robert's lower thigh, Joe tied it into a tourniquet and secured it tightly, apologising as Robert cried out in pain.

Walking over to Graham, he knelt beside him, gingerly moving the torn material of the old man's trousers as he examined the wound in his leg.

"I hope that mad bastard is going to get arrested for what he's done!" Graham whispered. Clinging desperately to the sentiment of a man being innocent until proven guilty, Joe chose his words carefully.

"I think the first thing we need to hope for is to get out of here safe and relatively well, don't you?" Graham chose not to answer, instead closing his eyes and breathing hard to try and deal with the intense pain.

"Thank you" Lisa whispered as Joe stood up.

"Don't thank him!" Steven commanded. "I've only let him keep them alive so that fate doesn't take the choice away!"

"What are you going on about?" Joe asked.

"Come on!" Steven said impatiently. "You've been hiding behind that curtain, listening to everything that's been going on! You know what that bastard did to me!" Joe didn't reply. Steven turned away from Joe and faced Joyce, who was still knelt by the side of her son, and was still fighting the suggestion that Graham was a paedophile

"You made the wrong choice once before!" Steven said as Joyce looked at him in confusion. "You knew what he was doing to me! You must have known! You chose your boyfriend over your son! I'm giving you the chance to choose again!"

"Steven! I don't understand! You're not making sense!" Joyce said.

"It makes perfect sense!" Steven snarled as he raised the weapon. Joe clenched his fists in a conscious effort not to try and grab the gun, realising that it would only make things worse. "You chose Graham over me when I needed you! Robert needs you! Graham needs you! Make your choice!"

"Make my choice?" Joyce repeated.

"One of them will die tonight!" Steven said with a wave of his hand, the gun aimed squarely at Joyce. "You have to choose which one!"

"No!" Joyce cried.

"Oh yes!" Steven said with a dark smile. "You either watch your lover die, or your son!" Joyce began sobbing. Amber was forcibly breathing in an attempt to ward off a panic attack; her full body seemed to be shivering. Joe slipped off his coat and placed it around Amber's shoulders. Steven glared at Joe.

"You just can't help but play the hero can you Tenby?"

"She's going into shock Kilkis!" Joe exclaimed. "How is she meant to make sure she records everything if she's in shock and unconscious?" Steven begrudgingly accepted Joe's logic.

"I can't do this!" Joyce sobbed. "I just can't! I've never killed anyone in my life! I've never even killed a spider! I'm not starting now!"

"Don't worry Mum" Steven soothed. "You won't be pulling the trigger!" She looked up at Steven questioningly, her eyes blinking through the tears.

"That honour falls to our resident knight in shining armour!" Steven switched the aim of the pistol back to Joe, who stepped back in surprise, his heart pounding.

"Me? What is this Kilkis?" Joe spat.

"This, Tenby, is justice!" Steven hissed. "Come on mother! Choose one, so the hero of the hour can put them out of their misery!"

Joe and Joyce stared at each other for a few seconds. Joyce

tried to speak, but the words wouldn't come out.

"Do it! Or I kill your precious grandchild!" Steven screamed, pointing the gun at Lisa's stomach.

"No, please!" Lisa screamed as her voice disintegrated into heaving sobs. Joyce was visibly shaking as her eyes darted left and right, her shoulders heaving as she cried softly.

Robert thrust his hands up at Joe. Stooping to lift him, Joe helped him to his feet, where he stood with his bloodied leg raised.

"Steven. Please, I'm begging you! Don't hurt my baby! Shoot me! Kill me now, do whatever, but let my baby live!" tears streamed down his face as he spoke. Lisa rushed to her husband's side, sliding her arms around his back and doing her best to support his wait as he wobbled back and forth.

"Aren't you a brave little bunny?" Steven said sarcastically.

"The decision is not mine to make!" Turning to Graham, Joyce bit her bottom lip as she stared into his eyes.

"I'm sorry" she whispered as she stepped back. "I can't let my boy die" Graham nodded before beginning to cry softly. Joe covered his face with his sweating palms.

"Come on Tenby!" Steven said with glee. Reaching down into his sock, he produced another hand pistol. Aiming it squarely at Joe, he handed him the original gun. Hesitantly, Joe accepted it, examining it minutely before looking down at the second gun.

"Call it insurance!" Steven explained before motioning with the pistol. "Come on Joe! Time to cross the line!"

Glen glanced down at his phone. Having just received another message from Joe, he momentarily lost concentration as he forwarded the message to Commander Carlton's phone, causing the car to wander across to the opposite side of the road.

"That was Joe! Steven Kilkis has 5 hostages, one of which is pregnant, and there have been 2 casualties from gunshot wounds!"

"Calm down Glen!" scolded Jessica as Glen threw the car violently around a tight bend in the road. The blue light that was sitting on the dashboard of the car was lighting up the air around the speeding car as it tore through the night time streets, its long beams of coloured light saving Glen, Jessica and Kevin from almost certain collision as the driver of a battered white van took evasive action.

"First rule of emergency response Glen" Kevin said. "You might want to get there first, but first you've got to get there!" Glen rolled his eyes as he changed gear. "I still can't get my head around all of this!" Kevin said as he watched a parade of brightly lit takeaways, and barricaded shop fronts flash past the window. "Your DCI is actually the guy you've been hunting for all this time?" Glen shrugged as he concentrated on the road ahead.

"Are you telling me that you would've caught him if he were your boss?"

"Not at all mate!" Kevin answered quickly, conscious of the perils of making enemies of the other two in the car. "I'm just saying that it's something that you usually read in some kind of crime thriller, not in an incident log! If you manage to arrest the guy he'll be a celebrity prisoner!"

"He's also my uncle Kevin, so no offence, but give it a rest please!" Jessica snapped. Glen looked at Kevin in the rear view mirror. Kevin's eyes were wide in disbelief. Mouthing "Wow" silently, Kevin shook his head as he concentrated on the urban scenery as it raced past his window.

A few minutes later, Glen brought the car to a violent halt at the police cordon that had been hastily set up at the end of Milward Street. The club was just in view from the cordon, and already a curious throng of onlookers were beginning to gather. Showing their identification badges, the three of them ducked under the tape and approached Commander Carlton, who was stood with the Duty Incident Officer, Inspector Mansfield, as they pored over the details of a piece of paper that was stretched out on the bonnet of a shoddily parked police van. The commander abruptly dismissed Inspector Mansfield, and turned to the three of them, her face solemn. "Who is this?" snapped the Commander as she gestured towards Kevin.

"Detective Constable Kevin McDonnell Ma'am" Kevin replied. "I have been assisting DS Tenby with some enquiries up in Newcastle" Commander Carlton studied Kevin intensely for a few seconds before nodding, and turning her attention to Jessica.

"Are you fully aware of what is happening Miss Hopewell?" Jessica nodded.

"DS Tenby is inside, shots have been fired, and there are hostages!" Commander Carlton's expression was grim.

"As if this weren't bad enough, one of the hostages is pregnant, and another is a prominent news reporter with a growing army of fans!" Jessica sighed. Despite the actions of her uncle, she couldn't shake a tiny piece of affinity to him that was stubbornly refusing to leave her. Still, she knew where her loyalties must continue to lie.

"I'm sure that we can create a plan that will lead to a safe exit for the hostages, and an arrest Ma'am!" Jessica said.

Commander Carlton looked around to make sure that nobody else other than the three of them could hear her.

"If this is going to be too awkward for you Jessica, you need to take yourself somewhere else. I cannot have clouded judgements within the police cordon. Are we clear on that?" she asked.

"Don't worry about me! I'm fine!" Jessica said. "I cannot think of anywhere else I want to be right now, other than right here. I need to be here for my colleagues"

"Just so long as you understand that your uncle is no longer to be considered as one of us. He is the subject to police operations, and will be treated accordingly. Is that understood?" Jessica nodded.

"So what are our options Ma'am?" Glen asked.

"Our options, DC Violet, are limited!" Commander Carlton said. "I take it from the fact that I have not received any further messages from you that DS Tenby has stopped communicating?" Glen nodded.

"Where is CO19 Ma'am?" Glen asked as he looked up and down the street.

"Armed response are half an hour away stuck in traffic DC Violet!" Commander Carlton snapped. "They're in a tailback behind a broken down bus in Denmark Hill"

"Half an hour Ma'am? Joe needs back up now Commander! Is there any possibility of entering the building?" Kevin asked.

Commander Carlton fixed him with a trademark stare.

"DC McDonnell, I do not know what the response policy is for the British Transport Police, but I can assure you that no Metropolitan Police officer will be entering that building without a thorough assessment being completed, and without appropriate armed response!" Before Kevin had an opportunity to reply Commander Carlton swiftly turned her back, punching the keypad of her mobile phone and pressing it to her ear as she returned her attention to the scribbled notes she had made during the impromptu briefing that had taken place on the bonnet of the police van moments before.

The three of them turned away from the Commander, unsure as to what to do next.

"This is too weird!" Jessica sighed, looking up into the glare of a streetlight.

"I can't fucking believe that we're in London and we're going to have to wait half an hour for armed assistance! I thought this was the centre of the universe? We get better response times than that in Newcastle!" Kevin said as he paced in small circles.

"We need to stay calm and follow procedure!" Glen said. A voice from the other side of the cordon interrupted the conversation. Glen looked across. It was Harry Crompton, Amber Rawson's editor. He was angrily shouting at the constable who was guarding the police cordon. Glen and Jessica walked over to try and help the increasingly flustered police officer calm Harry Crompton down. Kevin went to go with them, but stopped himself. Watching them until they were a few yards away, he looked over at Commander Carlton.

She was now stood in the road with Inspector Mansfield. They were pointing towards the far end of the road and were deep in conversation. Spying the alleyway at the side of the club, Kevin saw his chance. He took another look around, before easing himself gradually along the wall of the club, creeping as quietly as possible down the alleyway. Opening the yard gate, Kevin looked back towards the street, making sure that nobody had seen him. Cautiously, he entered the yard, peering into the darkness. Making a visual sweep, he quickly assessed the fire escape leading up the first floor, scaling the ladders two at a time. Looking into each of the windows, Kevin quickly satisfied himself that he was safe before trying the door. Silently giving his thanks as the door gently opened, Kevin slipped inside, being sure to leave the door open in the hope that help would soon be following him as he edged tentatively down the darkened corridor.

126

Joe gulped desperately as he rubbed his thumb repeatedly over the grip of the pistol. He stared disbelievingly at Steven, who waited impatiently for him to act.

"Come on Joe! You rode in here on your white horse! Be a man and finish the job for Christ's sake!"

"If you think I'm killing anyone, you're even further out of your mind than I already thought!" Joe said. Steven sighed.

"This is what happens when people like you get involved!" he said. "I told you when you arrived that you were out of your league Tenby! You're a traffic warden with a warrant card, and that's all you'll ever be!" Steven jabbed the barrel of his gun in Joe's direction. Joe stared intensely at the floor, as he flinched slightly, causing Steven to laugh mockingly. Joe's fingers gripped the grip of the pistol so tightly that they were actually painful as he struggled to remain calm in the face of what he was being commanded to do.

"I'm not standing for this!" Joe told himself as he fumed inwardly.

"Look at you!" snarled Steven. "Flinching like some kind of coward! Come on Joe! Prove to me that you're not a complete waste of fucking space! Shoot him!" Joe didn't move. Steven turned slightly away from him, clearly revelling in the opportunity to demean Joe and play to the captive audience at the same time.

"Look at this joker!" Steven said to the others. "He rushed in here to rescue you all from the big bad gunman, but he left his balls in the car, didn't you Joe?" Joe knew that this was his only chance.

"I don't have to prove anything to you!" he hissed, lurching forward and grabbing the gun. Steven stumbled backwards, and in the struggle, the gun fell to the floor, firing a bullet that embedded itself in the main door. As the two men struggled desperately, the four hostages screamed as the sound of gunfire filled the air, Robert trying and failing to throw himself across his pregnant wife. Steven grabbed Joe's left arm in an attempt to grab the remaining pistol. Joe resisted as hard as he could, sensing that Steven's sheer adrenaline and anger were making him impossible to repel. Aiming a harsh kick to Steven's kneecap, he managed to throw his attacker clear, scrambling to his feet as Steven cried out in pain, falling backwards, before regaining himself and rushing towards Joe, punching him squarely on the nose. Joe's vision and mouth were filled with the deep red of effervescent blood as his nose broke under the force of the punch. As his balance gave way, Joe managed to throw the gun across the room as he felt his grip loosen and begin to give way completely. As he fell against the wall, Joe breathed a sigh of relief as he watched the gun slide across the floor, disappearing under a table. Steven immediately launched himself across the room towards it, with Joe throwing himself at Steven in a bid to restrain him. Grabbing hold of Steven's trousers, Joe yanked them as hard as he could, forcing Steven's legs to give way under the combined weight of the two men. In an instant, Steven was on top of Joe, punching him repeatedly in the head and face, his expression chewed and twisted with hatred.

"Don't mess with me Tenby!" Steven shouted as blow after blow rained down on Joe, who was doing his best to defend himself. "You're a fucking amateur! All you've done is get yourself in the way of justice, just like you're old man did!" The mention of Joe's father threw him slightly, and Steven capitalised on Joe's slight hesitation, punching him once, twice and then a third time in the mouth in an attack that sent blood, saliva, and teeth skidding across the grubby floor. For a few seconds, Joe lost consciousness. As his eyes reopened, he did his best to focus on the figure standing over him. He was struggling to make out the details of the face, but there was no mistaking what the figure was holding. It was a gun, and it was aimed at Joe's forehead.

"It's such a same Joe!" Steven said mournfully as he steadily maintained the aim of the gun. "I was going to let you stick around long enough to watch the fun! Looks like I'm going to have to deal with you first!"

127

"Where's Kevin?" Glen said to nobody in particular as he and Jessica scanned the pavement and road.

"Why don't you ring him?" Jessica asked.

"I don't have his number!" Glen replied. "You don't think he's buggered off to the pub?" he asked. Jessica shook her head.

"Wouldn't be much of a copper if he had!" she said as she watched a transmission van pull up near the police cordon. "Joe seems impressed by him!"

"What does that prove?" Glen said snottily. Jessica smiled mischievously.

"Oh don't worry Glen! Joe still loves you too!" she said mockingly. "What I'm saying is that If he's happy to trust Kevin, then that's good enough for me! So bearing that in mind, I can't see him wandering off for a drink in the middle of an armed siege!" Glen nodded thoughtfully as he glanced at the alleyway leading down the side of the club. Tapping Jessica on the arm, he pointed at it.

"You don't think..?" Jessica said.

"I don't think he's gone in?" Glen replied. "I'd like to think he's got more sense, but I get the sinking feeling we might have another hostage to deal with!"

"What shall we do?" Jessica said.

"We need to find Commander Carlton!" Glen replied, already craning his neck as he scanned the growing crowd of police uniforms.

"I don't want to get him in trouble!" Jessica said.

"Neither do I!" Glen snapped. "But I don't want to get him killed either! If Commander Carlton found out we knew, and we didn't tell her, she'd have my warrant card! We have to tell her!"

"Tell me what?" said the Commander. Glen and Jessica froze. Turning to face her, Glen took a deep breath before speaking.

"Come on Violet!" Commander Carlton barked. "Out with it!"

The squeal of tyres diverted the Commander's attention as the Armed Response Unit arrived on scene under the hypnotic spray of yet more blue light. A tall man jumped out of the front passenger door and presented himself to Commander Carlton.

"Commander. I'm Sergeant Lloyd" he said.

"You took your bloody time!" Commander Carlton said. "We need to grab Inspector Mansfield and formulate an action plan, now!"

Kevin's heart was pounding furiously, and the sound seemed to be dominating his every sense as he struggled to remain calm

"What am I doing?" he said to himself. "I haven't even got a plan!" He made painfully slow progress as he placed one foot gently in front of the other, making slow sweeping motions with his boot as he lowered his foot to the well-worn carpet in an attempt to avoid knocking anything over and giving away his presence. Suddenly the silence was shattered by the sound of a gunshot. Kevin threw himself onto the floor, his hands covering the back of his head as he laid perfectly still, his ears desperately reaching through the bouncing sound waves of gunfire. Carefully getting to his feet, he forced himself to walk faster, becoming more aware of the sound of muffled voices. It sounded like a fight. He knew straight away that it was Joe, and that he was in trouble.

"Shit!" he said as he groped through the darkness as quickly as he could, following the sounds as they became louder, and quickly arriving at a door, easing it away from the door frame and peering through the gap. Across the room he could see Joe lying on the ground. A man was picking something up from the floor. As he straightened, Kevin could see that the man was holding a gun. He knew he had to act. Pushing the door as gently as he could, he managed to open it far enough to slip into the room and peek around the curtain. The armed man had his back to Kevin. As he levelled the gun at Joe, Kevin rushed forward, throwing the curtain to one side. With feet pounding the floor, he lowered his shoulder, smashing into Steven and wrenching him to the ground. Joe sat up, looking on in disbelief as the two men rolled over three times before Kevin levered himself on top of the disorientated gunman, grasping his collar and punching him twice in the face.

"Kevin?" Joe said, blinking through the pain. "What are you doing here?" Kevin looked across with a breathless grin as he straddled the unconscious Steven. Reaching into his pocket, he produced his warrant card and showed it to Joe.

"I told you I was coming down in my email! Are these things valid down here?" he said with a smile. Before Joe could reply, or Kevin could properly caution Steven, the air was filled with three malevolent thuds, followed by the main doors swinging wildly open as splinters of wood cascaded across the floor. The room filled with police officers dressed in black clothing. Everybody threw their hands into the air whilst armed officers made sure that the room was secure. The chaos gradually subsided as officers holstered weapons and tended to Graham, as well as Robert, his heavily pregnant wife, and Amber Rawson who had sunk to her knees and was sobbing uncontrollably. Joyce knelt next to Robert, absently stroking his hair as she stared coldly at Graham.

"We're police!" Joe said to the Sergeant.

"What?" The Sergeant barked. "Are you the hot head who came running in here without back up?" Joe stared at him, blinking rapidly. His initial reaction was to feel aggrieved by that assessment of his conduct, but he couldn't deny that he had put himself at serious risk. Deciding not to answer that question directly, he instead motioned to his trouser pocket. "I'm DS Tenby. Can I reach into my pocket and get my warrant card?" The Sergeant nodded impatiently. Joe slipped his hand inside his pocket and pulled out the leather wallet containing his police identification. "My colleague over there is a police officer too!" Joe said, motioning towards Kevin, who was still sitting astride Steven Kilkis. Steven was now conscious, and staring up at Kevin in a state of confusion. The police issue machine gun pointing at him however, was enough to keep him subdued for now.

"I'm very pleased to meet you Detective Sergeant!" Sergeant Lloyd said ironically. "Let's see your warrant card too!" Kevin reached inside his jacket and slid his card along the floor. Sgt Lloyd scooped up the warrant card, frowning as he read the detail. "British Transport Police?" he mused as he looked across at Kevin. "Why is a suspect in an armed siege on Metropolitan Police turf being restrained by one of the railway children?" Kevin looked down at Steven Kilkis.

"I thought you needed someone to come and show you how to do it properly!" he quipped with a smile. Sgt Lloyd was unmoved. Looking directly at Steven Kilkis' face for the first time, he breathed in sharply.

"Isn't that Detective Chief Inspector Whindle? Sgt Lloyd asked.

"It's a long and complicated story!" Joe said as he pulled himself gingerly to his feet and brushed the dirt from his trousers. "Sgt Lloyd, this man is the prime suspect in a murder enquiry!

"Is this some kind of joke?" snapped Sgt Lloyd. "He's a serving DCI!"

"He's under arrest!" Joe scolded.

"Actually Joe, he's not!" Kevin said.

"What?" Joe spluttered.

Kevin turned to Sgt Lloyd. "For the record Sergeant, the suspect was in the process of attempting to murder a police officer. I have been restraining him until I felt it safe to assist DS Tenby in completing his arrest"

"Very smooth DC McDonnell!" snapped Commander Carlton as she entered the room. Everyone turned and looked at her.

"You're just in time Commander!" Joe said, wiping blood and saliva from his mouth and chin, as he walked across to Steven Kilkis. "Steven Kilkis, you are under arrest for the offences of Murder, Attempted Murder, False Imprisonment, Assaulting a Police Officer, Possession of Controlled Substances, and Illegal Possession of Firearms. You do not have to say anything but it may harm your defence if you do not mention when questioned something you later rely on in court. Anything you do say may be taken down and used in evidence"

"Fuck you Tenby!" spat Steven. Commander Carlton watched

dispassionately for a few seconds as Joe and Kevin hauled Steven to his feet and placed his arms behind his back. As Joe fastened handcuffs onto Steven, Commander Carlton turned to Sgt Lloyd.

"Status report please, Sgt Lloyd! I have two paramedic units waiting for clearance to enter the building!"

"The building is secured Commander!" Sgt Lloyd said. "The two casualties have been given emergency aid and are stabilised, awaiting further medical assistance"

"Very good Sergeant!" Commander Carlton said sternly. "Let's get the scene sorted and processed as quickly as possible!" Sgt Lloyd nodded his agreement, pressing the transmit button on his radio, and informing Inspector Mansfield that the building was safe. "Detective Sergeant Tenby, and Detective Constable McDonnell! You both have many questions to answer once we're out of here! Count yourselves very lucky that you were not police victims 2 and 3 in this case!"

"Yes Ma'am!" Joe and Kevin replied in unison. Joe looked on as the paramedics clattered noisily into the room, their gurneys bouncing on the uneven floor as the men rushed to the stricken victims.

"Joe, get cleaned up and get ready to face the media! The Commander snapped. "Despite you dabbling with idiocy, the Commissioner wants to portray you as a hero!"

"Yes Ma'am!" Joe said quietly. Joe and Kevin turned to walk towards the door.

"Gentlemen!" Commander Carlton called after them. They turned to face her. "Good work!" Joe blushed slightly as he nursed his aching nose. "I suggest you get your statements completed ASAP!" With a nod they turned and made their way to the corridor, inwardly thanking the stars for the experience of leaving that room alive.

As they descended the stairs, Joe glanced at a picture of a face he would recognise anywhere. From behind the glass, the beaming face of a muscular black man surveyed the dimly lit corridor.

"Who's this?" Kevin asked. Pausing to study the subject of the picture,

"This is Clive Sullivan!" Joe said with a smile. "He played for Hull KR and Hull FC. He was part of the Rovers squad that beat Hull FC in the cup final in 1980, and he was the first black sportsman to captain a British international team!" As he spoke, Joe remembered the conversation he had with Phil only a day or two earlier when Phil had told Jessica about Sullivan. As he replayed it in his mind, his smile faded. Suddenly, Joe's stomach lurched.

"The dog!" Joe said, turning and bounding back up the staircase. "Where's the dog?"

"What dog?" Kevin asked. Joe didn't answer. Bursting into the function room, he strode breathlessly over to Steven, who was being lifted to his feet. "Where is he?" Steven ignored him. Joe grabbed Steven by the collar, yanking him violently forward. "I said, where's the dog?" he snarled. Steven looked Joe up and down, a sly smile on his face. After a few seconds, he let out an exaggerated sigh.

"It's in the office cupboard!" Steven said. "I can't allow myself to be seen as cruel now, can I?" he said sarcastically. Joe was already halfway across the room, heading for the side door that he had entered from when he had crept along the corridor.

"Prick!" he said over his shoulder as he rushed through the now open door. As he neared the office, he saw that forensic staff were already examining Phil. He paused at the door, his lead lowered. Taking a deep breath, he pushed on towards the office, rushing in and snatching the cupboard door open. The smell of urine and faeces was overpowering. Sully lay in the very corner of the cupboard, his dehydrated body shivering in fear and exhaustion. "Come on boy!" Joe said softly as he scooped him up and carried him out. Sully cried softly as he buried his face in Joe's neck. Joe squeezed him gently as he walked carefully down the stairs that avoided the commotion that was going on in the function room. Walking past Kevin, he headed stridently for the main doors, calling to Kevin as he went. "Are you coming then, or what?"

Letting themselves out of the front door of the club, they were both taken aback by the degree of activity in the street. The crowds at the cordon were three and four people deep, most desperately craning their necks to catch a glimpse of what was going on, others boldly recording the proceedings on their mobile phones. Joe hadn't realised it whilst inside, but he had been sweating profusely, and the cool night air was now biting at his moist skin as he realised that his jacket was still around the shoulders of Amber Rawson. A constable approached Joe, looking quizzically at Sully as he tried to bury his face in Joe's neck even further.

"Can you get me a bottle of water and some kind of container please?" Joe asked. Looking up and down the street, the Constable hesitated before disappearing for a moment, returning with water, and a plastic tub from one of the police vans. Joe hurried over to his car, managing to pull his keys from his trouser pocket and unlock the door. Gently placing Sully on the back seat, he filled the tub with water and placed it on the floor. He stood watching the dog drink enthusiastically for a few seconds before gently closing the car door, turning to Kevin and shaking his head.

"Poor thing!" he whispered. "He could've been locked in that cupboard for days!"

Walking over to one of the ambulances, the pair were directed to sit in the back by a paramedic, who dutifully draped blankets over their shoulders.

"Told you I still had it Joe!" Kevin said with a smirk. Joe took a long look at Kevin. Shaking his head, he laughed nervously.

"You saved my life in there mate!" he whispered. Kevin shrugged. "I won't forget that!"

"Looks like you've got company!" Kevin said, nodding towards the club.

As the pair looked across, the doors to the club crashed open. One of the gurneys was being manhandled onto the street by the paramedics. On the trolley was Graham. The sheet covering his leg was already stained with blood, and the dressings hastily applied were looking old and dirty. Joe walked across to the trolley as the Paramedics were preparing to slide it into the ambulance.

"Are you okay Mr Crosbie?" Joe asked softly. Graham looked up at him, his eyes struggling to focus.

"I need to thank you for all you did in there Sergeant Tenby!" Graham whispered, clutching for Joe's hand.

"You won't be thanking me Mr Crosbie" Joe said as he moved his hand away. "You're under arrest on suspicion of the statutory rape of a minor" Graham stared up at Joe with the same expression he gave Joyce when she questioned him. "Are you going to tell me it never happened?" Joe asked. Graham started to cry silently as Joe delivered the remainder of an official caution. Turning to a nearby constable, Joe beckoned him over.

"I need you to do a hospital watch on this suspect please! He's under arrest for statutory rape!" The constable nodded before clambering into the ambulance. Joe walked back to the ambulance where he and Kevin were awaiting a check-up and climbed back in, his brain filled with racing thoughts.

"Joe! Thank god you're okay!" Jessica shouted. Joe lifted himself from his seat and stepped down from the ambulance. Jessica sprinted, leaving Glen trailing in her wake as she threw her arms around him, causing him to cry out as she squeezed his bruised body.

"I'm alive anyway!" Joe said with a smile as their eyes met. Joe looked down at her flawless skin and delicate features as she held onto him, her eyes shut tight. "I'm bruised and cut a little bit Jess, but I'm okay!" he whispered. Her eyes were filling with tears as she looked up at him. Her expression transformed after a second into a sly smile as she spoke softly into his ear.

"I realised when you were in there just how much I want you Joe! I couldn't stop thinking about how devastated I would be if you were killed!" He looked down at her, his heart pounding and his eyes growing wider.

"So why are you smiling if you've been thinking like that?" he asked.

"I'm just glad that the next time I see you lying down won't be on a mortuary table!" she replied with a naughty grin.

"Miss Hopewell!" Joe hissed in shock. As he stared down at her open mouthed, she seized the opportunity and kissed him softly. "I suppose we'd better get you checked over" she said, breaking the kiss and struggling to tear her gaze away from his, as the buzz of activity continued to hum all around them.

"Interview terminated at 23:44" Glen sighed as he switched off the tape recorder. For the past three hours he had sat opposite his former boss. The only response that he had been able to illicit from Steven Kilkis was a terse "No comment" As he gathered together the pile of paperwork he had prepared for the interview, Glen stared thoughtfully at the warped and discoloured ceiling tiles.

"You don't actually think I'm going to tell you anything do you Violet?" Steven said as the duty solicitor stood up and put on his jacket.

"Three things you need to know Kilkis!" Glen said as casually as he could. "Firstly, we've got you! You're not going anywhere, other than Jail, for life!" Steven rolled his eyes dismissively. "Secondly, you're not my boss anymore! You made my life a complete misery from my first day in CID until the day you were finally kicked into touch by Commander Carlton!" Steven could barely conceal his rage. Despite the fact that he was now a suspect, he still expected to be treated with respect and deference, especially by the likes of Glen Violet. Glen looked at him with contempt as he rose from his chair and headed for the exit. Glen opened the door as a constable came in to take Steven back to the holding cells. As the constable pulled Steven to his feet, he leaned as far as he could towards Glen.

"So what was the third thing?"

"Pardon?" Glen replied as he checked his phone for messages.

"You said there were three things I needed to know you fucking idiot!" Steven snarled.

"Oh yeah" Glen said flatly "Detective Sergeant Tenby has arrested Graham Crosbie on suspicion of sexually assaulting you"

"Really? Why?" Steven asked as he stared at Glen.

"Mr Kilkis, I think this unofficial conversation has gone far enough!" said the duty solicitor sternly. Steven held his hand up as he continued to stare.

"I guess he believed you were telling the truth" Glen said with a shrug, closing his phone as he walked out into the corridor.

"Tell him I want to see him!" Steven shouted as Glen disappeared from view.

With her customary lack of ceremony, Commander Carlton thrust the door to the Executive Briefing Room open, and walked in, closely followed by Dr Rothesay. Striding over to the seat directly facing the door, she sat down and motioned for Dr Rothesay to follow suit. Joe had just finished pinning a series of photographs to a display board, was stood busily writing notes on the large whiteboard.

"Morning Joe!" she said forcefully as she checked her watch.

"We need to be getting a move on here! I need this case putting to bed!"

"Following recent developments, I have re-ordered toxicology tests on all victims, following the discovery of medazolene in the blood stream of Anna Brown. Each one came back positive, with the exception of PC Andy Mills" Joe said, launching straight into his briefing.

"So the theory that PC Mills was in the wrong place at the wrong time seems to be valid" said Commander Carlton. Joe nodded grimly.

"Russell Danton had medazolene in his blood stream, so it would seem logical to assume that PC Mills followed Kilkis for some reason, and was killed either accidentally, or because he tried to intervene" Joe waited a few seconds whilst Commander Carlton scribbled on her notepad. Looking up, she motioned for Joe to continue.

"Background enquiries have shown that each victim is linked to one common incident dating back over two decades." Joe pointed to the briefing board as he spoke. "All of them have relatives who were previously employed by the railway, and all of those relatives are shown to have been involved in a fatality that took place at Melsham West, where one Raymond Kilkis was hit by a train" Joe hesitated for her to complete the paragraph she was writing before he continuing. "At the home of Steven Kilkis, we found detailed documentation on each victim, their relatives, and their links to this single event." Joe glanced across at the board where he had arranged the photographs.

"Tina McBride is the niece of Stuart Mallon, the driver of the train. Anna Brown is the granddaughter of Jerry Pickford, the signaller on duty at the time Raymond Kilkis was hit, Sean Grant is the youngest son of Ian Ellison, the man in charge of the track maintenance crew, and Russell Danton was the nephew of Gary Fenley, the man in charge of the signal box. It's all laid out in detail within the evidence recovered from the house" Joe pointed to a photograph of the sinister black cupboard with its doors open, the photographs pinned to the back wall and in plain view of the camera.

"So why go after Graham Crosbie?" Commander Carlton asked.

"Crosbie was not only the step dad who had been abusing Steven Kilkis from an early age; he was also the look out on the track when Raymond Kilkis was run over by Stuart Mallon's train!" Joe said. Commander Carlton digested the information she had been given so far, clearing her throat as she scrutinised the photographs.

"So, what was your connection to the case Joe?" she asked. Joe took a deep breath.

"It was my late father who was the connection Commander" he said quietly. "He was the union official who defended the railway workers in the official inquiry. By all accounts, he stopped Jerry Pickford from losing his job and possibly facing criminal charges! I suppose that Steven Kilkis held him responsible for defending his father's colleagues" Commander Carlton nodded solemnly as she resumed making notes, her demeanour as clinical as ever. Before Joe could say anything further, the door slowly opened. It was Glen.

"Sorry to disturb your briefing Commander, but its Steven Kilkis"

"What about him?" Commander Carlton said. Joe immediately feared that Kilkis had committed suicide, and was sure from the tone of the Commander's voice that she was thinking along similar lines.

"He won't talk to anyone but Joe!"

"We won't be long Glen" Joe said as he turned back to the whiteboard.

"He's demanding to see you now!" Glen said. Joe looked at the Commander.

"Strike whilst the iron's hot DS Tenby!" Commander Carlton reached down into her case and produced a sealed white envelope and slid it across the table as she closed her notebook. "Take this Detective Sergeant Tenby and read it carefully. Don't be distracted though! This interview with Kilkis could be our best chance to get anything out of him!"

"This is becoming a bit of a pattern, you keeping me waiting Joe!" Steven Kilkis looked relaxed as he leant back in the chair. The duty solicitor cursed repeatedly under his breath as the nib of his fountain pen kept running dry of ink. Joe sat down opposite Kilkis, maintaining eye contact as he inserted a tape into the tape recorder and confirmed the identities of all concerned for the benefit of the recording.

"The way I see it Steven, you have all the time in the world, whereas I am currently a very busy man!" Joe said eventually.

"Was it the dog that really got you angry Joe?" Steven teased.

"I could've let him die you know! I found his cries quite soothing if I'm honest! They were almost melodic" Steven smiled darkly.

"Why am I here Steven?" Joe asked curtly. Steven leant forward.

"Why did you arrest Graham?" he asked. Joe thought for a

second before answering.

"You're a murderer, a thief, a liar, a bully and an abuser. But when it comes to what you said about Graham Crosbie, I think you're being truthful."

"What is this?" Steven scoffed, throwing himself back in the chair. "Another play from the book of modern detective psychobabble?"

"I don't need to play games with you" Joe said coldly. "I have witness testimony, I have you caught in the act of an armed attempted murder, I have your supply of medazolene, I have two illegal firearms with your fingerprints all over them, I have ballistic and forensic evidence and I have your precious black cupboard!" Steven visibly tensed at the mention of the cupboard and its contents. "I've got your list, your camera, and your silly little messages! I even have your mysterious pieces of mirror!" Steven chewed his bottom lip in frustration. "What was that all about Kilkis?" Joe asked as he sensed a weakness in Steven's armour. "Why do you use the shards of mirror glass? Is it because you see yourself in your victims?" Steven burst into laughter.

"You're priceless Tenby!" he said with a sigh. "You're such a frustrated psychologist! You've already stolen my job; I'll bet Tom Rothesay is looking over his shoulder now!"

"Come on Kilkis!" Joe persisted. "Don't hide behind your attitude! It didn't work when you were one of us, and it definitely won't work now you're just another convict! I've been looking at your service files, and you haven't shown any sign of a problem! These killings are the first anyone knows that you weren't Evan Whindle!"

"I couldn't believe my luck when I saw your name come across my desk as a candidate for the DS position Joe! Letting you have this job was almost like dropping the final piece of the jigsaw into position!"

"Almost!" Joe responded. "But you didn't bank on your new recruit catching you in the act did you?"

I think we've said all we have to say!" Steven said as he looked at his solicitor.

"That's fine by me!" Joe said as he got to his feet. "I've got a lot to be doing! I've got a case review with the Crown Prosecution Service this afternoon about Graham Crosbie's arrest" Joe walked towards the door and casually gripped the handle before turning to Steven, who was still seated. "You know what it's like! An old case, no forensic evidence, and only the word of a serial killer with a superiority complex to go on. You can't really blame the CPS for not pursuing the case!" Joe walked back to the table and leant into the microphone that sat on top of the tape recorder. "Such a shame really, not to mention ironic, given that all you ever wanted was justice! Interview terminated at 14:31"

"Wait!" Steven said "After all this, you can't just let him walk free!" Joe shrugged.

"I don't see what else I can do!" Joe said turning back towards the door. "Like you said Steven, I think we've said all we have to say!" Joe opened the door and stepped into the corridor.

"The mirror!" Steven called after him. Joe paused.

"What about the mirror?" he asked as he came back into the interview room and closed the door behind him. Steven covered his face with his hands as he lowered his head onto the table.

"When my dad was murdered by those bastards!" Steven

breathed hard as he fought back tears. "One of my earliest memories was this old mirror that my Gran had in her house. That day when the police came in and told my mum that dad was dead. She flipped, threw something across the room! It hit that mirror and smashed it into what seemed like millions of pieces. I remember staring at those pieces of glass with all the colours they made in the sun. I remember being mesmerised by my own eye being reflected in the mirror."

"This is all fascinating, but what use is it to me Steven?" Joe asked coolly.

"I can't see Graham go free! I just can't!" Steven said, almost pleading. Sensing the opportunity, Joe opened a drawer and pulled out some paper and a pen before leaning towards Steven.

"You tell me everything, and I promise you I will make it my business to ensure that Graham Crosbie is prosecuted for what he did to you!" Steven's eyes welled with tears as he searched for something to say. "Give me it all, in writing, and you have my word!" Joe said as he slid the paper across the table and tapped it with the pen. Taking a deep breath, and with a trembling hand, Steven pulled the paper closer to him, took hold of the pen, and began to write.

-132-

"Well, it was great to see you again mate, even though we didn't get chance for any beer, or rugby!" Kevin smiled warmly as he looked out over the station concourse. Kings Cross had just emerged from the morning rush, the bankers and office workers swiftly replaced with swarms of tourists. Joe placed a coffee in front of Kevin and sat down as they watched people filing in and out of the ticket barriers, one eye studiously monitoring the giant departure screens."You didn't have to bring those match tickets down in person you know!" Joe said with a smile. "But I'm glad you did! You saved my life mate!"

"Not to worry Joe!" Kevin said before taking a mouthful of coffee. "I was coming down to London anyway. The plan was to watch Newcastle Falcons play Harlequins, but there'll be other matches! I suppose the weekend was fun!" He took another healthy swig of coffee, and then put an envelope on the table.

"What's this?" asked Joe as he picked it up.

"Tickets!" Kevin said. "That'll get this Inspector Goodman off your back!"

Joe opened the envelope and scrutinised the details printed on each one before placing them back inside.

"Mate, I owe you!" Joe said. Kevin held up a hand.

"Please!" he said. "I look after my friends! How's the dog?"

Joe grimaced. "He'll be fine. He's stopped taking shits on my kitchen floor if that's anything to go by! Are you back to work on Monday?"

"Aye!" Kevin replied. "Back to the grindstone!"

"That's a shame!" Joe said. "I could do with a decent Detective Sergeant!"

"I don't follow!" Kevin said with a frown. Joe took an envelope from his inside pocket and dumped it on the table.

"My turn!" Joe said. Kevin scooped up the envelope and pulled out the letter inside.

"Bloody hell Joe!" Kevin spluttered. "Congratulations!"

"Cheers mate!" Joe replied. "I was serious by the way! If you ever fancy the big smoke, let me know!"

"I may just hold you to that one day!" Kevin said as he studied the departure board. "My train's up! I'd best make a move!" Joe rose from his seat. "Stay where you are and finish your coffee" Kevin said, offering Joe his hand.

"Thanks again Kevin!" Joe said. Kevin picked up his bag

"Thank you, Detective Inspector Tenby!" Joe smiled awkwardly. "That's got quite a ring to it!" Kevin said.

"You're right! It has, hasn't it?" Joe replied. "Have a safe journey Kevin!"

"Cheers mate!" Kevin said as he turned and walked to the escalator, stepping on and waving to Joe as he disappeared from view.

-133-

Jessica couldn't believe how cold it was as she got out of the car and quietly closed the door. Walking around to Joe, she reached up and straightened his tie. He smiled in gratitude. The strain of everything was starting to show on his face, and she worried about the burden of leadership, and its effect on him, especially given the fact that the case was far from resolved, and that he had just accepted promotion. They looked down at Sully as he fussed around their legs, his tail sweeping through the wintery air. Linking her arm through Joe's as they walked towards the imposing gothic stone gate of the crematorium, she leaned against him, partly for the warmth in the face of the biting, East Yorkshire wind, and also to give him some unspoken reassurance. The drive from London to Hull had been a largely silent one, both of them taking refuge in their own thoughts, and the music of the various radio stations that drifted in and out of range as they sped along the A1M, M18 and M62 motorways.

"Are you alright after seeing Kilkis, I mean your uncle, yesterday?" Joe asked Jessica.

"I think so" Jessica sighed. "He had a complete breakdown after we left! They had to sedate him Joe! The psychiatrist treating him thinks he'll be sent to Broadmoor!" Joe nodded in agreement.

"Has he said anymore about why he's done this?" Joe asked. "I know he told us quite a bit in his statement."

"He told the psychiatrist that he only became aware of what was happening over the last few months" Jessica said.

"Apparently he kept waking up in strange places not knowing where he was or what he was doing. As time went on it was happening more frequently. The psychiatrist said he thinks that was a symptom of completely separate identities being constructed within Evan's, I mean, Steven's head. He said he thinks it was a defence mechanism against the memories of the sexual abuse and the death of his father".

"That sounds like dissociative identity disorder" Joe said. "That's very rare!"

"That's what they said at the mental hospital" Jessica replied. "In their sessions, he kept mentioning staring at himself in an old mirror!

"He mentioned that in the interview I had with him too!" Joe said thoughtfully.

"The psychiatrist told me that he thinks that mirror could be the key to Steven's meltdown into violence. He says the theory is that he worked out what was happening in his own head and smashed the mirror at the sight of his own reflection! Somehow the mirror became a symbol of his campaign for justice!" Joe shook his head as he thought of all the needless death that had been played out as a result of one man's deep illness.

"Mr Tenby?" asked an unfamiliar voice. Joe looked across the small road. A thin, middle aged woman dressed in a sober black outfit walked across to them. "I'm Pamela" she said, her voice cracking with emotion.

"Phil's sister?" Joe asked as he placed his hand on her shoulder. She nodded, choking back tears. "This is Jessica" Joe said as he introduced the two women, who smiled cordially at each other.

"Thank you so much for coming" she said. "Phil told me about you when I rang him! He really thought highly of you Mr Tenby!"

"The feeling was mutual Pamela. Please, call me Joe"

"Joe. I was wondering if you would say a few words today?" Joe looked shocked.

"Oh, I'm really not sure Pamela" he said.

"It really would mean a lot to us" she said. "You knew the side of Phil we never really got to see!" Joe and Jessica exchanged surprised glances. Pamela looked down at Sully, who was excitedly sniffing at her skirt.

"Is this Phil's dog Sully?" she asked, stooping to ruffle Sully's ears. Joe nodded.

"I had to bring him!" he whispered quietly. Pamela glanced across to the vicar, who was repeatedly checking his watch.

"Thank you for bringing him Joe! I think that's our signal to go in!" she said with a forced smile. The three of them turned and filed into the crematorium as Joe grasped Jessica's hand, squeezing it gently.

Not having ever been interested in sports of any kind, Jessica was less than enthusiastic about the thought of standing in the biting wind for two hours. She clung to Joe as they walked down Hull's Preston Road, thinking about her uncle, the case, and the competing scenes of working class poverty, and shining new buildings that lined the street. Having just got off a bus that was packed with other fans heading for the game, they jostled for position in the growing crowds as they got nearer to the stadium.

"You do realise you're going to have to explain all the rules to me don't you?" she said as they walked.

"That's no problem" Joe said cheerily. His mood since Phil's funeral had lifted immensely. Jessica was unable to tell whether it was as a result of exorcising some demons at the crematorium, the anticipation of going to watch the game, or a mixture of both.

"I'll do my best Jess, but you probably won't be able to hear me anyway, what with all the noise!" Filtering through the turnstiles, Joe led Jessica into the East stand of the stadium, where they ducked into the bar. Having bought hot drinks and beer, Joe carefully picked his way through the crowd with Jessica following obediently in his wake. Settling for a viewpoint near the front of the stand, Joe put his arm around Jessica as she looked around, taking in the atmosphere as the crowd constantly bellowed their songs in a rising volume as they counted down to kick-off.

"Welcome to Craven Park!" Joe said grandly. "Isn't she a wonderful place?"

"When do you take over as Detective Inspector?" Jessica asked as she surveyed the stadium, trying to decipher the words of the song being sung by everyone around them.

"Straight away!" Joe replied. "I think we'd better enjoy these few days of freedom, because by the sound of Commander Carlton, we're going to be taking on the world!" Jessica laughed, still none the wiser as to the lyrics of the song.

"How did it go with Graham Crosbie?" she asked, her voice rose as she directed her mouth to Joe's ear.

"He admitted to everything" Joe said.

"Why did you go out of your way to help my uncle Joe?" Jessica asked. The both of them stopped talking as more fans manoeuvred past. The crowd roared in unison as the stadium announcer did his best to ramp up the excitement. As the teams emerged from the tunnel, the entire stand seemed to shake as supporters all around them went crazy. Joe thought long and hard before replying to Jessica's question.

"I didn't do it for him!" Joe said, as softly as the noise of the crowd would allow. "I did it because it was the right thing to do, and because it was justice!" He gazed into her eyes. "I hope that's okay?" he asked as they turned to the pitch. Craning her neck slightly, Jessica kissed Joe's cheek.

"That was all I needed to know!" she said with a smile. Joe's face beamed. He pulled her closer to him as she braced herself against the cutting winds of the Humber, the zealous roars of the crowd filling their ears.

Printed in Great Britain
by Amazon

16601662R00283